T0365924

SURROUNDED
BY ENEMIES
A BREAKPOINT NOVEL

BRYCE ZABEL

DIVERSIONBOOKS

Diversion Books
A Division of Diversion Publishing Corp.
443 Park Avenue South, Suite 1008
New York, New York 10016
www.DiversionBooks.com

For more information, email info@diversionbooks.com

First Diversion Books edition November 2015.
Print ISBN: 978-1-62681-829-3
eBook ISBN: 978-1-62681-828-6

For Jackie Z

FOREWORD

BY HARRY TURTLEDOVE

When I was a kid, I noticed that my parents—and everyone else of their generation—could (and, at the slightest excuse, would) tell you exactly where they were and what they were doing when they heard that Japan had attacked Pearl Harbor on December 7, 1941. I thought that was pretty strange...until November 22, 1963.

I was a high school sophomore. It was not quite half past eleven in the morning. I was walking from Spanish to PE when a guy who'd snuck a transistor radio into school told me John Kennedy had been shot. I said the first thing that popped into my head: "You're crazy." But maybe a minute later, I heard somebody coming the other way say the same thing. I started to think Frank wasn't crazy—I only wished he were.

Anybody my age can tell you a story like that. As with my folks' generation all those years before, it won't take much to get people my age to tell you what they were doing when they heard Kennedy was killed.

Eventually, I had three kids of my own. For a long time, they didn't understand how every so often my mind would slip back to that dark day in fall, 1963. Then September 11, 2001 rolled around. Two of them were in high school at the time, the youngest still in middle school. Now they get it, and their kids (I just had my first grandchild) will wonder what they're going on about...till those kids have their own black day on the calendar. And I'm afraid they will. Such horrible things do happen, however much we wish they wouldn't.

Even after half a century, we remember—or, if we aren't old enough to remember, we think about—John Kennedy's brief presidency with fondness. Those of us with white beards recall that we were young then, and had seen and been through a lot less sorrow. We remember the Kennedys' own youth, their vigor, their flair, their style.

Because we remember the times and the handsome martyred man with such affection, to this day we don't want to hear anything bad about him. We didn't hear much bad about him then. The press was different in those days, and cozied up to people in power. Reporters didn't try to catch them with their pants down; they mostly didn't write or say anything when they did catch them like that.

All of which went a long way toward keeping John Kennedy's reputation burnished bright. By what's come out since his death, he made later philanderers like Bill Clinton seem pikers by comparison. He would and did screw anything that moved, and gave it an experimental shake to see if he could get it moving in case it didn't. Some of the ladies of his intimate acquaintance had other intimate acquaintances who could easily have embarrassed or wanted to kill the President because he was boffing their women.

He and his brother Bobby, the Attorney General, weren't always the Constitution's best friends either. Bobby, let it not be forgotten, was appointed by Joe McCarthy as assistant counsel for the U.S. Senate Permanent Subcommittee on Investigations in 1951. Bobby had also served as John's campaign manager in 1960. He was, perhaps, not completely objective about everything he did in the Attorney General's office. After all these years, we still remember the Kennedys as ruthless, too.

So we could wonder whether John Kennedy's reputation shines so bright precisely because he was assassinated so early in his presidency. We could wonder what it would look like had he lived past that day in Dallas, campaigned for reelection in 1964, and gone on to a second term with all that added time for his excesses to become visible to the power brokers in Washington and to the

American people as a whole.

We could, and Bryce Zabel has. That's what *Surrounded by Enemies* is all about. It's an alarmingly believable look at what might have happened. Some of you will know that I've written a lot of alternate history, which is the usual name for this what-might-have-been kind of story. One of the things about which you need to warn readers, and especially readers unfamiliar with this sort of story, is that people don't write them to tell you what *would* have come next had the world turned left instead of right. By the nature of things, what would have come next is unknowable unless you happen to be God. People write alternate histories for two main reasons. One is to tell you what plausibly *could* have come next in a world after a particular kind of change. The other, and closely related to the first, is to make you think in a whole new way about what *did* come next. Imagine alternate history as a funhouse mirror, squeezing this and stretching that, and giving you a different picture of the ways things did work and all the myriad way they might have.

Plausible development—building from what we know about what really did go on—and a whacking good story are the two things you can reasonably expect from a good alternate history. *Surrounded by Enemies* delivers on both, big-time. So hold on to your hats, folks. You're in for quite a ride.

Harry Turtledove
Chatsworth, California

"Getting out of Dallas was the easy part."

President John Kennedy to his brother
Attorney General Robert Kennedy, March 21, 1966

FROM THE EDITORS
OF *TOP STORY*

This special edition detailing the fate of America's thirty-fifth President, John Fitzgerald Kennedy, takes its inspiration from the *Top Story* newsweekly coverage of the 1960s. That breaking news "instant history" has been revised and updated by our editorial staff to provide a perspective to the events of the 1961-1966 Kennedy Administration.

This endeavor draws heavily from the work of *Top Story* reporters Frank Altman and Steve Berkowitz and their journalistic efforts throughout, beginning with the national crisis that began in Dallas and continued for years through Washington's corridors, forever changing our national identity. On November 22, 1963, at the time those shots cracked through America's sense of well-being, *Top Story* had been publishing for barely a year and was teetering near bankruptcy. It's fair to say that in spite of acknowledged reportorial bright spots, the magazine was mired behind the two leading newsweeklies of that era, *Time* and *Newsweek*, both in circulation and gravitas. While those publications were headquartered in New York, *Top Story* was then, as now, based in Washington, D.C., and is more heavily tilted toward American policy and the people behind those issues.

This special fiftieth-anniversary compilation of John Kennedy's final days in office shows that times of extreme danger and uncertainty do not preclude politics but intensify its practice. In addition to our own archives, the dramatic scope of this work draws on the accumulation of five decades of history and journalistic digging, tell-all books from those who were involved, and even some private papers released in 1998 by the Kennedy family following the death of Robert Kennedy.

On that day in November, our nation and the world breathed a sigh of relief upon learning President Kennedy had miraculously avoided the bullets meant for him in Dallas. But that feeling was overshadowed by an almost unthinkable fact: Someone had tried to murder our President.

As the events broke that day, however, there erupted fear and confusion among all the President's men working in the White House. Many of their stories of shock and panic in Dallas have been told now, but other accounts have been lost in the fog of conspiracy. Historians still argue about the number of bullets, and who fired them and from where. We do know now that their intended target, President Kennedy, came away, miraculously, with only a minor shoulder wound.

Within the first hour after the event, both the President of the United States and the Attorney General believed the government they represented was under siege and their civilian authority was in serious jeopardy. How they came to that conclusion, and what they said to those working in the White House in those first days set the stage for an epic confrontation.

That the attack was coordinated by a conspiracy seems clear in retrospect, even though the confessed or convicted participants continue to contradict each other about roles and obfuscate the facts time and again through witness intimidation and murder, suppression of documents and even outright disinformation from government agencies.

The greatest clarity comes from our study of the events that took place in the aftermath of Dallas as a criminal investigation transformed into a political crisis. Rather than physical threats to President Kennedy from the barrels of rifles, we instead witnessed a period of hardball politics as aggressive and challenging as anything the United States had ever seen before. The Kennedy brothers, always known as savvy operators, did not accept this counterattack lightly and, in fact, fought back using every skill, resource and defense available.

Indeed, responding to a French journalist's question with characteristic élan at a contentious 1965 press conference, John Fitzgerald Kennedy gave the world some insight into why it all mattered. "Forgive your enemies," he said, repeating something he had first said years before, "but never forget their names."

Paula Reiss - Gordon Makela
Editors, *Top Story*
March 2016

Top Story

25c

CONN. DEAD

AMBUSH IN DALLAS

JFK's Close Call

BRUCE ZABEL
SURROUNDED BY ENEMIES
IFJFKLIVED.COM   2013
LYNDA KARR GRAPHICS

CHAPTER 1:
BREAKPOINT

NOVEMBER 22, 1963

DEALEY PLAZA

As the presidential motorcade turned left from Houston Street onto Elm Street and entered Dealey Plaza, Secret Service Special Agent Clinton J. Hill did not like what he saw. Hill, a stickler for following procedure, noticed that the driver of the presidential limo, fellow Secret Service Special Agent William Greer, had inexplicably hesitated and slowed his car to a near stop, a procedure opposite from what he had been trained to do.

In a series of photos taken by onlookers, Hill can be seen actually scowling in the direction to the left of the President's car as he looked at an open, landscaped area at the western end of downtown Dallas. The agent was already in a bad mood because he had been told to ride on the left running board of the follow-up car instead of the 1961 Lincoln Continental convertible carrying the President, Mrs. Kennedy, and Texas Governor John Connelly and his wife, Idanell, or Nellie.

In a photo taken from another angle a second later, Hill can be seen looking right, where he sees the Texas School Book Depository, toward which the President is waving. Hill's glance appears to be angled toward the building's higher floors. The driver of the follow car, Sam Kinney, thought he heard Hill bark "Sonofabitch. It's a kill zone."

Whatever he said, what this presidential bodyguard did changed the course of history.

It seems probable that he saw a glint of metal in the midday sun as it flashed from a window on the sixth floor. Whether Hill also saw a rifle barrel or a man holding it can't be known. He may even have seen, as was described by several witnesses, a spectator on the side of the street pumping an umbrella up and down in the air. In any case, there was no time to look, only to act. He launched himself from the running board of his own vehicle and sprinted toward the President's car, screaming, "Go! Go!" as he vaulted onto the trunk and scrambled forward where John Kennedy and his wife Jacqueline were riding in the back seat.

As the Kennedys turned to see what was happening, Hill screamed at them in a tone of voice usually reserved for men in combat, "Get down!" JFK, a war veteran, instinctively moved to push his wife down and cover her.

Hill was the agent assigned to the First Lady but, in an instant like this, his training was to cover the President, particularly when he saw that the agent in the front passenger seat, Roy Kellerman, whose actual job was to protect the President, was frozen.

Hill tried to push the President down, but Kennedy's body was stiff; it wouldn't bend, even under Hill's muscle. The Secret Service agent instantly readjusted so he could move both President Kennedy and the First Lady into prone positions across the seat. He supported his body over them with both arms. The result was that within just over a second, the First Lady was being squashed beneath her husband who was being crushed underneath Hill.

Even as Greer mashed his foot down on the gas, swerving out of his lane, the first shot rang out. It scored a direct hit on Clint Hill, entering his upper back, cutting through his interior organs and exiting above the navel. According to Nellie Connally, she could hear the President of the United States shouting from the back seat, "We got a sniper!"

What happened next has never, even to this day, been established with complete clarity. What is known is that multiple shots were fired, seemingly from a variety of directions, according to numerous witnesses.

During this six-second period, the President, by his own testimony, under oath before his interrogators at his U.S. Senate trial, told his wife, "Jesus Christ! They're going to kill all of us!"

The President was not alone in his fear. His advisers Kenneth O'Donnell and Dave Powers reacted similarly. O'Donnell was JFK's appointments secretary and political sounding board, and Powers was the President's long-time close friend. Because of their White House importance, the two men were riding in the car immediately behind Kennedy, and they, too, felt they were being targeted from at least two directions.

Agent Hill was hit once more after the bullet that shattered his spinal cord, and it was that bullet that ripped through his left temple, ending his life. The amateur film of Dallas resident Abraham Zapruder caught the action, including a spray of blood and brains that appeared to knock Hill's head back and to the left. For over fifty observers, the head shot did seem to indicate that at least one bullet was fired from a grassy knoll area nearby and not from the upper window of the book depository, the likely origin of the first spine-shattering explosion.

Later testimony from witnesses told a tale of Secret Service agents in other cars who seemed asleep or operating in slow motion. All that can be stated for certain is that the heroic Agent Hill's instant action had forced Greer to react quickly enough to make up for any other neglect. Kellerman had similarly snapped into delayed response and had climbed back to the jump seats that Governor Connally and his wife were using. Connally was bleeding badly but he wasn't Kellerman's concern. The Secret Service's job is to protect the President first and the First Lady second, at all costs. The description says nothing about the governor of Texas. And so, even as Kellerman lay across the Connallys, he looked directly past them to Kennedy. "Mr. President, are you hit?"

The President and First Lady were covered in blood from the shots that had nearly taken off an entire side of agent Hill's head and broken his back into pieces. Kennedy answered honestly, "I'm not sure. Maybe."

With Greer now driving evasively, two more shots appear to have hit the Kennedy vehicle in its furious escape. One shattered Agent Kellerman's shoulder, and entered Governor Connally's chest, causing severe internal bleeding and collapsing his right lung. A final bullet was fired out of desperation by a would-be assassin who knew his chance at the target was nearly over.

Since the President's condition was unknown, Greer zoomed the 350 horsepower Lincoln toward Parkland Memorial at speeds approaching eighty miles per hour. Even at this speed, driving with one hand on the wheel and another on the microphone, he managed to get off a concise status report to his superiors. "This is SS-100-X. I have Lancer and Lace," shouted Greer. "We're en route to Parkland. POTUS is conscious and responsive. FLOTUS same. Big Hat down. Agents down."

Inside the vehicle, although President Kennedy's condition seemed reasonable, the carnage among the other passengers was substantial enough to raise doubt. Hill was unconscious, probably dead, Governor Connally had been hit and badly injured, and agent Kellerman was losing a lot of blood. That left Jacqueline Kennedy and Nellie Connally still to account for but both of them appeared to have escaped being hit directly by gunfire. Even so, the agent with his foot on the gas pedal knew that there were no guarantees.

Later asked who "they" were, in response to his statement, "They're going to kill us all," President Kennedy famously told the investigators deposing him, "How much time do you have?"

HICKORY HILL

At his Hickory Hill estate, in suburban McLean, Virginia, purchased years earlier from JFK, thirty-eight-year-old Attorney General Robert Kennedy, lunched with U.S. Attorney Robert Morgenthau, who represented the southern district of New York, and Edwin Guthman, RFK's Justice Department spokesman. They ate hot clam chowder and tuna fish sandwiches.

The younger Kennedy had just finished a swim and was still

wet, a towel wrapped around his shoulders. He appeared to be trying to relax and not succeeding, according to Morgenthau. "He had a lot on his mind but he could only share a tiny bit with me. I could see he was frustrated."

The outside phone rang at about 1:45 p.m. on the other end of the pool and was picked up by Kennedy's wife, Ethel. "It's your office," she said to her husband. "They've got Hoover on the line for you." Kennedy moved quickly to take the call.

On the other end of the line was FBI director J. Edgar Hoover, someone who never called his ostensible boss at home. Neither man had ever had the slightest positive regard for the other. Never much of a conversationalist, Hoover said simply, "The motorcade was attacked in Dallas."

The Attorney General asked the first thing to come to mind: "How is the President?"

Hoover delivered a spare précis of the news that the President was alive and had been taken to Parkland Hospital. When RFK asked about Jacqueline Kennedy, Hoover brusquely told him, "I have a crime to investigate, Mister Attorney General." He recommended that Kennedy should call the hospital directly "if you have family concerns" and the two men hung up. In later years, each claimed to be the one to have ended the conversation.

Kennedy explained to Morgenthau and Guthman that the President's motorcade had been attacked. Both his guests remember the first thought the Attorney General expressed to them. "I thought they'd move on me, not Jack." They also both knew what this meant. The Mob.

Guthman immediately countered with the need for better security for his boss. "They could still be coming here," he warned, concerned that whoever was behind the Dallas ambush might be coming to Hickory Hill next.

Even though Robert Kennedy had been notoriously dismissive of his own security needs in the past, he offered up the idea that they should enlist the federal marshals. "McShane's loyal," he explained, but should be directed to keep his men at a distance, given that the Kennedy children would be scared enough when they heard the news from Dallas.

Morgenthau offered his help in any way. The New Yorker was instructed to call national security adviser McGeorge Bundy on RFK's authority. "Tell him to get the combinations on the President's locked files changed right away." Angry and focused, Kennedy left the men in order to work the phones from his upstairs bedroom. He did as much so feverishly that he would not change out of his wet swimsuit for more than two hours.

Within minutes, and without being ordered to, the Fairfax County police surrounded the grounds of the RFK compound. Within the hour, as discussed, Chief U.S. Marshal Jim McShane arrived. He brought seven agents and a collection of firearms with him. They dispatched the local police to an outer perimeter and assumed key positions in and around Kennedy's estate. As McShane testified in late 1964, "If someone was coming to kill that man, we were prepared to make them kill us first."

PARKLAND MEMORIAL

By 12:36 p.m., just six minutes after the shooting at Dealey Plaza, the presidential limo, followed closely by other cars from the motorcade, roared into the parking lot of Parkland Memorial Hospital. The passengers were met by a team of doctors, nurses and orderlies who, having been alerted just minutes before, swarmed the car.

The team assigned to the Kennedy limo was led by senior surgeon Doctor Robert Shaw and head nurse Margaret Hinchcliffe. Shaw spoke directly to President Kennedy. "Mister President," he said, "are you hurt?"

To Shaw's great consternation, the commander-in-chief ignored his question and spoke instead to Greer, his driver. "Get me O'Donnell."

The First Lady, already seen favoring her left arm, tried to answer for her husband. "It happened so fast," she told Shaw and Hinchcliffe.

Other teams, lead by surgical resident Doctor Charles Carrico, were on hand to deal with the other cars. They were met first by a team of Secret Service agents from the follow-up car who collectively sprang from it, revolvers drawn, and with one agent wielding a machine gun. That wave was followed by another composed of Dallas police officers on motorcycles.

Kennedy, seeing the state of Connally and Hill, ordered Shaw to tend to them first, a request that Shaw refused. "I can personally vouch for the teams working on both of them, sir," he told the President. "But you're my concern and the country's." Kennedy looked at the First Lady, who nodded that he should do as he was told.

Service chief Forrest Sorrels arrived at that moment with a team of agents who surrounded Kennedy, forming a human shield with their own bodies. Even here, the President balked, demanding that his wife had to come with him. "I'm the President, Forrest," he said. "Do as I say." Sorrels complied.

With that, the medical team, the Kennedys, and the agents moved en masse into the front door of Parkland Memorial where they continued on into the room designated as Trauma One. As they did, Shaw observed how over-stuffed the room had become with men carrying guns.

"We need to clear the room for the President," he said. Not a man moved a muscle. The doctor turned his attention to his patient, helping him out of his blood-soaked suit coat. "Sir, lie down on this gurney here. Immediately."

Kennedy looked around at the pale tile, sterile instruments, and the clock that read 12:38 p.m. Then he flashed his famous charm. "Well, Doctor, I can assure you I would like very much to lie down on that gurney, but I can't right now." Kennedy began to unbutton his shirt, which was heavily splattered with blood from Connally and Hill.

As the President's shirt came off, Shaw was surprised to see an unusually constrictive shoulder-to-groin brace on the President. "Pulled my back," said Kennedy, wincing. "Bit worse now." In subsequent interviews, Shaw remembered being startled by the President's compromised appearance, which was so uncharacteristic of his normal image. In truth, Kennedy had aggravated his back during a sexual encounter in the White House pool nearly two months earlier.

As Shaw helped him out of his back supports, Kennedy indicated Trauma Two, where Texas Governor John Connally was fighting for his life. Inside, Dr. Carrico—only two years a practicing physician—and two nurses were using surgical shears to cut the clothes away from the Texas governor. What they saw was not good; he had actually been hit three times, most grievously through the chest. Carrico checked for a pulse and blood pressure, and pronounced both "palpable."

Shaw explained the scene to the Kennedy party. "The governor's in the care of Doctor Carrico. He's on his way to the OR as soon as he can be stabilized."

From the side of the room, Jacqueline Kennedy spoke softly. "What about the agents? Where are they?"

Without taking his eyes off the President's body, now prone on the exam table, Shaw answered. "One of the agents was alert and is being attended in an OR. The other agent, Agent Hill, suffered extensive head trauma and spinal damage and has not survived his wounds. I'm very sorry."

As those words were spoken, the First Lady gasped, looked as if she might faint, and was given a chair by a nurse. His death made Secret Service Special Agent Clint Hill only the second member of the organization to be killed while protecting a United States President during an assassination attempt, along with Leslie Coffelt, who had died protecting President Harry Truman in 1950.

Mrs. Kennedy was taken to get an x-ray on her wrist. It was done as much to assess her injury, Hinchcliffe told investigators, as to spare her having to watch her husband's own examination.

Shaw carefully examined the President's body, looking for wounds. In a few cases, he used cotton gauze and alcohol to wipe away blood in order to satisfy himself that it had not originated from the President himself. He spent the most time on the President's right shoulder area. After several minutes, Shaw offered his initial conclusion, spoken to a nurse who took notes: "I see one visible entry wound, right shoulder, entrance and exit, minor damage."

President Kennedy was allowed to dress and did so in the same bloody clothes that he had entered with. He had discussed trading shirts and jackets with O'Donnell, but Jackie was adamant that he not do that: "Let them see what they've done." The Kennedys resolved then to wear their same clothes until this day was over.

Shaw instructed the President to remain in Trauma One for at least an hour for observation. Kennedy said he wanted to meet privately with Nellie Connally but was told such a conversation would have to wait. She was at her husband's side, moving with the trauma team to the OR. Kennedy nodded, turned to O'Donnell. "Right before this happened, Kenny, she said to us, 'You can't say Texas doesn't love you, Mr. President.'"

All across Parkland Memorial, chaos reigned. Dallas police officers, FBI agents, and Secret Service agents were everywhere, most of them with guns drawn. An intern was nearly shot when he tried to hide in a linen closet to deal with a panic attack.

The strangest encounter occurred when Greer and two Dallas Police officers came across a burly man in his fifties, wearing a hat. The man, Jack Ruby, stopped the team, asking if the President was okay. The officers told Greer that Ruby was a man they knew well, the proprietor of a local nightclub.

According to the sworn testimony of both police officers, Greer addressed Ruby directly, telling him, "The President is lucky to be alive."

Ruby was still not satisfied. "He's going to make it?" he asked.

Greer nodded in the affirmative but added, "You can't be here, Mister Ruby." The Secret Service agent then instructed the officer to "get him the hell outside our perimeter."

Neither officer remembered telling Greer Jack Ruby's full name. Greer denied using it. The dissonance in their testimony raised questions that kept at least two committee counsels speculating about a connection between the shooting and Greer himself. That kind of contradiction, however, would be dissected in the future. On November 22, 1963, there was simply no time to consider such matters.

Agent Hill was dead, and Governor Connally was near death. Only agent Kellerman looked like he would survive. Yet, despite the blood and carnage, the President of the United States had escaped with a relatively minor wound to his right shoulder that was stitched up in seventeen minutes. The First Lady had a hairline fracture in her right wrist, something that would suspend her personal note writing for nearly two months.

In the middle of this, Kennedy, scheduler Kenneth O'Donnell, and presidential factotum David Powers commandeered Trauma One as a temporary Oval Office, given Dr. Shaw's instructions that the President must stay for medical reasons. Finally, Jack Kennedy heard what he wanted to hear: "Your brother is on the phone."

"They fucking tried to kill us," the President told the Attorney General, based on the testimony of Dr. Shaw, who had refused to leave Kennedy's side in case he went into shock. He later said, "It was odd. Aside from the curse word, which hardly surprised me under the circumstances, it was the way he phrased it. *They* tried to kill us."

Attorney General Robert Kennedy did not trust their connection. "This phone may not be secure, Jack," he told his brother. "Just follow my lead." Bobby's lead, as it turned out, involved the two brothers speaking in a code where suspects became the cities they hailed from.

"Is Chicago behind this?" asked the Attorney General, referring to the local mob boss, Sam Giancana.

"You've got New Orleans in court," replied the President, referring to the greatest thorn in Robert Kennedy's side, Carlos Marcello. In fact, that very day the Attorney General was waiting to hear about a verdict in the Carlos Marcello deportation case. "He's got motive and Chicago's got the resources," said Bobby.

The President responded, "We both know plenty of people

with motives and resources to put me in the ground." Powers and O'Donnell, who would be called to testify about these events multiple times in the years ahead, each remembered the President's words exactly the same way.

One of the men who wished Kennedy ill, in fact, was the controversial leader of the Teamsters labor union, Jimmy Hoffa. The squat, bull-faced leader had been lunching in Nashville when the news of the attack broke. He stood on a table and declared, "If he's dead, I'm buying lunch for everybody." Hoffa told his dining companion that he only hoped that if JFK was dead that he had suffered first.

This behavior was unknown, of course, between the two brothers on the telephone. "I have people checking," said Bobby, "but we can't count on Hoover or McCone for a straight take." He was referring to the FBI director, and the CIA's leader, John McCone.

It became obvious the attempt at a code was not likely to fool anyone and, worse, anything further said was going to become testimony that made them sound paranoid and vengeful. Bobby then changed the subject of guilt to getting the President and First Lady out of Dallas immediately. President Kennedy argued that he could not do that so long as Texas Governor John Connally was still fighting for his life.

In later investigations the FBI would disclose that it had transcripts of the call. In that written record, the Attorney General advised the President in no uncertain terms:

> *You can leave now, Jack, and you must. Our country may be at war with an enemy, or at war with itself. Either way, it's too dangerous for you to stay there.*

Jack and Bobby Kennedy then agreed to meet that night in the Oval Office, as soon as possible after JFK came back to Washington. The Kennedys had begun the search for suspects on the phone and would have to finish it there.

Less than two hours after his arrival at Parkland Memorial Hospital, Governor John Connally died in the main OR. Although the surgical team labored to save him with the same urgency they would have given President Kennedy, Connally's injuries were too grave. His time of death was called at 2:17 p.m. Nellie Connally, who had been so upbeat moments before the attack, refused a sedative offered to help her "calm down" by stating, "I will never calm down in this lifetime."

President Kennedy wasn't at the hospital to share his own support with her. He and Mrs. Kennedy had already been driven in separate cars to Love Field, the public airport in Dallas, where they would reunite for the trip home on Air Force One.

LOVE FIELD

Still grounded six miles northwest of the downtown on the tarmac at Love Field, Air Force One was a hotbed of paranoia. The Boeing VC-137C jet was jammed full, with speculation of all manner underway. Vice President Johnson had arrived minutes before and was arguing with the assistant special agent in charge, Emory Roberts, who had taken over leadership duties for the Secret Service detail as Roy Kellerman was still in surgery. Roberts, trying to get Johnson to leave the plane immediately, blamed it on "protocol," but Johnson fired back that it was "bullshit" and said he would stay right where he was.

Seeing President Kennedy entering, Johnson pushed through the crowded plane to intercept him, grabbed him by the collar and pulled him close (the so-called "Johnson Treatment"). "It's your goddamned friend Khrushchev," he growled. "We may be at war. We need to get our heads together on this right now." Calling the leader of the Soviet Union the United States President's "friend" seemed inappropriate and revealing at the same time, but this was hardly the time to take offense.

Agent Roberts physically pulled Johnson away from Kennedy. His training made clear that no one is allowed to touch the President without permission, something that was particularly important under the existing conditions. The agent spoke directly to President

Kennedy: "Mr. President, I've told the Vice President that he cannot be on this plane, that he must depart on Air Force Two. Particularly now that you are here, sir, we need you two separated to assure continuity of authority." Looking between the President and the Vice President, the agent made his case crystal clear: "You can't fly together. He needs to leave now."

President Kennedy nodded to Johnson. "Lyndon, I have to get back. People will need to see that happen. I need you to stay here in Texas."

Johnson processed the political implications of sticking around Dallas surrounded by death and shame against the idea of returning to Washington to assure the continuity of the government. "Mr. President, that seems ill-advised."

Kennedy leaned forward, collared Johnson somewhat more gently than Johnson had just collared him and so many others, pulled close to his ear and said, "I don't have time to fuck around with you, Lyndon."

Kennedy let go, and simply nodded to Roberts. Within seconds, Secret Service agents Jack Ready and Donald Lawton lifted a humiliated Lyndon Johnson almost off his feet and escorted him from the plane with his aide Jack Valenti trailing behind. Using a long-distance lens, AP photographer Ralph Philpott captured the scene. It was a necessary moment to secure national leadership but, to Lyndon Johnson, it always looked as if he was being treated like "a two-bit poker cheat."

Indeed, in the time that followed, Johnson told practically anyone who would listen about this "ball-crushing" moment, confiding to them that this was when he felt his fate on the 1964 Democratic ticket was sealed. That Johnson would even be engaging in such political speculation on the day that the President of the United States had been targeted for murder is perhaps egocentric on his part. But the truth is that both Jack and Bobby Kennedy were thinking the same thing.

DALLAS POLICE DEPARTMENT

News of the events out of Dallas rocketed around the world. Nothing since Pearl Harbor seemed to have touched the American nation as powerfully. This was the first true breaking news television event of the modern age, driving audiences to record numbers, both in the United States and abroad. And, as is true for all good television dramas, it had a hero people could root for and a villain they could jeer.

Inside the Dallas police building, suspect Lee Harvey Oswald, captures less than two hours earlier hiding in a movie theater, was half-heartedly advised that anything he said could be used against him and that he was entitled to an attorney. He made several telephone calls seeking representation. He also spoke with the head of the Dallas Bar Association, who offered to find a lawyer for him. He declined, saying he preferred to secure one himself.

Under questioning, Oswald denied shooting Governor Connally or Agent Hill, claiming that he was eating lunch when the Dealey Plaza gunfire took place. When he was placed in a lineup, however, several eyewitnesses identified him as the man responsible for shooting Dallas policeman Officer J.D. Tippit who had been killed miles away from the motorcade but near Oswald's residence.

"I didn't shoot anybody," Oswald stated forcefully.

"Maybe it would be smart for you to come clean, Mr. Oswald. Maybe you don't understand how much trouble you're in," Captain Will Fritz said. The Dallas Police Department veteran had been on duty at the Trade Mart when the shots were fired and immediately reported to Dealey Plaza, where he had been part of the team that had found a rifle on the sixth floor of the Texas School Book Depository. Police Chief Jesse Curry picked Fritz, who had a reputation as an effective interrogator, to speak to Lee Oswald first. "Son, we've got witnesses who saw you shoot a police officer. And we've got strong evidence that you shot the governor and the Secret Service agent, too. Those murders are all capital crimes. If you're convicted, you'll go to the electric chair."

Although no stenographer was present at those early interrogations and no tape recorder was used, Officer Dan Selkirk took notes. These were later compared to a report written afterwards by Captain Fritz, who noted that Oswald, already pale, turned "white as a sheet" when the death penalty was mentioned. Selkirk's notes, however, state that Oswald leaned back in his chair and smiled.

"That's funny to you?" Fritz allegedly asked.

"You'll see. This'll all get straightened out" came the answer. Fritz asked for further clarification. "I'm not at liberty to discuss it," said Lee Harvey Oswald who subsequently refused to answer any further questions during that session.

While trying to lead the suspect to his secure location for safekeeping, two Dallas cops unwittingly led him into a sea of reporters instead. The scene, already chaotic, became threatening to the physical safety of the prisoner as well as the news reporters and the officers.

Top Story's Steve Berkowitz, a reporter with just three years' experience, was covering his first major news event for the magazine. At the moment of Oswald's transfer, he had been arguing with local CBS reporter Dan Rather over a pay phone that Rather had staked out because he was on hold to speak to network anchorman Walter Cronkite.

No shrinking violet, Berkowitz waded deep into the building fray, pushing toward Oswald and the officers where he summoned his most authoritative voice to rise above the cacophony: "Did you do it, Mr. Oswald?"

Oswald stopped, allowing the reporters clogging the hallway to quickly close ranks around him and the officers, trapping them for questions. He looked straight at Berkowitz and said, "I didn't do anything except go to work today." His refusal to speak only applied, it seemed, to police officers.

"So who hired you to kill the President?" Berkowitz was not above using sarcasm to address his sources, a trait that had gotten him dressed down by both editors and press secretaries. In this case, however, it seemed more appropriate than usual.

"The truth on that matter will come out if they'll let it," said Oswald, looking angry and offended. "But me? I'm just a patsy."

Meanwhile, with President and Mrs. Kennedy in mid-flight, Bobby Kennedy was still working the phone feverishly from his Virginia home office, watched over by his wife Ethel. Although he rarely smoked, Bobby had taken a stale pack of Kents from his drawer and was on his fifth cigarette. Like everyone else in America, he was watching the television and making his assessment of Oswald. The Attorney General thought the alleged killer looked smaller than he had imagined, expecting his assassins big and threatening.

Close on the heels of the Oswald proclamation of innocence, Dallas District Attorney Henry Wade put on his jacket, straightened his tie, and went out to the press area, where reporters and photographers and TV crews were standing mob vigil in the hallway outside, having been whipped into near-hysteria by Oswald's walk-by. Wade started by threatening to charge the reporters with obstruction of justice and throw them in jail if they did not allow the prisoner to be transported properly.

With Oswald sent on his way, Wade acknowledged that there were already calls for turning the whole thing over to federal authorities. That was what the FBI agents in Washington, D.C., wanted. "This crime took place in Dallas," the DA declared. "We know how to prosecute murder here."

Asked why he should trump federal authority in an attack on the President of the United States, Wade replied, "They missed. The President is healthy. The top public official who was murdered here earlier today was the governor who was, last I checked, a Texas resident."

Robert Kennedy could not believe what he was seeing. He hurled his ashtray across the room, furious that people from Lyndon Johnson's home state were sticking their noses where they had no real business. He left for the White House to begin the counter-attack against the forces that has targeted his brother.

THE WORKING GROUP

Before the sun had gone down in Washington, D.C., Attorney General Robert Kennedy had brought together an elite group of investigators and prosecutors at his office in the Justice Department. They included both Morgenthau and Guthman. They were supplemented by Deputy Attorney General Nicholas Katzenbach, investigator Carmine Bellino and special assistant Walter Sheridan who, on this day, sat at the back of the room cradling a loaded rifle.

"Four hours ago, the government of the United States was attacked," were the words chosen by RFK to bring the group to order. He indicated that U.S. Attorney Morgenthau would lead the investigation he contemplated.

"None of us will publicly or privately acknowledge the existence of this group," stated Morgenthau. He added that no direct calls would be made by its members to either the Justice Department or the White House. Instead, he indicated a fresh-faced Yale intern Adam Walinsky who, when not busy pouring coffee for them, would also coordinate all communications.

The meeting began with each member naming persons of interest to them in the assassination attempt. The names that came up included mobsters Carlos Marcello, Sam Trafficante, and Johnny Roselli. Others were interested in hearing from Cubans, both pro- and anti-Castro. Former CIA director Allen Dulles and "his boy" Angleton did not escape attention. Neither did Teamsters leader Jimmy Hoffa. And there was the Texas connection that included right-wing extremists like Clint Murchison. It was a long list.

At the end of what was characterized by Morgenthau as the "spitballing" session, the President's brother who had listened but not spoken, preferring to scowl and drum a pencil on his desk, asked what would happen if they brought the whole bunch of them in for questioning.

"You'll bring a shitstorm of historical proportions on this Administration," his Justice Department spokesman Guthman told him.

Without missing a beat, RFK fired back, "And what would you

call what just happened, Ed?"

In the end, the decision was made to do nothing overt, to put these persons of interest under surveillance of the federal marshals, yet let them believe the Administration was in shock over its close call with death. Kennedy ended the meeting with these words:

> *Gentlemen, today someone tried to instigate a coup d'etat in America and they failed. Now it is our job and sacred duty to find them and make them pay. I know you won't let your country down.*

ANDREWS AIR FORCE BASE

When President Kennedy landed in Washington, D.C., he felt compelled to respond to the rapidly changing story. Reporters had gathered near Air Force One, buzzing with the day's news, oblivious to both the temperature and the chill wind. One of them, *Top Story*'s Frank Altman, noted how this story would have changed if the President were coming back in a casket. Then he reminded himself that if JFK had died that day, Texas authorities would not have released his body until they'd had a chance to perform an autopsy. Those were rules, almost universally respected.

Emerging from Air Force One with his wife Jacqueline, John Kennedy shrugged up his jacket. Both actually still had on the same bloody clothes they had worn all day long, resolved that the nation and the guilty parties should face what had happened in Dallas.

So, looking more like he'd come in off a battlefield than a cross-country flight, Kennedy was uncharacteristically terse with the freezing press corps, offering prayers for the Connally, Hill, Tippit and Kellerman families. He explained that he was on his way to the White House to meet with the Attorney General and that they would receive a personal briefing at the Oval Office from FBI Director Hoover. For the nation, however, he offered resolve and firmness:

> *I would simply like to state at this time that the government is secure. I have instructed General Taylor of the Joint Chiefs to increase the armed forces state of alert. He has done so.*

The irony, we later learned, was that this was a lie and the President of the United States knew it. On the way to Washington, aboard Air Force One, Kennedy has learned that General Maxwell Taylor had indeed raised the armed forces state of alert without speaking to the President or anyone else. This happened after Taylor had heard that his own Air Force Chief of Staff General Curtis LeMay had already raised the alert status of the U.S. fleet of nuclear bombers. None of this was even close to the established policy and the fact that the U.S. military had been taken to DEFCON 2 status without presidential authority was unprecedented. After the fact, however, Kennedy preferred the public believe he had made this decision himself.

After his statement on the tarmac, the President was supposed to walk away from the microphones but instead went off his talking points, taking a question from the *Washington Post*'s Bart Barnes and replying, "I want whoever did this to know that last night was the last good night of sleep they'll ever have." It was angry and aggressive, spoken like a surrounded general, who had decided to fight rather than surrender.

As Kennedy moved toward a waiting limo, *Top Story*'s Altman maneuvered himself into a position directly in the President's line of sight and asked the simple, personal question on everyone's mind: "Mr. President how are you and the First Lady holding up?" Although softer-spoken than Berkowitz, Altman knew how to command attention.

Bone-weary, Kennedy paused as if he hadn't quite heard the question, buying time to decide the exact tenor of his answer. He looked to his wife, her own face downcast and tired. He answered Altman with the unvarnished truth. "Frank," said the President, "we've both had better days."

The President of the United States stiffly got into the limo, helped by a Secret Service agent. His presumption that the FBI was just beginning an investigation would soon be proven incorrect. In fact, the Bureau was doing all it could to wrap up its investigation immediately around the theme of a lone nut who was now, thankfully, in custody.

In future testimony, the First Lady was asked what she and her husband talked about in the limousine ride to the White House. She replied that she did not recall them speaking, only that they had held hands. In her memoirs, however, the famously private First Lady admitted that they did speak. "I was angry," she admitted. "I told John that these men had nearly orphaned our children."

Jacqueline Kennedy wanted to know how they would break the news to their children. Her husband offered the idea that "some very bad men tried to hurt daddy and mommy but we're okay." This would not do, she countered, since the idea of "bad men" implied that some of them were still out there at-large. The President corrected himself. "A bad man the police caught who can't hurt us now."

"Yes," said Jackie. "Better." That, she remembered, is when they actually did hold hands and ride home in silence.

First Brothers

According to the controversial entrance logs that were later subpoenaed and found to have been altered, President and Mrs. Kennedy arrived together at the White House at 8:39 p.m. EST on the night of November 22, 1963. Kennedy's secretary, Evelyn Lincoln, in all her testimony given to multiple committees over time, always used the word "disturbing" to describe their appearance.

"I'm so very happy to see you both tonight, Mrs. Kennedy, Mr. President," said Lincoln, re-directing to JFK. "The Attorney General is waiting for you in the Oval Office. Director Hoover should be here soon."

Kennedy kissed his wife goodnight. Lincoln overheard him saying, "I'll be up late." As the First Lady departed, Mrs. Lincoln informed the President that a change of clothes was in the office for him when he was ready. The President nodded his tired agreement, then entered his office on that cool evening, finding Bobby Kennedy looking at a bank of three televisions featuring the three

TV network newscasts. Only Walter Cronkite—by now running on pure adrenaline—was audible. Bobby was monitoring CBS because the nation preferred that network's news by big numbers; he wanted to hear what the people were hearing when they heard it.

When testifying two years later, Mrs. Lincoln had to be reminded of her oath twice before she could recall what she saw and heard before the door closed. Lincoln described the two brothers embracing in a strong hug. Using words best left out of the history books, Bobby Kennedy apparently summed up their mutual feelings toward those who had brought this situation down on them. "Fucking assholes" were the first words spoken by the Attorney General to the President.

Based on the private papers of Bobby Kennedy, released after his 1998 death, JFK responded as if he was picking up the conversation he and his brother had been having on the phone less than an hour after the shootings in Texas. "Before Hoover comes over here and lies to us," he said, "tell me what you know."

Bobby Kennedy quickly turned, picking up a pencil from his brother's desk. He scribbled on a notepad, "We can't talk here!" and held the message up for the President's eyes. JFK stopped himself from responding and moved with his brother into a small side alcove adjacent to the Oval Office, a place where the President had been known to nap. It had the distinction of being the only room in the White House that was swept for electronic surveillance bugs on a daily basis. Aside from the outside portico, it was the most secure spot on the White House grounds, and it was warm. But as secure as it was, whenever you came into this room, you still whispered.

As President Kennedy changed from his bloodstained clothes into a crisp blue suit, his younger brother, ever the prosecutor building a case, characterized the attack in Dealey Plaza as an attempt to execute the President of the United States in broad daylight on a public street. "More importantly to me," the President concluded, showing his trademark JFK humor, "they failed."

If only White House photographer Cecil Stoughton had been allowed to record this moment, a request denied by both Robert

Kennedy and Evelyn Lincoln, he might have captured an image that would have become as famous as any from his White House service. While attempting to knot his tie after changing into his new clothes, John Kennedy winced from his shoulder wound. While continuing their conversation, Bobby simply took the tie from his brother and tied it for him with no mention. The image would have said so much about that moment and their relationship but the idea that it was not allowed because of their need for privacy says perhaps even more.

In any case, the younger brother worried openly that the failure of the assassination made those who attempted it even more dangerous, setting events in motion that threatened to tear apart the Administration. Yet here the Kennedys were, locked up in the White House prison, where they were suddenly unsure who, if anyone, could be trusted.

The President directed his brother to get some friendly shoes running down the details immediately. Of course, the Attorney General had been on that from the beginning, protecting his brother from the details but laying out the formidable enemies they faced from the worlds of organized crime, Cuban freedom fighters, the FBI's Hoover, an overtly hostile CIA, the combative Joint Chiefs of Staff and, of course, Castro or Khrushchev. Analyzing his position, JFK's gallows humor again prevailed. "Well, Bobby," said the President. "Based on this discussion, the question is not who would want to kill me but who wouldn't."

The two men were silent for as much as a minute as they considered the possibilities, Cronkite's voice continuing to summarize the same basic fact set on the TV in the background. When they were together, with no one else, the brothers would often sit in long silences while thinking, knowing that the first one of them who had something important to say would say it. Finally, the Attorney General offered his assessment, "It's better for the White House at this point if Oswald keeps his mouth shut."

They also felt that, as much as possible, the President should follow the same policy for the foreseeable future. Although both knew the President would have to show his face publicly, they decided that it would only be in a carefully controlled event like a news conference. There would be no more of what Bobby described with disgust as "that clusterfuck ambush Lyndon dragged you into."

The priority action item was security. Clearly, in the aftermath of Dallas, the Secret Service organization was going to come in for its heaviest criticism ever, since its creation by Abraham Lincoln in 1865. Ironically, it came into existence on April 15 of that year, the same day that Lincoln himself had been assassinated. Its original mission of suppressing counterfeiting was not expanded to include presidential protection until the assassination of President William McKinley in 1901.

Maybe those agents reacted slowly in Texas for a reason, thought the Attorney General, and if so, there could be someone armed, already close to President Kennedy, who would be willing to trade his life for the President's. It would be necessary for every member of the Secret Service to be vetted for loyalty. Lie detector tests were ordered and administered by military police officers flown in from Florida within twelve hours of the attack. In addition to the standard screening questions, Robert Kennedy instructed that all agents be asked, "Do you recognize John Kennedy as the legitimate leader of the United States government?"

The matter did not end there. Bobby produced a typed document and slid it across the table. "This is an executive order for you to sign replacing the entire presidential Secret Service detail with federal marshals until further notice."

Jack studied the document. "An agent died trying to save me. This'll be controversial."

"Your safety is my only concern," said his brother. "I don't care who thinks what."

"Then neither do I," was the response. President John Fitzgerald Kennedy, the thirty-fifth president, signed Executive Order #11128, and slid it back across the table.

At that point, presidential secretary Lincoln called on the private line to inform the brothers that FBI director Hoover had arrived. The President, once again looking like the leader of the most powerful nation on Earth in his blue suit, took his seat behind his desk. Despite the late hour and his aching back, Hoover would not be allowed to see him in the more comfortable rocking chair. The Attorney General took his place strategically to the side so that Hoover would be forced to address any comments to both the President and the leader of the United States Department of Justice—two men for whom he theoretically worked.

In the seconds before Hoover entered, RFK made a final comment. "Remember," he said, "Oswald's probably a fairy tale and he knows it."

Hoover, to his credit, paid more respect to the President than he had to his brother earlier in the day. "It is a great relief to see you alive, Mr. President," Hoover stated at the outset. He made no other comments of a personal nature nor did he ask the most important eyewitness to the event to tell his story. Instead, he laid out the case against Lee Harvey Oswald, an update that had been relayed to him by his agents on the ground in Dallas.

After Hoover completed his briefing, Robert Kennedy read back the details from a yellow legal pad: "Ex-Marine. Lived in Russia from 1959 to 1962—claimed to be a Marxist. Tried to renounce his citizenship but didn't. Came back in June of '62 with a Russian wife, Marina. Lived in New Orleans earlier this year—there's a photo of him passing out leaflets for something called the Fair Play for Cuba Committee. Is that basically it, Mr. Director?"

Hoover nodded, barely.

The exhausted President Kennedy acidly pointed out to Hoover that the news he was hearing from the FBI was barely as comprehensive as what he was already hearing from Walter Cronkite. The President indicated the televisions in the Oval Office itself. "They've been parading the son of a bitch all around Dallas. He says he's innocent."

Hoover assured his superiors that Oswald was hardly innocent but nothing less than lies could be expected from a Communist sympathizer deranged loner. Since the point of the briefing was not to get facts but to assert authority, President Kennedy thanked the

FBI director for making the effort to visit him so late at night and dismissed him.

That was followed by another thirty minutes of terse back-and-forth between the Kennedy brothers, toward the end of which Bobby took note of the dark circles formed under his brother's nearly closed eyes. He knew tomorrow would be another tough day in a presidency already full of tough days. He ordered the President off to bed and received no argument. For years, Robert Kennedy's own recollection of these events remained a mystery, as he cited executive privilege and attorney-client privilege and refused to furnish investigators with any information, despite ultimately being cited for contempt.

Before retiring himself, however, the equally exhausted younger brother balled up the paper that he'd been nervously folding and unfolding during the recent conversation and tossed it into the wastebasket. The paper that said, "We can't talk here!" in his own tightly scribbled and recognizable handwriting.

That single piece of twenty-four-pound, antique laid paper with a presidential seal watermark would be collected the next morning by Francis Mullen of the White House janitorial staff and kept as a memento of the day President John F. Kennedy was nearly killed. Although neither Kennedy brother knew it at the time, Bobby had created Exhibit 517, so described and numbered by the Senate and House staff lawyers for the Joint Committee on the Attempted Assassination of the President, or JCAAP. Bobby Kennedy's written exclamation raised a compelling question. What did the President of the United States and the Attorney General have to talk about that was so secret it couldn't be discussed in the Oval Office itself?

The question had many answers, each one raising another set of questions. None of the questions were as succinct as the one that President Kennedy was asked when he arrived in the upstairs family quarters, where he found the First Lady still awake, sitting in the near-darkness. Her bloody pink dress was thrown on the floor, along with her pillbox hat, and she was wearing a bathrobe with her hair wrapped in a towel. The ashtray was full of L&Ms that she'd been chain-smoking, and she was drinking an uncharacteristic glass of Scotch. Her husband lit an uncharacteristic cigarette for himself.

Both acting out of character, they sat quietly together outside the rooms where their children slept with no knowledge of what had happened. "I made you go to Dallas," the President finally said, breaking the silence. "You should never have been there."

Jackie removed the towel and shook her hair out. Her response was heart-achingly simple: "Why do they want to kill you, Jack? What have you done?"

CHAPTER 2:
SEVEN DAYS IN NOVEMBER

NOVEMBER 23, 1963 -
NOVEMBER 28, 1963

THE MORNING AFTER

Robert Kennedy did not go home the night of November 22. Instead, he took a fitful two-hour nap on a couch in Kenny O'Donnell's office, covered by a crimson Harvard blanket that last saw duty at a frigid football game against Yale two years earlier.

On Saturday morning, November 23, Kennedy was awakened by Mrs. Lincoln, carrying a steaming mug of coffee. According to Lincoln's testimony, she had been directed the night before to wake the Attorney General by 8:00 a.m. if he ended up staying at the White House.

Bobby Kennedy was highly agitated. "They're going to look at everything that ever happened now," Mrs. Lincoln quoted him as saying. She said the Attorney General went on to explain his fear that a wide-ranging investigation into the events of the day before was imminent. As his first order of business, Bobby Kennedy asked for and took possession of Lincoln's handwritten telephone log as well as President Kennedy's appointment book. He also wanted to know where the records of people who had been upstairs to visit the President's living quarters were kept and by whom.

In earlier Administrations, these lists of personal visitors were considered public record. Chief White House usher J.B. West testified that he was surprised when the Attorney General asked for them and was told they were needed for safekeeping. West, who thought they were safe enough in the White House, was told they would go to a "more secure place." West surrendered the logs to Robert Kennedy who was, after all, the chief law enforcement officer of the United States at the time he asked for them.

With the Attorney General's business dispatched, Mrs. Lincoln had an agenda item of her own. "A Mary Meyers called again to speak to the President," she began, reading from her own notes.

Kennedy cut her off abruptly. "No, no, no," he said. "Absolutely not."

Later, on Saturday morning, Secret Service agent Robert Bouck was contacted by Deputy Attorney General Nicholas Katzenbach, RFK's number two man at the Justice Department and a key member of the newly formed Working Group. "If you have knowledge of any recordings of private Oval Office or telephonic conversations with the President of the United States that exist under your protection, Mr. Bouck—and I am not saying that I have confirmed personal knowledge of such existence," he said, parsing his words, "those recordings would need to be securely stored on the third floor of the Executive Office Building immediately."

When asked by congressional investigators if he felt any hesitation in obeying Katzenbach's order, Bouck replied, "I believed he was speaking for the Attorney General and that anything the AG had to say came straight from the President of the United States." Bouck immediately collected the recording equipment and all the tapes at his disposal and took them to the discussed location in the newly constructed Executive Office Building, not far from the White House. That floor also headquartered the Special Group for Counterinsurgency, a bureau dedicated to finding ways and means of defeating Communist guerrillas in South Vietnam and elsewhere around the world. Because of its highly secret operations, armed guards patrolled the third floor around the clock.

After one of those guards tried and failed to relieve Bouck of his equipment and tapes, the two men placed them under lock and key with the logs that Robert Kennedy had confiscated earlier in the morning. There was no more secure depository for those vital records that the Attorney General could have chosen, or at least none that were under his control.

While all this was in motion, the replacement of the Secret Service by federal marshals was underway. The lie detector tests were conducted in the cabinet room itself where Chief Marshal Jim McShane had set up. The first agent to pass both the machine's test and the Irish-American McShane's eyeball-to-eyeball analysis was Secret Service agent Abraham Bolden, the first and only African-American member of the Secret Service on November 23, 1963. To McShane's question about whether he believed the Secret Service provided proper protection to the President in Dallas, Bolden had answered "no."

In the morning, when Kennedy emerged from the family quarters, Bolden was there to greet him, having already been standing for hours in the West Sitting Hall. JFK had always liked Bolden and was pleased to hear that he had been assigned to cover him full-time until further notice. "What does Mrs. Bolden think of this new assignment?" asked the President. After the agent told him that she was in favor based on her desire to get her husband out of the house as often as possible, President Kennedy laughed. It had not yet been twenty-four hours since the shots fired in Dallas. When the Kennedy children, Caroline and John-John, emerged with their nanny to see their father, it was Bolden who helped lift both youngsters into the President's arms.

President Kennedy presented himself for work the next morning at 9:32 a.m. He took coffee from Mrs. Lincoln, entered the Oval Office and closed the door. Appointmenst Secretary (and de facto Chief of Staff) Kenneth O'Donnell was seated on the sofa, making notes. He said, "They won't get away with this, Mr. President." Then O'Donnell nodded toward the alcove where Robert Kennedy had spent the rest of his morning making phone calls on the secure line that had been installed there the year before. By the time lunch was served, the first twenty-four hours were over, but the work was just beginning.

At this point, although transfixed by the close call for President
Kennedy and the related deaths, the public was already being told
as fact that the would-be assassin had been caught. Every source
from *The New York Times* and the *Washington Post* to the nation's three
television networks seemed to be making that assumption based on
apparently definitive information from the FBI.

While the public watched an endless rehash of events on TV,
the White House heated up with most of the high-level officials
there knowing in their bones there was much more to be concerned
about than a lone gunman who had just been arrested. To a man,
they seemed to understand that grave forces building up for years
had just been ferociously unleashed on the streets of Dallas.

Indeed, Defense Secretary Robert McNamara, a man who had
been through the thirteen days of danger that had come to be known
as the Cuban Missile Crisis, felt immediately that this situation was at
least as dangerous. "If the President of the United States had been
targeted by a conspiracy," the man with the computer-like brain
wrote in his 1992 memoir, "then the government was not secure,
and if the government was not secure, then neither were the nation's
nuclear weapons."

At first the halls of the West Wing were home to whispers
about who could have truly been behind it all. Staffers up and
down the chain of command knew that a duly elected President
of the United States had been targeted for murder by forces that
probably considered their acts reasonable and necessary and not
treason. Everyone had a theory. The suspects included: the CIA,
organized crime, Soviet agents, key members of the U.S. military
going all the way to the Joint Chiefs, anti-Castro Cubans, Castro
himself, and even Lyndon Johnson. Only one man, speechwriter
Ted Sorensen, held out hope that Oswald could have actually acted
alone, and his belief was, by his own admission, "more a matter of
denial than conviction."

What to do about it was equally confusing. Everyone wanted to
obliterate this craven attempt to control U.S. policy through murder,
but they knew the fight ahead had the potential to cripple JFK's

presidency with as much finality as a fatal bullet would have.

There was much to fear. Most of the prime suspects could be prevented from gaining access to the White House to do actual physical harm to the President and his staff. There was one force, however, that could not be restrained—the military power of the United States. The nation's military readiness had been advanced to DEFCON 2—one step short of actual nuclear missiles flying. The decision had been made without the sign-off of the commander-in-chief, who had been notified three hours later as an afterthought.

Kenny O'Donnell bluntly worried about the *Seven Days in May* scenario, based on a popular book about a military coup in the United States. (The film starring Burt Lancaster and Kirk Douglas would be released only a few months later.) Well before Dallas turned up the paranoia, President Kennedy had told friends in private conversations after reading the book that he feared something similar could happen to him. He had experienced first-hand the insubordination of the Joint Chiefs, particularly the Air Force's chief General Curtis LeMay. Even General Lyman Lemnitzer, the former chair and now Supreme Allied Commander of NATO, seemed to have a first response that questioned any order from the White House rather than simply following it.

Only one thing was crystal clear at this moment. The cold war that had been taking place within the Kennedy Administration had gone searingly hot on the streets of Dallas. Things would not—*could not*—go back to normal.

Dark Forces

By Saturday morning, no one had any doubt that the true target of Friday's gun attack in Dallas was President John Kennedy and that Governor John Connally, Special Agent Clint Hill, Police Officer J.D. Tippit and even injured Special Agent Roy Kellerman were all just collateral damage. Most Americans never seriously considered any other scenario, even though Connally, like Kennedy, had his own share of dark forces that wished him ill.

Indeed, the hatred for President Kennedy in certain circles ran deep. Those people kept their feelings to themselves for the most part, but they were of the strong opinion that it was a shame that the assassin or assassins had missed. Around the globe many citizens thought the fact that things like this happened in America was not surprising. Many observers were only surprised that Kennedy had cheated death, given the lethality of his enemies.

For most Americans, though, the idea that anyone should try to snuff out the life of the young, vital President seemed particularly outrageous. This may have been true in Dallas even more than elsewhere, amplified by the belief that the shootings had stained the city's reputation, perhaps forever.

Police operators lost track of the number of telephoned death threats against Oswald. Some were explicit enough to alarm Dallas Police Chief Jesse Curry. For the first weekend, the suspect stayed in a maximum-security cell on the fifth floor of the Dallas Police Department. Fearing a possible lynch mob, Curry also called back off-duty policemen to help protect his besieged headquarters.

Outside his window, Curry could see an angry mob demanding that justice be delivered to the man they assumed was the killer. They shouted curses and shook fists. One man threw a stone. A flying squad of police waded into the crowd, billy clubs swinging, and arrested him without challenge. Their bold action, and the implicit promise of more if necessary, squelched a potential explosion.

Curry, however, had seen enough. Referring to Oswald, he told Captain Fritz, "We've got to get that little shit out of here."

In Nashville, Tennessee, Jimmy Hoffa, the leader of the most powerful labor union in America, was in an upbeat mood despite fighting a jury tampering charge brought by the Justice Department. The working group's Walter Sheridan had returned to Nashville to sound the Teamsters leader out about yesterday's events during a booking procedure.

Hoffa sucker-punched Sheridan by calling Dallas a "great tragedy" so that when the investigator agreed, Hoffa could follow with "that they missed." Even so, Sheridan probed Hoffa's potential involvement, telling the pugnacious leader, "If you gave the order, then God Himself can't help you." But if someone else gave the order and Hoffa gave them up, he might be able to get off without doing any time at all, "much as I hate to hear those words come out of my mouth."

Hoffa's profane response, characterizing Sheridan's mouth as already involved with oral sex with another man, ended the conversation. If James Riddle Hoffa was going to be implicated in the attempt on John Kennedy's life, it would involve more than threats or plea bargains to accomplish it.

THE FORTRESS AT 1600
PENNSYLVANIA AVENUE

During this first weekend after the assassination attempt, the residence and workplace for the nation's chief executive had a siege quality. The idea of "blinding" the White House fence with sheet metal was rejected in favor of driving in a collection of military buses on Saturday night and using them to form a cordon around the grounds. The perimeter was effectively pushed back across the street further into Lafayette Square. Even beyond that, D.C. police patrolled in record numbers.

White House reporters spotted Attorney General Robert Kennedy coming and going on several occasions, always in the company of large, hard-faced men carrying briefcases and wearing jackets that bulged from shoulder holsters they made no effort to conceal. This was shocking because Kennedy had an aversion to security, thinking it intrusive. Even after receiving death threats in 1962, he had said, "Kennedys don't need bodyguards," and gone on about his business of confronting organized crime and trying to jail its leaders.

Dallas had changed all that. The President of the United States had been targeted by a man who may or may not have been working alone, and probably by a larger conspiracy, the makeup of which he had not yet determined. No precaution was too much. Not now.

As a result, a half-dozen military snipers with spotters were posted on the roof of the White House, each man armed with a bolt-action 30.06 Springfield rifle, capable of knocking a bison off its feet at distance. All were in radio contact with marshals who walked the perimeter. Each sniper was fully prepared to shoot at anyone considered to be a threat to the safety of the President.

There had been calls to activate National Guard troops to watch over the White House in the first hours, but RFK had refused the offer. While others debated his motivation, the truth was that he did not want the Guard called in because he felt the country might well be in the middle of a coup attempt. If National Guard troops were deployed around the White House, treasonous leaders in the extreme right wing of the U.S. military might cause U.S. Army forces to move on them, spilling American blood in the worst fratricide since the Civil War.

The younger Kennedy was not in a trusting mood. As savvy politically as any two people operating in the nation's capital, John and Robert Kennedy knew they might be hurt by the executive order evicting the Secret Service. The problem was, there would be no politics or scandal to worry about if they did not survive the next few days. That was central. They could not allow themselves to think of this any other way. They had families to protect and they were, said the Attorney General, "surrounded by enemies."

Yet Robert Kennedy could not turn to the federal forces under his true command as Attorney General, those of the Federal Bureau of Investigation. J. Edgar Hoover's FBI had little use for the Kennedy brothers, spying on them and keeping files of all manner of indiscretion. Some of the incidents on file were concocted or overblown, but a good portion were true and incriminating enough to force President Kennedy to keep Hoover on the job when everyone else assumed he would fire him. The FBI under Hoover was compromised and not to be trusted.

Having rejected the services of the U.S. Army, the National Guard, the FBI and the Secret Service, the remaining list of capable security assistants was extremely short. In fact, it had only one name on it. Jim McShane.

Fellow Irish-American Chief U.S. Marshal Jim McShane ran the federal marshals. These people were loyal to McShane, and McShane was loyal to the Kennedys. He had started his career as a New York cop and had worked with Bobby as an investigator for the Senate Rackets Committee. He had even been a bodyguard for candidate John Kennedy during the 1960 election.

McShane and his marshals were called off their assignment protecting Bobby Kennedy's Hickory Hill estate early Saturday afternoon and told to come to the White House immediately, and to bring "other men you can personally vouch for" directly as well.

It is difficult to assess whether this action of embracing the federal marshals was needed or not. In the heat of the moment, all parties to these discussions have described over the years a sense of panic over personal safety that passed like an infection from one Administration player to another. With the hindsight of fifty years, it now seems to have escalated a conflict that was already high to a level at least equal to the days of the Cuban Missile Crisis.

The President of the United States, however, was not ready to speak publicly or answer hard questions about this issue or any other. Press Secretary Pierre Salinger got that assignment. His opening statement expressed that the President was shocked and saddened by the loss of Connally, Hill and Tippit. He fed the assembled journalists a tidbit about Jackie, describing her as "still shaken but recovering," noting that her wrist fracture was expected to heal fully with no loss of mobility.

The reporters, on the other hand, wanted to know if the White House's use of federal marshals meant the Administration was convinced the Secret Service and FBI were riddled with spies or conspirators. It was a fair, although uncomfortable, question, and certainly not one the President intended to answer until he absolutely had to.

Salinger fell on that sword, acting as the point man for the politically attuned machinery of the White House. He cast the decision as a temporary reassignment and nothing more. It was designed to give the Secret Service a chance to concentrate on its internal review of the failure in Dallas and adjust rather than focus on the demanding job of securing the White House, which others could do. Salinger tried to sell the idea that these agencies had their own problems to take care of, but nobody seemed to be completely buying it. In frustration, he blurted out the awful truth. "You try getting shot at," said the usually gregarious talking head for the Administration, "and see if you want to trust the people who were supposed to protect you." Even the candid Salinger knew immediately he had said too much too soon.

Even so, immediate polls showed that the public bought the Administration's argument. This was a testament to John Kennedy's power to evoke empathy, which would be his strongest asset in the years ahead. On the other hand, winning the debate was not winning the battle. Feeling shamed and humiliated, regardless of presidential explanations, Secret Service agents who had routinely covered up an array of presidential misbehavior since they got the assignment to protect "Lancer" (JFK's codename) suddenly felt a little bit less committed to the cause.

By the evening of Saturday, November 23, it was clear to those who were in Washington, D.C., that the White House was bristling with firepower and coiled like a snake, ready to strike if it had to. Even under these extraordinary circumstances, however, politics could not be put aside. The executive order banning the Secret Service from doing its job protecting the President was a tactical necessity that created a political storm. As soon as it had been signed, Republicans on Capitol Hill began whispering about this act as an overreaction. With an election less than a year away, Dallas had provided them with their first issue. The first battlefield would be the Sunday talk shows.

ON THE RECORD

In late 1963, Sunday morning talk shows were thriving in numbers and important to the national dialogue. On this particular Sunday morning, November 24, they became an emotionally wrought hybrid for national mourning, breaking news and serving as the political starting gun of the 1964 presidential election campaign.

Attorney General Robert Kennedy appeared on all three network talk shows, an unprecedented feat of logic and stamina. He taped CBS's second-place *Face the Nation* first, sped across town to open up NBC's top-rated *Meet the Press,* and then closed out the hour with ABC's third-place *Issues and Answers.* All shows drew record numbers of viewers to their broadcasts.

"American democracy is strong enough today that no cowardly bullets can stop the long arc of progress," the Attorney General told CBS moderator Paul Niven, as if this were breaking news, on his first stop at *Face the Nation.* On the security issue, Kennedy stated the Administration's premise that there was no need to surround the nation's residence with actual troops from the Army or the National Guard, that the Secret Service needed to focus on its internal investigation, and that the FBI had its hands full running point on the investigation that he had begun at his brother's direction. He tried to describe the federal marshals as the logical choice. Niven did not contest this analysis, and the Attorney General was out the door into a waiting limousine before the newsman could think of a follow-up.

Over on ABC's *Issues and Answers,* however, Senator Barry Goldwater called the Secret Service decision "reckless" and "knee-jerk," citing it as just another example that the Kennedy Administration "continues to make policy based on emotions, not facts." When moderator Howard K. Smith pointed out that as the leading Republican candidate to run against President Kennedy in 1964, Goldwater's criticism might be seen as political, the irascible senator refused to back down. "If I was president, and someone shot at me," he argued, "I'd be focused on finding and punishing those responsible, and not on expelling the people who had already paid a blood sacrifice, as Agent Hill did."

NBC's *Meet the Press* featured Vice President Lyndon Johnson being interviewed by moderator Ned Brooks at the top of the hour.

Only the day before, Johnson had forced his young aide Jack Valenti to suffer the indignity of prepping his boss for the appearance while LBJ sat on his office toilet with the door open. Valenti's advice, uncomfortably given, was still spot on. Johnson had been obsessed with what he was sure was the public perception that he was the man who nearly let the President be murdered in his home state of Texas. Valenti argued that during times of crisis, sins are forgiven. "You love President Kennedy," began Valenti, ticking off LBJ's talking points for the broadcast. "You hope that justice for this insane murderer Oswald will come swiftly and that you will do anything in your power to see that it does."

On the live broadcast, Johnson embraced a guilty solo Oswald with Southern gusto. "We already know that this was the work of some lone nut, someone who wasn't even a Texan in the first place," he drawled. "The people of Texas love President Kennedy like I do." This, of course, was a lie. The people of Texas were sharply divided about Kennedy, and the Vice President harbored deep resentments toward the President and his Eastern establishment inner circle.

On the way to the ABC studios that morning, Bobby Kennedy wrote out his potential responses to the Goldwater attacks in longhand on a yellow legal pad in order to better field the issue when it came up. When moderator Howard Smith gave Kennedy the opening, he was ready. "This is no time for partisan politics or launching campaigns," he said. "Senator Goldwater needs to think before he speaks. President Kennedy knows this from deep experience, and that is why he is studying the situation now and gathering information before he briefs the American people."

Senator Goldwater, too, had appeared on more than one show that day, also being interviewed by Ned Brooks on *Meet the Press* after Vice President Johnson had left the studio. It was there that he managed to use Lee Harvey Oswald as a chance to bolster his anti-Communist credentials. Calling the accused assassin both a "Communist sympathizer" and "pro-Castro," the Arizonan stated, "If he was taking orders from the Soviets or the Cubans to attack the President, then there should be hell to pay. Right now." Asked by

Brooks if he was talking about a military response, he replied that he "wouldn't take anything off the table."

President Kennedy, Kenneth O'Donnell, and Defense Secretary Robert McNamara watched all three talk shows simultaneously in the Oval Office that morning. When O'Donnell noted that Goldwater was as bad as the Joint Chiefs, their Commander-in-Chief remarked, "Why do you suppose these people all think nuking the Russians is the solution to everything?" He was, by all accounts, only half kidding.

Goldwater's pugnacious and partisan attitude was widely covered and soon forgotten but it did allow the Kennedy Administration to look calmer by comparison and allowed them to defuse the Secret Service issue before it gained real traction. It also added to the already great public sympathy for the President of the United States, whose job approval rating was measured at seventy-nine percent, the highest it had been since it soared in the aftermath of the Bay of Pigs disaster in 1961. Privately, Republicans groused that the worse things got for President Kennedy, the more the public seemed to like him. It was a premise that would eventually be tested to the limit.

THANKING GOD

The television appearances of Robert Kennedy and Lyndon Johnson on Sunday only half-completed the White House strategy. Next on the itinerary was St. Matthew's Cathedral on Rhode Island Avenue in Washington where the Kennedys worshipped. The cross-shaped, redbrick building with the weathered, green copper dome was a conspicuous landmark and would prove to be an excellent backdrop for a family show of support.

Bishop Philip Hannan celebrated a Thanksgiving Mass for the Kennedy family in sonorous Latin, but when he preached his sermon, Hannan switched to a language all could understand:

> *We thank God and His son Jesus Christ and the glorious Virgin that John and Jacqueline Kennedy are preserved alive today. Our*

*hearts are heavy because of what they have suffered, yet also glad,
because the President and First Lady walked through the valley
of the shadow of death, and the Lord saw fit to spare them for
further service.*

While Hannan spoke, Chief Marshal McShane was outside the cathedral, directing the security operation on the exterior perimeter, plus coordinating five undercover marshals inside the building. Almost pitiably, the Secret Service dispatched a unit as they always did, but this time they stood on the side, quietly fuming and smoking cigarettes.

Inside, after the services, President Kennedy met privately with Hannan to give confession. Hannan did not speak about this until shortly before his death in 2011 at the age of ninety-eight. He recalled telling Kennedy that he was "only the intermediary" and that the President should consider his words as being delivered to God.

In the privacy of a confession booth, John Kennedy told Bishop Hannan, "I'm afraid my sins have caught up with me." Hannan wanted to know if they had been committed in the service of the Lord. "Maybe a few" was Kennedy's reply. Told to say ten Hail Marys for each sin that was personal, Kennedy showed his humor even then. "I'm not sure the American people want me to be away from the job that long." Hannan told him to start with ten that Sunday and the President agreed.

Then, as the Kennedy family exited into the watery November gloom, they were swarmed by reporters. Every national media outlet had sent someone; international reporters were arriving by the hour; even local papers and TV stations had their own teams in both Dallas and Washington to cover the assassination attempt and its aftermath. Kennedy ignored the questions the Johnny-come-latelies shouted at him. He engaged with some of the regular press corps, though. The chief executive understood his relationship with the media better than any of his predecessors. He knew reporters wanted to be in his field of vision, literally and symbolically, and they would often slant stories to stay in favor at the White House. JFK had created a club everyone wanted to join.

Standing next to each other, both dressed for Sunday services, the President and First Lady provided quite a contrast from the bloody examples they had been only forty-eight hours earlier. "Today, we mourn the victims as is appropriate," said the man who had nearly been among them. "Tomorrow, we will return our attention to finding the guilty parties and holding them accountable."

Pierre Salinger visibly winced from the sidelines. Particularly when reporters shouted the obvious question: "When you say 'guilty parties,' are you saying you believe this was a conspiracy?"

"I'm withholding judgment until the facts are clear. It's irresponsible to speculate," concluded the President, even though that is exactly what he and his inner circle had been doing almost nonstop for two days.

Jackie Kennedy, seeing Salinger's discomfort, pulled at her husband's arm. "If you'll excuse us," she said to the press in her now trademark whisper, and she pulled the President away, allowing herself to be used as a human shield.

At this point, Salinger was set upon by the reporters. He clarified that President Kennedy had been using the term "guilty parties" only in a generic sense, that they were aware that the early investigation seemed to be focusing on Lee Harvey Oswald as a lone gunman. He promised a news conference where the President would take all questions. Pressed on a date, he offered Tuesday as a likely candidate, buying time under the pretext of needing to bury the dead.

The federal marshals around President and Mrs. Kennedy were a collection of clean-cut men in off-the-rack suits, eyes constantly shifting. As several escorted the first couple toward a waiting Lincoln limousine, others moved quickly to put themselves in front of the pack of reporters, roughly shoving them back.

The President and First Lady got into the waiting Lincoln. It was a closed car, not a convertible like the one in Dallas. Never again would such an exposed vehicle be used by an American president.

Motorcycle cops fore and aft, it sped away. Even those uniformed officers had been personally approved by RFK's right-hand man at the Justice Department, Nicholas Katzenbach, that morning before church. He had asked for a dozen local police officers to be sent over, from which he randomly selected four at the last possible minute. When it came to personal security, no one was taking any chances.

JOHNSON AGONIZES

After his appearance on *Meet the Press*, Vice President Lyndon Johnson, a member of the Disciples of Christ, had been driven by Jack Valenti across town to the National City Christian Church where he took a seat in the front pew next to his wife, Claudia "Lady Bird" Johnson. The Vice President looked ravaged, having put all his energy into his televised performance. Every so often, Lady Bird would touch his hand or pat him on the arm. He kept shaking her off. His outsize features showed outsize anxiety. Years later, it seems clear he was not concerned for the Kennedys or the Connallys, but for himself.

Later, at his own impromptu news encounter outside the church, Johnson was asked about his emotions and said, "I am sadder than I know how to tell you. John Connally was a friend. I've known him since he was a very young man, and liked him and admired him, too. He worked for me for a spell and he made a wonderful, just a wonderful, governor of Texas. I looked to see him on the national stage one day before too long. I wouldn't have been surprised to see him run for President, and I wouldn't have been surprised to see him win."

More than a few reporters noted Johnson's focus on Connally without mentioning Kennedy but reasoned that Connally was dead and the President still among the living. It was an oversight that could easily be made by a man enduring profound grief for a friend and fellow Texan. And they noted Johnson's invoking the presidential chances of his protégé when his own were always on his mind. All in all, it felt tone deaf but, to those who knew him, that was LBJ.

Was Johnson upset because he had come within half a second of being the President of the United States? Or was he aware that with Kennedy's survival and continued viability in the 1964 presidential election that he, Johnson, might now more easily be dumped from the ticket he had blackmailed his way onto in 1960?

Or did it go beyond even that?

An astute politician, LBJ knew that if he was now going to run for President, he'd have to wait until 1968 whether JFK kept him on the ticket or not. He'd be sixty by then—not too old, but not young either, particularly with his record of heart troubles. If he ran, he probably wouldn't run unopposed. Bobby Kennedy seemed unlikely to wait in line while somebody else succeeded his brother. "That ruthless little shit doesn't wait for anybody, except maybe Jack," LBJ had told another of his young assistants, Bill Moyers. "Bobby Kennedy's the kind of guy who gets into a revolving door behind you and comes out in front."

All that was interesting, but not for today. Even the 1964 election lay almost a year away, and a politician's year was longer than a dog's.

Johnson did not need a heart attack or an imposing opponent to cause him concern, however. There was also the growing scandal that had begun last summer over Johnson's protégé, Bobby "Little Lyndon" Baker, one that involved trading money and women for votes and government contracts. And if that weren't enough, another Johnson associate, Billie Sol Estes, was up to his ears in a scandal from the year before that threatened to send Johnson to jail amid charges involving suitcases of money and implications of being an accessory to murder.

As it turned out, on the very day that LBJ was watching the carnage from his own limo in the presidential motorcade, a Senate Rules Committee in Washington, D.C. was hearing testimony in closed session from a Donald Reynolds about a $100,000 payoff that had been made to Bobby Baker intended for Johnson.

Possibly just as threatening for LBJ was the fact that in the New York offices of *Life* magazine, managing editor George Hunt had convened a gathering of nine reporters, all working on a story about Johnson's path from poverty to wealth while pursuing a life in politics. Several of these reporters, including Pulitzer Prize-winning reporter William Lambert, had just returned from Texas with information that was going to be split up and investigated by the entire team. That Sunday morning, however, their work was postponed indefinitely while the journalists were instructed to pursue the more interesting angle of a potential assassination of a popular president.

The news of the assassination attempt in Dallas had re-focused priorities in both the Senate committee and at *Life* magazine. Suspicious financial practices by the Vice President hardly merited attention when the President's life had just been threatened.

CHANGE OF PLANS

With the world watching what was happening at the Dallas Police Department, Chief Jesse Curry fretted in his office on Sunday morning about a promise he had made to the media that wasn't sitting well with him. He had agreed to allow them to film the transfer of Lee Oswald to the county jail. In order to do that, the accused assassin would be led through the parking basement of the headquarters on Sunday at 12:30 p.m., nearly two days to the hour after he was alleged to have shot at the presidential motorcade. Curry sat in his office, drinking coffee from a thermos that his wife had handed him on his way out the door at 6 a.m. After watching all the morning news shows, he'd started to have buyer's remorse. After all, the White House was treating security as a national priority. Could he do any less?

Curry voiced these doubts to none other than Jack Ruby, the nightclub owner who had been chased out of Parkland Hospital when the presidential party arrived. Ruby, a regular presence around Dallas police, had brought take-out scrambled eggs for Curry to eat. Ruby wanted to know what Oswald had said so far to the police. "Jack," said Curry, "I appreciate everything you do for this department, but I can't talk to you about the prisoner."

"I know, I know," agreed Ruby. "Just makes me mad as hell to see this dark cloud he's put over Texas."

At that point, Detective James Leavelle presented himself at the chief's door and asked if he could have a moment. Leavelle cut a distinctive appearance in his cream-colored suit and his silverbelly Stetson "Open Road" hat. He was to be the man handcuffed to Oswald for the transfer, something that didn't bother him nearly as much as the logistics. Leavelle looked uncomfortable to say more and Curry dismissed Ruby with another thanks for the breakfast run he had made.

Leavelle then made a strong case to Curry that the elevator at the Dallas Police Department should be stopped on the first floor where they should take the prisoner off, put him in a car on Main Street, and whisk him off to the county jail before the media in the basement even realized he'd been moved.

Curry considered this carefully. "You want me to lie to the press?"

"Only if our priority is to keep the prisoner alive long enough to give him the death sentence," answered Leavelle.

Curry thought about it. He'd been an all-district tackle for Dallas Technical High School and led their football team all the way to the state finals back in 1933. "A feint might be just what we need here." Curry gave Leavelle the go-ahead and they agreed that the press would be told only after Oswald was already on the way. Sure, the TV networks with their live cameras down in the basement would be furious but they didn't run the show, he thought. He was still in charge.

When the time came for the transfer, the basement was packed with nearly forty newsmen, seventy police officers, three large "live" television cameras, an armored truck, and Jack Ruby. None of those many officers, it turned out, had bothered to even question Ruby about being there. He was simply a part of the scene in this town and he poured free drinks for cops at the Carousel Club.

Instead of Oswald coming off the elevator, however, it was

Chief Curry stepping forward. "Now boys, I know this may make you all mad as hornets," he began, "but the prisoner has already been transferred to county jail."

The disapproval recorded by the television cameras was cacophonous and angry. Even Jack Ruby pushed his way toward Curry, his morning breakfast companion, and yelled, "You lied to me, Chief!" As Ruby parted the crowd, he gestured, revealing a .38 caliber revolver under his jacket. A cry went up from a nearby reporter, "He's got a gun!" Suddenly, officers were all over their patron, wrestling him to the ground.

Curry would normally have let Ruby go with a warning and thanked his lucky stars that things had gone no further. But there were so many reporters who witnessed Ruby's takedown that it could not be ignored—particularly since the fifty-two-year-old seemed irrational.

Under questioning, the nightclub operator said he'd come to the basement on the spur of the moment, wanting to see for himself the face of the man who had darkened the good name of Texas and terrorized the Kennedy family.

What Curry and many in the Dallas Police Department knew was that Ruby had a reputation for being mobbed up with deep contacts in the organized crime underworld. What if he wasn't telling the truth about his motives? What if Jack Ruby had been sent to silence Lee Harvey Oswald from talking?

After a few hours, however, Ruby's gun was confiscated, and he was released with a warning not to make the same mistake twice.

A TALE OF TWO FUNERALS

Through circumstance, bad planning, and, quite possibly, political motivations, both the funerals of Secret Service agent Clint Hill in Washington, D.C., and Governor John Connally and police officer J.D. Tippit in Texas were scheduled at the same time on Monday. Based on long-established protocols of rank, the original plans called for President Kennedy to return to Texas to be at the funeral of the governor and for Vice President Lyndon Johnson to cover Hill's funeral at Arlington National Cemetery. LBJ made no secret of his displeasure at being forced to miss out on the funeral of a man he had known since 1939. Coming on the heels of being escorted off Air Force One, this new slight left him "sucking hind tit again," as he told Moyers, Valenti and anyone else who would listen.

Both Kenny O'Donnell and Pierre Salinger confronted the President and his brother about this plan and told them it must be stopped immediately. There was no way that Kennedy could go back to Texas so soon. That was a non-starter. And there was no way he could miss the funeral of the Secret Service agent who gave his life to save him, particularly when the Kennedys had rewarded that sacrifice by banishing the Secret Service from the White House. Protocol made no difference in this situation.

Both Kennedys felt the analysis was correct. They accepted the reality of the situation and made it work for them. If you get to deliver good news to someone, take credit for it if you can.

JFK called LBJ first. "Lyndon, I just told these people that you have to represent this Administration back in Texas at the funeral for Governor Connally," said the President. "I need you get on Air Force Two and return there now so you can pay all our respect to your friend on behalf of the United States of America. Will you do that for your country, Lyndon?" Johnson barked out a fast yes and effusively thanked the President he had been cursing all weekend.

The President then called the head of the Secret Service, Chief James Rowley, and told him there was no way that protocol would keep him from Arlington National Cemetery on Monday and that he would like to say a few words, if Rowley would allow it. He knew that the situation in the past day had been "misinterpreted" by some of his political opponents, said Kennedy, but this was a good way to send the message that there was "no daylight" between the President and the brave agents who put their lives on the line to protect him. Rowley also effusively thanked the President he had been cursing since the day before.

Figuring they had caught a break, Robert Kennedy returned to

Hickory Hill under escort of the federal marshals to shower, shave and change into some clean clothes. John Kennedy took lunch with his wife and children. With the help of the nanny, both Caroline and John-John had made craft-paper cards for the President to welcome him home.

Monday in Washington, D.C., was raw and chilly, with a biting wind blustering down from the north. Arlington National Cemetery, at one time Robert E. Lee's mansion and grounds, had since become the chief military burial ground for the country Lee had fought so hard to defeat. Most of the leaves were off the trees at the cemetery across the Potomac. The grass had started to go yellow. The waiting grave stood open, a new wound in the earth. By the grave, the Secret Service had set up a portable lectern with a bulletproof glass shield in front.

Secret Service Special Agent Clint Hill was to be buried here based on having served in the U.S. Army from 1954 to 1957. A special presidential order had waived any other issues that might have been raised under normal circumstances. Hill, in the view of almost everyone, had given his life on the field of battle at Dealey Plaza.

The U.S. Secret Service had a staff of nearly two hundred agents working for it nationwide. Thirty-four of them had been in the presidential detail, responsible for protecting John F. Kennedy around the clock. They worked in eight-hour shifts, rotating the duty times every two weeks.

Clint Hill had been assigned to the Jacqueline Kennedy detail as the special agent in charge. He had been positioned in the follow-up car behind the one with the Kennedys and the Connallys when he saw something and leaped instinctively to shield the President and First Lady, saving their lives and giving up his own in the process. While the President and the Attorney General had strategized and acted over the past forty-eight hours, Jackie Kennedy had been left alone with her grief. Ever since the attack in Dallas, there was speculation among a few wags that Hill and the First Lady had been involved in an extramarital affair, something that has never been confirmed and was, in fact, denied by both parties while they were alive. What is clear, however, is that Clint Hill had become Mrs. Kennedy's close friend, and she found the pain of his loss unbearable.

The assistant special agent in charge in Dallas had been Roy Kellerman, who was advised to stay there to recuperate from a shoulder wound that had required extensive surgery. Kellerman refused this advice and came to Arlington, where he sat with the contingent of Secret Service agents come to mourn their fallen friend. These men were easy to spot, and not just because they sat together. They were fairly young and tough and clean-cut. Many of them had to be wondering if, faced with identical circumstances, they would have responded as quickly and as bravely as Clint Hill did.

President and Mrs. Kennedy were seated strategically out of view of any potential line of fire. For this event, the Secret Service had been allowed to provide security, even though the Attorney General had seen to it that a generous contingent of federal marshals was also on the job to watch the watchers. While it was obvious that fence-mending needed to be done, the President being at the service was seen as a clear sign that his rearranging of White House security was temporary, as he'd said all along through his spokesmen, including his brother. Regardless of the politics, security was heavy. Some carried pistols, some tommy guns, and some scope-sighted rifles. They all wore don't-tread-on-me expressions. All agents regarded anyone they were unfamiliar with through hard eyes. To a man, they looked jumpy as hell.

The surprise of the event, however, was yet to come. After Chief James Rowley spoke about courage, self-sacrifice and duty, it was expected that President Kennedy would speak briefly. He did not. Instead, it was the First Lady who walked to the lectern. All three networks had TV cameras on hand to record the emotional moment:

A good man I called my friend is dead. Clint Hill gave his own life so that my husband and I might live. No one made him jump up on the trunk of our car. No one would have thought less of him if he didn't do it, but he did, and now he is gone. If God ever needs a bodyguard up in Heaven, He will find one in Clint Hill. He

protected us as he would his own family. He made the whole country
his family in Dallas on Friday afternoon. Thank you.

The entire speech by Jackie Kennedy was so short that it
was replayed in its entirety over and over on November 25. Her
husband did not speak, but after the service he presented Hill's wife,
Gwen, with a folded, cased flag, the kind any veteran's widow was
entitled to have. He gave her a warm, long hug and in an image
made famous, he removed his white pocket-handkerchief to dry
the tears from Gwen Hill's eyes. After that, Kennedy and his wife
walked over to the Secret Service contingent and spoke to agents for
seventeen minutes.

Those pictures of the Kennedys offering grief counseling in
the shadow of their own brush with death seemed for the moment
to completely eliminate the issue of the Secret Service. What the
First Lady did not know, but surely suspected, was that a number of
these agents knew a great deal more about her husband's activities
when he was not with his family than she did. If they were to speak,
the damage to the reputation of the First Family simply could not
be calculated.

ANOTHER PROFILE IN COURAGE

By Tuesday, the initial shock had worn off, the bodies of the dead
had been buried, and the White House knew that the President of
the United States needed to speak to the American people. John
Kennedy had made statements, but they were limited in scope and
general in information. It was time to say more in a press conference,
an art form he had mastered in sixty-four different appearances
before Dallas.

Far more reporters than usual crowded the State Department
auditorium waiting for Kennedy to appear. Because of the
international reporters in town and the local reporters flown in
from around the country, seating was at such a premium that many
others had been turned away, put into a nearby room with a closed-

circuit feed.

Top Story reporters Frank Altman and Adam Berkowitz had come to cover the President as a team. They had shared their first byline in the current week's magazine under the headline: "Ambush in Dallas: JFK's Close Call." They passed the time arguing—about seats, about protocol in the asking of questions, and even about whether or not Ruby would make bail. Theirs was a shotgun marriage that made more sense to news management at the magazine than to the concerned parties.

Normally, press secretary Pierre Salinger would have introduced the President, but Kennedy told him to hold off. It was not like he was an unknown quantity. Asked what his strategy would be, the President shrugged. "Kennedys smile, Pierre. That's how we do it."

As the event was being televised live, JFK entered precisely on cue at 9 p.m., primetime on the East Coast and dinnertime on the West Coast. He looked tanned and fit as usual. Seeing him enter, so masculine, so presidential, and so alive, the White House press corps burst into authentic and spontaneous applause out of the sheer spirit of it all.

He was there in the room for the reporters and there on the screens for the rest of America to accept the outpouring of emotion in a give-and-take that was cathartic for everyone. Unlike Truman and Eisenhower, presidents past their prime and not especially good-looking to begin with, this president understood what TV could do for him, the bond it could forge with the people who voted for him.

"I've never looked forward to taking your questions so much before," said the President, and the reporters broke up. How could they help it?

The President said he had a brief statement before those questions, and continued:

> *First, I'd like to speak to our friends from around the world. They should know that although we have been hurt, we are also a strong nation that knows how to rise to a great challenge. And to our adversaries, they should take no advantage of these times. The*

*United States is as confident today as we were last Friday before any
shots were fired. Let's begin.*

"Mr. President!" A sea of hands flew into the air. Kennedy
pointed to Kevin Barnes, the White House correspondent from the
Washington Post, who wanted to know if the President was as yet
satisfied that Lee Harvey Oswald was the lone shooter.

"That certainly seems to be what the FBI believes," responded
Kennedy. "They seem confident that the accused assassin is in
the hands of the law. For myself, I am confident the truth will
come out during the investigation and at this man's trial." His face
hardened. "Political murder of any kind has no place in a civil,
democratic society."

The man from the *Post* got a follow-up. Why did the President
refuse to say Oswald's name?

"The Greek historian Herodotus tells of a man who burned a
great temple to win everlasting fame. 'I know his name,' Herodotus
said, 'but I will not set it down here.' And that man who burned
the temple because he wanted to be remembered forever has been
forgotten for twenty-five hundred years." It was pure JFK. As it
turned out, the story of the ancient Greek had been dredged up by
his speechwriter Ted Sorensen, but Kennedy made the lines his own
when he delivered them. That talent he had in abundance.

"Mr. President, maybe you don't want to use his name because
you think there are other names that should go along with his. Could
he have been part of a larger conspiracy?" This question came from
Helen Thomas of UPI.

"Helen, there you go again, always asking these easy questions."
Kennedy's disarming grin and the subsequent reaction gave him
time to collect his thoughts. He had some pretty definite ideas about
who might want to shoot him besides Lee Harvey Oswald. His inner
circle was already looking into them.

"If the evidence against the accused is strong enough, they'll
indict him," he said. "If they indict him, he'll go to trial. If he's
convicted, he'll suffer the appropriate penalties under the law. If

there were others involved, I expect that they will have the same treatment, but I do not have any personal knowledge that there are."

"Do you expect to be called as a witness?" This came from NBC's Chet Huntley.

JFK looked surprised, as it was not something he'd given any thought to yet. "I'm not sure a sitting President can be," he said slowly. "I'd have to consult with the Justice Department before I gave you a firm answer." He meant he would have to talk to his brother. He went on, "The courts might also have to speak to that issue. It's an interesting question, Chet. I have already given a statement to FBI agents and, of course, I'll cooperate with any investigations where I can be helpful."

That statement took Kennedy into even more uncertain territory. The questions flew fast and furious. Who was investigating now? Would the President appoint a special investigatory panel of his own? What was the next step?

President Kennedy soon found himself discussing the intricacies of jurisdiction, given that the crime happened in Dallas, and then supporting the FBI's investigation, even though he personally had no trust whatsoever in any agents working for J. Edgar Hoover. His answer was a stall, one that he knew he could not let stand for long.

If the federal marshals had to stand in for the Secret Service, what agency or investigatory body could be called in to replace the Federal Bureau of Investigation?

This would need to be worked out and soon. The question of who would write the official record of what happened in Dallas, determine who was guilty and of what crime or crimes, had to be decided.

INSIDE THE RUSSIAN BOX

In the midst of the chaotic news conference, Frank Altman had risen to his feet and asked, "What about the Soviets?" He was drowned out by other reporters.

As JFK scanned the room, he was about to pick another

questioner when Adam Berkowitz shot to his feet. "What about the Soviets!" Berkowitz shouted his repeat of his partner's question so loudly that it shocked the room into near silence. It also got the attention of the President.

"I've spoken to Chairman Khrushchev briefly," said Kennedy. "He assured me that his country was in no way involved in the attack in Dallas, planning or operationally."

Before a new question could arise from the crowd, Berkowitz followed up. "Do you believe him?" Backstage, both O'Donnell and Salinger were observed to wince.

President Kennedy answered with his usual poise. "I told the Chairman *doveryai no proveryai*. I learned that phrase last year during the Nuclear Test Ban negotiations. In English, I believe it means trust but verify." JFK paused, a hint of smile, and coated his message in the honey of humor. "The Chairman thought my Russian accent could use a great deal of work but I believe he did get the message anyway."

In actual fact, Khrushchev had gotten the message so directly that the next day he dispatched Anatoly Dobrynin, the Soviet ambassador to the United States, to meet with Robert Kennedy. The two men had back-channeled the deal that defused the Cuban Missile Crisis just over a year earlier. Back then it had been Bobby coming to the Soviets with information about President Kennedy's true feelings and problems. This time it was reversed with Dobrynin bringing something directly from the Soviet Chairman.

Dobrynin opened a locked attaché case from which he produced a folder that was heavily marked with Russian security stamps. He gave it to the U.S. Attorney General who scanned it and, despite it being in Russian, stated, "This is the KGB's file on Lee Harvey Oswald then?"

Providing Kennedy with an English translation of the document, Dobrynin began by detailing how the KGB had been following Oswald for years. Not because he was a Soviet agent, the Soviet diplomat made clear, but because they suspected he was an American spy. Kennedy asked if that meant the Soviet intelligence apparatus believed that an American agent was behind the attack in Dallas. "My people believe only one thing," replied the Soviet ambassador. "He is not ours."

The Soviet insider had not come to see Robert Kennedy simply to show him a file, however. He also came bearing a message for President Kennedy from Premier Khrushchev, something that was so sensitive it could not be conveyed through any of the usual channels. "He believes the same people who tried to put our two countries into war last year intended for your brother's death to finish the job," he began. "He asks President Kennedy to be very, very careful and to look for his enemies to be very close to him."

With that, Dobrynin said he was authorized to say no more. He took back the document, snapped it into the attaché case, and left the Attorney General alone in his office thinking about enemies close at hand.

Chapter 3:
Battle Lines Being Drawn

November 28, 1963 -
December 31, 1963

Giving Thanks

When Thanksgiving came on Thursday, November 28 in 1963, millions of Americans gave thanks for the survival of President Kennedy at their holiday tables. Pope Paul VI, whom Kennedy had visited in the Vatican only in July, offered a special Thanksgiving blessing for the first Catholic president. In it, he called President Kennedy a "peacemaker" and implied that he had been spared by God to continue his mission.

Look magazine devoted more than a dozen pages and twenty-seven photos to that 1963 celebration. Despite its focus on average 'Americans, the most famous image from the *Look* spread was that of the President's mother, Rose, as she took her son's face in her hands when she first saw him arrive at the Kennedy compound in Hyannis Port and kissed his cheek. "The Lord is not done with you, Jack," she reminded him. "I hope you've said your prayers." The President had done so, religiously, since Dallas. Now he was celebrating with the First Lady, their children, and both their extended families. Every cousin, brother, mother or anyone else related to the Kennedy name was there as a show of support for John.

The country was also trying to come together a week after Dallas. The shock of the near assassination had proved to be so unnerving that country music populist Jimmy Dean scored an instant hit—released on Thanksgiving day—with his upbeat ballad, "The Day JFK Dodged a Bullet," writing new lyrics to match the Burt Bacharach-Hal David song, "The Man Who Shot Liberty Valance," originally made popular by singer Gene Pitney only the year before:

> *When John Kennedy rode to town, the womenfolk would smile, they'd smile.*
> *When John Kennedy waved at them, the men would doff their hats and bow.*
> *But the point of a gun was aiming strong at JFK. When it came to shooting straight and fast, they were mighty good.*

Although it fell far short of art, the phrasing fit right in with the mythos that had been so carefully cultivated since a young, brave, PT boat officer named John F. Kennedy began seeking office almost twenty years earlier. It was a way to see the unnerving current circumstances as proof of the President's charmed life rather than a shattering of our national calm.

Primetime television had retreated back to regular schedules days before, although there were more news cut-ins—the greatest volume ever since the invention of TV news. As in the White House, three televisions were in the study of the Hyannis Port main house so that Jack and Bobby could keep an eye on ABC, CBS and NBC simultaneously during the network news block.

Six days out from the ambush at Dealey Plaza, the Kennedys had to come to realize how many moving parts now existed in the management of what had happened there. There were federal and state investigations, a laundry list of potential suspects and a clear battle brewing over jurisdiction.

The Kennedy brothers, however, knew how to multi-task and that included the youngest—Massachusetts's newly elected Senator Edward Kennedy, or Teddy as the youngest brother was called. He had been appointed by Rose to be the emcee of the Kennedy Thanksgiving table. One thing he had learned from his oldest brother was the use of humor. After making his shy wife Joan read a truncated version of a Vatican statement, he directed his comments to Jack. "The Pope goes on but because we want to eat while the food is warm, I've used my senatorial privilege to have Joan give the table the abridged version."

Jack Kennedy missed not a beat. "Another thing we can be thankful for today," he said.

Teddy had been told by Jack and Bobby to stay clear of strategy sessions on the grounds that he needed "plausible deniability," a term then gaining currency in the intelligence community. They had kept him at arm's length to this point, because they wanted Teddy to be able to hear what was being said in the shadows of the Senate without having to offer up any real insight from the White House. At his insistence, however, they relented and brought him into their conversations at Hyannis Port.

On Friday, the blood relations were joined by the political family. The White House team contributed Kenny O'Donnell, Pierre Salinger, Dave Powers and Ted Sorensen. This self-described group of "all the President's men" was brought together to review the options that would be under consideration when Congress returned from the Thanksgiving break in less than seventy-two hours.

It began with them all seated outside at a round table on a cold, dreary afternoon, looking out over the water. Although the federal lawmen had established a cordon around the property, they still advised against an outdoor meeting but had been overruled by the President himself.

WEB OF SUSPICION

As the men gathered outside, Teddy, being a United States senator, confirmed the news that everyone had been dreading. Senator Everett Dirksen, the Republican leader of the Senate, was going to call for a congressional investigation of the botched assassination at an afternoon news conference. Dirksen's actions were no surprise to anyone, particularly the President who had served with the GOP's top legislator in the Senate and seen his penchant for "shit-stirring" up close.

After some small talk, Bobby announced that they would now begin a spitball session on the issue of what collection of killers might have planned the ambush of last Friday afternoon. It would be free flowing and off the record; no one would ever confirm or deny anything said today on this subject.

Bobby did not brief the men gathered at Hyannis Port that he had already gone through exactly the same process with his Justice Department "Working Group." He had told only his brother of its existence and, even then, he had refused to provide any details of who was in it, what they knew and what they might be planning. "It's better this way," he had explained in the Oval Office, citing the advantages of independent minds examining the situation without prejudice from others, particularly at this crucial juncture.

As the Hyannis Port group settled in, O'Donnell stopped the conversation when he asked, "What if we were put under oath?"

"Well, Kenny, we would never allow that to happen," assured the President. He turned to his kid brother. "Of course, the Attorney General may have another opinion."

Bobby assured everyone that no oath-taking was contemplated but that, even if it came to pass, this conversation was protected under the umbrella of "executive privilege." Under oath, all participants would confirm that they were at a meeting, but any other questions would require them to invoke privilege and refuse to answer. "It is my opinion," said the top law enforcement officer in the United States, "that this conversation as well as any other conversations you may have had on these subjects, both in the past and in the future, are protected by privilege."

If there was anyone uncomfortable with accepting this legal strategy and supporting it for the Administration, Bobby advised them to leave now. The choice was simple: stay and learn everything going forward, or resign. Everyone stayed.

The middle Kennedy brother then explained the ground rules for the next hour. He would propose the name of an individual or a group, and O'Donnell, Powers, Salinger, Sorensen and Teddy Kennedy would speculate about what they knew. The President and the Attorney General would only contribute after everyone else had spoken. They needed to hear independently what the others had to say. It was safer that way.

The following assessments have, over time, now been confirmed by multiple participants and represent the thinking of the Kennedy inner circle just one week after the shooting.

LEE HARVEY OSWALD

Hardly anyone in the post-Thanksgiving huddle believed Oswald had acted alone. The information they heard from internal reports and the media shouted otherwise. Emerging facts included Oswald's working with U2 intelligence at the Naval Air Facility Atsugi in Japan, which was the CIA presence in the Far East. The fact that he had renounced his U.S. citizenship to live in the Soviet Union, then returned and was never arrested for treason, seemed to be of key importance. His contradictory work with the violent anti-Castro Cuban community while making public appearances supporting Castro raised another red flag. There were already rumors that Oswald had been on the FBI payroll at $200 a month.

From his jail cell in Dallas, Oswald had found himself a fire-breathing New York attorney by the name of William Kunstler. Kunstler was making a name for himself by defending clients no other lawyer wanted to take on. Oswald phoned Kunstler—he was given free access to a telephone by the Dallas Police Department—and Kunstler agreed to defend him pro bono for as long as his case lasted. In conducting the Oswald legal update, RFK referred to him as "Kuntsler," deliberately transposing the "t" and "s" in the attorney's name.

The consensus among the group was that there was a great deal more to this Oswald than met the eye. The fingerprints of the intelligence community were all over him. Even so, it was clear that there was a powerful counter-narrative at work, particularly in the American media, that claimed he had acted alone.

THE SOVIET UNION

In the minutes and hours after the shooting in Dallas, suspicion had focused on the Soviet Union. The fear, not unfounded, was that the Soviets might try to decapitate the American government as a distraction for a nuclear showdown. After President Kennedy's peace speech before the American University on June 10, 1963, both sides had feared that such an overt peace feeler could trigger a counter-reaction from hard-liners on either side of the Iron Curtain. There was also the hard fact that Lee Harvey Oswald had lived in the Soviet Union and come back to America with a Soviet wife.

For the men drinking coffee that day in Hyannis Port, Soviet involvement had to be taken seriously. What they were blind to, however, was the experience of Bobby Kennedy back-channeling with Soviet Ambassador Dobrynin less than a week earlier. Seeing the alleged KGB Oswald file, and hearing about Khrushchev's warning to JFK to look to the people closest to him for suspects and not to the Soviet Union, made the oldest Kennedy brothers less prone to embrace Russian complicity than they might have otherwise been. On the other hand, in the world of Cold War espionage, files were often faked and Khrushchev's message could have been no more than disinformation.

The Kennedy inner circle knew their Cold War suspicions were grounded in hard experience and knew that with arsenals on both sides pushing toward fifty thousand nuclear weapons, the fact that the Soviet Union might be a prime suspect in an attack on a U.S. President was raw, ugly news.

When the elder Kennedys weighed in, it was only to acknowledge that the President had spoken to Khrushchev and felt that he sincerely was shocked by the events in Dallas. The Attorney General did not mention his own experiences, but acknowledged that a Soviet role was still a possibility.

CUBA

Fidel Castro was another matter. So was his country. And so were the Cubans who hated Castro and had come to hate Kennedy with the same vehemence. This island nation, just ninety miles away from the Florida Keys, had become a centerpiece of the Cold War sound and fury since the Cuban revolution had toppled Fulgencio Batista in 1959.

No one doubted for a moment that Cuba was involved in some way. Mutual antipathy and mistrust had dogged the U.S. and Cuba since the Kennedy Administration's disastrous April 1961 Bay of Pigs invasion. The only question was whether Cuban hostility was the organizing principle behind the Dallas attack or whether our Communist neighbor was being used as a smokescreen by other adversaries.

Certainly, Oswald's membership in the Fair Play for Cuba Committee alarmed both John and Robert Kennedy. With covert help from the Mafia (which was highly involved in Cuban gambling before the Cuban revolution), the CIA had unsuccessfully sought to murder the new Cuban strongman. Was Castro trying to pay the Americans back in the same coin? Or were angry anti-Castro Cubans, based in New Orleans and Miami, the ones who wanted Kennedy to pay the price for not fully supporting the Bay of Pigs fiasco and for taking an invasion of Cuba off the table during the Missile Crisis?

As recently as the previous month, the Administration had been sending out peace-feelers to Castro through more of its increasingly common back-channel diplomacy, to the great alarm of Washington national security hard-liners. While it was possible Castro wanted JFK dead, it seemed much more likely that he would know such a situation would be used against him, eventually as a rationale to end his own life and leadership in Cuba.

The issue had another level, however. In order to appease his hard-liners long enough to have a chance at making an accommodation over Cuba, the President had approved continuing a plan known as "Operation Mongoose." It was aimed at destabilizing the Castro regime by any covert means necessary. There was no doubt that from a Cuban perspective, the U.S. was sending some mixed signals out of the White House.

Bobby eventually ended this debate, saying, "I'll give this one top priority."

The President admonished him with a dry smile. "Not so fast, Bobby. We're just getting started."

ORGANIZED CRIME

If the Kennedys had a challenging relationship with Cuba, they had no less of one with the powers of the United States Mafia. Despite—or perhaps because of—the common knowledge that family patriarch Joseph Kennedy had accumulated much of his wealth through illegal activity during Prohibition, Bobby Kennedy had chosen, in the late 1950s, to plant his personal and political flag square in the midst of the organized crime issue. He'd made his national debut as chief counsel for the Senate Labor Rackets Committee, squaring off *mano-a-mano* on national TV against Teamsters Union president Jimmy Hoffa and other highly placed mob figures. He'd also written a 1960 bestseller, *The Enemy Within*, which attacked organized crime as a greater threat to America than communism.

Indeed, as Attorney General, Kennedy had told his fellow crusaders at the Justice Department that failure was no option—they had to crush the Mob or the Mob would run the country.

That antagonistic relationship alone made a Mob hit a real possibility. Yet the thinking went that if the Mafia wanted to kill a Kennedy, they'd probably go for Bobby, the very first thought he had expressed at Hickory Hill when he heard the news from Dallas. After all, the Mafia godfathers had expected leniency from the Kennedy Administration after their cozy friendship with Joe Kennedy, but instead they were the targets of a declaration of war by his children, particularly Bobby.

Still, as with all the suspects, there were twists and turns that made thinking about the Mob far more complex than could be seen at first blush. There was the fact that Joseph Kennedy had convinced some organized crime members to help out with John Kennedy's 1960 election, despite the fact that Robert's recent efforts to put them out of business were starting to border on obsession.

The greatest twist was that leaders of organized crime had been working hand-in-glove with members of U.S. intelligence to assassinate Castro in a classic "enemy-of-my-enemy" operation.

When President Kennedy excused himself to take a phone call, Bobby took the opportunity to alert the others to a "sensitive situation." JFK had, from 1960 through 1962, an affair with the Los Angeles socialite Judith Campbell, who was also involved with Chicago mob boss Sam Giancana. Kennedy had used Campbell as a messenger to communicate with Giancana, hoping to enlist support for the assassination attempts against Castro. Now the question was whether the mobster's jealousy prompted him to try to rub out the President.

Bobby reminded the group of the need for discretion in this matter and stated that the only reason Campbell was even relevant to today's conversation was her connection to Giancana. In other words, anything else in the area of "relationships" was none of the group's business.

Before the President returned, the Attorney General had another "priority" on his list to go along with the entire Cuban problem.

JOINT CHIEFS OF STAFF

From the beginning of the Kennedy Administration, the leaders of the United States military establishment had treated JFK disrespectfully. He was berated behind his back, undermined whenever possible, and often lectured to his face by members of the Joint Chiefs as if he were a schoolboy. The worst offender here was Air Force General Curtis LeMay, an aggressively confrontational character willing to face doomsday by launching preemptive attacks on both Cuba and the Soviet Union. LeMay was not alone. There were many military officers angry at Kennedy for trying to put some brakes on the "military-industrial complex" that President Eisenhower had warned the nation about.

The military chiefs were outraged at Kennedy's plans to withdraw from Vietnam, furious about his dramatic peace overtures to Soviet Premier Khrushchev, livid about his back-channel approaches to Fidel Castro, and utterly hostile to his plans to end the Cold War while they were determined to win it, even at the cost of a nuclear war.

The men in Hyannis Port agreed that the U.S. military had motive. They also had guns. But would they use them against their own commander-in-chief? Everyone in attendance had read the 1962 thriller *Seven Days in May* and knew the idea was out there in the air. It was possible.

It seemed more likely, however, that the sour, self-righteous attitude in the military might have unleashed a few freelancers who thought they were ridding the country of a treasonous leader and thus acting as patriots. Even that, however, didn't quite feel right.

The on-going belligerence of the military kept them off the priority list of suspects. The Kennedy men simply felt that had these powerful generals wanted to seize control of the government they would have done so with the military force they wanted to use in Cuba, Berlin and other hotspots. The military was used to a big flexing of muscle; they lived in a world of invasions, air strikes and nuclear payloads. The idea of triangulating an assassination was more of a finesse job.

The U.S. military, it was agreed, probably wouldn't have lost any sleep had the Dallas plot succeeded, but the operation itself didn't look like one of theirs.

FEDERAL BUREAU OF INVESTIGATION (FBI)

President Kennedy was also out of the room when the question of FBI involvement was broached. This was yet another government organization that had taken a hostile attitude toward the new president from the moment he took office back in January of 1961.

J. Edgar Hoover had been running the Federal Bureau of Investigation since its 1935 inception, and he now treated it as a lifetime appointment. Both Kennedy brothers had wanted to replace him, but he had blackmailed his way to a reappointment, one of the first that John Kennedy had made after his election. Hoover had simply made clear the vast knowledge he possessed based on surveillance, files, interviews and so forth, all of it aimed at finding embarrassing and politically devastating personal failings of the President-elect and others. Hoover's files went all the way back to the years before World War II. It was a powerful sledgehammer, and it worked.

Hoover did not like John Kennedy, went the thinking of the group at Hyannis Port, but he had no reason to see him dead. He enjoyed the power he had over the President too much. Hoover did not like Robert Kennedy, either, particularly since RFK was, as Attorney General, Hoover's boss. Yet Hoover also enjoyed tweaking RFK whenever he could.

There was another angle still. Hoover lived down the street from Vice President Lyndon Johnson. They were close friends and had been for some years. The Kennedy men had always assumed that LBJ got all his blackmail material on JFK that landed the Texan on the 1960 ticket in the first place from Hoover.

So even though J. Edgar Hoover was clearly an implacable foe of the Kennedys, he was not seen as a force behind an assassination attempt as much as he was seen as a force behind the current cover-up. Hoover, for reasons not a hundred percent clear, seemed to be taking the position through his investigation of the ambush that Oswald had likely acted alone. This would be a productive way to misdirect an investigation, the thinking went, particularly if Hoover was part of the conspiracy.

CENTRAL INTELLIGENCE AGENCY (CIA)

The already distrustful relationship between the Kennedys and the

Central Intelligence Agency was shattered completely when the shots were fired on November 22.

Ironically, at the beginning of his term, JFK supported the agency's aim to accomplish strategic objectives without hurtling toward Armageddon. Spying was also far less expensive than actually fighting wars. Plus, the cloak-and-dagger aspect had appealed to the new President's dash and style. He was actually a James Bond fan of both the books and the new films, *Dr. No* and *From Russia with Love*.

The honeymoon had ended less than three months after JFK's inauguration. The Bay of Pigs invasion was a CIA plan that was a leftover from the previous Administration. As presented by CIA spymaster Allen Dulles, President Kennedy had been open to it. The fact that it had supposedly been vetted by President Dwight Eisenhower, the general who had succeeded at D-Day, made it even more attractive. In reality, the President's men hugging up their jackets against the November cold thought it had been a con job, a setup all the way.

In the aftermath of its failure, the Kennedys had come to think of the men who ran the Central Intelligence Agency as "virtually treasonous," the same that the CIA apparently thought of them. President Kennedy, as angry as he had ever been in his life, threatened to break the agency into a thousand pieces and scatter it to the wind. Soon he had fired Dulles and two other key players, Richard Bissell and Charles Cabell (whose brother Earle Cabell was, ironically, the current mayor of Dallas, Texas). To say that Allen Dulles was embittered was a grand understatement. By all accounts, he felt a deep and powerful antipathy toward the man who had terminated his career so ignobly. To have bad blood exist with an organization that increasingly considered coups and assassinations as mere policy choices seemed particularly dangerous.

The list of priority suspects that Robert Kennedy had started now included the CIA.

SECRET SERVICE

There was no doubt in anyone's mind that November 22, 1963 was not the Secret Service's proudest day. While the President had survived, his life was saved by agent Clint Hill and not by the organization. It was as if the entire group of agents had been asleep at the switch. The question was why?

It might have been unintentional sloppiness. The Secret Service detail assigned to Dallas had been incredibly "off-procedure" the night before, with multiple agents up until 3 a.m. drinking. None of those agents were likely to have been at the top of their game.

Or it could have been more than incompetence. Were they drinking because they knew what was going to happen and weren't going to stop it?

The route had not been properly secured. Instructions to Dallas Police had not maximized their effort but minimized it. The motorcade at Dealey Plaza was traveling below the minimum speed. The agents in the President's car reacted poorly, responding only after Hill, a man who had just been shot, shouted them out of their somnambulation. Certainly the driver, William Greer, would be called before investigators and asked for an explanation for his leaden reflexes behind the wheel of the President's car.

There were so many loose ends. There was, for example, the issue of the decision not to go with the protective bubble-top glass for the President's limousine. It was a Secret Service call, according to protocol, but Lyndon Johnson, as part of his trip-planning responsibilities, had asked directly that it not be used.

The head of the Secret Service, James Rowley, was no fan of President Kennedy either. He knew better than most that there were more than a few of his agents who had open disdain for the President. Unlike the CIA, their hostility was not about policy; rather, this emotion came from seeing Kennedy's personal behavior up close.

It was a mixed bag. JFK had made friends with many agents, often asking about their families, vacations and sporting affiliations.

He was particularly fond of Abraham Bolden who had been with him every day since Dallas and, in fact, was standing just out of earshot of this gathering. Yet, as the Hyannis Port meeting was made aware, other than Bolden not a single Secret Service agent was currently on presidential detail. All of them were working outside perimeter duties or otherwise assigned until further notice.

Extremely troubling were the reports of Secret Service agents showing identification cards in Dealey Plaza, although there were no such agents deployed, at least officially. The Attorney General had heard from a source who had heard from someone else that they were the work of the CIA's Technical Services Division.

That would mean that there were CIA agents in Dealey Plaza doing the job of Secret Service agents, and Secret Service agents that had abandoned their own jobs by standing down in their defense of the President.

None of it was definitive proof of anything. The CIA may have learned of the plot and only been monitoring it from the sidelines, and maybe even working to stop it. The Secret Service may have had its agents intimidated and manipulated into adverse choices without support or knowledge of a full plot.

The conclusion was that as an institution, the Secret Service would have no motivation to see the President dead, although some elements inside the organization may have had a role among the plotters. As of now, with the information available, it was simply unclear.

VICE PRESIDENT LYNDON JOHNSON

While the jury was out on the Secret Service, virtually everyone who voiced an opinion had a greater suspicion of Vice President Johnson, a statement that by itself spoke volumes about the man and his reputation.

Johnson was considered to be a devious viper in the nest who, with the help of J. Edgar Hoover, had blackmailed his way onto the 1960 presidential ticket. Bobby Kennedy loathed Lyndon Johnson and the feeling was mutual. In fact, RFK's enmity toward LBJ was so strong he was unable to follow his own instructions and wait until everyone else had spoken.

He reminded all that back in Washington, particularly before Dallas, a potential scandal for Johnson had been slowly building, as the Senate rules committee looked into the activities of the man whom Johnson had appointed to serve as his secretary for the majority of his days on the Hill. Bobby "Little Lyndon" Baker had resigned under pressure from the probe, but the scandal was growing, and it threatened to embroil Baker's former boss. *Life* magazine had chronicled it all and, unlike prior press coverage, had tied the whole metastasizing mess directly to Johnson. The magazine had bigger targets in mind, too. That very morning of the assassination attempt, editors and reporters were meeting to discuss angles for a broader investigation, this one into the Vice President's personal finances.

LBJ also had strong reason to believe he was about to be indicted and could very well go to prison for his provable role in the Bobby Baker and Billie Sol Estes scandals. There was no doubt that the Texan's lifelong lust and endless scheming for the presidency was relentless. But murder? There were rumors back in Texas about suspicious deaths that LBJ had connections to that a few of Robert Kennedy's young turks actually thought were sufficiently grounded that a grand jury would indict the sitting VP if presented with the facts.

"If this line of reasoning is correct," said O'Donnell, "it would make Lyndon Baines Johnson the greatest conspirator since Brutus."

The room grew quiet. Finally, Bobby Kennedy leaned forward. "Exactly."

ALL OR SOME OF THE ABOVE

There were other possibilities, each one bending and twisting into a Mobius strip of suspicion. In addition to what had already been said, there were other questions:

- Was it Big Oil, which Kennedy was threatening by eliminating the industry's depletion allowance worth billions?
- Was it Big Money, which Kennedy was threatening by printing U.S. Treasury notes, thereby ending the Fed's monopoly on currency?
- Was it Big Steel, which Kennedy had stared down over price increases just a year ago and which never forgave him?

So many theories and possibilities existed that it truly seemed like a joke. How could anyone get into this and find success? Where would one even start?

Clearly there was the chance of some network of hostile adversaries who had come together to solve mutual problems by removing the President of the United States through extreme action. In fact, this seemed to be a far greater probability than the idea that the President would be attacked at the hand of a loser with no affiliations or connections to any of the other players. Still, until direct proof was offered to the contrary, Oswald remained the prime suspect—either acting by himself or in concert with others.

The team gathered that November day at Hyannis Port strongly suspected this brazen attack had to have been perpetrated with varying degrees of complicity, collusion and coordination from a variety of possibly interrelated players that included the CIA, organized crime, Cubans, and even Texas oil moneymen.

Reluctant to use the actual word "conspiracy," they pointed the finger of blame instead at what was called the "nexus," a word that the Justice Department's working group had already adopted to be used in place of conspiracy. Its use bled over into White House meetings, particularly those that were recorded. Later, once things got ugly, the word "conspiracy" was openly used as a matter of policy by members of the Kennedy Administration, including the President and the Attorney General.

Fight for Jurisdiction

Inside, fortified by hot chocolates made by the Kennedy children, the Hyannis Port collective turned its attention to the subject of who should serve as point man in sorting out the entire situation. The need was made critical by the press conference that Senator Everett Dirksen was now giving on live television.

Each of three TV sets was tuned to a different network, all featuring the Illinois Republican, a moderate only by the standards of his own Party. JFK, who admired a winning performance, knew that Dirksen was good TV and that such a quality could always be dangerous. The Senate Minority Leader had curls that came close to rivaling Harpo Marx's. And his voice was a pipe organ he could use for any sort of sound effect under the sun. He was, said Dave Powers, "the biggest ham outside an Armour can."

Dirksen did not disappoint, calling for a Senate investigation that would, presumably, include himself in a key position. He also promised legislative leadership. "Why, gentlemen, do you know it's not even a federal crime to assassinate the President of the United States or any other official of the government? This man in custody should be on trial here, but we can't do it. That is a shame and a disgrace that we shall remedy with legislation shortly."

Prosecution was one thing but investigation was another. Dirksen immediately ran into the same line of questioning the President had fielded at his recent primetime news conference. The issue was jurisdiction, and reporters wanted to know if Congress and the state of Texas wouldn't be stepping all over each other to conduct what was essentially the same kind of investigation. He argued that the U.S. Congress was capable of casting a broader net with finer mesh. He implied that the Dallas Police Department might be good at investigating what happened in Dallas last Friday, but for what led up to it, for what led Oswald to do the deed— if, in fact, Oswald was the culprit—a federal investigation seemed more appropriate.

Having declared his jurisdictional intentions, Dirksen was asked whether the White House was encouraging him in his pursuit of a congressional investigation.

The senator rolled his eyes. "Any President naturally wishes Congress would roll over on its back and wave its legs in the air. The executive branch believes that to be our proper role. This Administration seems no different."

As the networks cut away from Dirksen's conference, the Kennedy team adjourned to the study. The President's back was torturing him again, and he didn't want to have to use crutches. Everyone packed into a space that was much smaller than was comfortable. Ethel sat outside the door to keep out interruptions.

As the men took their seats behind that closed door, Bobby shrugged. "Well?"

The first answer came from Kenny O'Donnell, who held up a yellow legal pad where he had written one word in one of the new, inexpensive Bic Cristal pens: "Clusterfuck."

After seeing the sensitivity of their situation over the last hour of conversation, everyone knew that jurisdiction was everything. It defined the winners and the losers that would need to be sorted out. It was clear that things could soon be spinning out of control, what with Dirksen making his play and that Dallas Police Chief What's-His-Name enjoying sticking it to Washington.

JFK nodded his agreement. "We have to get in the game."

Bobby corrected him. "We are in the game, like it or not. We have to control it."

The single greatest asset the White House could manipulate on the day after Thanksgiving 1963 was what a previous occupant, Theodore Roosevelt, had called the "bully pulpit." Americans generally wanted answers, and they would want them soon on this matter of shooting at the President at high noon. But there was no consensus as to what should be done. JFK's press conference on Tuesday had only added more fog to the confusion. The good news was that the White House was still the most legitimate entity to lead on the subject.

The question was, lead where?

THE THREE BAD OPTIONS

After the review of facts and suspicions, it seemed clear to everyone in this discussion that the nation and the government were at a tipping point. While there was lots of room for improvisation within the options, there were only three basic ways to look at the big picture, none of them particularly good.

- **Option One:** Allowing the Soviets and/or Cubans to be blamed.
  This was deemed unacceptable because it was likely not true and, in any case, stopping nuclear war—not encouraging it—had now become the mission of the Kennedy Administration.
- **Option Two:** Taking on the conspiracy directly.
  This could quite possibly lead to a military coup that might destroy the country and would destabilize institutions that control nuclear weapons.
- **Option Three:** Covering it all up, at least temporarily.

President Kennedy had spoken only a few times in this discussion, but had listened carefully. He broke in with a call to "return to the issue of the Constitution."

The President noted his oath of office called for him to "preserve, protect and defend the Constitution of the United States of America." He reviewed the options as such. If the nation were to be destroyed in a nuclear war with the Soviet Union, the Constitution would be rendered meaningless. If the military were to seize control of the government from its legitimate civilian authority, that would be a direct violation of the oath's objective. The third option, however unpalatable, risked neither the destruction of the nation nor the destruction of the Constitution. "Indeed, if navigated properly, it might be possible to buy a year to tack away from the calls for war," posited the President, "get elected on that platform and, in the end, simply postpone the day of reckoning for any potential conspirators by kicking it down the road."

If their decision to choose the third option was an overreach or in any way adverse to the Constitution, said the Attorney General, the Constitution itself provided the remedy of impeachment by the House, and trial and removal by the Senate. If that remedy were to be required, the system would survive and the oath would be maintained. Abraham Lincoln felt that way about many of the measures he implemented during the Civil War that some considered unconstitutional. Lincoln believed that could all be sorted out after the war was over and so could be ignored in the middle of the conflict.

"I'm with President Lincoln on this one," said the President.

"Contain and maintain," agreed Kenny O'Donnell.

They reassured themselves that they would still seek the truth in time; their actions now merely meant that the truth could be managed to the benefit of the country, particularly in an election year. The President needed a nonpolitical body quietly investigating in order to assure the public. Either a House or Senate committee (or, God forbid, both) would be a circus of the kind not seen since the days of Joseph McCarthy. Bobby, who had worked for McCarthy and retained some affinity for those memories of the man if not his ideals, knew this better than most.

A congressional investigation into Dallas, complete with massive egos dying to get on TV at any cost, simply could not be allowed to happen. It would open doors during an election season that could escalate into political gridlock and chaos. That situation could be exploited by the conspirators and might trigger a coup. Worse, it could inflame Cold War adversaries in both the U.S. and the U.S.S.R. to miscalculate. The Cuban Missile Crisis had been a terrible near miss.

"The world might not be so lucky a second time," reminded the President.

SOUNDS OF SILENCE

By now, the meeting at Hyannis Port was being fueled by a third pot of coffee. "How do we stop them?" O'Donnell asked. "How do we stop the U.S. House and the Senate from doing what they have a legitimate right to do without making them wonder why we're stopping them?"

"National security," Bobby Kennedy said at once.

John Kennedy lit a rare cigar and drew on it before speaking. "We can't use that without scaring people and making them ask even more questions." The statement hung in the air like cigar smoke, as people read between the lines: asking questions in an election year was to be avoided at almost any cost.

Pierre Salinger could hold forth with reporters for hours on end but when he was in with the President and his men, he often held back. So it was surprising when he blurted out, "It's simple. Congress can't do the job right during an election, and the people will recognize that after we explain it properly."

It was almost December, argued the press secretary. The 1964 election, just eleven months away, would feature a hotly contested presidential race, made even more unpredictable by current events. Therefore, the U.S. Congress could hardly be trusted to investigate the attack in Dallas. They would be reaching conclusions in the midst of highly charged partisan wars that were certain to exist. Impartiality would be impossible.

Kenneth O'Donnell agreed to that line of reasoning. "The Administration has a moral obligation to set up an honest non-partisan investigation. The matter is too important to be left to Congress. We need to form an independent committee." It was quite an argument, given that Congress was exactly where the Constitution said important matters had to go.

Kennedy exhaled cigar smoke. "In the Navy, we'd call that a gun deck job," he said, using a term usually reserved for an exercise that was bullshit from top to bottom. "But it's probably the way to go."

As a general rule, President Kennedy had little patience for committees and the meetings they liked to have. His back pain made sitting through them excruciating, and usually they had no real purpose and accomplished nothing of value. If you wanted something done, you surely shouldn't ask a committee to do it. Even during the Cuban Missile Crisis, he'd been happy to let Bobby run the ExComm and not just because those attending would speak more freely if the President wasn't in the room.

In his own mind, JFK thought a committee would be no more competent at its work than most of the ones he had served on since going to Congress. It would, however, keep the work private until the election. Then, with a second term, the facts could fall where they may. In retrospect, it was an unusually optimistic position.

Everyone had his own opinion about what needed to happen next, particularly who should head any committee, but all waited for Bobby to go first. This happened often, and it was clear that he was speaking for his brother. "I've received some suggestions, but there's one in particular we may want to explore." He was asked where that suggestion came from. "It's better for all of us if we keep the source confidential," he said, ending that line of questioning.

The suggestion was Earl Warren, Chief Justice of the United States Supreme Court.

"We talked this morning. I asked him hypothetically if he would lead such a committee, and he said he would seriously consider it. He said he was honored, as a matter of fact, and that taking the matter out of the political arena was the right call to make."

So there it was. "That's not bad," thought O'Donnell out loud. "But can we trust him not to go wandering off on his own?"

It was a valid question. Earl Warren was a Republican. He'd been the Attorney General and the Governor of California, and he'd run for vice president with Thomas Dewey back in 1948 against Truman. He wanted to run for the presidency on his own in 1952. After being appointed to the Supreme Court by President Eisenhower, Warren had, to many, veered left during his years as Chief Justice. Now the John Birch Society had him targeted. "Impeach Earl Warren" billboards dotted the landscape, especially throughout the South.

The President weighed in. "He understands that we can't let a nuclear war start because a few congressmen need to distract voters from their own incompetence."

Bobby nodded. "We can get Warren to play ball. I'll put Hoover in charge of the investigation. He's already made up his mind about Oswald. We'll just see that they don't report until after November."

The meeting broke up a few minutes later. The Administration had a plan.

THE WARREN OMISSION

On Monday, December 2, 1963, President John Fitzgerald Kennedy signed Executive Order No. 11130, creating a commission to investigate the assassination of Governor John B. Connally of Texas, the death of Special Agent Clint Hill, and the death of Dallas Police Officer J.D. Tippit on November 22, 1963. The commission was directed to evaluate all the facts and circumstances surrounding the ambush, including whether or not it was specifically targeted against the President, and to report its findings and conclusions to the President for submission to the U.S. Congress with all due haste. Kennedy explained the mandate of the commission to reporters in the White House Briefing Room:

> *The subject of the inquiry is a chain of events that saddened and shocked the people of the United States and, indeed, the world. By my order establishing this commission, I hope to avoid parallel investigations and to concentrate fact-finding in a body having the broadest national mandate.*

Then the President introduced Chief Justice Earl Warren, who looked like everybody's kindly grandfather. Joining President Kennedy for the announcement, Warren addressed the assembled press in a dark brown suit, solid blue tie and white squared pocket-handkerchief instead of his usual judicial robes:

> *We will conduct a thorough and independent investigation of these tragic events. We will cooperate with the Dallas Police Department in any way we can. Obviously, they have a criminal investigation and trial to conduct. We do not want to interfere with Mr. Oswald's right to a fair trial. If he is found guilty, we do hope to determine*

whether his role was of his own device or whether he acted as part of a possible conspiracy.

The Chief Justice announced the makeup of what was nearly instantly called the Warren Commission: two senators and two representatives, split evenly between the Republicans and Democrats; plus four members from outside the Beltway who were not actively serving in Congress; and Warren himself.

The senators were Washington Democrat Warren Magnuson and none other than Illinois Republican Everett Dirksen. Kennedy and his team had decided that the devil they knew was better than the devil they didn't. Dirksen wanted the status of being on the committee. But even his ego would not be enough for him to try to take over the spokesman's position from the Chief Justice of the Supreme Court. With his own position in history secured, Dirksen was the first to condemn his own idea of a congressional investigation as "duplicative."

As far as senators went, Warren Magnuson was deeply experienced, well liked and certainly of Dirksen's stature, if not his prominence. Magnuson, it was also pointed out by a few news reports, had been the beneficiary of a 1961 fundraiser where President Kennedy had come to Seattle and gotten three thousand people to pay $100 each to hear JFK sing the senator's praises. The two men had history in the club that was the U.S. Senate. The Kennedy team felt he would be loyal if they needed him on a particular issue.

The representatives were Democrat Hale Boggs of Arkansas and Republican Florence Dwyer of New Jersey. Boggs was the Majority Whip in the House and got the job after Majority Leader Carl Albert said he could not run the House and serve on the commission at the same time. Dwyer was one of the very few women in either the House or Senate. The Kennedy team liked her because she had sponsored the so-called Equal Pay Act that had just passed. Looking ahead to the 1964 election, it would be good to have appointed a woman who believed in equal rights and was from the opposing party. When President Kennedy had first met her, Dwyer had said, "A Congresswoman must look like a girl, act like a lady, and think like a man." For Kennedy, she was the perfect Republican.

Even better, the thinking went, the four "politicians" could be balanced out with four others who could be presented as keeping the Warren Commission impartial. Appointed were former president of the World Bank, John J. McCloy; civil rights leader James Farmer; ailing news legend Edward R. Murrow; and New York City's young superintendent of schools, Calvin Gross.

The time estimated for the job was about a year, plus or minus. The public reaction to Oswald's trial and whether any further arrests would be made were unknown elements in the equation. As for the hot potato that this could become, given next year's presidential primaries and general election, both the President and the Chief Justice agreed the report would not be delayed or moved forward based on any political considerations, be they favorable or unfavorable to the Administration.

What the Kennedys already knew and the public had yet to fully comprehend, was that the Warren Commission would be receiving testimony, files and theories from the FBI which, at that time, seemed to be leaning strongly toward pinning the matter on Oswald and moving on.

The commission had no funds or authority for independent investigation. It would have to make whatever case it felt needed to be made from other people's evidence. Whether that evidence would include the product of the Working Group, operating under the direction of Attorney General Robert Kennedy, was still an open question.

Oswald Casts a Shadow

Against the backdrop of this high-stakes gamesmanship, the trial of Lee Harvey Oswald loomed large. Oswald, who at the beginning had talked much more than anyone had expected, had suddenly gone quiet at the insistence of his attorney, William Kunstler. The New Yorker, however, was anything but quiet, arguing his client's innocence regularly to all takers. The one thing that Kunstler said that grabbed everyone's attention, however, was the fact that Lee Harvey Oswald was going to take the stand in his own defense. Kunstler dropped this bombshell on a crowd of reporters outside the Dallas courts building after a hearing about whether Oswald's federal troubles might supersede local jurisdiction:

> *My client is innocent. It is not up to him to prove that, as you all know, and he is under no legal obligation to testify, a right protected by the U.S. Constitution. It is up to the Dallas District Attorney to prove that he is guilty. Lee Oswald, however, will testify, under oath, that the only mistake he made on November 22 was coming to work at the Texas School Book Depository on a day when someone chose to shoot at the President of the United States. Powerful forces have framed him, ladies and gentlemen. He is exactly what he said on the day he was arrested. A patsy.*

Day in and day out, Kunstler embellished his reputation as a radical firebrand and showed that he intended to carry out an aggressive defense of Lee Harvey Oswald. Besides proclaiming his client's innocence, he declared that all of Oswald's statements before he gained legal representation were obtained under duress and were therefore "inoperative"—the attorney's word, which was later widely quoted and ridiculed.

When confronted with a statement from Dallas D.A. Henry Wade that a recovered bullet matched the gun that Oswald had bought by mail-order before the shooting, Kunstler was unfazed. "Henry Wade can say whatever he damn well pleases. He's a state lackey, and they pay him to get convictions. He doesn't care that he's prejudicing the jury pool against my client."

Kunstler would later say in his 1967 book *The People Versus Lee Harvey Oswald* that he was "preparing the battlefield." He wanted to be the underdog, citing the fact that he was a New York Jew fighting in the buckle of the Bible Belt, and hoping that some of that would rub off on his client. He continually invoked his theory of a grand right-wing conspiracy that decided the President was too progressive. He railed against conspirators, real and imagined, with a vested interest in nipping change in the bud. By "change," Kunstler meant peace talks, black civil rights, and strengthening organized labor.

The irony, of course, is that the Kennedy men all seemed to agree with William Kunstler about the likelihood of conspiracy, even as they hoped the Warren Commission—which they had empowered as the official investigation—would come to the opposite conclusion. It was, to use a word favored by psychologists, a "cognitive dissonance" that would make living in the White House during 1964 the trickiest year yet.

CHRISTMAS TRUCE

By mid-December 1963 the nation was exhausted. It had been hit with the impact of what felt like a brush-with-death of a family member, combined with the unsettled feeling that won't go away after being mugged. America was high-strung and stressed-out.

Holiday shopping sales figures were headed for a historic low. Retail organizations implored President and Mrs. Kennedy to consider lighting more public Christmas trees but were rebuffed for security reasons. The First Lady's new social secretary Nancy Tuckerman explained the feeling in her own memoirs, tying the public's down mood in part to the loss of the Kennedys' infant son from respiratory stress disease. "People understood that the President and Mrs. Kennedy needed some time alone. They'd suffered the death of their son that year as well, and then what happened in November. It was just a bit too much for anyone."

The mood of Christmas 1963 was one of somber and earnest prayer for many people. After the shadow of the Cuban Missile Crisis hung over the 1962 holiday season, now the ambush in Dallas hung over this one. America's holidays had been hijacked by a couple of frightening and disturbing near misses. Many people did without holiday parties and spent time with their families.

No one talked about politics, at least publicly. December had been declared the lull before the storm by both parties, but politics, particularly presidential politics, were gone only temporarily. In many homes of America's political elite, there was a great deal of thinking and strategizing.

This current quiet, sold as respect for the dead, would end soon.

Top Story

FEBRUARY 24, 1964

35c

THE WILD 1964 ELECTION BEGINS

Beatles in America

Chapter 4:
An Election with
Consequences

January 1, 1964 -
December 31, 1964

A Family Retreat

As a political matter, President Kennedy's survival had taken an already uncertain electoral map and made it more fluid. Before Dallas, it had been assumed that the election would be close. Nothing had changed the White House perspective, even the bullets of an assassin.

One thing had taken a turn, however. John Kennedy had made separate comments to his brother, Kenneth O'Donnell, and Theodore Sorensen that maybe he would surprise them all and "not go through it again." It was a trial balloon, said without conviction, but still, it bothered them. They understood, however, that being shot at is something that changes a man.

Jacqueline Kennedy had been traumatized by Dallas even more than her husband. She would not accept any more public invitations until further notice. She said so in such a way that it seemed untoward to even think of asking a follow-up question. In reality, the First Lady had practically moved out of the White House by January 1, heading with her children to Wexford, the newly-constructed family home on thirty-nine acres in the Middleburg, Virginia area, a place where the President himself had only been twice before. After a week there, however, she felt the entire area had been too commonly identified as a Kennedy retreat, and she began a cycle of visiting several locations short-term, moving out almost before she and the family had settled in, trying to keep her whereabouts and those of her children a mystery. To calm her decidedly manic behavior, she had been prescribed sedatives by her husband's personal physician, Dr. Janet Travell.

And so, it was against this backdrop that Jackie Kennedy told John Kennedy that she was going into virtual hiding and that she expected him to curtail his own public activities as well. He could still do his news conferences and Rose Garden activities with guests if he wanted, but only if Bobby approved of security. Most importantly, she instructed him to stop taking risks outside the gates. No more wading into crowds, no more convertibles, no more windows for assassins. "I started to argue with her," Kennedy explained in the last interview before his death, "but I concluded she was right."

The First Lady further demanded of the President that there would be no planned travel or public appearances for either of them for the entire month of January. They needed time to assess the situation. The President pointed out that he had spent plenty of time lately assessing the situation. "Not with me," she countered.

With her husband's agreement secured, Jackie left with Caroline and John Jr. The President instructed his secretary, Evelyn Lincoln, to make certain there was a daily note on his desk with the family's current whereabouts. He also wanted to make certain he spoke to his wife and children every day. He instructed her to see to it that it was scheduled. Those who overheard any of these conversations confirmed that although the President was always polite and concerned when speaking with his wife, he spent far more time on each call with Caroline and John-John.

STATE OF WHOSE UNION?

President Kennedy then turned his attention to the January 8 State of the Union. It had only a short mention of Dallas in it, a reference to the strength of America being tested again, as the country once more proved itself to be stronger than any adversity thrown in its path. He did, however, throw his support behind the Dirksen bill to make it a federal crime to murder the president, something that until Dallas had been considered a state matter.

JFK also talked about his budget, cutting a full $1 billion in Defense Department spending, owing mostly to Secretary McNamara's campaign for better procurement practices and a shutdown of unneeded military bases. The total number of Americans working to support the Cold War effort was 990,000, a number that represented cuts to the civilian employment in the Defense Department by seventeen thousand employees, so determined was Kennedy to bring that number below one million.

The President also cut funding to the Atomic Energy Commission, limiting production of enriched uranium by twenty-five percent and shutting down four plutonium piles. Kennedy also called for more attention to the nation's impoverished citizens, swift congressional passage of a civil rights bill, and a tax cut.

It was a businesslike speech, not a great one, certainly not by Kennedy standards. If anything, the rapid criticism delivered by Republican officials did show how fast the country was moving on beyond Dallas. Said House GOP leader Charles Halleck: "I hope that the Administration's newfound enthusiasm for economy is as great in June as it is in January."

House Minority Whip Les Arends called the President's speech "patently a 1964 political campaign document."

When asked about the Republican response the next day by O'Donnell, Kennedy responded, "Obviously, Kenny, my getting out of Dallas alive has seriously hurt our legislative agenda."

LIFE IN A FOXHOLE

With the Union addressed, and Jackie and the children in motion, Jack Kennedy hunkered down in the White House. The entire inner circle began to refer to the Oval Office as "the Foxhole." The President clearly displayed signs of what came to be called battle fatigue during World War II. He had tried to ignore or laugh off his feelings in November and December. Now, as the rest of the nation seemed to be turning a corner, he was turning inward.

A major snowstorm turned into a blizzard for portions of the northeastern United States between January 11-16 of 1964. All of the major cities from Washington, D.C., to Philadelphia, New York City and Boston reported about ten inches of snowfall or more.

For those five days in Washington, D.C., it was so difficult to get around that the President could actually cancel nearly all of his meetings and obligations and just get some work done. Plus, he was in a lot of pain, and the cold seemed to aggravate his back. The bad weather did not, however, prevent one of Kennedy's many lovers, Mary Pinchot Meyer, from stopping by twice, according to the testimony of Evelyn Lincoln, who had made sure the visits were no longer being recorded in the White House log.

Jackie was snowed in up in Massachusetts, chain-smoking L&M filtered cigarettes and trying to calm down. It didn't help that on the first day of the blizzard, Surgeon General Luther Terry issued a report finding that cigarettes can cause cancer and urging all smokers to stop, advice the First Lady ignored. Health issues were often hidden away from prying eyes in the Kennedy White House. What no one in America knew at the time was how important Dr. Travell had become to the health of the President and First Lady. During the fall of 1961, Travell had been giving the President up to several injections daily of the local anesthetic procaine. He was under her personal treatment for an adrenal ailment he lived with since his youth, constant high fevers, extremely high cholesterol levels, the inability to get a good night's sleep, and colon, prostate and stomach problems.

The wide variety of pills and shots that Travell was administering to the President of the United States for these issues filled out the "Administration medical record" she kept. Yet it was not a complete accounting, not by far.

Dr. Max Jacobson had entered John Kennedy's life back during the 1960 campaign. Known informally among patients as

"Dr. Feelgood," he had continued to make house calls to the White House and even shadowed the President on trips to foreign capitals, such as Paris and Vienna. Jacobson's injections were also being enjoyed by the First Lady.

At Bobby's request, the President's medications were submitted to the Food and Drug Administration for analysis. The agency reported back that Jacobson's injections included amphetamines and steroids. The President told his brother, "I don't care if it's horse piss. It works."

Based on the testimony of a nurse who had worked with Jacobson, the injections appear to have also included hormones, vitamins, enzymes and even animal cells. The result was what another client, author Truman Capote, called "Instant Superman," a condition where the injectee could ofter stay awake for three days or more without sleep. The bottom line was that at least some of the "vigor" that was so embraced as a description of JFK's activity level was chemically induced.

A future Congress eventually raised concerns about the potential national security consequences of such a concoction. These shots, while alleviating pain, made their recipients experience an exaggerated sense of personal power, something that Kennedy might have experienced often, including during the Cuban Missile Crisis, given that he took them throughout the years he'd been in office. Other side effects included hypertension, impaired judgment and elevated anxiety. Between doses, mood swings were common. Over a long period, the dosages the President had been using could produce paranoia, schizophrenia, memory loss and even hallucinations.

In the beginning, both Jack and Jackie Kennedy were making use of the physician's injections at least once a week and sometimes as often as three to four times weekly. Over the years, they had tapered off the regular use of Dr. Jacobson's injections, at one point quitting altogether. It was too much. They needed to be in control. But that was before someone had tried to kill him. Jacobson had literally been welcomed back to the White House on the morning of November 23, and multiple times after that.

Now, as the New Year began, JFK once again picked up the phone in the side office and told the operator to get him an outside line. Once connected, Jacobson asked what the President what he could do to help. "I just need to take the edge off and prepare myself for battle," answered Kennedy. Within the hour, Dr. Max Jacobson was making a house call to the President's quarters.

To Run or Not to Run?

Feeling energetic thanks to a snowbound Washington, D.C., with a schedule that had been cleared by his wife's decree, John Kennedy reached out to the usual suspects. He invited the team from Hyannis Port to the Oval Office for lunch. The subject was the 1964 election.

To a man, Robert Kennedy, Kenneth O'Donnell, Pierre Salinger, Arthur Schlesinger Jr., Theodore Sorensen, Dave Powers and Teddy Kennedy thought the President might be summoning them to tell them he would not be running for reelection. "First of all," said the President, "I have made no decision yet on whether or not to run. I want to see where we stand politically."

Before Dallas, when they did discuss the political situation, the Kennedys and their team of advisers believed the Republican nominee would be Arizona Senator Barry Goldwater, a plainspoken Westerner whom the right wing of his Party adored. In fact, Kennedy and Goldwater were friends, going back to their days serving in the U.S. Senate together. They agreed on very little politically, but they enjoyed each other's company.

Goldwater had announced his candidacy on January 3, describing the choice ahead between the Democrats and Republicans as a stark one. "As a general rule, one Party has emphasized individual liberty and the other has favored the extension of government power," claimed Goldwater. "I'm convinced that today a majority of the American people believe in the essential emphasis on individual liberty." Goldwater then famously added the impromptu words that, paraphrased, would become his campaign slogan. "And in your heart, you know I'm right."

What Goldwater could not possibly understand as he uttered those words was how much his likely opponent John Kennedy agreed with him on the subject. Wherever Kennedy had been politically at the start of his term in 1961, by early 1964 he wanted to accomplish only one thing before he left office, whether it be a year later in 1965 or, God and voters willing, early 1969. As much as anybody in politics, he wanted to curb the power of government to defy civilian authority.

Goldwater still had to win the nomination from a Republican Party that tended to support mainstream conservatives like Dwight Eisenhower over political ideologues like Robert Taft. This meant that New York's liberal Governor Nelson Rockefeller and moderate Governor Bill Scranton out of Pennsylvania had an outside shot at the nomination, too. O'Donnell said he wouldn't put it past the Republicans to run Dick Nixon again either, although Nixon had lost the California governor's race in 1962 and declared his retirement from politics.

"It'll be Goldwater," stated Bobby, cutting the debate short. "At least we have to plan as if it will be. How do we assess his electability?"

The consensus was uncertainty. Before shots were fired, it was going to be possible to paint Goldwater as a reckless man who could only drag the nation into trouble. Now, on their watch, the Kennedy Administration had dragged the people close to a nuclear war one year and barely avoided a public execution of the President the next. Goldwater might start to look like the conservative choice in more ways than one.

President Kennedy listened to it all and summed up. "We can beat Barry if we can keep things calm and keep the economic numbers solid. If Dallas becomes an issue, I don't know. I think it could be as close as '60, with a chance that one of us gets more electoral votes and the other gets more popular votes. The nation is stirred up and restless, and we're in a street fight." No one in the room disagreed with his assessment.

The discussion pivoted to what, if anything, needed to get done now, regardless of the President's reelection decision. Bobby said they needed to form a committee to run the campaign.

The President shook his head, bemused. "First, as someone with no use for committees, I formed all of you into a committee up in Hyannis Port, and then we formed Earl's commission, and now we have reconvened the original committee to form a new committee. Maybe we should adjourn while we're ahead, gentlemen."

Bobby continued with the news that he had cleared a name, just in case. It would be called the Committee to Re-Elect Kennedy. It was pointed out that the acronym sounded like CREEK, as in something you were up without a paddle. It stuck, however, as no one offered up a better name.

The meeting adjourned when the President was called into an urgent national security briefing. Panama had just broken diplomatic ties with the United States. John Kennedy, always able to compartmentalize, dispatched the political meeting and was on to the next.

PARALLEL TRACKS

The reality of the United States presidential election was set by the calendar. Primaries and caucuses happened as the established order had set them, and the 1964 election would happen on Tuesday, November 3, just three weeks shy of the one-year anniversary of the attack in Dealey Plaza.

Woven into this tapestry of national politics were the parallel tracks of the investigation of the Dallas ambush.

Even as the Warren Commission began its work, Dallas District Attorney Henry Wade moved to aggressively prosecute Lee Harvey Oswald. The Warren Commission and the district attorney's office had been on a collision course, and neither one had blinked.

The nation was following the investigation like a soap opera narrative at odds with itself. On the one hand, there was the powerful, establishment-supported Warren Commission, quietly and soberly gathering its evidence within the reassuring confines of the nation's capital. This was the cerebral approach.

The visceral side of the equation could be found in Dallas, where the loud trial of the assassin was boisterously in full bloom. Every day brought new attempts at headline-grabbing and new heights of grandstanding to get there. The stakes were life and death here in this rough-hewn Texas city.

One young man in a cowboy hat, driving a pickup truck slowly past the courthouse, said it best: "You screw up in Washington, all you get is spanked. But you mess up in Texas, you're gonna fry."

BACK CHANNELS

John Kennedy had not yet ended the speculation as to whether or not he would run. Refusing to declare too early was a long-held tradition among incumbent Presidents, but this was different. It felt like Kennedy might just walk away, and if he did, who could blame him? Still, it left open the real possibility that he would take a pass. Lyndon Johnson, Hubert Humphrey and Stuart Symington were all positioning themselves to jump in if Kennedy bowed out.

Outside the Kennedy inner circle, there were powerful men who watched the situation in early 1964 and found it too unsettled for their liking. And so, these men decided to move the process along through a back channel. They chose Edwin Guthman, the press spokesman for the Justice Department, a member of the Working Group, and a close enough friend of Attorney General Robert Kennedy that they were having lunch together when the news from Dallas arrived at Hickory Hill that awful day.

Guthman came to see his boss on the morning of January 24, and his face was grave enough that RFK immediately poured him a glass of water from the pitcher on his desk. He told Bobby he'd been phoned the night before by a man who refused to give his identity yet clearly came from the intelligence community based on who he knew and the details he revealed about multiple operations of which he was clearly aware. The man said that some "concerned patriots" had a message for President Kennedy and Guthman should be their point-of-access.

As Guthman explained the threatening conversation, the bottom line was that President Kennedy had a week to announce his intention to not seek reelection. He could blame it on his personal feelings about what happened in Dallas or a desire to spend more time with his family. It made no difference. He just had to get out of the race fast.

"Please, Ed," Bobby said with fierce irony, "let me know how my brother and I might have the pleasure of communicating with these new friends."

Guthman informed Bobby no direct response was needed. The messenger had told him, "My friends and I will know whether he heard our message based on the President's actions, and we will react accordingly, in our best interests, exercising our Constitutional rights as free Americans."

Kennedy took a moment to process this phrasing, thinking it sounded like the rhetoric of the extreme hard right, the way people like LeMay and his crowd would talk. He asked Guthman a series of questions designed to determine how real this message was. After all, the White House routinely received threats from all manner of cranks and dismissed them as the cost of doing business. Of course, this was before Dallas.

The Attorney General immediately cleared his schedule and went to see the President in person. He laid out the circumstances of Guthman's message and engaged in spirited speculation about who this messenger might be. When Bobby told him about the demand that he immediately take himself out of the presidential race, his brother's stare grew hard.

"Nice of them to ask this time," said President Kennedy.

Interviewed repeatedly about this moment, both under oath and in memoirs, JFK never deviated from his description of the impact it had on him. "I had been feeling better for almost a week at this point, starting to see some daylight," said Kennedy. "This news from the Attorney General, well, I hadn't felt that way since the shooting happened."

'TIL THERE WAS YOU

By February of 1964, not quite three months after Dallas, the deadline imparted by the conspirators to Guthman had just passed, and the President still had not decided what to do about it. He and Bobby discussed one option, that the threat should be made public, but rejected it because it would inflame the nation's mood. Besides, it would be difficult to prove, and the White House would look paranoid and shaken—not exactly the image required for the times.

The President told his brother that he would think about it a bit longer. "If I don't run, there's no problem," he explained. "If I do run, then we see what they do before we react. Nobody wins if all hell breaks loose. It's possible they're bluffing."

Before Bobby left, JFK pointed at *The New York Times* front page. The Big Apple was in turmoil over the arrival of a British rock-and-roll sensation called The Beatles. They were coming to play on the *Ed Sullivan Show* Sunday night. The issue of the moment seemed to be providing security against mobs of screaming girls. To better understand this, the President called in Priscilla Wear and Jill Cowen, two young women with White House secretarial jobs known to the Secret Service as "Fiddle" and "Faddle", respectively. Mrs. Lincoln then put on a 45-rpm record, a song called "Love Me Do," that had been sent up by the mailroom at Pierre Salinger's request. Both men teased the young women about how much they liked the music but admitted it did have a lot of energy.

The Beatles were coming to America whether America was ready for them or not. Predictions were everywhere that Ed Sullivan would attract the highest ratings in his show's history, even higher than they had been for Elvis Presley's appearances. There would be more security outside and inside CBS-TV Studio 50 (later renamed the Ed Sullivan Theater) than there currently was at the White House.

"Great," said the President. "Maybe it would be safe for me to see them." JFK had taken lately to complaining to his younger brother that he was a virtual prisoner in the White House, with the heavy security and his wife's declared moratorium on public trips. Now, JFK was looking to come out of his shell, even if Jackie and the security teams said he couldn't. Bobby took this as a sign of progress, though in the brothers' typical way of joking with each other, he wouldn't show it.

"Don't go to any theaters, Jack," Bobby deadpanned. "You know what happened to Lincoln."

And yet, that is exactly what President John F. Kennedy did on February 9, 1964. He went to the theater.

The Beatles played two sets of their music that seemed the perfect medicine to lift the national depression. Sullivan smiled, girls screamed, and during the second set Kennedy was escorted backstage, where he watched along with Bobby and Ethel. The two White House secretaries who had danced to The Beatles record in the Oval Office—Wear and Cowen—had seats in the audience that night and, apparently, also received a private audience with The Beatles in their hotel rooms.

The Kennedy brothers had decided to send the conspirators a message, publicly, that they, too, could keep a secret and pull off an operation. Kenny O'Donnell knew someone who knew someone, and discrete calls were made from secure lines. It came so fast and from so far out of left field that absolutely no one saw it coming.

Millions of Americans and nearly everyone under twenty-five, it seems, remembers the night when the President of the United States appeared on the *Ed Sullivan Show* to greet The Beatles after their second set as the greatest jolt of pop cultural intensity they'd ever experienced. Seeing The Beatles was beyond huge to millions and millions of people. Seeing the President smiling was an unbeatable relief. Together, the two images were off the charts. It was, said Sammy Davis Jr. to *Newsweek*, "magic times magic, man."

"I wanted to come up to New York to welcome you young men to the United States," grinned the President as the shocked Fab Four shook his hand on live television. "Now, which one of you is the leader?" Kennedy held out an over-large gold key that had been given him by a stagehand.

John Lennon and Paul McCartney exchanged glances. Neither one wanted to discuss this with the President of the United States. Lennon grinned back. "We don't have a leader in The Beatles," he declared. "We just all go off in different directions at the same time."

Kennedy did not miss a beat. "Probably safer that way." He winked and smiled and that black-and-white video image of the President laughing with The Beatles as they all stood together seemed to instantly dispel the rumors that he was shaken and brooding in the Oval Office.

Later, after the show, the President posed for a photo on the stage with The Beatles that did not include the gold key. In fact, by this point, both George Harrison and Ringo Starr had already changed out of their trademark Beatle suits. This is the image that everyone remembers. Kennedy smiling broadly, surrounded by four slightly stunned Mop Tops, an arm on the backs of Harrison and his band mate John Lennon. Heralding how "The Wild 1964 Election Begins," *Top Story* ran it as the cover of its February 24 issue, which quickly sold out on the newsstand, went into a second printing, and sold out again.

Whether President Kennedy had just tweaked the treasonous conspirators who wanted him dead, it was clear he couldn't have picked a better coming-out party. The record shows that the President of the United States did not look afraid at all and seemed to be enjoying himself as much as these four English lads from Liverpool.

THE PRIMARY THING

Campaigning in the Currier and Ives landscape of snow-covered New Hampshire, presidential candidate Barry Goldwater took on an issue that had been bothering him since the President's State of the Union speech. It was the implication that Dallas was caused by hate and that the hate had been inspired by conservatives. The Arizona senator practically cried out his indignation: "Immediately after the trigger was pulled, a hate attack against conservative Americans was started by the Communists and taken up by radical columnists and kept going. I never use the word 'hate,'" he continued. "I think it is the most despicable word in the English language."

The White House watched the Republican candidates carefully. Goldwater was clearly claiming communism was behind the ambush and that, by implication, if Oswald acted alone, it must have been out of his Communist sympathies. In order to move to the right, where the votes in the GOP primaries would be, New York Governor Nelson Rockefeller actually managed to accuse his far-right opponent of being soft on communism himself. "My God," said President Kennedy to an office gathering, "how can we resist this?"

JFK called his 1960 campaign manager, his brother, over the phone. "The issue we've been discussing," he said, and Bobby knew what he meant, "I think we have to just go ahead with it. So I'm working with Ted now." Working with Ted meant that the President was writing a speech or a statement with Theodore Sorensen, not Teddy Kennedy.

"If you're in it, then I'm in it with you," said Bobby. They discussed how as Attorney General he would need to stay out of politics and in the Justice Department and that, this time, Kenny O'Donnell would have to run the campaign by taking on the leadership duties at CREEK.

While his surprise appearance with The Beatles kicked off the election cycle's charm offensive, it had also drawn its own fair share of criticism. There were complaints that it demeaned the office, that it took unfair advantage over political opponents, and that it showed the President as a person who was not as serious as the times demanded. These comments came largely from Republicans. The party of the Kennedys, the Democrats, said it just proved that GOP stood for "Grand Old Partypoopers" and tried to laugh it off.

Still, the White House political team felt that an official announcement had to tack away from the criticism. All three network anchormen (Ron Cochran, ABC; Walter Cronkite, CBS; David Brinkley, NBC) were summoned to the White House for a discussion in the Oval Office. Seeing Kennedy taking their questions in his familiar rocking chair reminded viewers that the President still was on the job, and when he had something to say, the networks wanted to hear it and cover it. Goldwater and Rockefeller could not make that happen.

Under ordinary circumstances the partisan nature of all three networks giving primetime to a sitting president in an election year might have led them to decline the invitation. But this was a President of the United States who had been shot at on live TV, survived, and was back on the job. The American people had a right to see and hear from him in this way. If a little politics seeped into this news, that couldn't be helped, could it?

At one point, ABC's Cochran, knowing his network was in a distant third place, went for the score, actually interrupting President Kennedy during an answer he was giving to CBS's Cronkite. "Mr. President," interjected Cochran, "you sound like a man who's running for reelection. Are you?" While Cronkite glowered at Cochran off-camera, JFK bit his lip, then smiled.

"There are some people," said the President, "who won't be happy with what I have to say on that subject…"

The President paused for a full three seconds before speaking again, giving his plotters ample time to assume he had taken their threat seriously and was getting out of the race.

"I'm talking about the people we have working for us over at the Democratic Party headquarters here in Washington who say there is a right way and a wrong way to handle these things. The right way I'm pretty sure involves a big, important speech with flags." Then came that charming smile. "But yes, let's make it official. I intend to stand for reelection this year."

There it was. Inside the Pentagon where the Joint Chiefs of Staff had offices, there were reports of shattered drink glasses and cursing. More than a few CIA operatives narrowed their eyes and wondered how this was going to be handled. And at the Dallas County Courthouse, Lee Harvey Oswald told guard Chester Northridge, "Good for him."

"I'll campaign hard and on the issues facing our country," Kennedy said. He listed the pursuit of peace with America's enemies abroad, cutting the budget, civil rights, and the growing poverty gap between America's haves and have-nots. He did not mention arresting and trying alleged conspirators in an attempted presidential assassination.

Asked how the events in Dallas would impact the type of campaign he would be able to conduct, he replied, "As you know, Mrs. Kennedy and I have promised each other to avoid public spaces and events until such time as an entire review of security can be conducted. So whether that leads to a less public campaign than we had in 1960 or not will have to be determined later. However, I feel confident that will not be a defining issue. The people know who I am and what I stand for and that I stand with them."

If the conspirators were watching this performance on their television sets that night, they knew that this man they hated, this man they had tried to kill, had just given them the finger.

Spoiling for a Fight

February had been a much better month for John Kennedy than it was for his brother Robert. The Attorney General had seen his investigation into Dallas stall, the Working Group that RFK had established within the Justice Department had met only three times since the assassination attempt. They had many theories but found that trying to run them down ran the double risk of telegraphing their suspicions to their enemies while also sending out a message to the press that the Administration wasn't as satisfied with the Warren Commission investigation as it said it was.

This conundrum weighed heavily on Bobby's mind on the morning of February 25, 1964. He felt that he was in a box of his own making and he wanted out so that he could find answers and hold the guilty accountable. As he sat at his Justice Department desk chewing through one pencil after another, he discussed the problem with Working Group leader Robert Morgenthau, who had come by to discuss strategy. Kennedy was seemingly more convinced than ever that the nexus for the heinous act in Dallas could be found among the leadership of organized crime, men that he hated and had sworn to take down.

Kennedy and Morgenthau were interrupted by press spokesman Ed Guthman, who wanted to know if they could put on the television in the AG's office. "It's the weigh-in," he explained.

The nation, having been in thrall to The Beatles during their two *Ed Sullivan Show* appearances this month, had moved on to a hysterical fascination with the heavyweight championship bout that would pit title holder Sonny Liston against loud-mouthed upstart Cassius Clay that very night in Miami, Florida, the hotbed of the anti-Castro fervor that may have been a breeding ground for conspiracy and assassination.

As they tuned the television to the live coverage out of Miami, they were treated to the spectacle of Clay, wearing a denim jacket with the words "Bear Huntin'" stitched on the back, barging into the crowded room with his entourage. Clay banged his walking stick on the floor and screamed at Liston like a madman that he would "float like a butterfly and sting like a bee" and that Liston would be gone in eight rounds. "I can't be beat!" yelled Clay. "I'm ready to rumble!" He lunged at Liston while his entourage held him back and he kept talking and gesturing even as the doctor checked his pulse and blood pressure.

Morgenthau and Guthman seemed convinced that Clay was scared to death about facing Liston in the ring that night and had simply lost his mind with fright. Indeed, reporters relayed the confirming news that Clay's heart rate registered at 120 beats per minute and his blood pressure was 200/100.

"Cassius Clay is crazy like a fox," noted Bobby, studying the TV screen intently. "It's an act. He's not afraid of Sonny Liston." They continued to watch together until RFK offered his conclusion. "If he wins this fight, we should take a lesson."

The lesson Bobby had in mind was that of the schoolyard: any adversary could be taken down, and the most important action was to show him that you did not fear him. Fear was the advantage people thought Liston had going into the fight, but this weigh-in was all about Clay taking that away from the champ.

In this analogy, the President had shown the conspirators he did not fear them or their threats. Going on Sullivan and summoning the network news anchors to the Oval Office were symbolic acts of a confident man. Yet even as Clay had to back his boisterous behavior with action to win the fight that evening, the President would need to follow up his symbolic acts with something concrete. He needed to land a few punches of his own.

Bobby picked up one of his chewed pencils and began to scribble furiously on his yellow legal pad. Within the hour, the Working Group had a time urgent mission.

In the world of organized crime, reasoned Kennedy, there are few sporting events as powerful and compelling as a high-profile boxing match. On a visceral level, it pits man against man in a brutal contest of violence where death is always a possibility. It always involves gambling and the chance to make money, even if it involves fixing fights, something that might even apply to the Miami showdown, given the mobbed up background of Liston. And fights gave men the chance to hang with other men, bonding in a way that was primal to the core.

Because the Liston-Clay fight had been considered a mismatch that the champion would make short order of, fewer than 9,000 tickets had been sold to see it in person in Miami. But as Clay had intensified his antics during training, it had captured the imagination of average Americans. Theater Network Television (TNT) had put together over 350 arenas and theaters across North America to see the fight. These ranged from large capacity stadiums like the Los Angeles Sports Arena and Detroit's Cobo Hall to many smaller theaters across the country, including drive-ins. From those seats, over a million Americans were expected to watch the closed circuit telecast of the fight, announced by Steve Ellis and former heavyweight champion Joe Louis. Many more would listen to the fight "live" as it was being broadcast on ABC Radio with announcers Les Keiter and Howard Cosell doing the play-by-play, with another former champ Rocky Marciano and pro football star Jim Brown providing insight and commentary.

Attorney General Robert Kennedy knew that pinning down the whereabouts of anyone was notoriously unreliable business without confidential informants under ordinary circumstances. On the other hand, most of the people he wanted to talk to about the Mob's possible role in the Dallas attack had probably made plans to attend the fight, see it on closed circuit, or listen to it with their fellow wise guys.

The Working Group, assisted by McShane's federal marshals, were dispatched to determine as quickly as possible where the biggest names on the list might be on fight night. Highest priority was given to the organized crime figures on it, but it also included several other persons of interest.

That night, as Liston and Clay climbed into the ring to do battle against each other, the Working Group made its move. Using Justice Department agents and federal marshals, five men were brought in for questioning. For most, it was a double-blow. They were taken away in front of friends and, in most cases, they missed the fight itself.

Agents and marshals had been instructed to make their move immediately after the first round to achieve the greatest chance of surprise. As a sidebar, that round ended with the clanging of a bell, yet both fighters continued to punch at each other for nearly seven seconds. Bobby Kennedy listened to the fight from his command station at the Justice Department. "Clay isn't interested in going to his corner any more than we are," he concluded.

The men taken into custody included Sam Giancana, Carlos Marcello, and Johnny Roselli from the world of organized crime. Also taken in were Cuban exile leader Antonio Veciana and CIA Counter-Intelligence officer James Angleton. They were pulled out of homes, theaters, and, in the cases of Veciana and Marcello, from the actual fight location, the Miami Beach Convention Center.

Before the fight was even over, the five men whose tickets had been revoked were in federal facilities in their respective cities being questioned about what they knew about the attempt on the life of the President of the United States. At the Justice Department, the Attorney General and Morgenthau directed the details of each interrogation.

"I'm not saying a word," stated Chicago boss Sam Giancana, "until I know how the fight turned out." He was informed that Clay's prediction had come true when, after seven rounds, Liston refused to come out of his corner to fight the eighth, causing him to lose by TKO. Giancana smiled with the relief of a man who had just made a great deal of money.

Over the course of the next twenty-four hours, each man demanded legal representation and each man told the lawmen questioning them that they knew absolutely nothing about what happened in Dallas last November. They offered various theories that favored blaming Khrushchev or Castro while casually stating that it was all very obvious to them that President Kennedy had brought this on himself. When it came to offering alibis for their whereabouts, each of them had a detailed story that seemed to place them as far away from Texas as possible.

All of this was done without the knowledge of President Kennedy. The next day the two brothers talked by phone about the fight that neither had seen. It would have been nice to invite this young champion to the White House, but he had troubling associations with the Black Muslims and was friends with Malcolm X. He was radioactive to a politician seeking reelection. The subject of the five men still being held under Department of Justice warrants did not come up.

Only after the operation was over, the men questioned and released, did Bobby go the White House to tell the President what had happened. "We're surrounded by enemies, Jack," RFK told him. "We had to go on the offensive."

The President said he understood the need for him to be kept out of the planning on the takedowns. "It's an example of the independence of the Justice Department," he said, knowing that the press would jump all over it. He asked his brother if they had gained any actionable intelligence.

"They're all innocent men as they'll proudly tell you," said Bobby. "But their stories are on record now and if they change them later, we can use that." From the Attorney General's point-of-view, his brother was the heavyweight champion of politics, the victim of a low blow from his opponent. They were only in the middle rounds but they had shown they could take a punch and still fight back as hard as ever.

BALANCING THE TICKET

Vice President Lyndon Johnson was a man held in such low regard at the White House that Kennedy's team of advisers actually wondered if he might have been involved in approving or supporting the assassination attempt in his home state of Texas. The enmity between RFK and LBJ was particularly personal and harsh. On one level it was political, but on another it went back to 1958, when Johnson had invited the younger Kennedy to his Texas ranch and tried to intimidate him during a hunting trip. He had given RFK a 38-gauge shotgun, capable of blowing a deer in half, without warning him about the kick it would have. Bobby had been knocked off his feet, and the gunstock had opened a wound on his forehead. In response, LBJ gave RFK a hand up and noted that he was going to have to "learn to shoot like a man."

The Kennedys were forced to let LBJ on the ticket in 1960. The details were tightly held by the brothers as well as Johnson and to this day are not clear. Historians now believe Johnson's Georgetown neighbor, J. Edgar Hoover, had provided him damning evidence about JFK's extramarital affairs, and that Johnson had used the information straight-out, Texas-style to get the number two spot he coveted.

Both John and Robert Kennedy made mental notes to avoid being in such a position again where they could be attacked with the weapon they had given an enemy. It had been impossible to keep that pledge entirely. The mere existence of J. Edgar Hoover in their lives assured that. Now, however, that dynamic would work in their favor. LBJ had given them what they needed to get rid of him.

The black eye of Dallas alone could probably not have toppled LBJ, but the VP's choice of friends put him on shaky ground indeed. Johnson's close associate, Texas financier Billie Sol Estes, had just been tried and convicted of fraud against the U.S. government for a scandal that threatened to engulf the Vice President. The con man had been sentenced to twenty-four years in jail after enduring a corruption trial that followed a congressional investigation into his contacts with the federal government. More than eighty FBI agents had been assigned to look into the business dealings of Estes.

What they'd found so far was massive fraud against the United States government. There was also a mysterious suicide that looked like murder, and a trail of generous support for powerful Democrats including, most particularly, Lyndon Baines Johnson. Now, with his fate swinging in the wind, Estes was said to be teasing grand jury testimony that would implicate Johnson not only in a direct cash-for-services bribery scandal but also, incredibly, in the murder of the dogged Henry Marshall who had been investigating the Billie Sol Estes case for the Agricultural Adjustment Agency starting in 1960. The next year, Marshall was found dead on his farm, shot five times by his own rifle. Although the death was ruled a suicide, there were many who were skeptical that it took Marshall five self-inflicted shotgun shells to kill himself in his car.

Feeling confident that even Lyndon Johnson would know when he was beat, President Kennedy already had a short list of replacements in mind. There was Missouri Senator Stuart Symington, the man he'd originally wanted on the ticket before LBJ's power play. There was also Florida Senator George Smathers, a man JFK enjoyed socially and who had the discretion to attend parties with dubious guest lists and say nothing to anyone later. And, if Johnson's southern roots were considered necessary to prevail in 1964, there was also Governor Terry Sanford of North Carolina, who unlike Smathers, would be completely untainted by presidential skirt-chasing.

The only decision of the moment, however, was who would

tell LBJ that the clock had run out on his prospects. All agreed it shouldn't be the President, who must be kept out of the fray. Bobby would enjoy the job the most, seeing LBJ suffer after all the headaches Johnson had caused the Kennedys. But the President said Teddy should do it. "He's got to get some experience at this someday," is how he phrased it.

So it became the task of the youngest of the Kennedy brothers to tell Lyndon Johnson face-to-face that he was being dropped from the 1964 Democratic presidential ticket. The new senator from Massachusetts started the job by focusing on his talking points, only to be cut off by Johnson.

"Your brother sent you to tell me I'm off the damn ticket," said LBJ, nailing it, "because he wants me to understand I don't rate the President, I don't even rate the Attorney General. What I rate is some turd-blossom named Junior." Johnson stood toe-to-toe with Teddy, his face just an inch from the other man's, and put an arm on his shoulder so he could not escape. "Now, I don't dislike you, Teddy; I know it's hard for you, growin' up with a couple of brothers like you got, but what makes you think that I should even entertain this proposition you've come to make?"

Teddy said it wasn't a negotiation, that the President could certainly decide who his running mate should be. And there were the various financial scandals that made LBJ's tenure untenable. The implication was that if Johnson used the dirt he had on the President, the Administration would be very diligent in supporting investigations into Johnson's own behavior.

Johnson pursed his lip and glared at this "junior" senator. If he surrendered to the Kennedys now, Johnson thought, he faced a dismal future. He would be remembered only as the first Vice President sentenced to the penitentiary for tax fraud, extortion, illegal campaign funding, bribery, influence peddling, and, if investigators were working under the thumb of Bobby Kennedy, just possibly his own involvement in a number of murders in his home state.

His heart had leaped when he heard the shots in Dealey Plaza. Had they connected with their target as intended, he would be the

President now, and all these charges would have melted away in the interest of continuity and national security. Now, despite his hatred of the vice presidency, his only choice was to hold onto the office and force the Kennedys to see it was in their best interests to save him.

"You can throw all the ten-dollar words you want at me," said Johnson, "but I've done nothing wrong but help my country, and no Senate committee or picture magazine is ever gonna say otherwise. You'll see."

Seeing that Johnson was not taking no for an answer and panicking at the large Texan's physical proximity, Teddy said he would run Johnson's position past the Attorney General. Johnson blocked his escape from the office and handed him a telephone, calling out to his assistant for an outside line. Once Teddy had explained the situation to his brother, Johnson grabbed the phone from him and said, "Mr. Attorney General, whatever happened to being innocent until proven guilty?"

Robert Kennedy replied that such a concept applied to the legal system but not to politics. The Democratic Party simply could not afford to have LBJ's situation flare up in the middle of a presidential campaign. "We've had enough instability with a Texas address," he stated. "What we need now are solutions, not more problems."

"The Democrat Party loves me, Bobby, always has. What you mean to say is that you and your brother need a reason to say to me what you've wanted to say since 1960." As he said this to Robert Kennedy, Johnson winked at the youngest Kennedy brother as if they were now a couple of kids having fun with the neighbor. After hearing RFK's response, LBJ said, "That won't be a problem. You tell the President how much I look forward to our campaign."

Hanging up the phone, LBJ turned to Teddy, "It's all worked out." What the Attorney General had actually told him was that he had two months to straighten things out and, if LBJ's financial dealings had reached public scandal proportions, he would be expected to resign. What Johnson said to Teddy, however, was, "You don't threaten to put the fucking Vice President of the United

States behind bars. It's goddamn disrespectful. This will bite your big brother in the ass if he doesn't wise up."

To his enduring credit, Teddy did not run for cover. He stared right back at the Vice President and said, "It's a very serious matter to threaten the President of the United States, particularly given the recent attempt on his life that's yet to be resolved. You wouldn't be threatening the President now, would you, Mr. Vice President?"

Johnson smiled, knowing the point had been made. "No, I am not," he said. "I support the President of the United States as any proud American does during this time of trouble for our nation."

THE STATE OF TEXAS VS. LEE HARVEY OSWALD

It seemed to many that it had taken forever to get to the business of prosecuting Lee Harvey Oswald. In reality, it had taken only five months, and the miracle was that they could navigate the cacophony of accusations, insinuations, and demonstrations with any sanity at all.

In retrospect, perhaps the first sign that it would be a troubled trial was the resignation of Oswald attorney William Kunstler, who left with an uncommonly terse statement: "I'm making this change in the service of my client." He was replaced by San Francisco trial attorney F. Lee Bailey. Media wags immediately took to calling the lawyer and his client "the two Lees."

"Every American deserves a fair trial," said Bailey when he first announced his presence on the case. "My client is a man accused of a crime that he did not commit, and on that one level, it is just that simple. The men who tried to murder our president are still at large."

Bailey had distinguished himself in the mid-'50s case of Sam Sheppard (which TV's *The Fugitive* was based on). With Kunstler's near-daily diatribes, the American Bar Association had begun a whisper campaign among its members and the press designed to undermine him. The ABA leadership had come to believe that the verdict in the Oswald trial would never be embraced by the people if his defense was seen as showboating and self-serving. Bailey also had flair and a style, but he was clearly the more buttoned-down type, and his demeanor simply shouted competence.

The question that hung over the trial was always the same: would Lee Harvey Oswald take the stand in his own defense?

"Next question," said F. Lee Bailey.

Opening Arguments

The circus-like atmosphere on the streets of Dallas, Texas was unsettling and inappropriate, yet no one seemed able to resist it. It was like the Scopes trial in sheer, high-wattage sensationalism, but it was being televised with an intensity that had only been seen before during the McCarthy hearings of the early '50s. If the Warren Commission wanted to stay behind closed doors, it was almost as if nature had created its polar opposite force in Texas. Every network featured "live" coverage, and the pre-trial hullaballoo led the evening news on all three networks with amazing regularity.

The trial was set to begin April 20, 1964 but was delayed, based on a prosecution request, to Monday, May 18.

After a two-week jury selection process, the trial began with both prosecutor Henry Wade and defense attorney F. Lee Bailey given an entire day to lay out their opening arguments. While each seemed to have marshaled an incredible assortment of facts, testimony and theories, the basic brief each man brought to his argument was clear.

The prosecution intended to prove only that Lee Harvey Oswald was the shooter in the Texas School Book Depository. Witnesses would place Oswald as the man in that sixth floor "sniper's nest" who shot at the Kennedy motorcade with a Mannlicher-Carcano rifle. The jury would be presented with evidence that would convince them beyond a reasonable doubt that Oswald murdered Connally, Hill, and Tippit, and attempted to murder President Kennedy.

The defense meant to obscure Oswald's role by raising grave doubts about the lone-actor theory and disputing testimony that placed him at the Texas School Book Depository. Moreover, Oswald was only a puppet, ultimately manipulated by a shadowy, wide-reaching conspiracy to appear guilty when he was, in fact, a victim himself. By the end of the trial, the jury would see so many holes in the lone-gunman theory that they would have honest and reasonable doubt and would have to acquit on all charges.

In the opening days, when the prosecution presented its case, Henry Wade used his down-home Texas demeanor to hammer witnesses over and over in ways that portrayed Oswald's involvement as just another crime that needed sorting out before the guilty man is sent away. The victims of gunfire were famous, but it did not change the nature of the crime. "Murder is still murder," said Wade, and he said this mantra seven times in this opening statement so no one could mistake his belief.

The evidence favored Oswald acting alone, argued Wade, but so long as he pulled a trigger in an act of premeditated assassination, he was guilty as charged. Wade believed the conspiracy charges were a big smokescreen and, in any event, could be addressed at a later date in another venue.

Bailey saw the entire trial as a Kafkaesque masquerade of conspiracy, mirrors within mirrors, secrets and lies. And in the center of this madness, said Bailey, was Lee Harvey Oswald, the puppet who was being danced against his will. Kunstler had always used the word "patsy" to describe his client, because it was the word Oswald himself had used. Bailey felt it sounded like a word that Al Capone would favor and so abandoned it.

Oswald was a puppet, Bailey thundered. The people on that Dallas jury, he imagined, would like the chance to cut those strings, and freeing his client was the best possible way for them to express their outrage.

Nowhere to Hide

After just nine days, the prosecution was about to rest. Henry Wade didn't believe in gilding the lily and, in any case, felt he should not overreach. Wade had presented eyewitnesses to both the shooting in Dealey Plaza and the physical location of Lee Harvey Oswald in the Texas School Book Depository. He brought in witnesses and evidence that placed Oswald as a supporter of communism who had lived in the Soviet Union and had returned to the United States to agitate against the government's policy in Cuba. This was a man, said the prosecution, who deeply hated his country and showed his contempt for it by shooting at the President himself.

Wade felt, and most agreed, that he had established a crime, presented evidence that placed Oswald at the crime location, tied him to the gun that had been found, and revealed his anti-American motive.

F. Lee Bailey had not really been able to touch his opponent during this phase, and the case against Oswald seemed to be strong. At the same time, Bailey always said he would win his case during the testimony of the defense witnesses who would raise question upon question about the prosecution's case. Bailey also teased his ace in the hole to the hundreds of reporters and cameramen gathered outside the Dallas Courthouse. Lee Harvey Oswald had a powerful and confounding tale to tell and, if he should tell it, "the heavens shall fall." At the same time, he refused to confirm that Oswald would testify, always pointing out that he had every constitutional right to refuse and was keeping his options open until the last moment.

June 3, 1964 was, by the calendar, exactly two days until that moment when the defense would mount its own case. Lee Harvey Oswald sat quietly in his cell that morning and waited. He was in a special holding cell and was allowed only an hour of exercise with other inmates once a day. The case was literally driving him crazy, and he had come to have a maniacal focus on his getting fresh air and exercise in the jail yard.

What happened next was never made explicitly clear. What is known as fact is that at 1:37 p.m., Oswald was found by fellow inmate, Clyde Melville, in a pool of his own blood inside a side entrance off the exercise yard. He was unconscious from a severe beating and barely breathing when orderlies, responding to Melville's frantic shouts, summoned the prison doctor on call.

Dr. Joseph Nowotny was not capable of delivering a level of care that would have guaranteed Oswald's survival, but he got lucky when Melville revealed he had worked briefly as a hospital attendant in Houston before his arrest. Together, Melville and Dr. Nowotny managed to stabilize the injured Oswald. Soon after, Oswald was taken to Parkland Hospital, the same place where Oswald's alleged shooting victims had been treated.

The trial was immediately suspended, pending an investigation and a judgment on Oswald's condition. Judge Harlan Epel locked the jury down in a local hotel while the legal teams debated the issues. Within forty-eight hours, everyone realized the judge had no choice but to declare a mistrial, which he did immediately.

The one-two punch of Dealey Plaza and now the Dallas Jail gave Texas a public relations black eye that it took decades to recover from.

In the aftermath, F. Lee Bailey had this to say:

> *There are no accidents and certainly none in prison. A man this important to the nation's sense of justice does not get beaten within an inch of his life unless someone wants to send a message. You must ask yourself today who wants to send a message to my client, and what would that message be?*

The internal investigation blamed the attack on inmates angry at Oswald for trying to kill the President. Oswald was not able to voice his response given the swelling in his broken and wired jaw. He did write three words on a doctor's prescription pad: "Get me Warren." Oswald had determined there was only one person in America worth talking to more than his lawyer and that was the nation's top judge, Chief Justice Earl Warren.

A PLEA TO LEAVE
The trial was left in chaos after the beating of Lee Oswald. It would

not be a fast recovery, the doctors at Parkland advised. The trial had been ordered postponed for a month, but the delay was expected to be extended again when the first one ran out. It was just as well. With the mistrial sending all the jurors home, it was clear that the wheels of justice would have to start turning all over again if they were going to turn at all.

While Oswald recovered under police guard at Parkland for the first two weeks before he was shipped back to the Dallas County Jail, defense attorney Bailey was busy. He relayed an urgent message to Earl Warren, saying his client wanted to meet with the Chief Justice in Texas.

The men who run the Supreme Court are not accustomed to being summoned anywhere by a lowly defense attorney. When the accused, however, is suspected of trying to kill the President of the United States, it pays to listen. Bailey said his client was adamant. He would no longer tell his story in a Texas courtroom. That was off the table forever now. But he would tell it to the Chief Justice, man-to-man.

At the same time, Nicholas Katzenbach, another in RFK's inner circle, had been presenting a case to a federal grand jury convened by the AG's office that sought to indict Lee Harvey Oswald for the murder of Secret Service agent Clint Hill. For while it was true that a law still needed to be passed making it a federal crime to murder the president instead of leaving it up to state prosecution, there was federal jurisdiction established for the Secret Service.

So Earl Warren traveled to Dallas, Texas to hear from Oswald. The meeting was set up in a secure conference building. Warren insisted that several commission staff attorneys accompany him. Afterward, they all characterized Oswald as practically begging them to charge him under federal statutes and drag him back to Washington, D.C. Only then, said Oswald, would it be possible for him to confide what he truly knew about the Kennedy "hit." Oswald argued that telling the truth while he was still physically in Dallas would get him killed for sure next time. He wanted to be granted immunity and moved to Washington, D.C.

The Chief Justice was stunned. "Immunity?" he asked. "Sir, you are on trial for attempting to murder the President of the United States and succeeding at murdering the governor of Texas, a police officer, and a Secret Service agent. All of these people have families."

Oswald stood his ground. "You want to know what's happening, Mr. Chief Justice sir, and you want to get the responsible people placed in one of these cells instead of some puppet like me, then I have to demand protection." Even Oswald had changed the P-word from patsy to puppet.

After the hour-long interview of Oswald ended, he was taken back to his prison hospital bed. He was limping with a cane as he left, and his left jaw still looked as if he had a plum inside his cheek.

Eventually, the content of the talk with Oswald leaked. When it did, District Attorney Henry Wade made it clear he had asked Police Chief Jesse Curry to double security over Oswald and said the only way the feds would ever get their hands on Lee Harvey Oswald was after the state of Texas was good and done with him.

In the Department of Justice in Washington, D.C., Robert Kennedy met with his team of attorneys to discuss what to do next. They were inclined toward action because the witness roundup they conducted during the February Liston-Clay fight had barely been noticed by the pack mentality of the period's news media. It was so much easier to cover a trial than to try to ascribe motivation to bringing people in for questioning. That required hard work to cover and to analyze.

Attorney General Robert Kennedy had taken the offensive then and he argued strongly that they should give up no ground but continue to press the case. As it turned out, RFK's Working Group had developed a confidential informant with deep contacts within Dallas law enforcement. This man was feeding them regular reports on the prisoner's status and what was being said about him by others. This intelligence would soon become urgent and actionable.

CURSED

On June 19, 1964, just seven months after John Kennedy had been targeted in Dallas, death nearly struck the Kennedy family again, when the youngest surviving brother, Massachusetts Senator Edward Kennedy, nearly died in a small plane crash. He was only thirty-two years old and had won his seat just two years earlier (the one vacated by his brother's election as president).

Kennedy and his friend and fellow senator, Birch Bayh, were on their way from Washington National Airport to the Massachusetts State Democratic Convention where Kennedy was to accept his senate re-nomination in advance of a weekend where the two would campaign together. Instead, late at night, with poor visibility, the twin-engine Aero Commander 680, flown by experienced pilot Edwin Zimny, made a sharp right turn, then went down into an apple orchard three miles short of the runway they were approaching.

Zimny and a young Kennedy aide, Edwin Moss, died in the crash. Bayh and his wife, Marvella, survived but Teddy was badly injured with three vertebrae and two ribs broken as well as a collapsed lung. Bayh pulled his friend from the plane, but by the time rescue workers got him to Cooley-Dickinson Hospital, the youngest Kennedy brother had no pulse and blood pressure that Dr. Thomas Corriden described as "almost nonexistent," necessitating the transfusion of three units of blood to save his life.

Even the official report filed by the local authorities contained the phrase "lucky to be alive" in describing the senator's condition.

Both John and Robert dropped everything to come to his side at the hospital, as they had done earlier when their father had his stroke, and which the family had repeated for Jack the previous November. The idea of the Kennedys rallying around their own touched a national nerve, particularly the image of the two oldest Kennedy brothers standing next to Teddy who was laying prone in a special orthopedic bed.

Because President Kennedy had survived his own brush with death the year before, his words carried special weight and significance. "Senator Kennedy has great work to complete in the U.S. Senate and I'm happy to say he will be around to pursue those activities," he told the assembled reporters. "For me, of course, he's my little brother and I thank God that He has seen fit to save Teddy for my family and the country." The President went on to give his condolences to the families of those who had not survived the crash, an eerie repeat of his statements immediately after the Dallas shooting.

One reporter wondered out loud if the Kennedys might somehow be cursed, given that the eldest Kennedy brother, Joe Kennedy Jr., and their sister, Kathleen Kennedy, had also both been killed in air crashes.

The very idea of an affliction specific to his family incited RFK to anger. "There is no Kennedy curse," he fairly spit out. "Life carries risk, and Kennedys live our lives to the fullest. That's all there is to it."

STROKE OF MIDNIGHT

Attorney General Robert Kennedy's appetite for risk was about to be tested to the extreme. By July, the demand for action was reaching a fever pitch in Washington, D.C. The idea was widely discussed that Lee Harvey Oswald should be a federal prisoner and that the Texas authorities had demonstrated grave incompetence, going back to November 22, 1963, and certainly culminating with Oswald's beating. Even so, on an official level, the Department of Justice was getting nowhere in its negotiations with Texas authorities on the idea that Oswald should be brought back to D.C. to stand trial for the death of federal employee Clint Hill and then, after that trial, returned to Texas.

At the same time, the confidential informant in Dallas had been saying from the moment of Oswald's beating that the trial would never be completed in Texas. "That little communist will never get out of here alive," he claimed, saying this was a truth widely understood by all who worked at the Dallas County Jail

and particularly in the Police and Courts Building, the gray stone
structure in downtown Dallas that housed the headquarters of the
Dallas Police Department and the city jail. Everybody just knew, he
stated. This inside man was not as forthcoming with information as
to how a murder might go down or when. "Days, not weeks," is all
he said to his contact on RFK's Working Group.

What the people demanding action did not know at the
time was that an elite team of federal marshals—activated by the
signature of the Attorney General himself—was training in Virginia
to take control of prisoner Oswald in a raid the following Sunday
night. The plan was bold and a little bit reckless. It involved serving
a warrant, seizing Oswald, and signaling to a helicopter that would
pick him up off the rooftop and whisk him to Love Field, where
a waiting plane would fly him to D.C. Once there, he would be
charged with a civil rights violation, which was a stretch, and the
death of Hill, which wasn't.

Somehow the bare essence of this plan had leaked to *Top Story*
reporter Adam Berkowitz. Fresh off his high-profile coverage in
Dallas and the weeks following, he was increasingly being seen as an
aggressive newsman who wasn't afraid to rock boats to get what he
wanted. Berkowitz and his continuing partner Frank Altman were
trying to find another source to lock down this controversial story
about a federal plan to kidnap a state prisoner, the law be damned.

By late afternoon Thursday, the Attorney General was
contemplating exactly what to say to the *Top Story* reporters who
were calling every hour on the hour when he received an update
from Dallas. Oswald was going to be taken out this weekend, one
way or another. His time was up.

RFK immediately demanded an assessment from Chief Marshal
Jim McShane about the team's readiness for action. McShane told
him that the situation was "dicey, but doable." The variables included
just about everything from weather to the level of resistance that
could be expected from Dallas police officers. Of key interest to the
AG was the likelihood that shots would be fired. "We won't fire first
unless they give us no choice" was all McShane would say, providing

cold comfort to Kennedy.

Robert Kennedy knew that the one person whose advice and consent would be of most value, the President of the United States, simply could not be brought into this loop. If things went wrong, RFK wanted his brother to be able to fire him and not be tied to the action in any way whatsoever. With key members of his team waiting in the outer lobby, the Attorney General sat alone at his desk in his darkened office and thought through everything. After ninety minutes, he summoned everyone in. "The interests of the nation demand that we bring that prisoner back here for trial as quickly and as safely as possible."

The operational decision was to make the move in the early morning hours of Saturday before the weekend shift took over and the regular officers would be at minimum alertness. Twelve marshals, spread between five vehicles, would be driven to the Dallas County Criminal Courts Building in a coordinated approach. As they arrived and engaged, other marshals would arrive at the homes of Police Chief Curry and Sheriff J. E. Decker, serving them with warrants explaining the federal action, and preventing them from entering into phone contact or other activities that could undermine the plan.

Nothing, however, went according to that plan. One of the vehicles ended up with a flat tire, and while carrying on toward the location, was stopped by a Dallas Police vehicle. The federal agents ended up taking the officer into their custody but not before he had begun to radio in his suspicions that something was not right. Once at the target location, one of the teams found that the side door, expected to be left open, was instead double-locked with a chain. As this minute-by-minute activity was relayed piecemeal to the Department of Justice command post, RFK chewed through a half-dozen pencils yet refused to call the operation off.

Eventually, by 3:45 a.m. on Friday, July 11, all twelve marshals were inside the Dallas County Jail, moving toward the infirmary where Oswald was being held. Their entry into the building was difficult. Even with warrants being waved, several Dallas deputies refused to back down. In two cases, guns were drawn and threats to use them made at shouted volumes.

The first marshals, having taken keys at gunpoint, entered the infirmary and found Oswald awake and listening carefully. "Did Warren send you?" he asked.

"We're here under orders from the Department of Justice," he was told. "And your orders are to shut up." The prisoner was roughly escorted toward the hallway to enter a stairway that would lead to the top of the building and a helicopter that was on landing approach at that moment.

As six federal marshals ran into an equal sized force of Dallas deputies blocking the stairway, the situation reached critical mass. Again, all had guns drawn, and both sides were shouting threats. The marshals pivoted toward the stairs at the other end of the hallway.

What no one had accounted for, however, was the ultimate wild card. Jack Ruby, the nightclub owner who had made it his job to be in the good graces of Dallas law enforcement, was in the building, smoking cigarettes and drinking coffee with two deputies in the break room waiting for their shift to end. It was not a coincidence.

Ranking as one of the greatest mistakes in the history of law enforcement, it would later be revealed that Ruby was, in fact, the confidential informant. A chain-of-command that ran through the FBI, federal marshals and the Department of Justice had managed to disguise his identity on a "need-to-know" basis to such a degree that everyone but the original two agents who became his conduits knew him simply as "X."

In any case, it was Ruby who emerged from the break room. He pushed his way forward, directly inserting himself in the melee. He closed toward the marshals who loudly threatened to shoot him, and produced his own handgun so quickly he had discharged it into the belly of Lee Harvey Oswald before he was forced to drop his weapon and submit to arrest.

The exact sequence of these events and those that follow has never been perfectly understood or accepted as both the marshals and the local authorities told stories that differed significantly in their details. What is known as fact, however, is that both Oswald and Ruby were subsequently taken up a single flight of stairs to a rooftop where agents placed them into the waiting helicopter while other agents held the perimeter against the Dallas authorities who now seemed less motivated to hold onto the bleeding bodies involved in the tug-of-war.

The helicopter was flown directly to Love Field as basic first aid was rendered. There, Ruby and Oswald were placed on a waiting unmarked government jet. Once airborne, the decision was made that the flight would be stopped in Kansas City because of the medical facilities available and the concern that Oswald was not likely to make it to Washington, D.C.

Lee Harvey Oswald died in the emergency room of the University of Kansas Medical Center within an hour of his arrival. On one level, Oswald's death certainly ended the jurisdictional dispute about who should get to try him first. He would never testify at a legitimate trial, nor would he survive long enough to make a confession before an execution. One of the marshals on the plane thought he heard Oswald say "not me" during the flight but, even if that was accurate, it was clearly a statement open to wide interpretation.

The nation was shocked and seething with anger. *What the hell was happening in this country?* they wondered. The President isn't safe in broad daylight, and the most important prisoner in the nation can't be kept safe in order to stand trial. It was outrageous and, coming so close to the still-vivid Cuban Missile Crisis, it felt like the nation was in the middle of a nervous breakdown.

People did not cry as they did after Dallas. This time they were coldly furious.

CHOICES AND ECHOES

Coming in the middle of a national election's convention summer, the anger cut across party lines, liberal and conservative talking points, and status quo calculations. Suddenly, an election that seemed destined for the Democratic column was shaken up.

It certainly didn't help that the Dallas prisoner disaster had taken place just days before the 28th Republican convention nominated Senator Barry Goldwater for president at an enthusiastic celebration at the Cow Palace in San Francisco. Still, it wasn't only timing that worked for the GOP candidate, it was the issue that the entire chapter had laid at his feet: states' rights. "The federal government's Mickey Mouse operation is a violation of the constitutional rights granted states and an embarrassment to the people of this great country."

Goldwater wasted no time in latching on to the issue in public even though privately he had been voicing concern that Oswald was "dead meat" given the Texas-size beating he received during the trial. Now Goldwater came out swinging, accusing Robert Kennedy of using the federal marshals as his "brownshirts and stormtroopers," and calling for his resignation.

RFK, as it turned out, was ahead of the curve on quitting. Within two hours of the bungled operation, he had a letter of resignation on his brother's desk. President Kennedy read it quietly, and then slid it back across the desk. "You can't do this to me now, Bobby," he said. "Not now. We've always been in this together and that hasn't changed."

The Attorney General pointed out that he was now going to be an issue in the fall campaign and argued that resignation would end that. The President felt it would make matters worse. "You were trying to save this man's life so he could be brought to trial, tell his story, and allow the people of this nation to see for themselves whether they thought he was telling the truth," he stated. "There's no shame in that."

The shame for Robert Kennedy was something he could not yet tell his brother. He had been informed, only an hour before their meeting, that the man who shot Lee Harvey Oswald was also the confidential informant whose word that the authorization for the raid was based on. Somehow, Jack Ruby had been unable to get close to Oswald since the Sunday after the assassination when he was waiting for him in the basement of the Police and Courts Building.

By helping to trigger the federal government's capture attempt, Ruby had been able to seize a singular moment of vulnerability. He knew to be in the Dallas County Jail because he knew the operation was underway and he knew because he had triggered it.

Both the FBI and the Justice Department would bury this salient fact over a year until the trial of Jack Ruby on murder charges. The Attorney General would brief the President in advance of this reveal, but not by more than a few days.

That was the future. For now, it was the election looming, and a slightly less incendiary point and counter-point of Oswald's untimely death was established. The Republicans would argue that it was federal hubris that got him killed, and the Democrats would argue that he was a marked man they were trying to save and that he was collateral damage in the war that had opened on the streets of Dallas less than a year before.

Privately, both Republicans and Democrats were relieved that the Oswald death came during the dog days of summer as no one had a handle on how it might have played during the presidential primaries. The timing gave both sides time to hone their arguments.

Senator Goldwater ultimately picked Pennsylvania Governor William Scranton as his running mate. The moderate Republican had lost to Goldwater on the first ballot but had made it known he would accept the vice presidency. Goldwater needed an in-road into the Northeast, and Scranton would serve that purpose.

Before announcing his choice, however, Goldwater forced a humiliating march of defeated candidates to his Phoenix ranch house to discuss the job, none more famous or humiliated as New York Governor Nelson Rockefeller who was forced to tell the press he would take the job if offered, then not offered it. In his biography, Rockefeller was blunt about the experience, "From that point on, I knew that if I ever found myself lost in that awful desert with Barry Goldwater with a single glass of water between us that I would drink it as fast as I could gulp it down."

Rockefeller's opinion of Goldwater roughly mirrored the way the Kennedy brothers felt about the sitting Vice President Lyndon

Johnson. Yet, on the eve of their own convention, LBJ's fate on the Democratic ticket was trickier than ever.

ALL THE WAY WITH LBJ

In late August, over a month after the Republicans picked Goldwater to lead their Party, the Democrats convened at Boardwalk Hall in Atlantic City, New Jersey. Both JFK and RFK could be forgiven if they were feeling a sense of déjà vu about the affair. In Los Angeles in 1960, they had been forced by intimidation and bribery to accept LBJ as the ticket's vice presidential candidate. Four years later, it was all coming down to another power play by the Texan at the convention that was supposed to be about the re-nomination of John Fitzgerald Kennedy to serve a second term as President of the United States.

Nothing humiliated Bobby Kennedy more than taking a meeting with Lyndon Johnson during a Democratic convention to talk about the vice presidency. But there he was, sitting across from his enemy, in another hotel suite with only a fruit plate on a coffee table separating them.

"Bobby, I did what you Kennedys asked me to do, and I got my house in order. Right?" RFK had to agree that he had.

Mixing threats, bravado, payoffs, and sycophancy, LBJ had actually managed to stand down both the investigation of the Senate Rules Committee and the articles that had been contemplated by *Life* magazine.

The Senate investigation disappeared, said LBJ, "like smoke from a barbecue after the steer's been cooked." This had less to do with Johnson's innocence as it did with the second thoughts of a number of senior politicians in Congress whom LBJ promised would "rot in jail with me" if he had to take a fall. It also had to do with having Bobby Baker take the rap on his own, after receiving Johnson's pledge that he would be taken care of and that it would be worth his while if he did.

The *Life* magazine article was not so much killed as ignored.

By the time it was published, Baker was looking more and more guilty of deceiving not only LBJ but other astute politicians as well. In the aftermath, Johnson made a public mea culpa about how disappointed he was to have been "sold out" by a good friend. He promised to be more careful in the future but implied that any mistakes that were made had occurred because he had focused on his political service at the exclusion of careful business practices. He had "paid more attention to the country than to myself," he said. He added that if these matters were considered serious, he would expect the Congress to investigate, something he had already taken great pains to assure would never happen. The public accepted this explanation and that was that.

In the end, John Kennedy had given Lyndon Johnson two months to get his house in order, and it had taken LBJ barely half that time.

"And when you bungled the Oswald snatch, I zipped my lips even though that cost me a lot with people I care about. Right?" Again, RFK had to agree that he had.

The prevailing opinion in Texas, from Democrats and Republicans, was that the state had been dealt with badly by a high-handed federal government. Johnson had, indeed, stayed out of sight, although he went to great pains to let both the President and the Attorney General know that this was a great sacrifice he was making on behalf of the Democratic Party and the Administration.

"You have no right to deny the nomination to me this year any more than you did last time," declared Johnson. "I won't have it. I can't have it. Do you understand?" RFK wanted to know if LBJ was making a threat.

"Not at all. I'm stating the facts. As the Vice President, it is my duty to support the actions of this Administration and President Kennedy, even when I might disagree," LBJ explained. "On the other hand, if I am not the Vice President, then my duty is to the people of the great state of Texas. And those people have been dealt a terrible blow to their pride at your own hand."

What Johnson was making clear was that any chance the

Democrats had of hanging on to Texas and its important electoral votes in the general election hinged on LBJ arguing the party line about the Oswald situation. And that he would do the exact opposite if he were dumped from the ticket.

"Do you think we can hold Texas with your support, Lyndon?" Bobby asked.

"Texas is conflicted," said LBJ. "On the one hand, they're angry as hornets about what you did to them but you're not the President, just his little shit of a brother. On the other hand, they're deeply ashamed that the President was shot at on our streets. I think if I explain things properly to them, we can win another close one."

Bobby Kennedy extended his hand to his bitter rival who had just called him a "little shit."

"On behalf of my brother, Mr. Vice President," he said, "I'd like to welcome you back to the 1964 Democratic ticket."

Two days later, Vice President Lyndon Baines Johnson was nominated by acclamation by the delegates of the Democratic National Convention to serve a second time as the running mate of President Kennedy. Johnson was immediately dispatched to hit the road on behalf of the Democratic ticket with an emphasis on Texas fence-mending.

The general election strategy the Kennedy team envisioned was simple. JFK would stay in the White House or travel discreetly, while acting presidential, and LBJ would find the Party faithful in all the states that were likely to be in play in November.

Everyone knew that no vice presidential candidate, even an incumbent one, would make a real difference. The nation had to decide if John Kennedy had been up to the job and, even if they had doubts, they had to consider replacing him with the untested Goldwater.

TWO NATIONS, DIVISIBLE

The general election was conducted against a backdrop of two news stories that told conflicting narratives about who Lee Harvey

Oswald was and his involvement in the assassination attempt and related murders. The narrative a person chose to accept was often a better indicator of their personality type than any of the question-and-answer surveys that were so popular in the nation's magazines.

In the deep background, as always, resided the Warren Commission. It had chosen to present itself as the sober group of professionals going on about the great work of the nation. The commission's meetings were not public, and its members had strictly honored their vow to withhold comment for the duration. Thus, none could grandstand on his own behalf.

Witnesses rarely walked in the front door of their proceedings but were driven by town car to drop points. Eventually, news organizations gave up assigning reporters to the thankless task. Instead the press corps contented itself with speculation that the commissioners were doing a "deliberate" job, implying a slow and steady approach to the truth.

The other alternative narrative came with loud cries that the fix was in and that shadowy forces were keeping the truth from the American people. This passionate belief came from a growing coterie of opinionated men who would shout from street corners and occasional TV shows about conspiracy. Oswald's beating was portrayed as a "warning" by guilty men, and his subsequent death was commonly accepted as a murder staged to stop a man bent on telling an inconvenient truth.

A slight majority of the jury, taking to the Sunday talk shows after the Oswald death, confirmed their belief that the ex-military drifter was what he claimed—a puppet. Still, they all believed he was guilty of firing on the presidential limousine in an attempt to murder President Kennedy. Most jurors felt he would have been convicted had the trial gone forward. Several of the most vocal jurors, however, believed that multiple gunmen were involved, and therefore, they were reluctant to convict on the actual murder charges of Governor Connally, agent Hill or Officer Tippit, and wanted to instruct a grand jury to bring charges against other gunmen they were sure must have been involved. It seems that the jury might just as easily have ended up deadlocked had they gone all the way.

Shortly before Labor Day, the unofficial start of the general election, Chief Justice Earl Warren met privately with President Kennedy and Attorney General Kennedy to brief them on the commission's progress. He told them the preponderance of current evidence seemed to lead to the conclusion that Oswald acted alone and there was no evidence of a conspiracy. Still, he felt the death of Oswald and the federal intent to seize the prisoner (and its disastrous ending) indicated the situation had clearly gotten out of hand. The Supreme Court would likely be asked to rule in the future on issues arising from this very battle, pitting the rights of states against those of the federal government. If that should happen, Warren would be unable to take part in one of the Court's most central decisions of his time. He should never have taken the assignment, he fretted, no matter how well intentioned, and now he realized the mistake. The Chief Justice said, "I must do the right thing, and I am compelled by a love of this country to do it immediately." Warren resigned his commission, as it were.

The Kennedy brothers shared a brief glance. They both felt strongly that someone had gotten to Warren, but they knew they couldn't address that for fear of introducing the "paranoia" issue into the national conversation. Even so, Bobby Kennedy took a hard stance. "Mr. Chief Justice, you know the political world well, and you know that it simply will not do for the nation to have its confidence in your mission undermined by your recusal," he argued. "You must do no such thing as resign; it is imperative that you see this through."

John Kennedy nodded his slow agreement. "I have to agree with the Attorney General," he told Warren. "None of us will win if our efforts to assess blame do not have the impartial power of the judiciary behind them. And it may be even worse if you leave before the job is done."

Warren agreed to reconsider his position, went home to think on it, and sent over the following letter in the morning: "I resign, effective immediately, the chairmanship of this commission. I recommend that the commission staff work with congressional staff to support an appropriate congressional committee, operating under public oversight."

With those words, Warren threw a bomb into the middle of America's public square. He had left, and he had taken his commission with him. In the middle of a presidential election, the Chief Justice of the Supreme Court had told the White House not to investigate its own crime but to let the U.S. Congress do the job.

In a move that struck the White House as clearly choreographed, the moment Warren's resignation and recommendation were released to the press, Senator Everett Dirksen was standing before the cameras, pledging his patriotic effort to follow Warren's sage advice.

Soon, even though it was not quite a political autumn, both the House and the Senate had taken a seat at the table by creating the Joint Committee on the Attempted Assassination of the President, or JCAAP. The public immediately pronounced this, "J-Cap," and the name stuck. Whatever it was called, though, its existence would change everything.

TIEBREAKER

The political cover that Congress gave itself when it created JCAAP was that it would take several months to fold the work of the Warren Commission into the congressional system, and so it would not begin its own fact-finding and deliberations until after the November election. The fact that this was a full year after the crime was committed was conveniently ignored whenever possible.

The non-congressional members of the Warren Commission (McCloy, Farmer, Murrow and Gross) were thanked for their service and dismissed. They were replaced by a contentiously assembled group of representatives and senators from each party. All were assembled under the election year mandate that the public needed to know there would be no cover-up and that their representatives would follow where the facts led. People in 1964 still trusted Congress, and many thought that, yes, their elected representatives probably ought to earn their paychecks and look into this.

With the Warren Commission leaning toward the lone-gunman theory, and the Dallas jury leaning toward conspiracy, JCAAP immediately became known as the "tiebreaker." The first two rounds had been split, and now Congress would settle it.

While Congress stipulated, in an effort to appear nonpartisan, that public hearings would not begin in earnest until after the election, being selected for the committee clearly propelled six representatives and three of six senators toward reelection in November. The committee was composed of all the congressional names from the Warren Commission roster (Dirksen and Magnuson for the Senate; Boggs and Dwyer for the House), plus eight others— four Republicans and four Democrats.

Because the Democrats controlled both the Senate and the House, the chairman of the committee became Democratic Senator Magnuson of Washington. It was the biggest political matter ever placed on his desk, and it would overwhelm him. Magnuson described the experience by saying, "It seemed so straightforward when we started, and it became so impossible so quickly."

DISTANT THUNDER

The fact that the assassination attempt had become what often seemed like a national obsession did not stop real events from needing presidential attention. The Cold War continually threatened to become hot. Always, there was the forward march of the civil rights movement and the Kennedy commitment to the cause of racial equality.

Also demanding much of President Kennedy's attention was the Southeast Asian nation of Vietnam. The Joint Chiefs had never given up pitching a beefier response to the Communist menace there. Lately, after Dallas, it seemed that their frustration grew greater and their impatience at the President's restraint more visible. Kennedy did not believe in land wars in Asia and had said so often. He had been to Vietnam in the early '50s with his brother, heard the advice from the diplomats there, and taken it to heart.

Then, on August 2, 1964, the *USS Maddox*, an American naval destroyer, got into a shooting incident with three North Vietnamese navy torpedo boats. The *Maddox* expended more than 280 shells, and four USN F-8 Crusader jet fighter-bombers strafed the torpedo boats. Four North Vietnamese sailors were killed, but no Americans.

The upshot, however, was a "rally 'round the flag" effect and a demand for action. John and Robert Kennedy brought together a smallish new ExComm structure and sat all its members down in the Cabinet room. After an alleged second incident had happened on August 4, the military leaders all believed that the United States must stand ready to fight.

"Do I need a formal declaration of war to take offensive action?" the President asked his Attorney General.

The answer was probably not. Nonetheless, Capitol Hill was alive with a Southeast Asia Resolution that conveyed full congressional authority to the commander-in-chief to "take all necessary measures to repel any armed attack against the forces of the United States and to prevent further aggression." It looked like it might even pass unanimously, but obviously the White House would have to ask for permission before it could be granted.

Suddenly, Kennedy found himself with both the U.S. Congress and his Joint Chiefs of Staff pushing him toward deploying combat troops in Vietnam. He had already made up his mind to withdraw more or less completely after his reelection, but that was a closely held secret within the Administration's inner circle of advisers.

During a break, JFK brought Bobby to the outside patio. They had taken to doing all their talking there; it just felt safer. "I wouldn't be surprised if this entire affair in the Gulf of Tonkin has been cooked up," he raged, "and those men will not tell me the truth." It was a tragic testament to the divide between the civilian and military leadership that the President would question the facts as they were brought to him. Yet he did question them, and deeply.

In the early afternoon, Vice President Lyndon Johnson joined the Executive Committee after cutting short a campaign swing through Illinois, a state that could have gone either way in the last election, and may in fact have been decided through voter fraud by both parties. The Vice President had visited South Vietnam only last year and had come back as a strong supporter of doing what was necessary to hold off the Communists.

"What would happen if I just said, 'We assume it was an accident, and we also assume it will not be repeated'?" asked Kennedy. He could argue that if either of those assumptions were incorrect, he would act according to that new information. The Administration, however, did not need or want a statement backing military force. If it needed to act, it would do so, and Congress would then be brought into the picture. The Administration did not wish for a blank check.

"Mr. President, the problem with that tactic," said the increasingly confident and disparaging Vice President, "is that you can't keep splittin' the damn baby, because half a baby's no good for anybody." He went on to clarify that he believed his boss had split the baby by giving the go-ahead to the Bay of Pigs invasion but withholding air power, and he had done it again with the Cuban Missile Crisis by putting a blockade around Cuba instead of taking out the Soviet missiles.

In the end, the House of Representatives unanimously passed the Gulf of Tonkin Resolution, as did the Senate by a vote of 88-2. Senator Wayne Morse of Oregon, one of the two dissenters, called President Kennedy before the vote. "You do not need this resolution, Mr. President, and I will not support it."

"I appreciate that straight talk from you, Senator Morse, and I fully expect you to offer your seasoned advice to me as you judge I need it."

Morse confided to friends that he wondered if the President wasn't putting him in his place. The next time they met, he reminded himself, he would need to set that right.

President Kennedy told his circle of advisers at a meeting the next day not to be concerned. "Just because they said I can do whatever I want, doesn't mean I have to do anything at all."

GENERAL ANXIETY

Tradition holds that American presidential campaigns get started on Labor Day weekend, and 1964 was no exception. Over the three days of September 5-7, both President Kennedy and Senator Barry Goldwater hit multiple campaign events across the nation. Goldwater looked every bit as suntanned and confident as President John Kennedy, and much more relaxed. Reporters who had little respect for Goldwater judged his persona on the campaign trail, framed through his ever-present, black, horn-rimmed glasses, as being like that of a "square Kennedy." The Republican had a conservative, plainspoken charisma of his own.

Goldwater and Kennedy created a dynamic that no one had foreseen. Each brought the other's game up a great deal. Both spoke more extemporaneously than the average politician, and each man seemed to particularly disgust and frighten supporters of the other. Passion, light and dark, surrounded each campaign from the beginning.

Goldwater's crowds were large, wild and enthusiastic on Labor Day weekend. Kennedy's would have been the same way, except that the Democratic campaign had severely limited the types of campaign events it would allow the President to attend. The larger the event, the more time and resources were devoted to protecting it. The upshot was that JFK did smaller and safer events. Kennedy seemed like a boxer trying to fight somebody else's style and not his own. He wanted to jump out into crowds, but the men in his corner said that he could not.

This allowed Barry Goldwater to wrap himself up in the relaxed, western lifestyle he represented, presenting himself as more of a common man. The President seemed less fluid and friendly without the adoring crowds surrounding him. Every day that President Kennedy read the political coverage and saw the photos in his pile of morning newspapers, he became more and more dissatisfied with his team.

The problem was corrected by the middle of September, when

the young Minnesota Attorney General, Walter Mondale, took over the Committee to Re-Elect Kennedy from Kenneth O'Donnell who JFK wanted back by his side in the White House. Mondale was a rising star in the Democratic Party; he'd been elected the state's AG just four years out of law school. He shared Kennedy's "vigor" in his public image. On the other hand, very little was known about him, something that was considered a plus for how it might confuse the GOP.

As Mondale laid out his vision, the President would, in fact, do fewer events than Goldwater, but the ones he did do would be designed to perfection. There would be crowds and audiences, but they would be like extras in a film production. Commercial camera crews were turned loose on each one of these events. They came back to editing rooms with stunning images of John Kennedy, a man who had nearly been martyred in Dallas, now surrounded by people, touching them, shaking hands, smiling, even kissing babies.

Mondale had been pitched this idea by Tony Schwartz of the advertising giant Doyle Dane Bernbach, a company itching to create the ad campaign for CREEK. "The subliminal message of every JFK commercial," said Schwartz, "is that John Kennedy is a good guy who'd just come through a close call, and the nation was lucky to have him around, agreeing to finish the job he had started." The tone of the reelection campaign had been set.

Goldwater's media buys, in contrast, were often sharp and aggressive. He usually looked like a man who was just mad enough to grab the bull by the horns, stop all the foolishness and get the job done. Several were aimed at humanizing him, showing the Arizona politician saddling up to ride his horse, and stealing a line he'd heard from one of his supporters, Hollywood actor Ronald Reagan. "There's nothing so good for the inside of a man," borrowed Goldwater, "than the outside of a horse." Then he rode off to, ostensibly, face a High Noon showdown with the federal government.

JFK's team portrayed Goldwater as a lunatic who would get America into a nuclear war that would destroy the world. Goldwater's team portrayed JFK as an entitled rich boy who was in over his head.

It got very, very ugly. There were accusations from both sides in October that each had bugged the other's campaign headquarters. Goldwater's campaign went further, accusing the Administration of ordering illegal wiretaps of his personal phone conversations. No evidence was ever produced. The White House vigorously denied this charge.

The Goldwater campaign slogan was adapted from his announcement speech into the now famous, "In your heart, you know he's right." The phrase was successfully parodied by the Kennedy campaign as, "In your guts, you know he's nuts." Many voters found themselves agreeing with both versions.

Dallas continued to spin its dark magic over the campaign. The Kennedy campaign acted most often to downplay conspiracy, letting the lone-gunman theory take the day, even though the team knew otherwise. The Goldwater campaign, in ironic contrast, felt strongly that Oswald was the likely killer who worked alone but that any suspicion of conspiracy reflected badly on their opponent. Both sides seemed to be in hot disagreement, even though each side was publicly arguing the other side's private position.

No one seriously thought Barry Goldwater could win the general election, and that included most Republicans. Yet there was something unsettled in America that said anything could happen. A Gallup poll released after the Republican convention suggested Goldwater was within five points of Kennedy. Such a bump for a new nominee was not unusual and would likely fade. The conventional wisdom felt that Kennedy would likely win unless something happened. Yet something always did seem to happen with President Kennedy. His lead increased after his own convention, but only slightly. The game wasn't over.

On a campaign stop, Barry Goldwater sighted through a replica scope of the Mannlicher-Carcano-style rifle reportedly used by Lee Harvey Oswald and quipped, "I don't care if he was a Marine sharpshooter. Nobody could get three shots off in that time, let alone four or five." Goldwater further implied that Kennedy himself may have had something to do with creating the conditions of his assassination attempt. "I make no specific charge," he said. "I simply question whether President Kennedy has leveled completely with the American people about what he really knows about the events in Dallas."

All this was in addition to Goldwater's standard stump speech that attacked the Kennedy brothers for using federal marshals as their personal police force. The issue had sufficient traction that the White House was forced to clarify that the Secret Service was now fully in charge of presidential protection and the federal marshals were back to their old jobs.

On one level, Goldwater's belligerent comments seemed like more of the same from a man prone to gaffes. Yet there was a large constituency out there for the Arizonan who felt he was only getting in trouble because he spoke the truth too plainly. The White House knew that no matter how extreme he might sound, it would be a grave mistake to dismiss the threat he posed.

THE ARGUMENTS

The fall campaign had gotten so nasty and just plain angry, particularly on the Goldwater side, that the two presidential debates of 1964 became known as "The Arguments."

The Kennedy and Goldwater teams agreed to only two debates, or as JFK said, "two more than are absolutely necessary." One would be on domestic policy and the other on foreign policy issues. The Kennedy campaign team briefly considered not debating Goldwater, but given the President had debated Nixon four years ago, they felt they would have to match that commitment or be seen as being afraid of a fair fight. They did draw the line on a vice presidential debate that would pit Lyndon Johnson against William Scranton because, as Kenny O'Donnell put it, "With those two on the stage, who would speak up for the Administration?"

In the first domestic policy debate, Goldwater aides had prepped him to "soften his image" a bit, to appear more calm and presidential. He had been branded as an extremist by his opponents within his own Party in the primaries and had seemed to embrace the characterization, famously saying that "extremism in defense of liberty is no vice" in his acceptance speech.

The debate started with Goldwater trying to portray his opponent as out of touch in contrast to his own common touch. "This President cares that a sailboat named *Constellation* won the America's Cup this year, but I don't, and neither do you people at home," Goldwater told the audience.

Kennedy smiled, *"Constellation* won? I didn't know that." Kennedy had not lost his ability at political jujitsu.

The debate certainly began with its share of genial moments as both Kennedy and Goldwater had served in the Senate together and were on friendly terms. It also had sharp jabs, witty asides, reckless accusations, lies, feints and dodges. Before the halfway mark, Goldwater gave up trying to "look presidential" and reverted to form, trying to demonstrate that John Kennedy should never have been president in the first place.

Goldwater even deployed the comparisons to stormtroopers. It prompted a sharp rebuke from the President. "I fought in World War II to preserve American democracy and the rights of free men," he said to his opponent. "That includes, I suppose, tolerating your free speech, even when it is exercised in contradiction of the facts."

In the end, the press declared the debate a tie, then declared that ties go to the incumbent. The narrative being developed was that Goldwater was going to lose on points if he didn't go for a knockout the next time he and Kennedy got in the ring.

The good news for Goldwater in all this was that the 1964 Summer Olympics were being beamed by satellite around the world for the first time ever, and ratings for the debate were depressed. The second debate, however, was scheduled for October 25, the day after the Olympics sent all the athletes home.

Prior to that second debate, polls showed Goldwater now losing by double digits (49-38, Gallup). His campaign advisers knew that they had to shake things up or they could lose in a landslide. Goldwater friend and campaign adviser George Shadegg could not restrain himself, leaping to his feet. "Take the battle to Kennedy, hit him hard, knock him down, and if he gets up, knock him down again," Shadegg implored. The entire group urged the senator on: "Be who you are, a warrior for truth." This way, the reasoning went, even if they lost on November 3, they could feel good about showing the electorate what was really at stake with this "big government at home and appeasement abroad" operation that Kennedy was running.

Democrats knew this change of tactics was in the wind. Goldwater aides claimed they had knowledge only because CREEK had seen fit to bug Republican headquarters, a complaint they never grew tired of making. That belief would turn out to be just one of more than a dozen extreme disagreements in the second debate's ninety minutes of back-and-forth.

Within minutes, Goldwater's aggressive behavior had triggered a lot of that pent-up stress that Kennedy had suppressed over the past year. Ordinarily, he might have held that in check and delivered one of his measured and good-natured performances. But an hour before the debate, Kennedy had received yet another injection from Dr. Max Jacobson that contained a strong shot of amphetamine. The President of the United States was buzzing when he took the stage that night.

So, for different reasons and with different strategies, Goldwater, by design, and Kennedy, by circumstance, punched hard the entire time. It resulted in a bruising presidential debate, the political equivalent of a heavyweight championship fight.

Goldwater immediately tried to put Kennedy on the defensive over the Atomic Test Ban Treaty, mocking the agreement as something "you and your Harvard friends think will bring peace and happiness to the world."

"No, Senator," said Kennedy, cutting him off. "We will still probably have our share of local wars and unhappiness on this Earth, but at least we will all be alive to have that experience."

Goldwater attacked Kennedy for having supported selling wheat to the Soviet Union in 1963 or as he put it, "buying dinner for your friend Nikita." Soviet leader Nikita Khrushchev had only recently survived an attempt to remove him from power by Supreme Soviet head Leonid Brezhnev, who was now under arrest in Moscow. The two leaders who had nearly come to war two years earlier, Kennedy and Khrushchev, now found themselves sharing a common brush with conspiracies designed to remove them from office. In private correspondence in 1964, each man had stated to the other their belief that they had been targeted by domestic political enemies angered over actions and statements they had made together in the pursuit of world peace.

In the debate with Goldwater, Kennedy did not acknowledge his communications with Khrushchev but did call the Soviet leader an "adversary America can and should do business with" to advance the cause of peace between the Cold War rivals. This immediately was seized upon by Goldwater, who claimed the statement represented Kennedy's problem in a nutshell. "There is no doing business with Communists, Mr. President," he said. "All you can do is prepare to defend yourself."

During the 1960 debates, Kennedy had successfully boxed in his opponent Richard Nixon by talking tough about Cuba and implying Nixon was weak on the issue, knowing full well that Nixon could not talk about classified activities that might prove otherwise. Now it was JFK's turn to be boxed in. He could not reveal the private exchange he'd had with Khrushchev only the day before, when the Soviet premier confided that the only reason he'd fought to keep his office was his strong desire to work with Kennedy to end the Cold War.

The debate over China's October 16 detonation of an atomic bomb drew a similar back-and-forth. As far as nuclear policy went, Goldwater argued against the increasing dependence on intercontinental missiles instead of SAC (Strategic Air Command) bombers. "I don't feel safe at all about our missiles," he answered moderator John Chancellor of NBC. "I wish President Kennedy would tell the American people how undependable the missiles in our silos actually are."

The President declined, stating that the matter was classified. "I am, however, glad to hear Senator Goldwater agrees with our goal to reduce global tensions by reducing the world's nuclear stockpiles." Goldwater shot back his outrage that his words could be twisted so terribly.

The real fireworks came when Goldwater, who had backed the populist nature of following the Oswald jury's conspiratorial leanings, hinted at dark secrets in the Kennedy White House that could have triggered such ugliness. Kennedy had been fully briefed on this line of attack and was quick to respond. "For Senator Goldwater to come before the American people and say in so many words that somehow the President of the United States is the responsible party for an attempt on his life and the lives of others is reckless behavior in the extreme." Kennedy looked straight at Barry Goldwater, the friendlier times seemingly forgotten. "Senator, if you believe that, then you need to say it to my face, and let the people you would ask to lead, hear you say it and judge your own character for themselves."

It was political dynamite, the most shocking moment in the televised presidential debate. It was a moment that transcended politics and felt more like the beginning of a brawl. Instead of backing down and saying he had been misinterpreted, Goldwater fixed Kennedy with his own steely gaze. "I will say it, Mr. President, and to your face. I believe that the way you ran your White House caught up with you in Dallas. Oh, I don't know the specifics, and maybe we never will, but we do know your record of reckless appeasement of the Soviets. That kind of weakness incites a response from your enemies. It's not pleasant to hear, sir, I know that, but someone must say it."

Rather than further escalate the fireworks, the President smiled cryptically to himself. Audiences perhaps got a glimpse of what was on his mind moments later, when NBC's Chancellor said it was time for the candidates to deliver their closing statements. Kennedy looked straight at Barry Goldwater and began:

Barry, we've been colleagues for years, and I've seen you express true outrage. But tonight it just seems that you have come to pick a fight. Now my opportunities for retaliation and justice are few. I could refuse to shake your hand at the end of our debate here, or maybe, and this is purely hypothetical, but if I were angry enough, as angry as you seem to be, I could stride over to your podium and take a punch at you. But that's it—my fist, your face, as it might be. But what if nuclear weapons were involved? What if you're feeling like you were tonight, like you wanted to pick a fight, and you succeed, and the other guy feels like punching back. And he has nuclear bombs a thousand times more destructive than Hiroshima. What then?

At that point, President Kennedy turned from Goldwater to the camera, and directly asked, "What then?"

Many believe that the chance Barry Goldwater had to be President of the United States evaporated into thin air at that moment on the University of Wisconsin stage. A clear majority of undecided voters decided that the Republicans had nominated someone who was politically suicidal and potentially insane. The election was over, even though it had twelve days yet to go.

The headline had been set, as had the tone of the rest of the campaign. *The New York Times* titled its article, "Desperate Goldwater Blames JFK for Dallas." *Top Story* headlined its own coverage, "Goldwater KOs Himself."

The polling data that the GOP establishment started getting was dismal. The country, still unsettled, had nonetheless collectively decided that Kennedy deserved a second term, particularly given Goldwater as his opponent. In the final ten days of the campaign, a veritable GOP all-star team of Richard Nixon, Nelson Rockefeller, George Romney, and Everett Dirksen all hit the road, not for Barry Goldwater, whom they felt was a lost cause, but for Republican candidates in the House and the Senate. They urged Kennedy-leaning voters to avoid giving the incumbent President a "liberal blank check" by handing him congressional super-majorities. *Top*

Story called it, "The Drive to Bury Barry," and it stuck.

Then, with only two days to go until the election, Vietnam came alive again as an issue when Viet Cong guerrillas hit a U.S. air base at Bien Hoa, killing four Americans and wounding a dozen more. Five planes were destroyed and many others were heavily damaged. All of this happened just ten miles northeast of Saigon.

Goldwater called for immediate retaliation, saying, "Let's take the planes they didn't get and anything else we need and go after them."

Kennedy, knowing he only had to straddle the fence a matter of hours, used it to play into the prevailing theme of his campaign that Goldwater was a hothead who would drag the country into danger. "This is a very serious matter," said Kennedy somberly, "and those who have done this should expect our response soon. What I won't do is treat real-time foreign policy as a political game and, frankly, my opponent shouldn't either."

Now What?

The election that year was an odd one. Pundits had openly speculated about what might have happened had John Kennedy died in Dallas. LBJ would have become President Johnson. He could probably have passed a civil rights bill based on Kennedy's martyrdom, a bill that was still stalled in Congress in the real world. Johnson might have crushed Goldwater under the right conditions.

By surviving, John Kennedy remained fair game. He got the tough race he always expected, albeit made so much more unpredictable by the events in Texas.

What happened on the electoral map surprised everyone. Kennedy had benefitted by the rejection of Barry Goldwater in the final days of the campaign as a serious candidate. In the end, the more than seventy million popular votes were split fifty-three percent to forty-four percent in Kennedy's favor, with three percent going to other candidates. Voters gave the South solidly to Goldwater, who had only sporadic success elsewhere. LBJ managed to lose his home state of Texas, but the Democrats picked up California, a state they had lost to Nixon in 1960. It was an Electoral College rout, 366-172.

At the same time, though, voters had shown their discontent in the November election by splitting tickets in absolutely unprecedented numbers and sending a divided government to Washington. The appeal made by the GOP establishment to focus the electorate on Congress and not the presidential race had worked. When the smoke cleared, the Democrats lost six Senate seats and a whopping thirty-eight House seats. Although this left the President's Party still in control of the Senate by a reduced but comfortable 59-41 margin, the Republicans had taken control of the much larger House by the slimmest possible margin, 218-217.

HOPE FOR A NEW YEAR

The Kennedy families came together for Thanksgiving once again in 1964. Given the horrible dark cloud that had hung over the last year's gathering, this one seemed to be about rebirth. Edward Kennedy had just been reelected senator from Massachusetts, despite being confined to a hospital bed while recovering from his near-fatal plane crash. Against his doctors' wishes, he was transported by ambulance and allowed to recuperate in the Hyannis Port compound in a special hospital bed that had been moved there for him. On Thanksgiving Day, John Kennedy helped his youngest brother put on a back brace and walk to the dinner table, where they posed for a picture together. They shared a special bond in that they had each cheated death in the last year. Until this day, it had always been Jack and Bobby. For the first time, friends and family members saw them as Jack and Teddy, their own duo with its own potential.

John Kennedy was alive and had just retained the presidency. His family was unified. They could begin to pick up the pieces and move forward again, after a year of difficulties.

During the holidays, President Kennedy spent a great deal of time reading and consulting over the two big events of the next month—the State of the Union, followed by his second presidential inauguration. Pierre Salinger told *The New York Times* that the President had read Winston Churchill's *A History of the English-Speaking Peoples*. While that may have been true, it was later learned he had also re-read one of his favorite books, *Melbourne* by David Cecil. This biography of Lord Melbourne, Queen Victoria's prime minister and political adviser, includes many anecdotes of the young aristocracy in England, which held honor above all else but often spent weekends at country estates, where parties and extramarital sexual relations were the order of the day (and night). When it was time to get back to business, however, no one talked about these events, and divorce was considered disgrace.

Clearly by his choice of reading material, John Kennedy was considering both his public and his private life during these weeks.

Kenny O'Donnell, wearing the hat of political strategist, argued during the entire month of December that the January 3 State of the Union and the January 20 inauguration speech had to be considered a double shot to address the American people and the world about where America stood. The first speech would be for U.S. consumption and the second for the world at large. The opportunity could not be wasted.

The New Frontier had taken the world to the brink of nuclear holocaust, featured man's inhumanity to man in the Deep South, and shattered the domestic tranquility on the streets of Dallas, Texas. The one area of agreement for everyone in the Administration was that this second chance could not be wasted.

Top Story

NE 14, 1965   35c

THE SECRET LIFE
OF THE PRESIDENT

by Frank Altman and
Steve Berkowitz

Chapter 5:
Proxy Wars

January 1, 1965 -
August 23, 1965

Second Chances

1965 was shaping up to be an ugly, tumultuous year. More than thirteen months had passed since the dismal fall of 1963, and yet the reality about what went down in Dallas, and why, had yet to be made clear. If anything, the truth seemed to be slipping away. The nation's shock had turned to anger.

Indeed, two separate investigations had foundered during this recent past: the Oswald trial, because of the suspect's beating; and the Warren Commission, because of the suspect's death. The reasons and excuses were what they were, but the public was unhappy with the lack of results. A majority of people felt that the truth about Oswald had been covered up and that the Warren Commission was a sham.

That single seat margin of GOP control in the new House of Representatives set the stage for an epic struggle to control Congress and, by extension, to decide the fate of the newly reelected President and his agenda. As an example, Democratic Congressman Albert Watson of South Carolina's Second District supported Barry Goldwater. Ordinarily the Democrats would have thrown him out of the Party, forcing a vacancy that would have called for a special election. Now they needed him, no matter what his politics were. There were many senators and representatives like Watson, all from the southern states, who were now questioning their allegiance to the Democratic Party. They could not be trusted to vote with their Party on individual issues, particularly those concerning social justice. With a virtually tied House of Representatives, they would have to be dealt with.

For now, though, the Republicans had the House, and that meant they had the Speaker. The position went to Congressman Gerald R. Ford of Michigan, a man known to his colleagues as a congressman's congressman. It was the accomplishment of Ford's personal agenda to be the Speaker of the House, a position he had dreamed of since the 1950s, when he declined offers to run for both the Senate and the Michigan governorship. He had become Minority Leader in 1964 in a closely contested race, replacing Indiana's Charles Halleck. That Ford had also served on the now-imploded Warren Commission made Democrats nervous.

Ford's stated position was that by splitting tickets in 1964, voters had shown John Kennedy their sympathy for what happened at Dallas but were reminding him not to interpret his victory as a mandate for a liberal agenda. This would be much easier to enforce now that Republicans, by virtue of their paper-thin majority in the House, got to chair all the committees. The new numbers meant nothing was going to be easy for the Democrats going forward.

John Kennedy's "luck of the Irish" in surviving both the assassination attempt in Dallas and an unexpectedly spirited GOP reelection challenge also had the White House in a more combative mood. With those boxes checked off, JFK's inner circle now felt the time had come to strike back somehow and hold accountable those who had been a part of this crime. They had to seize the momentum. Whatever people thought about the lone-nut-versus-conspiracy debate, John Fitzgerald Kennedy still needed to make it clear that he was in charge.

A more activist approach brought with it grave danger: the exposure of the President's extramarital private life and drug use; the real depth of dissatisfaction the nation's military and intelligence agencies felt toward him; and the possibility that the conspirators would try again, with force, and this time succeed. Still, the Kennedy White House knew that the election, then the State of the Union address, and even the second inauguration could not forestall the inevitable.

The one-two punch of the two looming speeches needed to launch a new theme. It was time to turn a page in the history of the 1960s, and if any man had the rhetorical skills and personal charisma to do that, it was John Kennedy.

NIGHT VISION

In his January 3, 1965 State of the Union address delivered to both houses of the Eighty-Ninth Congress, President Kennedy looked out across the faces in the room and joked that it was good to see so many old friends and be given the opportunity by the nation's voters to make so many new ones. It was one of the few lines that got a positive reaction from both sides of the aisle. Any applause line the President offered was guaranteed to be accompanied by TV images showing half of the new Congress sitting on their hands.

Three weeks earlier, while planning for the address, John Kennedy had, in a moment of keen political clarity, realized exactly that TV dynamic and planned accordingly. He knew that Americans would see those sour images and be disgusted. He would use television and speak past the congressmen and senators, engaging the camera as directly as possible, and speak to the people at home who had just reelected him. And he would direct their attention to the humorless Republicans who sat motionless, without response.

The Kennedy White House added a dramatic touch, to justify a feeling of greater importance and potential for bipartisanship. They borrowed from the great Franklin Delano Roosevelt and scheduled the speech for delivery at night, the first time this had been done since FDR's State of the Union message in 1936. By doing so, Kennedy thus assured himself a nationwide television audience of more than thirty-one million of his fellow citizens.

The rhetoric of the election was toned down and, in its place, was a President Kennedy simply acknowledging Dallas and its aftermath, lamenting the "political stagnation" of the previous year. His word choice and his demeanor addressed his comments to the viewer at home:

> *We are weary of this crime and wonder why more than a year later this Congress is just now beginning its own investigation, the so-called Joint Committee on the Attempted Assassination of the President. This committee will have the cooperation of the President's office, but it should do its work expeditiously. Those of you listening at home without jobs, farmers who need help, auto workers in Detroit, and so many other Americans, you all want answers and an end. And you want Congress to turn its attention to the great issues that still challenge our society. Congress will be tested this year and it must not fail.*

With that, JFK did his best to put Congress in a box, knowing that in most minds, their new committee should have been up and operating a full year ago. New staff members had been sifting through the voluminous amount of material that had been collected by the Warren Commission. Most of it was gathered and distributed to committee members on the very day that the President was making his address.

In order to give Congress reasons not to turn all of its attention to Dallas, the State of the Union needed to put serious policy matters before the legislative branch and challenge them to show the same enthusiasm for bill-passing as crime investigation. With that in mind, President Kennedy unveiled a laundry list of activity.

At the top of the President's list, however, remained his call for profound civil rights legislation, something that would probably have been introduced and passed if he had actually succumbed to injuries in Dallas, but had been put on hold by Congress during the 1964 election cycle. Kennedy renewed his call to outlaw discrimination based on race, color, religion, sex, or national origin. Once again, his proposed legislation would end unequal application of voter registration requirements and racial segregation in schools, at the workplace and by public accommodations.

In a bid to re-start the nation's business after what felt like a year off, the President also asked for fresh congressional action on several bills that got by the Senate but failed to pass the House in 1964: Medicare under Social Security, aid to Appalachia, and liberalization of the immigration laws. As a stimulus to the economy and a follow-up to last year's $11.6 billion tax cut, he asked for heavy cuts in excise taxes. He also promoted a bigger war on waste, a new regional redevelopment program, and more money for housing and urban renewal.

The national budget was now close to $100 billion and could not be increased without a fight. So frugality in government had to be stressed over bold, new programs. Kennedy called for the full development of all national resources, human and natural—but not for more spending—to improve the quality of life in the U.S.

Kennedy declared that the phrase, "America, the beautiful" was itself in danger. "The water we drink, the food we eat, the very air we breathe, are threatened with pollution," argued President Kennedy. "Our parks are overcrowded, and our seashore overburdened. Green fields and dense forests are disappearing."

He said he did not regard the Administration's agenda for a second term as pushing for "a final objective, finished work," but rather as a "challenge constantly renewed."

As it turned out, JCAAP met formally for the first time, three days after the State of the Union. That first call-to-order was pro forma and businesslike, actually avoiding the sense of partisan fighting that most people were expecting. Instead, the committee focused on which witnesses to call back and whether to do so publicly. It also decided which witnesses to add to the lists that had been forwarded. Most tellingly, it made clear that its mandate now included all aspects—state and federal—of the miserable handling of prisoner Lee Harvey Oswald.

Everyone, from the President to the committee members to the conspirators themselves, knew this was the calm before the storm.

MOVING ON

John Fitzgerald Kennedy took his second oath of office on January 20, 1965, administered by Chief Justice Earl Warren, the man who had run from the commission named after him and hung the President of the United States out to dry. An estimated 1.2 million people attended this inauguration, a record for any such event held at the National Mall. It was also the last time an inauguration was covered by newsreels.

All in all, it took little more than an hour to transact the business of the occasion—to swear John Kennedy in again for a second full term as the thirty-fifth U.S. President and Lyndon Johnson once more as the thirty-seventh Vice President. While the pundits did not consider it as dramatic as the 1961 inauguration, in which the torch was passed from the World War II generation's Eisenhower to a new generation led by Kennedy, it had its own sense of history. Covering it for CBS, Walter Cronkite noted, "No one who is watching can help thinking how close the nation came to having another man standing there with his hand on the Bible." As he delivered that line, the camera lingered on Vice President Lyndon Johnson who seemed downcast and somber.

The problem that President Kennedy faced for his second inaugural address was that his first one had been declared certainly one of the best ever. He was in competition with himself. Knowing this, Kennedy had tried to be smarter. In 1961, he had stayed out until 4 a.m. partying with friends and even, rumor had it, sleeping with a woman who wasn't his wife. In 1965, he was in bed by 9 p.m. the night before, and with Jacqueline Kennedy. We now know she had told him that if he wasn't home with her by midnight that she would come down with a serious bout of the flu and miss his speech.

Kennedy had also gone through five full drafts of his comments with Theodore Sorensen, including one done on the morning of the Inauguration. Kennedy woke his speechwriter up at 6 a.m., telling him on the phone that the version they had written had too much "treacle" in it and summoning him to the Oval Office. Together they ended up cutting it down to less than three-fourths of its original length, leaving out an entire section that dealt with the need to refocus energy on the economy, something they both agreed had been amply covered just two weeks earlier. Instead they substituted words aimed at the international, and not the domestic, audience:

> *The United States seeks no dominion over our fellow man, but only man's dominion over tyranny and misery. Let us now transform our unity of interest into a unity of purpose, to achieve progress without strife, change without hatred; not without difference of opinion, but without the deep and abiding divisions which scar the world for generations.*

Kennedy said the New Frontier, still the destination of his Administration, was "not a set of promises, but a set of challenges." It would only be built, he said, by the combined efforts of government and the public and not by a series of laws and edicts. The journey had to be personal for everyone.

During the policy debates leading up to the speech, Sorensen had noted that even before Dallas, Vice President Johnson had been promoting the idea that the second term should be about "the Great Society." He wondered if, just possibly, it might be the one good idea LBJ had given them during his tenure and that they might want to borrow it. Kennedy thought the phrase smacked of press agentry, and a particularly grandiose kind at that. "Spare me from another Johnson Treatment" is how he put it, sticking in the final knife.

While the New Frontier had no room at all for a Great Society, as it turns out, it could be a place where people could get a second chance. Kennedy tackled the shadow of assassination by rhetorically sailing past it:

> *It is time to move past our recent divisions and begin again to address the issues of war and peace, the human rights of men and women of all nations, and the pursuit of justice. Let our work begin anew. Let Americans and the world enjoy the redemption that only a second chance can offer.*

John F. Kennedy's "Second Chance" speech was meant to get the country moving again. He used the metaphorical power of the phrase over and over as he ran through his Administration's record from the success of the early space launches, but also defending and deflecting the record on the Bay of Pigs, the Cuban Missile Crisis, the civil rights protests, the Berlin Wall, and Vietnam.

President Kennedy then transitioned to the biggest headline of his speech. If the first term had a too-close brush with war, then the second term would be about the search for peace. Echoing many of the themes from his 1963 American University speech and 1963 United Nations address, he cast 1964 as a dramatic pause that must now end. He had accepted an offer from Soviet Premier Nikita Khrushchev to visit Moscow and would do so before the year was out. Together, they would discuss ways to reduce international tensions and seek new ways to work together.

After the speech, the Kennedys and the Johnsons enjoyed what looked like a long, glittering toast offered up by the capital and the nation, even though at this time, JFK and LBJ were barely speaking to each other. First came the parade where they stood beaming in a glassed-in and bulletproof box outside the White House and saluted the paraders marching past. Then came a visit back to the Oval Office for Kennedy to do a little business and change into evening clothes, while the Vice President went to a local club for a few scotches with friends.

The long evening came with five inaugural balls where the President and First Lady danced late into the night. "My husband rarely dances with me but when he does, there is no one finer," explained Jackie Kennedy, adding a comment that made a few observers wonder if she was discussing the ballroom or the bedroom. "Of course, all the ladies seem to want to dance with the President."

The smiles and toasts were observed by heavily armed men who were part of security measures that were nearly double what had been in place four years earlier. At one point, Kenneth O'Donnell pointed this out to Dave Powers and asked, "If Oswald acted alone, and he's dead, then why are so many of these guys still on the job?"

These two men, who had personally felt the hot fire of bullets coming from behind the grassy knoll along with that from the now-infamous sixth floor of the School Book Depository, knew the answer. The men who had planned Dallas were still at large.

SHADOW VOICES

It has always been a truth of politics that what is publicly discussed is never the whole story. With the President now on the job for his second term, the man-on-the-street probably saw things as going back to normal. Kennedy was back at work, the new Congress was digging in, Russians were still threatening to bury us, blacks were planning new demonstrations, and kids were back to listening to incomprehensible music their parents could never fully understand.

Many were even hopeful that the Joint Committee on the Attempted Assassination of the President might finally straighten out the entire mess that Texas had become and get to the bottom of who did what. Under the surface, however, Republicans were looking to use the committee as a blunt instrument to break into the White House and do political damage. Democrats sought to keep things under control. What was clear to everyone on Capitol Hill, however, was that it was going to be as contentious as the McCarthy hearings or even the rackets hearings, and maybe even more so.

Congress was hardly the only group simmering with the potential to shatter this fragile return to normalcy. The heavy scrutiny for the past year had made the kind of communications that hatched the conspiracy in the first place even more difficult. Even so, chance meetings and hushed utterances began happening with a greater frequency after the election.

From the point of view of the conspirators, the situation was dire. Kennedy had been targeted because he was seen as taking America off a cliff. They had lain low for nearly a year after the failure in Dallas, covering their tracks, destroying evidence, even seeing that a few key witnesses met untimely ends. Even in their retreat, though, they had kept their objective in mind. Kennedy had been given a chance for a graceful exit and had refused it.

Seeing him campaigning for reelection was hard enough. When he began his new term in 1965 by naively reaching out again to the Soviet Communists, it was simply too much to bear. All bets were off now, the conspirators told themselves (as if hiring gunmen had been only a half-measure). Still, they were ever mindful that the direct tactic of assassination had failed and could not be tried again. In quiet moments inside shadowed offices, the conversation continued. Something had to be done, and soon.

Two new books were being read by a lot of Americans, both punching holes in the lone-gunman theory. The first was F. Lee Bailey's *The Puppeteers*, a work that seemed to be more about the San Francisco attorney than his client or even the men he claimed had conspired to use that client for the nefarious purpose of killing the President. None of this prevented the book from shooting to the top of *The New York Times* best sellers list the week it was released.

More threatening to the actual conspirators, however, was *Rush to Judgement*, a book that unabashedly presented strong evidence that Lee Harvey Oswald had not acted alone and, possibly, hadn't even fired a shot at the motorcade. Authored by New York lawyer Mark Lane, it methodically assembled the case that the fingerprints of the intelligence community could be seen everywhere, from the moment those shots were fired in Dealey Plaza.

These powerful men (and, yes, they were all men) knew that the national discussion could not be allowed to focus on taking revenge against the people who had tried to kill their beloved President. Goldwater had floated the idea that Kennedy had brought the whole thing down on himself, but the charge had never gained traction. JFK seemed like one of those new frying pans, coated with that miracle substance Teflon that was becoming so popular. Nothing seemed to stick to the man. That had to change, too.

Equally worrisome was the fact that the Warren Commission, the only real chance for the cover-up's success, had given way to a far less controllable congressional investigation. No one was naming names yet, but could that really be far behind?

A battle for the perception of the American people now loomed. John and Bobby were two of the most skillful political forces ever to come to Washington, but the conspirators had access to vast sources of experience in espionage, intelligence, and disinformation. They had the will and the ability to change the subject.

There would be no more bullets, but Kennedy still had to go. There was more than one way to assassinate a man. It was time to change tactics.

JUSTICE DELAYED

From the beginning, Attorney General Robert Kennedy knew how to describe the difficulty in sorting out who did what before the ambush in Dallas. The term he used was first coined in counterintelligence circles to denote the feelings of paranoia and confusion that sometimes develop in the byzantine business of spy hunting, when one is no longer able to distinguish between what is real and what is illusion. "It's a wilderness of mirrors," he would say.

Quietly, since the 22nd of November 1963, RFK had been toiling with the Working Group—his gung-ho staff of young prosecutors and Kennedy loyalists—on the Dallas case, all through the 1964 election and beyond. Often, they would gather late at night or early in the morning, when their absence from other work duties would not draw anyone's attention. Because of their extreme discretion, the reality of their quest had leaked to virtually no one.

One such meeting took place at Bobby's Hickory Hill estate in mid-February 1965. The choice of location was convenient for the Attorney General, and also held the advantage of being private and secure. No matter how often he had his Justice Department office swept for bugs, Bobby was always aware of the chance that J. Edgar Hoover's prying ears might have worked their way inside. The need for secrecy was challenged by the sheer number of leads he and his team had to follow. Just the ones introduced at this meeting alone demonstrated the complexity.

One of these that particularly intrigued them was the story of Richard Case Nagell, who claimed he got himself arrested for attempted bank robbery in El Paso, Texas on September 20, 1963 in order to avoid being made a fall guy in a CIA plot to assassinate President Kennedy. Nagell looked like a man who preferred to spend the next few years in jail if that's what it took.

There was also the rumored existence of a 201 ("personality") file on Lee Harvey Oswald, a set of documents maintained by the U.S. government for members of the armed forces. It seemed that Oswald had been trained by the CIA and had actually been on the FBI's payroll. Famously, he had claimed he was a patsy. "It's fifty-fifty that he was telling the truth," RFK argued, "but the conspirators have their tentacles into our institutions to prove he worked alone, so we must ask the other questions, the harder questions."

Fueled by deli sandwiches and coffee, RFK and his six-person crew worked until almost eleven, at which point he sent them home with the understanding that they continue on their own in the days ahead, keeping in mind the same mandate he had described in his first crusade against organized crime in 1961. At that time, he had directed many of these same young prosecutors to stamp out "the conspiracy of evil" that the plotters represented. "Don't let anything get in your way," Bobby told them now. "If you have problems, come see me. Get the job done, and if you can't get the job done, get out."

Inevitably, everyone wanted to know who the United States Attorney General thought was behind the attempt on his brother's life on a regular basis, as if to gauge the latest trend. Kennedy now strongly believed the President had been the victim of a domestic conspiracy, he told his prosecutorial team. He did not believe it was the Soviet Union or the Cuban government that was involved. He believed others had concocted a trail of falsified evidence to lay blame on our Cold War opponents and trigger a new invasion of Cuba.

Both professionally and personally, Bobby Kennedy had obsessed on this issue for months now. He had mulled it over, studied the evidence and weighed the issues. His best guess now was that the hit had been planned and executed by elements of the United States intelligence community, exploiting elements of the Mafia, and anti-Castro Cubans, with key support from within the U.S. military, largely funded by Texas oil interests.

It sounded like a joke. The nation's top law enforcement officer believed the answer to "Who tried to kill President Kennedy?" was "All of the above."

RFK freely admitted his theory was based only on his gut suspicions and not yet on hard facts. He expected these prosecutors to get him those facts so they could make arrests and bring people to trial. He wanted to charge these conspirators with treason, the only crime specifically defined in the U.S. Constitution.

Kennedy had as little faith in JCAAP as he did the Warren Commission. He believed that the conspiracy would never be shattered and held accountable without the Department of Justice bringing charges against the suspects. It was only by shaking the trees that they could see what kind of interesting fruit might present itself.

What none of these eager avengers fully appreciated yet was how every lead would take them down a road that either turned into a dead end or splintered into a dozen new paths.

FLASHPOINTS

Political life in Washington was complicated by the fact that history was not taking a pause to let anyone sort out the past. There were two huge issues facing America that would not wait: the Civil Rights Movement and the Vietnam War.

The crisis in Southeast Asia was turning into the nightmare that John Kennedy had always feared. He had talked tough during 1963 to placate those who warned against the dominoes falling in Asia; then, to win the 1964 election, he'd had to play it both ways, speaking of firm resolve while characterizing his opponent as a man over-eager to bring America to war. Now, in 1965, it was becoming clear that decisions needed to be made. Already Kennedy had authorized air strikes on North Vietnam in retaliation for guerrilla attacks against the 23,500 American military "advisers" now on the ground. That offensive did not prevent the American Embassy or the major American air base at Da Nang from being bombed. The President had on his desk a proposal from the Joint Chiefs of Staff to commit two battalions of U.S. Marines to shore up protection.

In his 1974 book, *Flashpoints*, Robert Kennedy wrote that Dallas, making him bolder on some issues and more tentative on others, had heavily impacted his brother's thought process. In Vietnam, JFK had pulled back from his commitment to end American involvement completely, knowing full well that his intentions to do so, stated shortly before the assassination attempt, may have put his life in danger. On civil rights, however, he was more willing to line up behind decisive action, seeing the potential for a national race war if the government stayed aloof from the issue.

There was no doubt that America's troubled race relations were at the boiling point. Even Martin Luther King was having trouble keeping his flock united behind his idea of nonviolent resistance, particularly as their opponents continued to ratchet up their opposition with intimidation, beatings and even murder. Those who wanted to respond in kind, like the black militant Malcolm X, were under attack. Black Muslims had assassinated the fiery leader on February 21, proving that America was becoming a place where change was more often coming from the barrel of a gun.

From March 25 to March 28, more than twenty-five thousand civil rights demonstrators embarked on a fifty-mile walk for freedom from Selma, Alabama to the state Capitol in Montgomery. Led by the Rev. Dr. Martin Luther King Jr., it was a response to the mass arrests of Negroes protesting segregation and voting rights violations, and those protests were themselves a response to continued violent suppression of black Americans across the Deep South. The ultimate civil rights violation, of course, is murder, and JFK's own experience with it had changed his thinking about slow forward progress. He wanted action and he wanted it now.

President Kennedy had exercised federal authority before, but not since his brother's Dallas raid, and, in any case, the move was always tricky. It immediately turned the U.S. government against state authorities, who used the controversy to fan the flames of their own political bases, inevitably resulting in even more violence. Kennedy was particularly upset at a pattern he saw developing with the Federal Bureau of Investigation. Under J. Edgar Hoover's leadership, FBI agents assigned to the racial disturbances in the South were passive observers, taking notes and photos, but not acting when laws were being violated.

President Kennedy summoned Hoover to the Oval Office for a meeting on March 26, during the height of the march on Montgomery. Kennedy and Hoover had an awful relationship, but as officers of the government, they still needed to talk to get things done. Hoover was not happy when Attorney General Robert Kennedy joined them, but RFK ostensibly was Hoover's boss and had a right to be there. At the beginning of the conversation, President Kennedy pressed a button beneath his desk, activating the White House recording system.

The agenda began with the Kennedys requesting a more active response from Hoover's agents, stating that it was necessary to make certain this current protest march would not explode into violence and trigger even more violence around the country as a result.

"We don't guard anybody; we are fact-finders," stated Hoover. He was told that he needed to broaden his definition but refused to back down. "The FBI can't wet-nurse every Negro in the South or every do-gooder from the North who goes down there and tries to reform or educate them."

Robert Kennedy was livid. He called Hoover "insubordinate," a characteristic the director had maintained toward presidential authority since the beginning of President Kennedy's term in 1961. Hoover shot back that both Kennedys were in "over their heads" and needed to "change their tune."

As was his style, JFK watched this back-and-forth escalate. Clearly Bobby was speaking his brother's mind, but the tactic allowed the President to weigh in at the end. By this point, the President could not suppress his own anger.

"If the President of the United States and the Attorney General find their views in conflict with the Director of the Federal Bureau of Investigation, Mr. Hoover," said Kennedy, "what remedy do you think should be pursued?"

Hoover shot back that he was only trying to protect the Kennedys from themselves, a favor he was granting them out of respect for their offices.

"Mr. Hoover, you have enjoyed a long and distinguished career in the service of your country. I am quite sure that history will record your sense of duty." The President and the Attorney General traded looks. They had talked about this moment as being inevitable, but they had not discussed that it was imminent. "Perhaps it is time to close that chapter honorably and allow new blood into your organization."

There it was. The President of the United States had invited the man who had run the FBI like his own private business for decades to step down. Hoover's response was curt. "I will not resign," he said.

RFK tried to intercede. "There is no need for the nation to see conflict here. If you resign, both the President and I can sing your praises but if not…" He let the idea hang in the air.

Hoover ignored the younger Kennedy, addressing his remark straight to the President. "This is a bold gambit, Mr. President. Particularly for a man as vulnerable as you appear to be." It was obviously a reference to the thick files the FBI director had maintained on the Kennedys going back to the 1930s.

The President did not flinch. "This country and the Soviet Union have not been involved in a nuclear war, because both sides understand that such a war would destroy their own countries and not just their enemy's. We call this concept mutually assured destruction, and so far, it has kept the peace. Do you not believe that there are lessons learned from that policy that could be applied to our own situation?"

Hoover stood. "I will consider your ill-advised request and give you my answer." The FBI Director left the Oval Office without waiting for the President to end the meeting as was the custom and protocol.

STRANGELOVE LEAKS

The aftermath of Dallas had not been American journalism's finest hour. By and large, the nation's press corps capably covered the immediate excitement of gunfire, funerals, and trials, but they had shown little appetite to get beneath the surface of the story. Someone else could do that—the Dallas jury, the Warren Commission, now JCAAP—and the media would be content to report the findings and the process of arriving at them. This was completely true for the television networks, and the nation's newspapers weren't much different.

Perhaps that is why the financially struggling magazine *Top Story* became the lightning rod and the facilitator for a political explosion. Bob Dylan might have nailed the motivation with his impending release, *Highway 61 Revisited*, which included the classic anger anthem, "Like a Rolling Stone." The singer-songwriter's lyric summed up *Top Story*'s situation nicely: "When you ain't got nothing, you got nothing to lose."

By the winter of 1965, the investigative reporting team of Frank Altman and Adam Berkowitz was stymied internally and externally. The older, more conservative Altman felt it was probable that Lee Harvey Oswald, despite suspicions to the contrary, was just a disaffected Communist-sympathizer who wasn't as good a shot as he thought he was. The younger Berkowitz embraced conspiracy theory like a duck to water. He had spoken to at least a dozen direct witnesses from Dealey Plaza who had told him to his face that at least some of the shots came from in front of the motorcade. That meant two or more shooters, and that meant conspiracy.

While the reporters held daily and often angry debates, their work product suffered. Since the rule they operated under was that they would only write what they agreed on, and they agreed on practically nothing, they found themselves reduced to covering White House news conferences and attending JCAAP hearings, even the dull ones.

The State of the Union and the inaugural speeches had not exactly been riveting either. What they didn't know, however, but were soon to be the first to find out was that the inaugural announcement of the impending visit to the Soviet Union by the President had changed everything.

On January 24, 1965, just four days after Kennedy's "Second Chance" speech, the reporters were contacted by a potential source who claimed to have access to secret files and asked to meet just one of the reporters. The rendezvous was arranged in a Sambo's restaurant in Bethesda, Maryland at 8 p.m. Berkowitz drew the assignment because Altman, a married man, was under an ultimatum from his wife to be home in time for dinner with his children that night or face unspecified but disastrous consequences.

The man sitting in the orange vinyl booth wore sunglasses he refused to take off, and Berkowitz guessed he must have been in his mid-fifties. He also refused to give his name, instructing the young reporter to instead assign him one. Berkowitz, a movie fan, pulled the name "Strangelove" out of the cinematic zeitgeist, referencing a now-classic film that had made a marked impact on him when it was released the previous year. The man said something that Berkowitz found quite odd: "Do you think I am a homosexual, sir?" Berkowitz assured him that he had no opinion on the matter and was simply a fan of Stanley Kubrick's *Dr. Strangelove or: How I Learned to Stop Worrying and Love the Bomb*, a film about the madness of nuclear war. To that statement the man replied, "Madness was not using the superior weapons we had in 1962 to destroy the Soviet Communists when the advantage was ours."

After arguing with the waitress over whether he should be charged extra for ordering an omelet with tomatoes instead of potatoes, Strangelove then offered up the reason for requesting the meeting with Berkowitz. He had access to the FBI files on the

President, and they made clear that the nation's chief executive was nothing more than a "moral degenerate." He offered a manila envelope with a single file in it. He asked Berkowitz to share it with his partner Altman, and satisfy themselves that it was the real deal. They would be contacted again to see if they had the stomach to do the hard work that needed to be done. With that, he dismissed Berkowitz and dined alone on his nighttime breakfast.

The memo Strangelove had given Berkowitz was explosive. It dealt with FBI surveillance of German-born Ellen Rometsch, who in 1963 had allegedly begun an affair with President Kennedy. She was being investigated at the time as a possible East German spy and, as the report indicated, she'd been a member of the Communist Party before coming to the United States. She was also, it was alleged, a prostitute, who had been brought into the White House under the nose of the Secret Service and had sexual relations with Kennedy in the White House pool area. Supposedly, certain Republicans on Capitol Hill and other reporters had become aware of this in the fall of 1963, when Rometsch was suddenly deported at the request of Attorney General Robert Kennedy and allegedly paid hush money.

Altman and Berkowitz checked the memo out as discreetly as they could, and both became convinced that whether or not its contents were a hundred percent accurate, the memo itself was legitimate. They began to gather notes on the many allegations of extramarital affairs that had been swirling around John Kennedy going back to his days in the House of Representatives and the Senate. Some but not all of these they had heard whispers of before.

In the 1960s, reporters still looked the other way when it came to presidential romantic dalliances, believing they were private matters and even, perhaps, that a President must be allowed an extraordinary amount of personal leeway to relax in whatever way he saw fit. The problem with the Rometsch memo was that it raised questions about JFK's judgment that went beyond his right to enjoy a private life. The Secret Service had never been allowed to search Rometsch before her clandestine meetings with Kennedy. Had she been so inclined, she easily could have caused him physical harm or even killed him. Certainly, she could have held him up for blackmail.

Finally, an excruciating eleven days later, Berkowitz received a phone call. "Mr. Berkowitz," said the voice. "This is your Doctor Strangelove."

ASSASSINATION THEATER

The nation soon had a new soap opera. It was called the Joint Commission on the Attempted Assassination of the President. The hearings were open, except for frequent closed-door sessions when the CIA and other intelligence assets testified in ways that might impact national security, a situation that occurred by their estimation, every time they were called before the committee.

Still, the seemingly endless parade of eyewitnesses, police officers, government insiders, Mafia bosses, Cuban activists, Soviet experts, and agents of the FBI and Secret Service made for compelling viewing. The hearings were telecast live to the nation by the fledgling ABC network, something that was akin to political catnip for the committee members of both political parties, jostling for position and visibility. Chairman Magnuson nearly wore out his gavel trying to keep the egos in check.

During the hearings, Secret Service agent Robert Bouck testified about the existence of tape recording systems in the Oval Office, Cabinet Room and the President's living quarters on the second floor of the White House, and a separate Dictabelt recording system for use on the telephone lines in the President's office and his upstairs bedroom. All had been installed in the summer of 1962.

Lawyers for JCAAP immediately requested tapes of conversations before and after the Dallas ambush. The White House nearly as immediately turned them down, citing executive privilege; if the conversations of the President of the United States were no longer considered confidential, the President's attorneys claimed, it would create a chilling effect on the Oval Office, causing advisers to be less free in their advice to the nation's chief executive. That, they argued, could have a detrimental effect on his decision-making ability. The White House recorded these conversations for their own use and review, not for the inspection of Congress.

It seemed like a reasonable argument, and, for the moment, there were enough Democrats on the committee who agreed, and the situation went no further.

One of the men glued to the television set during all this was famed newsman and former Warren Commission member Edward R. Murrow, who was in the last days of his life. He had been battling cancer since a malignant tumor had caused the removal of his left lung in October 1963, after a lifetime of smoking up to seventy cigarettes a day. He had been in and out of the hospital ever since, but he'd been discharged from New York Hospital at the beginning of April and had gone home to die. On April 25, just two days before he passed away, Murrow allowed himself to smoke a final cigarette while watching the hearings and told his wife Janet that "they won't let this President finish."

Changing the Subject

In May of 1965, a single ticket to the rematch between Muhammad Ali (no longer known as Cassius Clay) and Sonny Liston had appeared in an envelope under the door of Steve Berkowitz's modest Georgetown apartment. He and Frank Altman drove up to Lewiston, Maine, where the fight was to take place. Ali was now publicly embracing the Nation of Islam, some adherents of which were widely suspected of having just assassinated Malcolm X, and there were rumors that Ali might be murdered in retaliation. It was a tense and sober fight, held in a very small-town ice rink.

Altman was a huge boxing fan, and Berkowitz barely knew Sonny Liston from Sonny Bono. Nonetheless, Altman had to sit in his car a few blocks away from the venue, while Berkowitz took his seat inside, as he suspected, next to the man known as Strangelove. The fight ended with Ali knocking out Liston in the first round. As the stunned crowd began to leave, Strangelove nodded under Berkowitz's seat where a thick manila envelope could be seen.

"Champions fall," he said, and departed.

On the way back from Maine, Berkowitz drove while Altman read aloud from the almost three dozen documents from Strangelove, each one seemingly more scandalous than the next. Hearing them spoken in a speeding car gave the documents a thrilling urgency to Berkowitz. He slammed at the dashboard, more than once shouting, "The floodgates are open!" They were also closed, as it turned out, as Strangelove was never heard from again.

Altman knew that none of what the documents contained was yet deemed publishable by the standards of journalism as practiced in the mid-1960s, where the private lives of public officials were not considered to be of sufficient importance to merit disclosure. "Roosevelt and Eisenhower had their mistresses that the public never heard about," he shrugged. "And the medical stuff, hell, Roosevelt was a cripple for his entire twelve years in office."

It wasn't just the falling of the barrier of past journalistic standards that bothered the older reporter. It was the powerful emotions he began to feel about President Kennedy, emotions he had never associated with a politician.

Indeed, when Frank Altman came to bed early in the morning after reading all the documents, his wife took one look at him and asked, "What are you so sad about, Frankie?"

Just as the government has always been plagued by leaks, the nation's fourth estate has not been immune. Through sources that have never been made public but are assumed to have emanated from the FBI, the White House advisers came to know that Altman and Berkowitz were up to something they didn't like. They heard, discreetly and indirectly, that John Kennedy's sex life was the subject of daily discussion at *Top Story* and possibly the *Washington Post*. The *Post* published *Newsweek* magazine, *Top Story*'s direct competition.

President Kennedy met privately with his brother to discuss this rumored turn of events. Bobby considered the matter carefully and concluded, "Jack, we always knew this could happen."

The problem was that no plan existed for what to do when that arrived, said JFK. Bobby countered that there was a plan but it was best that he not know what it was. The President agreed, "Just make sure it's a good plan." Even at their moment of maximum danger, there was a soldier's joking bravado.

Although it was not necessarily important where the leak originated, the President had allowed the impasse with J. Edgar Hoover to continue without his resignation or firing. The arrogant FBI director had left the Oval Office that day with only the slim promise that he would think about the President's request to step down and get back to him. The President concluded for his brother's benefit, "I guess now we have our answer." Hoover's retaliation was to use his files as a weapon.

Fearing a phone call from journalists asking to confirm or deny these reports, the Kennedys decided to move up the President's scheduled visit to Moscow. No responsible journalistic organization would dare publish such scandal, they felt, if the President of the United States was on foreign soil negotiating matters of global peace with a nuclear-armed adversary.

MISSION TO MOSCOW

Both John Kennedy and Nikita Khrushchev had survived attempts to remove them from office over the past year and a half, and each knew just how precarious his grip on power truly was. Khrushchev actually felt that had Kennedy been killed in Dallas, the impact would have extended all the way to Russia and led to his own removal by the Politburo. They both had reasons to change the subject and keep it changed as fast as possible.

Khrushchev had been to the United States before, back in September of 1959. He had debated Vice President Nixon, visited Hollywood, and even been barred from going to Disneyland, supposedly for security reasons. Now it was Kennedy's turn to visit the Soviet Union.

In mid-May, with JCAAP nearing the end of its hearings, and journalists in Washington sitting on a bombshell of sexual misconduct, President Kennedy stepped off a plane in Moscow and shook hands with Premier Khrushchev. The two men had already traveled a unique path together, from Cold War nuclear adversaries who nearly incinerated the planet, to men who understood that the mission of their times was to create the architecture of peace. They had been communicating regularly by private correspondence, the substance of which was known only to each other and their translators. They had achieved a Nuclear Test Ban Treaty in 1963 and started talks on global disarmament. Those talks had been scuttled by Kennedy's close call in Dallas and Khrushchev's close call with the Soviet Politburo.

They needed a big idea but one that would not set their generals off, as disarmament talks seemed to do. They needed to "Trojan Horse" peace into the public discussion. They needed the moon.

The idea was already on the table, just dying for lack of support. Back on September 20, 1963, President Kennedy had spoken before the United Nations Eighteenth General Assembly. In that speech, he had extended an invitation to the Soviet Union to join with the United States in a joint mission to the moon. At the end of that address, Kennedy said: "In a field where the United States and the Soviet Union have a special capacity—space—there is room for new cooperation, for further joint efforts."

Why, the President asked, should the United States and the Soviet Union conduct parallel efforts that would include "duplication of research, construction and expense?" He laid out a proposal for a joint series of space missions, which, if enacted, he said would "require a new approach to the Cold War."

Khrushchev told Kennedy at the time that he could not accept the offer even if he wanted to. Kennedy needed to win reelection, but Khrushchev needed to put down an insurrection from his own internal enemies who thought he had backed down and lost the Cuban Missile Crisis of 1962.

Now, two years later, the timing seemed to be right. Both men knew that a space race to the moon would be economically prohibitive and accomplish nothing. Better to share the costs and turn it into a win-win.

After four days and three nights touring the Soviet Union side-by-side, Kennedy and Khrushchev faced the press together. They proposed the Joint Lunar Exploration Treaty between the United States and the Soviet Union. They would join forces, share costs, and crew missions together. Sometime before 1970, they hoped, a Russian cosmonaut and an American astronaut would both set foot on the moon together. Kennedy let his former foe Khrushchev have the first word:

> *Space offers no problems of sovereignty; the members of the United Nations have already foresworn any claim to territorial rights in outer space or on celestial bodies, and declared that international law and the United Nations Charter will apply. Why, therefore, should man's first flight to the moon be a matter of national competition? Why should the United States and the Soviet Union, in preparing for such expeditions, become involved in immense duplications of research, construction, and expenditure?*

Khrushchev laid out the full legal framework. The man who'd slammed his shoe on his desk in the United Nations years before was now using the U.N.'s mission and charter as his own rationalization for action. Kennedy followed with the poetry:

> *Surely we should explore whether the scientists and astronauts of the United States, the Soviet Union and other countries can work together in the conquest of space. They will look back at the Earth while standing on the surface of the moon and they will see a fragile world that deserves the full measure of our devotion. While showing that Humankind can leave the Earth, we will also demonstrate why we must always return to our home.*

The only thing standing in the way of such a peaceful and cooperative enterprise was the approval of the Soviet Politburo and the American Senate.

For the most part, the Joint Lunar Exploration Treaty was embraced by Americans as a good idea. Conservative Republicans derided Kennedy's advocacy of the program and referred to him as

"Moonbeam Jack," although the phrase never seemed to catch on outside of their own political circles.

The real opposition came from within. The military establishments of both the Soviet Union and the United States were staunchly opposed. Both viewed implementation of the treaty as putting them in the unacceptable position of sharing treasured national technological advances with their rivals. Both sides worried that rockets that could take men to the moon could also carry nuclear weapons to the cities of their enemies.

After watching the coverage of Kennedy and Khrushchev on a live satellite feed out of Moscow, General Curtis LeMay turned to his fellow military careerists and said, "that treaty will pass over his dead body," while pointing at Kennedy. When asked to confirm this statement shortly before his death in 1990, LeMay said that it had been a slip of the tongue and he meant the conventional use of the phrase.

THE SECRET LIFE OF THE PRESIDENT

The visit to the Soviet Union had, in fact, worked its magic, holding off publication of any damaging information about John Kennedy's personal life until after his return. Even then, with internal debates raging, it was no sure thing that such details would ever see the light of day.

No one at *Top Story* who knew about the files felt they were anything other than the most explosive document leak in the history of politics and journalism combined. Certainly, that is how Berkowitz characterized them to Altman when they were first received, and Altman, who often felt it was his job to tone down his partner's natural exuberance, could not disagree. They were political dynamite.

By this point, the two men had determined that the files came to them from J. Edgar Hoover himself. Hoover had given them to his number two, Clyde Tolson. Then Tolson had given them to this connection of his, unidentified during the coverage cycle, known as "Strangelove," to pass on to Berkowitz, who brought them to *Top Story*.

THE DEBATE OVER PUBLISHING

Over at *Top Story*, editor Joseph Carlyle wrestled with their publication day and night for months. Even as he wondered if they could ever be published, Carlyle continued to insist that his reporters source them to perfection. Given all the calls being made by Altman and Berkowitz, the existence of these files was becoming an open secret. In the final week of May, one of the targets of Altman's investigation, a socialite and former runway model, told Altman, "Look, what happened between me and the President, or didn't happen, is none of the *Washington Post*'s business." Then she hung up the phone.

Altman mentioned the call at that day's conference held in Carlyle's office. "Sounds like the *Post* has it, too," he said. "We're ahead of them, but we won't be for long."

The line was out there now for all to see. It was publish or perish. But no story of this magnitude could be printed if the primary source was not contacted for comment or rebuttal. Someone had to call the President of the United States and ask him if it was true that he had turned the White House into what looked like a revolving door of sex partners while his wife and children were away.

Berkowitz volunteered. Altman shot that down. "No one in the Kennedy White House is going to talk to some kid who's out to make his bones on this story. I'll do it." Carlyle agreed.

Altman set a meeting with Pierre Salinger, feeling it was best to follow protocol. "Certain facts have come to our attention," said Altman, "facts that require the President to comment directly. I need to know from you that you will take this immediately to President Kennedy for a response."

Salinger protested that he could make no such assurance without knowing what they were talking about. Altman stated that they were talking about women that the President had extramarital affairs with. Salinger waved him off. "No, no, no. That's not news."

"It's news if these affairs happened in the White House," said Altman. "It's the people's house, paid for by the taxpayers. And it's news if some of these women have connections to mobsters, or foreign governments, or actually work in the White House."

Salinger said he didn't need to talk to the President. The White House position would be not to dignify these charges with an answer. Altman reminded him that he had a professional responsibility to his boss and to the ethics of journalism to take this to the President. *Top Story* would give him forty-eight hours to get back to them. If the President agreed, as he hoped he would, Altman and his partner, Steve Berkowitz, would like to schedule a sit-down with President Kennedy at his earliest convenience. They felt that at least two hours should be allocated and understood that the President could include anyone he wanted in such a meeting, including his lawyer or lawyers.

"Fine," barked Salinger, confirming that he would take this information to his boss. The press secretary would later contend to anyone who asked that, to his credit, the President took it like a man. He didn't rage or deny. Instead, he asked questions, trying to tie down exactly what was being said. Salinger told him everything he knew and was dismissed.

That night Kennedy visited with his friend Ben Bradlee, the newish editor of the *Washington Post* and someone who knew more than most about JFK's activities. Bradlee's wife, Antoinette (Toni), was the sister of Mary Pinchot Meyer, who seemed to enjoy both a sexual and a personal relationship with the President. Bradlee promised Kennedy the *Post* would not be first to publish these charges but that if *Top Story* or other reputable news organizations did, then his newspaper and probably *Newsweek* would have to follow suit. He assured the President that they would stick to the facts. "That's what I'm afraid of," Kennedy said, and even managed to flash his trademark smile to his close friend. In 1963, Bradlee, who with his wife had often dined with President and Mrs. Kennedy, had published what Kennedy considered unflattering material about the Administration and had suffered a three-month ban from White

House insider privileges. Both men knew this would go far beyond that skirmish and could lead to a lifetime estrangement.

The President wanted to know if there was anything that could be done to stop or delay *Top Story* from publishing the results of its investigation. Bradlee thought about it, then offered that they must know that the *Post* had the same material. If they thought the *Post* was determined to publish, then the race was on. But if they understood that the *Post* would not go first, they might think twice. With that analysis, however, Bradlee told Kennedy that he could say no more.

The next day, Pierre Salinger phoned Joseph Carlyle and told him the President of the United States would not be responding to Altman's inquiries as that would only give the magazine further incentive to publish its findings. He made it clear to Carlyle the White House knew that this same material had been distributed to the *Washington Post* and that they had been assured that the town's leading newspaper was not planning to publish anything. "They want us to go first," said Carlyle. The conversation, according to both men, lasted less than two minutes.

Carlyle and his two reporters, Altman and Berkowitz, plus *Top Story* publisher Dante Falcone and lawyers Rich Cortright and Susan Monteith, gathered in Carlyle's office to decide what to do next. It was impossible to underestimate the importance of the decision. If they published the story they had, it would likely destroy John Kennedy's marriage and maybe his presidency. It would put the nation's progress at risk, sow discord, and set in motion events that were, at best, unpredictable.

There was a series of questions that had to be asked and answered. Were all the allegations true? If true, were they news? If so, would they be seen as such, or would they destroy the magazine along with the President? And even if that were the case, was it the magazine's duty to print the story anyway?

Several of the magazine's top editors, along with Altman and Berkowitz, began an exhaustive review of everything they knew, starting with the contents of the leaked FBI files. There seemed to be little doubt that the documents were real. Many of them contained transcriptions of phone wiretaps between Kennedy and the various women. Others were based on surveillance. Still others included testimony of friends, family and former lovers about conversations the women had had that implicated the President in affairs. The numbers were staggering. Berkowitz counted all the allegations and names mentioned in the files and came up with a number: thirty-seven. Many of these preceded JFK's presidency, a few preceded his marriage, and many were based on rumor and gossip.

The aggregate, however, did highlight a pattern of behavior that could have compromised the nation's security and/or Kennedy's ability to appropriately manage the duties of the presidency. These women were not being adequately identified by the Secret Service and were not searched for listening devices or weapons. Some had prior allegiances to foreign governments. Almost all of these relationships would have exposed President Kennedy to potential blackmail. Just covering up the existence of these affairs had already caused the President to expend untold personal and government resources.

The review focused on the numerous potential sexual relationships and/or misconduct on Kennedy's part as alleged in the leaked FBI files. Much of the information, at this stage, was still rumor and speculation, but the fact that national journalists were discussing it was shocking and disturbing.

With publisher Dante Falcone listening from a corner, editor Carlyle and his two lawyers grilled the two reporters about not only the details of the files but also the work that had been done to substantiate them. Altman and Berkowitz had developed multiple unnamed sources among the women and their friends, multiple confirmations from disaffected Secret Service agents and one Kennedy insider. None of them were on the record, however, and the reporters declined to name them to their bosses.

The journalistic interrogation began with a heated debate about Marilyn Monroe, whose affair with John Kennedy was alleged to have begun before his election in 1960 when the two were introduced by Frank Sinatra at the Cal-Neva Lodge. One source was a Hollywood director who'd been at a party when JFK was in Los Angeles during the Democratic convention that nominated him that year. Held at Peter Lawford's home, the man told a story of Monroe and Kennedy disappearing together into the guesthouse and returning hours later with Marilyn wearing JFK's now-rumpled white shirt and no panties. The director's account further stated that the inebriated politician supposedly had to be physically pulled off the Pacific Coast Highway where the future president was standing in traffic shouting, "I'm going to be the fucking President of the United States." This part of the story was rejected as having occurred before JFK's term of office and was based on only a single source. Yet the files made clear that the relationship had become an open secret in Hollywood and the affair had continued once Kennedy took office in 1961 and was ended by the President shortly before Monroe's death in 1962.

If the files were to be believed, the President had many affairs with Hollywood starlets besides Monroe. Alleged and largely unconfirmed celebrity relationships included Audrey Hepburn, Jayne Mansfield, Angie Dickinson, Kim Novak, Janet Leigh, Gene Tierney, Rhonda Fleming, Joan Crawford, Marlene Dietrich, Zza Zza Gabor, Sophia Loren, Lee Remick, Hedy Lamarr, Olivia de Havilland, and others.

Inside the files, there were literally dozens of these kinds of anecdotal stories, compromised over relevance or lack of a reliable source. In order to fully comprehend the magnitude of the President's alleged transgressions, it was necessary to break the rest of the relationships into categories.

From a historical perspective, the files claimed that President Kennedy had begun his dangerous sexual behavior early in his life. There was the story of Inga Marie Arvadi, a Danish beauty queen turned married journalist who had actually socialized with Hitler before carrying on an affair with Kennedy when he was a naval intelligence officer.

It was even alleged that JFK had been married to socialite Durie Malcolm on January 24, 1947. Supposedly, Joseph Kennedy had Cardinal Cushing quietly grant an annulment, and the marriage record was removed from the Palm Beach County courthouse and destroyed.

In the 1950s, Kennedy supposedly had another affair with call girl Alicia Darr Clark that resulted in the birth of a child. The file stated that Clark had tried to extort the Kennedy family and had received $500,000.

Compelling and shocking as they were, the stories about Arvadi, Malcolm and Clark were all set aside, given that they had occurred long before Jack Kennedy became President Kennedy.

His behavior with female members of the White House staff, however, was another matter. A pattern was clear and there were numerous "girls" the President had entered into sexual relationships with, bolstered primarily by Secret Service reports, FBI wiretaps, and coerced interviews of the women's friends. They included presidential favorites like secretaries Priscilla Wear and Jill Cowan, so well known to the Secret Service agents that they were given code names Fiddle and Faddle, and were known to regularly swim nude along with President Kennedy in the White House pool when his wife was out of town. Two other White House employees thought to be having sex with the President included Pamela Turnure, Jackie Kennedy's press secretary, and Mimi Beardsley, a debutante from a prominent New Jersey family who had been given an internship position that on her first day on the job had ended with a visit to the First Lady's bedroom.

Carlyle gave his tentative approval to including this material because it took place in the White House or during official presidential travel, and it was not clear what justification could be offered that they were performing duties that could be considered the public's business.

There were stories of numerous prostitutes, some being brought into the White House and others procured during presidential travels. Ellen Rometsch, the German-born prostitute, had been the subject of an independent investigation by the FBI, based on its belief that she was working for the Communist leader of East Germany, when it was discovered she was seeing Kennedy. Two others in particular, Maria Novotny and Suzie Chang, were also troubling. The former was thought to be connected to a Soviet vice ring and the latter was involved in the British Profumo scandal at the same time she was thought to be seeing Kennedy.

Secretaries and prostitutes aside, however, there were two other names that raised equally serious questions about President Kennedy's seemingly reckless behavior and poor judgment.

The first was Judith Campbell, a California socialite and another Sinatra introduction. She was also a sometime-girlfriend of Mafia kingpin Sam Giancana, and had made at least twenty visits to the White House and had made more than seventy phone calls to the President. All of this was confirmed in early 1961 by way of a wiretap of the Mafia's Johnny Roselli.

The other woman raising eyebrows was Mary Pinchot Meyer. Even though she was married to the CIA's Cord Meyer, she had made at least thirty trips to the White House during JFK's presidency and was still active up to Dallas. She was Bobby Kennedy's next door neighbor, the sister-in-law of Ben Bradlee, a close friend of Timothy Leary, and active on the Washington party circuit. Her file explicitly claimed that she had used marijuana, cocaine and even LSD with President Kennedy.

At the end of an exhaustive (and exhausting) seven-hour session, Carlyle offered his judgment. The story should be written up for final analysis and approval. He wanted a first draft on his desk in three days.

Definitely ruled in was Marilyn Monroe, who was not a living subject who could sue the magazine, making her fair game. The other celebrities would be mentioned as a group but not by name.

All the White House employees would also be listed in that first draft. Carlyle felt that this was the public's house, not Kennedy's, and his behavior toward these women raised legitimate questions about the way the people's business had been conducted.

The *Top Story* editor felt even more strongly about the prostitutes and girlfriends who were connected to potential U.S. adversaries and to the one woman tied to the Mafia. These encounters not only endangered the President's life but they put him at risk for blackmail, something that simply could not be tolerated when it came to the nation's leader.

Finally, the quote from JFK that had surfaced from multiple sources—"I'm not through with a girl until I've had her three ways"—would not be included, period. They weren't *that* type of magazine.

It was also decided that at least the first draft of the article should include the rumors of drug use and abuse in passing, pointing out their unverified nature, but should focus most heavily on the President's medical condition, particularly his Addison's disease, its cover-up, and his routine use of substances that may have included amphetamines and other stimulants. The continuing relationship with Dr. Max Jacobson should be thoroughly vetted, but was fair game.

After the reporters were sent to their typewriters and the lawyers dismissed, Carlyle and Falcone remained to talk privately about the stakes. Carlyle, the editor, fretted that this explosive information had the potential to destroy the magazine. Falcone, a no-nonsense Italian-American, made explicit what Carlyle already suspected. "This magazine is six months away from bankruptcy," he said." The story has just as much chance of saving us." He told Carlyle that an editorial decision was needed, not a financial one, and that he, as publisher, was taking himself out of the equation.

The decision was Carlyle's to make.

THE FINAL HOURS

On Thursday, June 3, 1965, astronaut Edward White took a twenty-minute stroll, untethered, a hundred miles above the Earth, while James McDivitt stayed in the capsule of Gemini 4. Given the importance of this step in the U.S. planned moon mission, and the possibility that future missions might include cosmonauts, it ranked as the story of the week.

Newsweek, *Time* and *Top Story* all followed the same schedule, publishing every Monday. The cover for the coming week's issue seemed likely to be the space walk, unless bigger events interceded. The problem was that the Gemini crew would not be returned to Earth in time for glorious color photos to be made available from NASA.

As a publisher, Dante Falcone knew that *Time* would probably feature its usual piece of commissioned art on its cover, something showing White and McDivitt. *Newsweek* would likely go with a NASA simulation or a photo of a black-and-white TV screen. If the cover of *Top Story* featuring the President's extramarital affairs became the competition, it would potentially explode on the newsstand beyond any publishing figures the magazine had ever seen. He said to Joseph Carlyle, "As I said, the decision is yours, but the time for you to make your decision is now."

Carlyle knew the publisher was correct. He and the Altman-Berkowitz team had been through five drafts of the story that was being called "The Secret Life of the President." It was tight, fair and sensational. It left out as much as it left in. It was true, even if all the sources weren't on the record. And its timing was right.

Bobby Kennedy had called Carlyle earlier in the week to warn him that if the story were published, *Top Story* could be facing a lawsuit. "Are you telling me that as the Attorney General or as the family's lawyer?" asked Carlyle. Kennedy slammed the phone down and hung up.

Carlyle put a call through to the Attorney General's office. They were preparing to publish the story on Monday's cover, he said, but because of the sensitive, personal nature of the material involving the President of the United States, he was willing to take the unprecedented step of allowing a representative of the President to read the story in advance. The representative would have to come to read it at the *Top Story* offices, however. If so desired, he would be provided a conference room and a secure line to call the Oval Office and discuss the content. If the President then wished to comment, arrangements could be made to incorporate those responses into the story. Robert Kennedy heard him out and announced, "I'll be over in one hour."

The *Top Story* offices were emptied of most of their staff while the Secret Service swept the area for bugs, and the conference room was prepared. It included a solid mahogany table, a telephone, a yellow legal pad, three No. 2 sharpened pencils, and a photocopy of the entire five-thousand-word article by Frank Altman and Steve Berkowitz. Exactly fifty-eight minutes after hanging up the phone, the Attorney General arrived with two of his top aides, Ed Guthman and Nicholas Katzenbach. Carlyle tried to introduce himself and his reporters, but Kennedy brushed aside his pleasantries. "Where is the article in question?" he asked and was directed to the conference room.

Kennedy and his aides read the article with RFK finishing one page, handing it off to Katzenbach, who read it and handed the page to Guthman. From outside in the bullpen, the nervous journalists watched as all three men inside read the material. They could be seen in animated conversation with each other through the conference windows until Guthman noticed and closed the blinds. The last thing Frank Altman remembers seeing was the Attorney General picking up the receiver on the phone placed in the middle of the table.

Two hours later, Kennedy and Carlyle went into private session, leaving Katzenbach, Guthman, Altman, and Berkowitz all staring silently at each other. Carlyle remembers that the face of Robert Kennedy frightened him. "That article is malicious, defamatory, and intolerable," began the Attorney General. "If you publish it, you will do the President of the United States and this country a great disservice at a time of maximum danger. While a free press is something that President Kennedy has always believed in, it is also true that a great magazine should aspire to more than this level of vile character attack. We ask that you reconsider your decision to publish this material if that is, in fact, your intent."

Carlyle considered this and replied, "I understand that this is difficult material, and we are all aware of its potential for disruptive impact. However, at this time, there's only one thing that would cause us to reconsider our decision to publish."

Kennedy was ahead of the editor on that one. "You wish to know if it is true."

Carlyle nodded.

"There are elements of truth, elements of falsity, elements of misinterpretation, and an overall unappealing tone of hubris on the part of your reporters," said Kennedy. "Neither the President nor I will address these charges generally or specifically. If you publish this, Mr. Carlyle, your career as a serious journalist will be forever destroyed. And that, I can confirm, is true."

The meeting was over as quickly as it had begun. As Kennedy rose, Carlyle extended a hand that was not taken. "Please tell the President that this is not personal."

Kennedy replied, "I'll do no such thing." With that, he exited the office and left with his aides, refusing to make eye contact with Altman or Berkowitz.

THE TOP STORY AT *TOP STORY*

The Monday, June 14 issue of *Top Story* (released, as was practice in those days, on June 7) carried the title "The Secret Life of the President." It sold more than six million copies, almost all of them newsstand sales, more than three times its usual circulation of 1.6 million copies. This compares with *Time*'s circulation that week of about 3.3 million copies and *Newsweek*'s with 2.2 million copies. As predicted, *Time* featured a line drawing of the Gemini astronauts and *Newsweek* a photo of a space walk simulation.

In its final form, the article began:

> *Throughout his political career, John F. Kennedy has appeared to be the loving husband with a storybook marriage to his wife, Jacqueline Kennedy. A Top Story investigation, however, has revealed that this public image has not been matched by private reality. Documents from a secret FBI surveillance file on President Kennedy, supported by this magazine's own interviews and reporting, show another*

side. The John Kennedy who emerges here is a man foreign to most Americans and appears to be a serial adulterer who has engaged in sexual brinksmanship from his youngest days to more recent times as the resident of the nation's White House. His actions may have placed his life and, by extension, the well-being of the nation at risk.

It was tough copy, and for readers who had virtually no inkling that it was possible, it was even more shocking than the events that had transpired in Dallas just nineteen months earlier. In the final analysis, *Top Story* had decided that half-measures would not do justice to the story's comprehensiveness. Accordingly, it began in Kennedy's adulthood, wove through his political life as a Congressman and a senator, and landed harshly in the Oval Office as President.

The article named names when there were two or more sources that could be cited by Altman and Berkowitz beyond the FBI files. In other cases, it described the participants in more general terms. Still, even by today's standards of political scandals that seem to spring to life as regularly as the sunrise, it was unsparing.

The story it told began with the society marriage of Jack and Jackie Kennedy on September 12, 1953, and allegations that even in their first year of matrimony there were extramarital affairs.

The article laid out over a dozen sexual relationships with women who included foreign nationals, those with CIA connections, Mafia girlfriends, Hollywood starlets, and numerous White House employees. It reported the FBI files even included the possibility of drug abuse and use of prostitutes by the commander-in-chief during the Cuban Missile Crisis but noted that those allegations were unsubstantiated by other sources.

BETTER LATE THAN NEVER

In actual fact, the special edition facilitated one rare moment of agreement between the current occupant of the White House and the director of the Federal Bureau of Investigation. Both John

Kennedy and J. Edgar Hoover declined comment.

In the immediate aftermath, however, Hoover was summoned to the Oval Office, where President Kennedy demanded to know what Hoover knew about the leaked material. Hoover denied any personal involvement as well as having any knowledge of who might have done it. It was the first time the two men had met since Kennedy had asked for Hoover's resignation and had been rebuffed.

"While it is obviously too late to affect what has just transpired," the President told the director, "I instruct you to turn over all similar files regarding other government officials and civil rights leaders, including the Rev. Dr. Martin Luther King Jr., as it is my judgment that you have abused your authority and can no longer be trusted to maintain physical custody of such files."

Hoover replied, "I am unable to comply with your unjustified and misguided request. The files you seek do not exist."

President Kennedy fired Hoover from his position on the spot, effective immediately. He instructed him not to return to FBI headquarters but to appoint an individual to act on his behalf. That individual would return under the supervision of federal marshals to retrieve Hoover's personal belongings. With Hoover in the office, Kennedy called his brother, advised him that Hoover was no longer in charge, and directed him to see to it that the ex-director adhere to the policy he had just laid out.

Hoover replied, "Mr. President, you have made a serious mistake here."

"Yes, I have, Mr. Hoover," replied the President. "I made it back in 1960 when I allowed you to remain in this job. I was, apparently, ill-advised to believe that you would exercise discretion over your personal control of sensitive material." With that, Kennedy asked Hoover to leave, and he did so.

Hoover's first words as a private citizen were spoken to secretary Evelyn Lincoln. "Good day, Mrs. Lincoln. That dress looks lovely on you."

GROUND ZERO

The effect of "The Secret Life of the President" was immediate and monumental, impacting the body politic of Washington, D.C., the feelings of average Americans, the members of the conspiracy against the President, and the relationship between John Kennedy and his wife. People who lived through both the Dallas ambush and the revelation of the President's affairs have consistently in public opinion polls rated the second event as even more significant than the first.

Although the White House had known it was coming for days, seeing the actual magazine, feeling its heft and flipping through its pages, gave it a dark power beyond mere words. Kenneth O'Donnell felt strongly that refusing comment for the article was only postponing the inevitable. John Kennedy simply could not remain President and pretend this article never happened. After all, almost everyone on the planet was going to hear and talk about it soon, and the allegations were sensational enough that they would not simply go away on their own accord. O'Donnell felt the team had no more than twenty-four hours to get their response together. "What is Mrs. Kennedy's response?" he asked.

As of that moment, however, the President had not spoken to her and replied with heavy sarcasm. "I think she and I should talk before we brief to the press, don't you?" The meeting was interrupted by Evelyn Lincoln's call stating that Mrs. Kennedy would like to see the President in the family quarters at his earliest convenience. The meeting broke up momentarily with the President going upstairs and Pierre Salinger heading to the White House Briefing Room.

The White House issued the following statement through the press secretary: "The issues inside the President's marriage belong there and there alone, and are solely for the President and his wife to consider." Of course, even as he was reading them, Salinger knew that these words would not satisfy anyone, nor would they last longer than a single news cycle.

Neither John nor Jacqueline Kennedy has ever spoken to the media about the conversation that took place between them on the afternoon of June 7, 1965. Both, however, spoke to others who have spoken out.

It appears that Jackie was packing when the President arrived in the family living quarters. He asked her if she was packing for the weekend as she often did or perhaps something longer. "I haven't decided, Jack. I will let you know, which is more than you have done for me."

The President apologized and promised that such behavior had recently been curtailed and would not continue in the future. He asked for her forgiveness. The First Lady lit a second cigarette from the one she was smoking and acknowledged a small fact that could only be appreciated between the two of them. "You have been better since that awful day." It was the truth. Even before the events in Dallas, the First Couple had been working at falling back in love and had been making progress. After the loss of their newborn son Patrick, followed by Dallas, they both felt driven closer together by the force of the tragedy.

Still, she pointed out, she had agreed to look the other way only because his behavior was not public. Now that her husband's infidelity was no longer secret, he had humiliated her, embarrassed their children, and allowed his implicit promise of discretion to be broken beyond repair. Their relationship had been on the road to recovery after Dallas, but she did not believe they could recover from this.

The President was dismissed by the First Lady. There would be changes made, but she was not thinking clearly enough to make them today. She had one immediate demand. No actual copies of the magazine should be allowed in the White House, and under no circumstances were Caroline or John Jr. to see it.

By this point, Robert Kennedy and his wife, Ethel, had arrived through the back entrance to the White House. Jack and Bobby met privately in the Oval Office, as they had done so many times before, in so many crises, and the younger man who had, more than anyone else, truly been his brother's keeper informed him of Ethel's mission.

She was sharing a good cry with Jackie, said Bobby, and when the tears were over, they would discuss business. Trust funds would be set up for Jackie and both children, great enough to provide for all of them for the rest of their lives, the funds approved by both Joseph Kennedy and Rose Kennedy. All Jackie had to do was to meet the press with JFK tomorrow, stand by his side, and agree not to initiate divorce proceedings so long as Kennedy was in office.

"My God," said the President. "How did you get Dad to agree to this so quickly?"

Bobby shook his head. The truth was that this plan had been hatched back in 1959 and was ready to go if this day ever came to pass. The only real question was what Jacqueline Kennedy would do now.

The reputation of President Kennedy had been forever changed by the events of this day. That battle could, at best, be fought to a standstill. The current strategy, agreed to by all the President's men, was to shift tactics to basic political survival. John Kennedy would have to defeat attempts to drive him from office. That would be a bloody fight, but it could be won.

THE DAY AFTER

For the first hours after the article was published, the reporting duo of Altman and Berkowitz owned the story and appeared to own it alone. Not only was nobody else touching it, but many journalistic organizations were expressing chagrin that *Top Story* had cheapened journalism forever by printing it, whether or not its facts were accurate. The reporting team and its editors were starting to swing in the wind. As it turned out, however, this condition was only temporary.

By Tuesday morning, it was standing room only in the White House briefing room. Not only were the hundreds of questions raised by the *Top Story* article on the table, but so was the firing of

J. Edgar Hoover, which had become public overnight but had not yet been confirmed by the White House. Altman and Berkowitz were treated as celebrities by some of their fellow reporters and as pariahs by a substantial group as well. Everyone now knew their names and everyone had read their work.

In the Oval Office, President Kennedy huddled with his advisers, discussing how to handle the questions they knew were coming. The President would stand on privacy as regards to the actual names and allegations. That left plenty of room to discuss the peripheral issues. How was it possible that the FBI was keeping such a file on the President of the United States for so long? Why had it been leaked? By whom?

The firing of J. Edgar Hoover did much to draw the public's attention to those issues. Reaction ranged from, "JFK should have fired him a long time ago," the Democratic talking point, to, "This shows how dangerously out of control this President has become," on the Republican side. Kennedy caught one break, however, in that Hoover decided to go into hiding himself, refusing requests for interviews, cursing at photographers and generally looking like a guilty man.

Finally, Mrs. Lincoln interrupted. "The First Lady is here."

Together, President Kennedy and First Lady Jacqueline Kennedy walked from the Oval Office to the White House Briefing Room. This again was one of the times when the President needed no introduction, from Salinger or anyone else. There was an audible gasp from the hardened reporters when the First Couple entered. As they had in Dallas before the assassination attempt, the two of them looked sensational. If there had been crying or arguing since the article's publication, you could not tell by looking.

The President stepped to the microphone, and the First Lady stood to the side. She seemed quiet and subdued, but she did not look defeated. In contrast, observers thought the dark circles under JFK's eyes were larger than usual.

I'll make a short statement, and then I'll take your questions. Mrs.

SURROUNDED BY ENEMIES

*Kennedy will not be taking your questions at her request, and she
asks that you respect her wishes. As is always the case here at the
White House, multiple issues occupy our minds. The most important
today, from the position of government, is the issue of the firing of
FBI Director Hoover. I am the responsible officer of this government
and that decision was mine. I made it not because of the article that
appeared yesterday in* Top Story *magazine but because of what
that article represented. According to both Mr. Altman and Mr.
Berkowitz, who I see are here today, they began their reporting when
FBI files were released to them without authorization. Additionally,
those files deal with private matters that the Bureau should not have
been investigating. Until yesterday, Mr. Hoover was the responsible
officer at the FBI. I am satisfied that he has approved illegal wiretaps
of the President and also of other private citizens. Additionally, he
did not maintain proper custody of those files whether they were
legally or illegally obtained. That is a fireable offense and so, the
director has been fired. I'll take your questions.*

Those questions came in a full-throated roar from a room
that was already swooning from all the compressed body heat. By
prearrangement, JFK pointed to UPI's Helen Thomas for the first
question: "Whether or not Mr. Hoover deserves to be fired, Mr.
President, most Americans today are wondering, did you do all the
things that those FBI files say you did?"

Kennedy, now seemingly ignoring the larger audience, spoke
directly to the forty-five-year-old Thomas, one of the very few
women in the press corps:

*The short answer is no. The difficulty with that answer, however, is
that many of you would like me to go through those files and what
has been made of them and respond to each and every accusation,
and that is something that I cannot and will not do. I will say,
however, that the issues raised are deeply painful to my wife, and I
am humbled by the damage my actions have caused my marriage.
Jacqueline and I have been married for a dozen years now and hope
to be married for the rest of our lives. I will answer your question—*

not before this group but to her. I will ask her forgiveness in the privacy of our marriage, not in the publicity of the moment.

It was a good answer, particularly the look he gave his wife when talking about their marriage, but no one in the room thought for a moment that it would suffice. Reporters came after him in waves, and his answer was always a rephrasing of his response to Thomas. It is worth mentioning that neither Frank Altman nor Steve Berkowitz was called upon by the President that day, nor ever again, no matter how often or how loudly they shouted their questions.

The news conference was notable for one turn of a phrase that has often been credited to Theodore Sorensen, but actually came from President Kennedy himself, on the spur of the moment. He was asked by NBC's David Brinkley what he made of any possible motivation for the FBI to have gathered all this material for years only to unleash it now in 1965.

"There were apparently some who wished my presidency might have ended back in 1963," said Kennedy. "Yet here I am still in the White House in 1965 with a full term ahead of me. Perhaps some of those people feel that a sniper firing a rifle at a man is only one way to assassinate him."

The room, so boisterous at the beginning, fell momentarily silent. Rarely has the truth been spoken so clearly in a situation where it is so often hidden.

The press conference answered almost no questions except for one. Would Jackie Kennedy stand by her man? At least temporarily, it seemed, the answer was yes. On the way out with her husband, one reporter pushed his luck enough to shout at Jackie Kennedy, "Mrs. Kennedy, did you know about any of this before you read about it?"

She seemed taken aback and stammered only the word, "Oh," before the President grasped her forearm and led her from the room. First the *National Enquirer*, then other papers, began to call her "Jackie Oh" and it caught on as her nickname, used by tabloids for the rest of her life.

BLOWBACK

If Jackie Kennedy would not talk, then reporters seemed to be of the mind to find someone who would. The article and the news conference unleashed the investigative force of the Washington journalistic establishment as reporters sought response from all of the suspected paramours of the President. More than a few who had respected their vows of silence regarding their sexual liaisons with Kennedy now found themselves completely out of their depth. It was one thing to remain silent when few if anyone knew you had anything to say, and another thing entirely when reporters and photographers were waiting on the street outside your home.

The "other women" became household names. Within a week, arguments were breaking out as to whether Priscilla Wear was Fiddle or Faddle. But it was Jill Cowan (Faddle) who famously confirmed her relationship with the President when she told a reporter, "If you think it was just about sex, then you don't know President Kennedy at all."

All legal issues aside, the nation seemed transfixed by the state of the Kennedy marriage, with men and women often finding themselves on opposite sides of the issue. A Gallup Poll released at this time showed that fifty-eight percent of women—Republicans and Democrats in nearly equal numbers—agreed with the statement that "If current revelations of multiple affairs are true, Jackie Kennedy should consider divorce proceedings against President Kennedy." Only twenty-nine percent of men felt the same way.

Most of the pillars of the fourth estate, pressed for an honest reaction, admitted that news of Kennedy's secret life was widely known and probably would have dribbled out bit by bit over decades had the story been contained until his term expired in 1969. These explosive revelations, made suddenly and with a completeness that was stunning, simply demanded follow-up and independent investigation. By the end of the first week following publication, everyone had reporters on the job: *The New York Times*, *Washington Post*, *Wall Street Journal*, *Time*, *Newsweek* and all the TV networks.

Suddenly, things that were known about the President's medical condition, the allegations about associations with mobsters, election money-laundering and even attempts to assassinate foreign leaders like Castro were under investigation.

The American people were stunned. It wasn't as if the President had just been discovered having an affair. That might have been tolerable or understandable for some people (although not the Catholics in Kennedy's own church) but the sheer numbers of women he had been involved with said something else entirely. It was reckless to be sure, given his office, but it was more than that. It seemed to be completely unhinged behavior.

Initially, because the President wouldn't confirm or deny any specifics, it was the Republican Party that condemned him most strongly, while Democrats took a wait-and-see approach. The problem with that strategy was that the more anyone waited, the more they saw.

It was all anyone talked about. Americans felt they knew John Kennedy, so hearing the news of his fall from grace was like hearing the same thing about a close friend. The twin nature of the revelations—sexual feats and medical disabilities—led to a robust comedy take in the nation's barber shops and taverns, places where men gathered with other men out of earshot of the women in their lives.

The blue comedian Lenny Bruce had just over a year left to live when the story of the President's risk-taking private life surfaced and became a top item on the national agenda. Health aside, Bruce was feeling in a particularly angry mood, given his conviction the year before on obscenity charges arising from his act. No stranger to substance abuse or promiscuity, and looking for some material he could ride back to the top, Bruce embraced the Kennedy story as his new cause. Not even a call from Bobby Kennedy, thanking him for his support but asking him to tone down his act, could get him to back off. Two days after the article broke, Bruce had a microphone and a New York audience:

How about that fucking JFK? And by fucking JFK, well, that's exactly what I mean. This man, it turns out, is a complete fuck machine. Now, I know we're all supposed to be shocked and appalled by the fact that the man has seen more poontang in his time in office than anybody I know will see in a lifetime. I'm not shocked, I'm in awe. Look, say what you will, but instead of the man screwing us, he's out screwing Marilyn Monroe. This is progress folks. There is hope for democracy here.

Bruce went on to include some unkind remarks about Jackie Kennedy and found out that this was about the only line that even his audiences, who came expecting raunch and anger, would not let him cross. America loved her before and they felt sympathy for her now. She was off-limits.

Instead of making any public statement that might have implied she and her husband were now separated, Jacqueline Kennedy simply did what she had done during the first four and a half years in the White House. She quietly gathered up her things and her children and the support staff, and she left for the country. She would have had her press secretary Pamela Turnure explain it all away, except that it turned out that JFK had been having regular sexual relations with Turnure as well, and she had been given paid leave to find a new job. The young woman was hired by the office of Massachusetts Congressman Tip O'Neill and was ushered off to the relative safety of Capitol Hill. It was left to Jackie's social secretary Nancy Tuckerman to explain that the First Lady's absence was not that unusual.

Vice President Lyndon Johnson, sensing blood in the water, began raising his Washington profile, particularly hanging around the Senate, which was his right as the constitutional president of that body. What he was really doing, he told his own mistress, Madeline Brown, was "letting them know that this fox was in the henhouse."

The Los Angeles District Attorney Evelle Younger said that his office would reexamine the supposed suicide of Marilyn Monroe in light of the FBI files that were recently disclosed. He went to great lengths to state that he was not accusing the Kennedys of any foul play but was simply exercising the oversight that voters had trusted him to use when they elected him in 1964, more than two years after his predecessor had closed Monroe's case.

Although many, if not most, Americans were appalled at Kennedy's affairs and his treatment of Jackie, he was now something he had never been before—an underdog. For reasons that psychologists had a field day with, his problems actually increased his support among a prime demographic: young men eighteen to thirty-four. A significant number of these men actually found something to admire in a President who could sleep with that many women, get away with it for so long, still have a beautiful wife and run the country at the same time.

Within the first twenty-four hours, however, the political elites in Washington, D.C., began quietly asking about impeachment. It was as if *Top Story* had written the position paper that could serve as the basis for the charges, or articles.

Catch-25

The Twenty-Fifth Amendment did not exist yet. This created one of the most complex political equations ever seen in American history. One of the largest variables was Lyndon Johnson.

While the Kennedys' first choice was for JFK to remain in office, their back-up position was to be able to pick his successor. Yet as things stood, if President Kennedy were to be impeached, that would mean Johnson would become the next President, an option completely unacceptable to John and Bobby Kennedy, who both loathed him.

Johnson's recent legal troubles made him vulnerable as well, but even if he could be quickly forced to resign, President Kennedy could not appoint anyone to take his place. Based on the Constitution as of 1965, if the Vice President's office were to be left vacant for any reason, the position could not be filled until the next general election. Only when the Twenty-Fifth Amendment was ratified in 1969 were the terms of presidential succession finally clarified, allowing the President to appoint a new Vice President, subject to congressional approval.

This meant that if Johnson resigned and Kennedy was impeached, the next in line to assume the presidency would be the Speaker of the House. With the Republicans in control of the House of Representatives, that would mean that the genial but conservative Gerald Ford would get to serve out Kennedy's term.

The Republican hold on the House of Representatives also meant, oddly enough, that the more a Democrat felt a Kennedy impeachment was possible, the more likely that he would want to keep Vice President Johnson in office, corrupt or not. Otherwise, Congress could hand the presidency to Ford and the Republicans. For this reason, the GOP had joined the drumbeat in Washington, D.C., predicting Johnson's imminent political demise. They needed him out of office before they trained their fire on Kennedy.

It is a testament to just how much the Kennedy White House sought to block the ascension of Lyndon Johnson that they became fierce and uncompromising in the battle to force him out. Bobby had never liked anything about the man, but now he felt there was more to it. He actually began to believe that LBJ had foreknowledge of the Dallas assassination attempt. He and his brother were determined to prevent any possibility of Johnson becoming President, even if it meant handing the country's leadership to the Republicans. This created an unholy alliance of shared interest, never formal or even discussed, between JFK and the leaders of the Republican Party, to oust LBJ.

Robert Kennedy called a meeting of his young Turks in the Working Group and gave them a new mission. Behind closed doors and zipped lips, RFK announced that LBJ must be forced out, the sooner the better, despite LBJ's flirting with disaster just over a year ago during the 1964 election cycle. The Attorney General needed to know everything that was knowable about Lyndon Johnson, particularly anything that might have implicated him in any prior knowledge of the attack in Dallas. Even though Lyndon Johnson had to go and go soon, all the President's men still passionately believed that John Kennedy, however flawed and damaged he might be, had to stay in office. They did not intend to hand over the nation's stewardship, either to Johnson or to a Republican President Ford, without a fight.

A TALE OF TWO COMMITTEES

The revelations about John Kennedy shot through the Joint Committee on the Attempted Assassination of the President like a surge of electricity. Having already subpoenaed Chicago mob boss Sam Giancana, the way was now open to also force the girlfriend he had shared with Kennedy to testify. The ostensible reason that Judith Campbell was sworn in to testify was to see if she had been told anything by Giancana that would implicate him in ordering the Dallas hit. Once she was under oath, however, asking her about her relationship with JFK was simply too tempting. She spent two entire days being grilled. The most damning information she delivered was her confirmation that Giancana felt he had been "double-crossed" by the Kennedys and had been overheard speaking to his lieutenants about how he wished JFK were dead.

America was at a boiling point. While the hearings were winding down, the Watts Riots took place in Los Angeles from August 11-17 and provided a violent backdrop, leaving thirty-four dead, more than one thousand injured, and close to four thousand arrested. They also caused more than $40 million in property damage before the looting ended and the flames died down.

As the long, hot summer claimed its victims on the West Coast, JCAAP continued its work on Capitol Hill. On August 19, two days after what rioters called "the rebellion" in Los Angeles had ended under the thumb of the National Guard, the committee issued its report on Dallas:

> *The Joint Committee on the Attempted Assassination of the President finds that the rifle attack on the motorcade of President*

*Kennedy in Dallas, Texas on November 22, 1963 was probably
the result of a conspiracy. The Committee believes on the basis of all
available evidence that Lee Harvey Oswald did, in fact, participate
in the assassination attempt. The Committee also believes that
Oswald was not the sole assassin and that evidence supports the
existence of a second and, possibly, a third gunman.*

Beyond that, the Committee was vague. It did not name names
and expose whom it actually thought was a part of that conspiracy.
In fact, it ruled out several possibilities, saying that it did not believe
"on the basis of all available evidence" that the Soviet Union or
the Cuban government was behind what had happened. Ample
evidence had been found, however, to implicate "rogue elements"
of the CIA, the Cuban exile community, and organized crime. It did
not find sufficient reason to say that any single group had organized
it, only that the conspiracy had probably drawn resources and
manpower from a "linkage or connection" of these groups. In this
way, it held the institutions responsible for not policing their own
employees but not necessarily for planning the attack.

Of particular importance in the report's conjecture was the
"probability" that the assassination plot that had placed John
Kennedy in its crosshairs had its origin in an assassination plot that
had been intended for Fidel Castro. Under this scenario, the plot
was redirected at Kennedy based on pent-up frustration with the
President. The clear implication was that anti-Castro Cubans were
integral to the well-planned attack on the Kennedy motorcade.

On August 23, 1965, the first Monday after the Joint Committee
on the Attempted Assassination of the President made its report
public, the Republican Speaker of the House, Gerald Ford, held a
news conference to announce that the Committee on the Judiciary in
the House of Representatives would begin to consider impeachment
charges against President Kennedy. Most Democrats made a show
of halfheartedly accusing their Republican counterparts of playing
politics and reminded them that impeachment was not inevitable as
the GOP held control of the House by only a single vote. *National*

Review editor William F. Buckley wrote a column in which he stated his opinion on the subject: "I should think a single vote would do the trick."

The next day President John Kennedy gathered with his inner circle in the Oval Office to discuss strategy. "Maybe I have to go, but if I do," he warned everyone, "every treasonous bastard is going with me."

Top Story

CRIME OR POLITICS?

JANUARY 10, 1966

35c

BRYCE ZABEL
SURROUNDED BY ENEMIES
IFJFKLIVED.COM 2018
LYNDA KARR GRAPHICS

THE IMPEACHMENT AND TRIAL OF JOHN F. KENNEDY

Chapter 6:
Impeachment and Trial

August 23, 1965 -
February 25, 1966

Nightmare Scenario

On an unusually muggy August day, Gerald Ford stood before reporters, sweating heavily in a jacket he refused to take off, and said that as Speaker of the House, he would not take a position on whether President Kennedy should remain in office unless the House Committee on the Judiciary agreed on the articles of impeachment. He would simply see to it that the process ran as smoothly as possible until it had run its course. As he put it, "America's long, national nightmare since Dallas must come to an end one way or another." Ford, a strict constructionist of the U.S. Constitution, told Kennedy in a private phone conversation that he could see no other way than impeachment. No matter what the outcome, it would either legitimize the President's second term or end it altogether.

As events unfolded during the march toward impeachment, even John Kennedy's popularity could not hold off the blowback from his years of incautious behavior. The cascading revelations felt like a betrayal to most voters. Like Jackie Kennedy responding to her own marriage, the relationship with voters now felt like a sham. The question to be decided was whether or not the relationship could be saved.

Few would have enjoyed the resulting spectacle even if it had been unleashed in a vacuum where no attempt had been made on

Kennedy's life. As experienced in the shadow of that violence, everything seemed dirty and lethal at the same time. The curtain had been pulled back on anti-democratic plotters that would assassinate an American President as a matter of convenience, power or greed. Now it seemed as if the President might have unleashed some of these destructive forces on himself as his election opponent had unsuccessfully argued a year earlier.

One result of Kennedy's reckless behavior and all the arguments about it was confusion. Suddenly the ground under the debate about the attack on the President shifted to Kennedy himself. Shadowy conspiracies were difficult to understand and nearly impossible to prove. Affairs, sex scandals and drugs could be talked about by the common man and woman, and talk they did. The leaks of the FBI files accomplished exactly what the leakers had hoped. The subject was changed. It made no difference that it was a crime to gather some of this information or to leak it. Overnight, it seemed, there were so many potential crimes to discuss that the average person could hardly be blamed for throwing up his hands in frustration at the mess of it all.

John Kennedy is not the only president who has ever faced an impeachment by the House of Representatives and a trial in the United States Senate, but his story is surely the most tragic. In late 1965, it had been nearly a full century since the impeachment of any President of the United States had been seriously contemplated. Ironically, the story of how Lincoln's successor, Andrew Johnson, had been kept in office by a single vote in his Senate trial was one of the stories that John Kennedy had written about in his Pulitzer-winning book, *Profiles in Courage*. Not a single person with a conscious memory of that earlier event, however, was even alive in the mid-1960s. Everything in the process felt like the first time.

THE WAR NOT AT HOME

Historians now seem to agree that the implosion of John Kennedy's reputation shocked most Americans even more than the failure in

Vietnam. Yet revisionist thinking also has it that seeing his power slipping away through the fall and winter of 1965-66, Kennedy stiffened his resolve to prevent the United States from becoming fully involved in a land war in Asia while he still had the chance.

Even as Kennedy's efforts to save himself politically dissolved, so, too, did any chance to prop up the South Vietnamese government. His choices had narrowed. Having straddled the middle ground longer than he ever thought he would, JFK now realized he could either turn up the heat with a vast new commitment of American military power, or he could wind it down and let it end. There seemed to be no responsible choice in between.

So, even as the House and then the Senate debated what to do about the Kennedy presidency, the still-incumbent commander-in-chief decided the war in Vietnam must end. In a series of three executive orders, President Kennedy declared a halt to all aerial bombing of North Vietnam, forbade American military advisers from operating in active combat roles, and organized the U.S. forces in established military bases where they would plan their eventual return in six months' time.

The Kennedy Administration then asked the North Vietnamese for peace talks through diplomatic channels. The talks began, but the North's military campaign continued. Kennedy's withdrawal literally showed that the South Vietnamese forces had no real will to fight. It became only a matter of time, a deathwatch. The reorganization on the ground did not go smoothly. It was no secret that the Joint Chiefs felt this was a suicidal retreat and were slow to implement. One unnamed, high-ranking U.S. commander said, "We were hoping to run out the clock on him. Stall long enough for the bastard to get his ass thrown out of office, then cut a better deal with the next guy."

Back in the United States, the public was deeply divided. A plurality actually favored withdrawal of forces, but favoring it in the abstract and watching it happen on the nightly news was something else. And the people who were opposed saw this as another example of why Kennedy had to go. In their view, he was simply too weak and too naïve to continue to serve as President of the United States.

By refusing to deepen American involvement in the war under his own authority as commander-in-chief, President Kennedy had practically dared Congress to demand that troops be sent. As it turned out, the majority of representatives and senators favored war only if the President would take the ultimate responsibility. Without the cover of his leadership, the hawks in Congress fell surprisingly silent. The unexpected gift of Kennedy's troubles may very well have been the saving of hundreds of thousands of lives in Southeast Asia.

In the end, the Vietnam situation did not gain the President any support, and it probably cost him some. He took the actions he did for practical reasons. He opposed widening the war, and he knew he could end it if he moved quickly. His presidential power was waning.

In February 1966, the South Vietnamese government fell to forces loyal to North Vietnam's Ho Chi Minh. The American withdrawal was underway simultaneously. The TV newscasts juxtaposed images of Viet Cong raising their flag over the old American embassy, against film showing U.S. soldiers cutting and running with their tanks and planes and helicopters. It was ruinous theater of the national mood, raising anger, and it was in the news along with the latest events from the Kennedy impeachment story.

IMPEACHMENT

Under the leadership of Speaker Ford, the House Committee on the Judiciary was encouraged to get the job done on the issue of impeachment before adjournment. That was originally scheduled for late October, but Ford said he would keep the House working until Christmas Eve, if necessary. Ford's firewall was his determination that the fate of John F. Kennedy would be out of his House by 1966.

Impeachment, then, began with a ticking clock of approximately four months. That amount of time was considered short by virtually everyone but Ford, who remained adamant that JFK's fate not derail the upcoming second session of the Eighty-Ninth Congress.

The Speaker further argued that the President's fate was not a topic that should need great investigation, given the publicity to date, a statement that even members of his own party felt was simplistic and wrong. Yet it was Ford's decision to make, and he had made it. "Do whatever you feel is right," he seemed to be saying to the congress, "but do it fast."

THE PEOPLE'S GRAND JURY

Most constitutional scholars consider the House Committee on the Judiciary, backed up by the full body of the House of Representatives, to be the equivalent of a grand jury. The lower body of the U.S. government is empowered to conduct official proceedings to investigate potential criminal conduct (i.e., treason, bribery and other high crimes and misdemeanors) and to determine whether criminal charges should be brought before the upper body (i.e., sent to the U.S. Senate for trial). As with a grand jury, the Judiciary Committee can compel the production of documents and command witnesses to appear and offer sworn testimony.

It is a common misconception that to impeach a President is to remove him from office. In truth, it only means that the House believes the charges are sufficient to generate a trial in the Senate. Only by approving at least one article of impeachment by a two-thirds vote can the Senate remove the President from office.

As for the case of President Kennedy, the House Committee on the Judiciary was authorized in the late summer of 1965 to consider the specifics and to gather and review the evidence. If deemed sufficient, the committee would write and debate proposed articles of impeachment. If the committee voted them down, that would be that. If committee members voted to send the articles to the floor of the House, a simple majority would impeach the President and send the matter to the United States Senate in January for a trial.

Naturally, it was not that simple. The mere act of considering a President's impeachment can put the Congress and the executive branch into conflict and even trigger impeachable behavior that did not exist before impeachment was considered. The struggle over the recordings that were made by the White House, for example, became an issue debated by the Judiciary Committee as possibly justifying an article of impeachment.

HOUSE POLITICS

Since January 1965, the Republican Party had controlled the House of Representatives by a single vote, 218-217, making their leader, Gerald Ford, the Speaker of the House. The Republicans also controlled the committee chairmanships. This became extremely important during the impeachment proceedings, because William Moore McCulloch, the Republican representing Ohio's Fourth District, had replaced the previous chairman of the Judiciary Committee, Emanuel Celler, a Democrat from New York's Tenth District.

Over the course of any congressional session, seats are commonly vacated by death, disability or personal issues that might cause an incumbent to resign while in office. This usually leads to a special election held within a few months, or the next general election, if that is feasible. Normally these elections have little importance other than being symbolic bellwethers of the electorate's mood. The years 1965 and 1966 were anything but normal, though, given that House leadership teetered on a virtual tie between the parties.

On October 2, 1965, Edwin Edwards retained Louisiana's Seventh District for the Democrats after the incumbent T. Ashton Thompson was killed in an automobile accident. This left the House still in GOP control, 218-217. Had Edwards lost, it would have put the Democrats behind by three votes.

However, falling right in the middle of the impeachment debate, in which the Republicans barely controlled the House of Representatives, was another election to be held on November 2, and it had the power to change history.

Ohio's Seventh District had been Representative Clarence Brown's since 1939. Brown died on August 23 in a Bethesda hospital, the same day that Gerald Ford declared he would support impeachment hearings. With only two months to campaign, Brown's son, Clarence "Bud" Brown Jr., was set to run as a Republican against Democrat James Barry. If Barry could defeat the younger Brown, the Democrats would reverse the Republicans' 218-217 majority in the House. Democrat John McCormack would become the Speaker, and Emanuel Celler would get back control of the Judiciary Committee. The Democrats poured money and volunteers into the campaign, hoping to score an upset win over the late incumbent's son. In the end, though, Barry simply could not overcome Brown's name familiarity in such a short campaign, and lost by a margin of 54-46 percent.

The House might still change leadership from Republicans back to Democrats in the future, but not in time to save the President of the United States, if his fate were to be decided along party lines.

BLACKOUT

Republican Chairman William McCulloch called the House Committee on the Judiciary to order on September 15, 1966. Its first order of business was a decision not to allow its impeachment hearings or deliberations to be televised. The decision was on party lines, with McCulloch casting the deciding vote. The GOP, having been stung by the Kennedy charisma going back to his 1960 debates with Richard Nixon and his standout news conference performances, wanted to make sure that TV would not impact their work. Also, the spectacle of the JCAAP hearings was recent enough that it served to end the debate before it started.

Kennedy friend Clark Clifford represented the President's legal team in these proceedings. In 1960, Clifford was a member of Kennedy's Committee on the Defense Establishment and was appointed in May 1961 to the President's Foreign Intelligence Advisory Board, which he was chairing when asked to handle the impeachment defense. Over the years, Clifford served frequently as an unofficial White House counsel and sometimes undertook short-term official duties.

When the President asked him if he would have any problem leading the defense team, Clifford had answered, "Mr. President, I do not approve of much of what I have read lately, but I know that you have been a good President for this country, and I will gladly defend you on the basis of that record." Even though Bobby had no choice but to recuse himself officially, he continued to remain his brother's closest confidante, and worked in an unofficial capacity with Clifford from start to finish.

After settling the rules, the committee attempted to decide the scope of its investigation. Members seemed to focus their main concern on the following:

- Improper relationships that jeopardized the security of the United States or even the life of the President through reckless behavior.
- Undisclosed presidential medical conditions and treatments that could have affected the safety and security of the United States during times of crisis.
- Presidential approval and encouragement of extralegal activities of the CIA and the FBI, including misuse of the federal marshals.
- Use of government resources to prevent the President's activities from becoming public knowledge.

In addition to these areas of interest, it was also up to committee members to seek all relevant testimony and evidence.

From a testimony point of view, it was decided to bring no woman before the committee simply on the basis of her having engaged in sexual relations with Kennedy, whether inside or outside the White House. Members also decided to bring no cases before the committee that had occurred before January 20, 1961, ruling out a great deal of what was in the FBI files. The decision did, however, leave in some difficult cases, including those of Ellen Rometsch, Judith Campbell, and prostitutes such as Suzy Chang, who were not U.S. citizens. Even Democrats on the committee were forced to reluctantly agree to investigate these cases.

Where Republicans and Democrats sparred the most was on the issue of the young women who were White House employees and were involved in relationships with the President. The laws in the 1960s were undefined about what constituted an improper workplace environment, and it seemed clear that none of these young women were physical threats to the President. All were known by the Secret Service agents on duty. Republicans wanted these women interviewed by counsel at the very least and got their way with their one-vote majority.

There was also the question of whether Kennedy had abused his presidential power by using Kenneth O'Donnell, David Powers or Evelyn Lincoln to procure or schedule the women involved in these sexual liaisons. All were fair game for compelled testimony, the committee ruled.

The medical condition of President Kennedy was another matter. There was no specific law to prevent a President from lying to the American people about his health, but if the President could be shown to have directed his personal physician to lie about his records, that would be another matter. There was also the issue of what drugs Kennedy was taking when, and whether or not they could have clouded his judgment at crucial times, such as during his meetings with Khrushchev or the Cuban Missile Crisis. All records were then subpoenaed. Dr. Janet Travell and Dr. Max Jacobson would be brought before the committee.

The third leg of potential charges was perhaps the trickiest of all. It involved the role of the President in overseas assassinations and coups in the Congo, Vietnam, Cuba and other countries. In some of these cases, if not most, the CIA had pushed for action that Kennedy had reluctantly agreed to, but as chief executive, the responsibility was his. Even FBI wiretaps of Dr. Martin Luther King Jr. had been approved because Hoover wanted them and the Kennedys had agreed in order to keep their own vulnerabilities secret.

Then there was the larger issue of which of these conceivable charges could have generated possible assassination plots against Kennedy. Clearly, sleeping with a mobster's girlfriend could have triggered a reaction. Approving plots to kill Castro could likewise have triggered counter-plots to kill Kennedy.

William Foley, the general counsel to the Committee on the Judiciary, knew better than most that Ford's deadline was crushing and nearly impossible to meet. He saw two possible solutions: the committee would have to narrow the focus early, and it would have to fight the White House for the presidential recordings of Oval Office conversations.

"I believed that the committee would have to pick and choose its battles carefully, deciding which charges were most likely to lead to an article of impeachment in advance, and then investigate," said Foley, "rather than cast a wide net and see what we caught." In other words, they would have to make full use of what the Joint Committee on the Attempted Assassination of the President and the Warren Commission had learned, plus the journalistic output spawned by the FBI file leak, rather than start from scratch. The committee's investigation would have to be supplementary and not primary, whenever possible.

Most importantly, thought Foley, committee members would have to get their hands on the White House recordings that Secret Service Special Agent Robert Bouck had disclosed before the Joint Committee on the Attempted Assassination of the President. Chairman McCulloch agreed, and asked Foley and his lawyers to prepare for battle.

TALE OF THE TAPES

The White House was served with a subpoena requesting all recordings and responded that the request was too broad. The committee narrowed the request to a list of forty-five days' worth of tapes and was told by the White House that it would not comply, based on the concept of executive privilege.

The battle was on. Chairman McCulloch met the press on the Capitol steps to complain, "If the President did not want Congress to hear what is on these recordings, he should not have made them in the first place. They are evidence, and we are prepared to fight for them."

The Supreme Court agreed to hear the case immediately, because of its importance to the nation. Once again, Chief Justice Earl Warren was in the middle of the President's affairs. Once again, he refused to recuse himself.

For three days running, lawyers for the executive and legislative branches of the government made their arguments. The White House certainly had possession of the tapes, that much was clear, but having created them, the question could now legitimately be raised in a democracy as to who really owned them. Given they were considered crucial in a showdown between the two branches, the justices were heavily involved, asking dozens of sharp questions.

In the end, the Court ruled 6-3 that the tapes must be turned over. Warren wrote the majority opinion:

> *Presidential power is not absolute, but proportionate, and must exist within the framework of three-branch government. Checks and balances are real, and the executive branch may not deny the legislative branch evidence without sharing direct cause. The simple claim of privilege is not sufficient.*

On the afternoon of November 5, 1965, White House lawyer Clark Clifford informed Chairman McCulloch and General Counsel Foley that he had conducted his own review and found that the White House could not comply with the Supreme Court request. It was not because he did not recognize the ultimate authority of the Court or the committee, he said, but because the tapes apparently no longer existed.

While this conversation was taking place, New York was plunged into darkness, the result of a faulty power grid that threatened the entire East Coast. Staff Director Bess E. Dick interrupted the meeting shortly after 5:30 p.m. with the news. It was best for everyone to head home to their families while they still could; the legal wrangling would have to wait until later. It's unlikely that anyone in the room missed the obvious metaphor: this crisis, too, was about to bring the entire system down, if the players were not careful.

As it turned out, power was restored by 7 a.m. the next day across most of the affected areas, and in Washington, D.C., the lights remained on throughout. By 9:30 a.m., Kennedy aide Dave Powers had received a second subpoena, asking him to return to the committee the very next morning. Powers had already testified on charges that he had procured prostitutes for President Kennedy and had used his authority to prevent the Secret Service from doing its due diligence in vetting their identities and examining purses for drugs or weapons.

During that testimony, Powers had exercised his Fifth Amendment right to remain silent to all questions that were asked of him. Earlier, Powers had made news by first refusing to testify at all, but he had changed his mind on the advice of Attorney General Robert Kennedy.

Now the Attorney General had to discuss the situation with the President. "Where are these damned tapes, Bobby?" Kennedy had asked. He was informed that Powers had destroyed them. All of them. RFK had retrieved them all from their storage, sent them to Powers's office, and asked him to begin reviewing them from the moment the committee had asked for them.

Reconstructing the scene in his 1974 book, *Flashpoints*, Robert Kennedy recalls his brother delivering the following words cautiously: "Dave would never destroy those tapes on his own. We both know that."

The Attorney General chose his own words carefully. "I have just spoken to Dave, and it is his testimony that he took this action on his own volition in an obviously misguided attempt to protect the office of the presidency."

"They'll hold him in contempt. He'll go to prison," the President said. Jack Kennedy and Dave Powers had been friends going back to the first campaign for Congress in 1946.

"He knows," Bobby said. "Under no circumstances should you contact him. My advice is that you must fire him immediately before he testifies tomorrow."

Dave Powers was fired by the White House that afternoon. The next morning he went to Capitol Hill and appeared again before the House Committee on the Judiciary. Rather than take the Fifth Amendment again, he read the following statement:

> On October 13, 1965, I removed all of the boxes containing the audiotapes recorded in the White House during the presidency of John Kennedy. I did so with authorization papers on which I forged all necessary signatures. I took this action completely on my own. No one told me to do this, and I specifically state that this action was not taken at the directive of President Kennedy, Attorney General Robert Kennedy, Kenneth O'Donnell, Clark Clifford, nor any other member of the White House staff. I drove these tapes myself to a location in Virginia and supervised their destruction by burning. While this may not be the wish of the committee nor President Kennedy, I have taken this action on my own and am solely responsible.

The Judiciary Committee responded with fury. All of their questions were met by Powers once again invoking the Fifth Amendment. Powers was held immediately in contempt. He was later indicted for lying to Congress and convicted. Powers was sentenced to seven years in prison and fined $100,000.

This case has been hotly debated ever since. Many believe, as President Kennedy apparently did, that his friend would not have acted on his own. Yet Powers never spoke again on the subject, and his statement to the committee stands as his only comment. Many committee members felt that his actions seemed like prima facie evidence of criminality. West Virginia's Arch Moore Jr. was most outspoken: "The only reason one man agrees to go to jail is to keep another man from going."

The closest anyone ever came to a link to the White House was the admission by Kenny O'Donnell, who recalled that he had angrily said, "Somebody ought to burn those fucking tapes!" when the issue was first introduced. O'Donnell insisted, however, that he was not proposing a serious action but simply expressing his frustration at the process and how the tapes had become such a focus of the committee.

Yet the committee was instructed by its counsel that it could draw no conclusions about President Kennedy or the facts based on Powers's action. It did, however, have an extremely negative impact on the mood of everyone serving.

President Kennedy addressed the issue. "I have never advocated the destruction of evidence on any matter that has come before me in this White House. Mr. Powers, who has been a longtime friend, says he committed this act on his own. I know him to be a truthful man, and I have to take him at his word."

The Case for Impeachment

It has become an axiom of political scandal that the cover-up is more damning than the crime. But in the articles of impeachment drafted to strip John Kennedy of his office, alleged crime and cover-up were both amply cited. Certainly the House Committee on the Judiciary wrote up a varied menu of high crimes and misdemeanors for the Senate to choose from when deciding whether to truncate Kennedy's term.

The first draft of these articles became known as the "kitchen sink" impeachment by Democrats, who wanted to characterize the litany as a Republican fishing expedition. But no one doubted their chilling, dark power when rendered in the formal language of impeachment. They began directly:

> *These Articles of Impeachment are exhibited by the House of Representatives of the United States of America in the name of itself and of the people of the United States of America, against John Fitzgerald Kennedy, President of the United States of America, in maintenance and support of its impeachment against him for high crimes and misdemeanors. Resolved, that John Fitzgerald Kennedy, President of the United States, is impeached*

*for high crimes and misdemeanors, and that the following articles of
impeachment be exhibited to the United States Senate.*

The charges were broken into three categories: abuse of power,
obstruction of justice, and contempt of Congress. The high crimes
and misdemeanors, screamed the *New York Post* headlines, were
"Sex, Drugs, Murder!"

There it was. The stakes were instantly back at Dallas levels of
hysteria. The average person knew that John Kennedy screwed up, but
a lot of people clung to liking him anyway. Their opinion wasn't the
issue now. Congress would take over, and many of its representatives
believed that the President was guilty of something that was probably
impeachable if they were in the mood to see it that way.

In retrospect, the articles as drafted were overkill, sloppily
constructed, overlapping and unequal in importance. Yet,
underneath the verbiage lay a chilling reality for the White House.
Based on the Constitution itself, if only a single article made it out
of the Judiciary Committee and was approved by the entire House
of Representatives and then agreed to by the Senate, President
Kennedy would be out of a job.

ARTICLE ONE: ABUSE OF POWER

This came to be known in common terminology as "the sex article."
What the charges covered, however, were the improper relationships
that jeopardized the security of the United States or even the life of
the President through reckless behavior.

The abuse of power charges were, by far, the ones with the
greatest traction among the public. They specifically included misuse
of the FBI, something that was ironic at best, given the fact that the
impeachment itself had been caused by the illegal leaking of FBI
files against the President and, in some cases, the illegal wiretapping
of citizens by the FBI. Still, on at least one instance, the bugging
of Dr. Martin Luther King Jr., the President had authorized the
wiretapping. He had done it to stop Hoover from leaking the very

same files he had eventually leaked to damage Kennedy, but that was hardly an excuse. His only alibi, such as it was, was that he had given his approval through the Attorney General, acting on his behalf, and no record existed of their conversation. The President of the United States had plausible deniability.

Kennedy was also accused of the misuse of the Secret Service, another irony given the organization's poor job performance in Dallas in November 1963. The charges, however, predated that event for the most part, referring to the fact that Kennedy had forced the agents entrusted with his safety to look the other way when women were brought to the White House. Beyond even that, when prostitutes were brought in, it was argued that the agents were being asked to ignore personal knowledge of a crime being committed.

In the months since Dallas, Secret Service agent Abraham Bolden had become close to JFK, spending double-shifts with him more often than not. One late night, the President asked Bolden if the passage of time had changed his opinion about the Secret Service agents in Dallas. Bolden replied, "There were agents that day in Dallas who would not trade their lives for you, sir. I'm damn sorry to say that." Kennedy replied that Bolden couldn't be as sorry saying it as he was to be hearing it.

Beneath his usual wry veneer, the President was alarmed to hear his suspicions confirmed about some of the agents charged with protecting his life. What Bolden was suggesting went beyond simple dereliction of duty; it bordered on treason. Kennedy cared too much for Bolden personally to put him on the spot by asking him to name names, but he was visibly shaken. The following evening, he was surprised when the agent approached him at the entrance to the Oval Office, offering a folded slip of paper with three names handwritten inside. "If you need me to make some kind of a formal statement," Bolden told him, "I'd be willing to do so, sir."

Kennedy looked over the list, then regarded his friend warmly. "I don't think that will be necessary, Agent Bolden. Thank you for this."

In the coming weeks, one of the agents on Bolden's list was transferred to Gettysburg, Pennsylvania, where he was assigned to protect former First Lady Mamie Eisenhower at the farm where she lived with her husband. Two others were sent out of the country to work indefinitely on a currency investigation in the Philippines.

At the same time, the President could only sit back and watch as a divided House committee pondered its response to the charges against him. Two specific relationships formed the core of the issue of whether the President's behavior put himself and, by extension, the nation at risk: Ellen Rometsch and Judith Campbell. One was an alleged East German spy, and the other was an alleged Mafia girlfriend. Kennedy's best defense on these issues was the obvious one that guilt by association was not part of our judicial system. He could simply deny knowledge of their connections.

Also included in early drafts of the article was the entire Department of Justice use of federal marshals to swoop into Texas to bring what many saw as a state prisoner back to Washington, D.C.

Any one of those cases, if deemed substantive by the committee, would have been sufficient to send an abuse of power article to the floor of the House. There were also two more articles to be considered.

ARTICLE TWO: OBSTRUCTION OF JUSTICE

Article Two seemed to be a grab bag of sins, some more serious than others, but all difficult to prove. They involved, in several cases, trying to assess the intent of the Administration. The setting up of the Warren Commission was a prime example. Was Kennedy's appointment of that commission an attempt to delay the truth about Dallas, which the President would rather have kept quiet until after the 1964 election? Or, for another example, was the President's testimony—or the testimony of his staff at his direction—incorrect or incomplete by design? These were difficult questions to answer, and certainly to prove. They demanded the interpretation of both intent and action.

Ultimately, Article Two became known as "the drugs article" because it dealt with undisclosed presidential medical conditions and treatments that could have affected the safety and security of the United States during times of crisis. This was the angle that held steady traction from the beginning.

The President of the United States had serious ailments and was often taking powerful medications with serious side effects. Kennedy had taken an oath to perform the office of the presidency, "to the best of my ability." Did that mean he should take any drug to boost his performance on the job no matter what the risk or side effect, or did it mean that he needed to be straight about his health issues and seek appropriate measures to avoid risking mood alteration and possible drug addiction?

The House of Representatives needed to decide if Kennedy's medical treatment was a legitimate concern of the people and providing accurate details about the condition of his health was part of his oath. If it was, then the numerous times that the President had lied, covered-up, misled and hidden the truth, were attempts to stop the administration of justice and, thus, obstruction.

Both Dr. Travell and Dr. Jacobson had been compelled to testify about the drug cocktails they had personally administered to the President and First Lady. Both had also gone out of their way to prevent these ministrations from becoming part of the public record. Other medical experts had been brought in to testify about how such drug mixtures could have affected the President's performance at crucial times. There was actual talk of calling Elvis Presley as a witness because he, too, had been a patient of Dr. Jacobson's, although it never happened.

The voters, however, knew what it meant to lie about your health. Most of them had done it at one time or another. Would they hold the President to a higher standard? Were his lies more significant? Enough to end his career?

ARTICLE THREE: CONTEMPT OF CONGRESS

This became known as "the murder article" because it involved presidential approval and encouragement of extralegal activities of the CIA that included alleged assassinations of foreign leaders. It was a supreme irony to blame this on John Kennedy, given his own close call.

Kennedy stood accused of directly or indirectly through the Central Intelligence Agency targeting foreign leaders for death or coup. These targets included Prime Minister Patrice Lumumba of the Congo in January 1961; Prime Minister Rafael Trujillo of the Dominican Republic in May of 1961; and Premier Ngo Dinh Diem of South Vietnam in November of 1963. Those were the successful kills. There was also the matter of the Cuban leader Fidel Castro, a man both the CIA and the Administration seem to have been bent on killing for years, though without success.

Incredibly, the CIA that had carried out these missions and pushed for them so strongly was now in a position to use them to hang Kennedy. Several key witnesses managed to make it sound like it was all the President's idea. The bottom line still remained that Truman was right—the buck stopped on the President's desk—and if Kennedy approved something, it was the same as if it were his idea.

The contempt of Congress interpretation had been agreed to because of the constitutional war powers that favor the action of the chief executive with congressional oversight and approval. By not consulting Congress before or after these actions, the thinking went, President Kennedy was preventing the Senate and the House from performing its constitutional duty and, thus, showing it contempt.

The article also contained a key count about the defiance of the committee's subpoena by Dave Powers, who claimed to have destroyed certain documents and all of the Oval Office recordings by himself with no instruction from above. While hardly any member could believe this explanation as the truth, it was a far greater stretch to pin it directly on the President.

COAL FOR CHRISTMAS

On December 17, 1965, the Committee on the Judiciary of the House of Representatives decided all three articles of impeachment by a sharply partisan vote. The President's defenders called the committee's mission a "witch hunt," while the GOP insisted that they were merely performing their constitutional duty.

Committee chairman William Moore McCulloch, the Republican representing Ohio's Fourth District, said, "The office of President of the United States is the greatest position of responsibility in the history of the world. It demands respect, particularly from its occupant."

Leading Democrat Emanuel Celler, from New York's Tenth District, countered, "This man, John Kennedy, was shot at on the streets of an American city just two years ago. I will not vote to put him on trial while the traitors who plotted his murder walk free."

Within each of the three articles, subsections had been deleted. There were thirty-four members of the committee, divided in favor of the GOP, 18-16. The abuse of power article was approved by the largest margin, 19-15. The obstruction of justice article and the contempt of Congress article were each approved 18-16.

On the night that his impeachment by the House Judiciary Committee finally came to a vote, President Kennedy watched the final debate in the White House residence with his brothers, Bobby and Teddy, and others from his inner circle. Even before it was over, the President assessed the situation wryly: "It looks like Santa's bringing coal this Christmas," he said.

With two seats vacant and headed for special elections in February, the debate in the full House of Representatives was acrimonious and partisan, lasting nearly three days. The vote came on December 22, with Christmas recess on everyone's mind.

Speaker Gerald Ford ultimately agreed with the overwhelming majority of his Republican colleagues that it was his solemn duty to support the articles of impeachment. He tried to maintain his independence by voting against several of the specific counts, but, in the end, he made certain that all articles got sent to the U.S. Senate for trial. Ford's counterpart, Minority Leader John McCormack, no real fan of the Kennedys, mounted a public show of support but refused to trade valuable political capital he would need in 1966 to save the President. In that regard, both Ford and McCormack were united in a desire to get the impeachment out of the House and into the Senate.

Eager to get home for Christmas break, the House approved the Abuse of Power article 227-206, with three GOP members and seven southern Democrats breaking ranks. The House approved the Obstruction of Justice article, 219-214, but approved the Contempt of Congress citation by the slimmest of margins, 217-216.

Not all of the charges under each article were approved but at least one was. Notably stripped out were the sub-articles dealing with Dave Powers's destruction of the tapes and the alleged abuse of power through the use of the federal marshals. In the end, though, all three of the main articles of impeachment had passed.

With that, John Fitzgerald Kennedy became only the second President—and the first in almost one hundred years—to face a legal trial in the Senate. Afterward, on a freezing afternoon, the President forced the media to gather on the lawn near the Rose Garden, where he offered no hint he would resign. The vote margins had been thin and sharply partisan, he pointed out. His GOP foes, he said coolly, should find a way in the Senate to craft a "reasonable, bipartisan and proportionate" deal to avoid trial.

With more than sixty House Democrats standing behind him, Kennedy vowed to serve "until the last hour of the last day of my term in 1969," when he would legitimately turn power over to the next President. The tableau on the lawn had one clear message: the President would make a deal, but he'd never quit. Yet, he had reason to worry. A Gallup poll taken in the next twenty-four hours showed that after his impeachment, forty-three percent of the country felt he should resign immediately, compared to just forty-five percent who felt he should stay and fight.

After the Rose Garden freeze-out, President Kennedy, his aides and dozens of congressmen retired to the larger Cabinet room for hot chocolate. The atmosphere, it was said, was eerily giddy, with the death-be-not-proud bravado of an Irish wake. The Kennedys toasted to a battle in the Senate, a place where they felt JFK's service for eight years would be implicitly acknowledged in a friendlier forum. The President stepped forward. "I would give anything," he said, "to keep you from being in the position you were in today, and for me not to have acted in such a way as to put you there." Of course, he had acted that way, and the war would soon rage to judge the consequences.

In mortal political peril, however, his team knew that the next order of business was to make certain that no Democrats—inside or outside Washington—called for his resignation. Starting the next morning, President Kennedy would begin to roll calls with Mrs. Lincoln, and would not stop until he had spoken to each and every one of the Senate Democrats who would now sit in judgment of him.

At the same time, the idea was to stake out a bargaining position for an eventual deal. To that end, Kennedy would also call his two Republican opponents, Richard Nixon from the 1960 election and Barry Goldwater from 1964. He did not expect their support, but he was hoping they would work with him to craft a compromise deal, allowing him to accept censure and a fine to resolve the case. Both Nixon and Goldwater, while friendly with the President when they had served in the Senate together, harbored hard feelings over their general election losses and offered little comfort.

Congress adjourned on Tuesday, December 23, 1965. Every senator who went home for the recess knew that his constituents would have a lot to say about how to vote in the New Year.

FAILURE TO LAUNCH

It is perhaps only a sad side-note to impeachment that the once-vaunted Lunar Exploration Treaty binding the United States and the Soviet Union to a joint moon mission never even came up for a vote in the United States Senate. Perhaps it was a sign of Kennedy's declining influence and his upcoming trial, or the reality that Khrushchev finally appeared to be on his way out in the Soviet Union, or both.

Many senators explained the death of the treaty on practical grounds, saying it had taken so long to get around to it that the United States would now have to give up far too much by approving it. We were already winning the space race and the moon race in particular. Just last December, two Gemini capsules had docked in space. We could have astronauts walking on the moon by the summer of 1969 if we kept our eye on the ball. The Soviets, it was widely presumed, were nowhere close.

President Kennedy accepted this calmly. He knew when he came home with the idea that his generals would fight it to the end. He might have beaten them as he did with the Nuclear Test Ban Treaty. When that passed the Senate in 1963, he was as politically muscular as he'd ever been, and it took every ounce of strength to pull it off. Now, he was fighting just to keep his job.

If America was going to the moon, it was going solo. Back in Lyndon Johnson's home state of Texas, NASA was pouring plenty into the economy. If it wasn't for his ongoing efforts to keep scandal at bay, Johnson would have been sitting pretty.

LBJ knew in his gut that his benefactor and nemesis, John Kennedy, was going to get fired by his constituents in the next year. That, he knew, would open the door for the realization of a lifetime dream, a Johnson presidency.

According to a plea bargain statement later made by Johnson associate Bobby Baker, Lyndon Johnson had only one goal now, and it consumed his every waking hour. He had to hang on long enough to outlast Kennedy. The Congress would never impeach John Kennedy and then go after him, too. The public would never stand for it. He would be safe, finally.

Go Away, LBJ

During the Christmas recess, everyone in the Kennedy Administration knew they were in a fight for political survival. One would have to be in absolute denial not to realize that things could end badly. If they did, Lyndon Baines Johnson would take over as the President of the

United States unless he could be forced out first. This is something that John and Robert Kennedy wanted to avoid with almost the same passion as they wanted to avoid conviction in a Senate trial.

Fortunately, the Attorney General's Working Group had done its job well. They had accumulated enough testimony and evidence to take Johnson down by picking up where the derailed Senate investigation had left off. They had also, incredibly, found a plausible trail of suspicion that put Johnson in the middle of the conspiracy. He was not, to their way of thinking, definitively the ringleader, but they believed he had knowledge of what was going to happen well in advance of Dallas and had done nothing to stop it. At the very least, he had let John Kennedy ride into an ambush.

The suspicious behavior of LBJ generated its own kind of evidence. There was a classic photo of Johnson slumping so low in his limousine's seat that he disappears, and it was taken two seconds *before* shots were fired. His involvement in planning the trip was extreme, and he had interacted negatively on several security issues. Comments like the one made by oilman Clint Murchison that "Lyndon don't get no more ready [to be president] than he is now" looked particularly suspicious when they turned up in an FBI wiretap.

Robert Kennedy came to Lyndon Johnson's office on the morning of January 3, 1966 and laid out the situation. Deputy Attorney General Nicholas Katzenbach, whom LBJ had always claimed to like, assisted him. "We both know that you've been involved in dirty business, Lyndon—far worse than anything President Kennedy has ever contemplated," said the AG, obviously relishing the moment. "There is no way that you are ever going to be President of the United States. I hope we are absolutely clear on that."

Johnson was not clear, and so Katzenbach explained it further. His team of investigators had the Vice President on bribery, extortion, influence peddling, and probably murder. He rattled off names. Not just Billie Sol Estes and Bobby Baker, but Malcolm Wallace, Edward Clark, Henry Marshall and Clifton Carter. He mentioned John

Kinser and LBJ's own sister, Josefa. Each name contained the story of an illegal act that could manifest in Johnson's imprisonment.

Johnson exploded with rage aimed at Bobby. "Your brother's about to be yesterday's news around here, and you come into my office like that?"

"You have blood on your hands, Lyndon," responded Kennedy. He waved a sealed indictment, handed down from a grand jury, in front of Johnson. It named the Vice President as a co-conspirator in the death of his own friend, John Connally, and the attempted murder of the President. "Let me explain what happens next." Bobby instructed Johnson to write out two confessions: one for blackmail and influence-peddling in both the Bobby Baker and Billie Sol Estes cases, and another for complicity in the assassination attempt on JFK and the deaths of Connally, Tippit, and Hill.

LBJ said he would do no such thing, and the bargaining began.

"Much as I hate to do this," said the Attorney General, "I am here to offer you a deal. You will accept it while I am here in your office, or you will not accept it, and I will see that these matters are all turned over to the courts, including your involvement in this Dallas debacle."

Kennedy informed the Vice President that by writing his two confessions he could spare his family the shame he had brought on them, at least while he was alive. Only the first confession would be used against him by the Justice Department. LBJ would resign immediately, and he would plead to multiple charges of extortion and bribery. The other confession would be sealed until ten years after Johnson's death.

Johnson did not accept this fate easily. He fought back in every way he knew how. Yet the longer he disputed the conclusion that he had no choice but to sign, the more he realized that it was better to go to prison for some hardball politics and a kickback here and there than it was to be the man who tried to bump off the President of the United States so he could take his job.

The Vice President changed his tone from threats to pleas. "Those men were serious, Bobby," he said. "They'd have killed me."

Kennedy was surprised and a little exalted to see Johnson fighting back tears. LBJ tried to bargain, asking the Attorney General to push back the unsealing of the second confession until twenty-five years after his death. The Attorney General did not budge. Then Johnson asked if the President would consider pardoning him.

"Lyndon, you know the President cannot do that, given the situation in the Senate. Most particularly, he has hard feelings toward you now, as you might imagine." The Attorney General did agree to use his office to influence local authorities in Texas to stand down on their own investigations, given Johnson's plea bargain with federal authorities. Plus, he would see to it that LBJ would serve his time in a medium security facility in Texas, if that was his wish. That was the best he could do.

Kennedy said the Justice Department would need LBJ to testify against the other plotters. Johnson responded that if he did that, he would be dead. And if that was the price of the deal, then there would be no deal. They should charge him right then and there.

Within the hour, Kennedy and Katzenbach had the two confessions, and Johnson's letter of resignation. He would not cooperate on the mechanics of the assassination plot, but at least he would never, ever be President.

TRIAL

The second session of the Eighty-Ninth Congress convened on January 10, 1966. The House of Representatives officially approved a group of managers, a dozen Republicans led by Wisconsin's Melvin Laird, to take the impeachment case to the Senate. Some Democrats attempted to challenge the propriety of a lame duck House impeaching a President but found insufficient support.

By this time, Chief Justice Warren had spent the Christmas weeks boning up on rules and precedents. The trial was scheduled to begin in February, when the managers were to present the articles of impeachment to the full Senate. Before then, witnesses would be interviewed and evidence gathered, but there was little patience for too much investigation, given the scope of the JCAAP hearings and the House Judiciary Committee's findings. Besides, that scope had been narrowed from nearly two-dozen counts in the Committee's first draft. Now there were just eight counts, still distributed over the three articles.

One profound difference was that the Senate, as opposed to the House, had decided that all proceedings, except for the final deliberations of the senators, would be public and broadcast on TV.

THE WINTER OF OUR DISCONTENT

Although the dates do not perfectly line up with the seasons of the calendar, the nearly six months of intense drama in Washington, D.C., became known as the "winter of our discontent." The phrase gained greatest traction when President Kennedy used it himself in a February 1, 1966 news conference, causing it to be immediately picked up by the press and the public, and applied retroactively to the constitutional crisis that culminated during the end of 1965 and beginning of 1966.

The nation was dealing with a great nor'easter blizzard that had unleashed fourteen inches of snow on Washington, D.C., from January 30 to 31, and up to two feet along much of the East Coast. The weather had turned rapidly raw after the New Year, with snowdrifts forming and arctic air settling in and dropping temperatures into the teens.

President Kennedy had taken a question from Tom Wicker of *The New York Times* about the impact of the blizzard on transportation and the resulting effect on the economic recovery that everyone agreed was needed. Kennedy famously replied, "I'm just relieved, Tom, that the winter of our discontent you're asking about is meteorological and not political."

After an excellent briefing on how the storm's intense, drifting snow would keep roads closed for several more days, Kennedy discussed the restoration of crippled transportation lines and the by-products of a food shortage and rationing. He was at his best, competent and reassuring.

The next question came from *Newsweek's* Karl Fleming, who picked up on Kennedy's metaphor, baiting the President with the idea that "January came in mild and left with this blizzard. Do you think that's a metaphor for impeachment?"

Kennedy pointed out that starting the year as the first President to stand impeached by the House of Representatives since Andrew Johnson was hardly "mild" and, if it was to be considered as such, he would not be looking forward to the upcoming Senate trial, where he believed he would find sufficient support to remain in office.

THE CENTURY CLUB

During the winter of 1966, as the country prepared itself emotionally for their President's bad behavior to be fully explored and perhaps severely punished in the U.S. Senate. Journalists and Beltway insiders began using the term *Century Club* to refer to that legislative body, a term that had a double meaning. Its primary usage came from the idea that it was almost a full century ago that President Andrew Johnson was impeached and his case sent to the Senate for trial. The secondary usage referred to the cozy little club of one hundred (since Hawaii made it fifty states times two senators in 1959) that would be deciding the President's fate.

To begin the proceedings, each senator took the following oath:

> *I solemnly swear that in all things appertaining to the trial of John Fitzgerald Kennedy, now pending, I will do impartial justice, according to the Constitution and laws, so help me God.*

The trial began in the manner of an ordinary criminal trial, with the defense and the prosecution each allowed to give an opening statement. Both sides then presented and cross-examined witnesses and could introduce evidence. Senators could submit written questions or motions to the Chief Justice of the Supreme Court, whom the Constitution placed on call throughout the procedure to clarify any points of law. A simple majority vote could overturn any of Chief Justice Warren's decisions on matters of evidence or procedure. Clark Clifford once again represented the President.

DALLAS ON TRIAL AGAIN

Realizing that they fought and lost the impeachment vote in the Judiciary Committee by arguing the facts, the President and the Attorney General decided a change of tactics was needed. They had been stunned by the building chorus for the President to step down and spare the nation the trauma of a Senate trial that had the potential to embarrass the nation and, worse, to make public certain U.S. security procedures and private White House discussions. People wanted to see the entire mess go away.

Still, the President's men decided they would fight in the Senate based on the big-picture assassination conspiracy, and attempt to make the vote about that, instead of the alleged crimes and misdemeanors the President may or may not have committed. They decided to go on the offensive yet again, as crusaders for justice and American principles.

The Kennedy brothers felt strongly that JFK's best chance lay in the relationships he formed in the Senate in the 1950s. If the trial could be framed as a vote on the dangerous levels of power held by the nation's intelligence community and military-industrial complex, they could win. They resolved to use the trial to do what the Warren Commission, JCAAP and the Oswald trial could not: shine an intense, unwavering light directly on the conspirators, and make them pay.

The longer John and Robert Kennedy fought the march to impeachment, the stronger their belief grew that history would record not the President's personal failings and physical ailments, but instead would focus more on the profound menace to democracy that the conspiracy represented. That was the gamble they made.

NEW YORK STAKE

Once again, the one-vote margin of control in the House of Representatives was up for grabs. On February 5, 1966, with two seats vacant, the GOP led the Democrats 217-216. That day, Democrats regained one seat, when Walter B. Jones won a special election in North Carolina's First District. The House of Representatives was officially a 217-217 tie as a result, and would stay that way for three days.

On February 8, control of the House all came down to Republican Congressman John Lindsay's seat in New York. If any Republican could be said to have a Kennedy's looks and charisma, it was Lindsay, who had just used these natural advantages to get elected mayor of New York City. In the special congressional election to replace him, liberal Republican Theodore R. Kupferman was in a neck-and-neck race with liberal Democrat Orin Lehman. Under ordinary circumstances, both men would probably have voted the same on most issues. The main difference between them was that one of them would vote to organize with the GOP and the other with the Democrats.

Both parties threw everything they had into the New York race. Both parties drafted their top vote-getters in the state to walk point. The White House was silent at the request of the Democratic congressional committee.

As often happens in New York politics, fringe and third-party candidates can upset the mix, serving as game-changing anomalies. In this case, the wild card was right-leaning journalist Jeffrey St. John of the Conservative Party. The pressure was so intense for St. John to throw his support to the Republican candidate, he literally checked into the Plaza Hotel under an assumed name to consider what to do. St. John somehow came down with food poisoning from room service (Republicans always blamed Democrats) and was not well enough to make any endorsement before the election. When the votes were in, Lehman had forty-seven percent of the vote to forty-six percent for Kupferman and seven percent for St.

John. This tipped the House to the Democrats by the same margin Republicans had enjoyed all year, 218-217, making Massachusetts Congressman John McCormack the Speaker of the House by virtue of some undercooked chicken.

Seeing this in isolation, it is possible to say that while control of the House was a big deal for the two-party system in 1966, it had nothing to do with the political struggle being waged in the upper house of the U.S. Senate. Yet, as it turned out, it had everything to do with it. The new Speaker of the House, John McCormack, was now in line to advance to the presidency instead of Gerald Ford if John Kennedy were to go, but only if the Democrats retained or expanded on their one-vote lead. As a practical matter, however, it meant that Democratic fence-sitters could now vote JFK's impeachment while still retaining the presidency for the Party.

CLEAN-SLATERS

The so-called "clean-slaters" were Democrats who, while personally loyal to President Kennedy, had reached the conclusion that only his removal from office could wipe the slate clean and allow the Party to still compete in the next election. The rise of this group was a recognition that the White House strategy seemed to be weakening by the day. At one point, President Kennedy had hoped to defeat the articles with a majority vote. Eventually his team came to realize they were playing for a lesser victory, depriving Republicans of passing the articles by the two-thirds vote requirement and, thus, staying in office. But to achieve even that much, the ranks of the clean-slaters had to remain small.

Oregon Senator Wayne Morse led a delegation of these political pragmatists to the White House. The group of Democratic senators was becoming vocal about the need for President Kennedy to step down so their Party's candidates would not be tarred in the upcoming midterm elections by the aftermath of an ugly Senate trial.

John Kennedy had argued with his advisers about even letting them come to visit. The media would cover it as an ultimatum.

Bobby convinced him to hear them out on the theory that they might be bringing the outlines of a deal. Maybe the Senate could still be convinced to formally censure the President and allow him to remain in office.

The senators started the meeting over coffee in the Oval Office by agreeing with Kennedy's stated position that the greatest crime had been done to the American nation by the forces that conspired to murder a sitting president. "We get a lot of mail here, senators," said Kennedy, pointing to a pile of letters that had been arranged on a side table. "And most of it lately is from constituents who wonder how it works that someone tries to kill the President, but we put the target on trial."

"What those evil men, those plotters with murder in their hearts, have done to their country can never be forgiven," Morse agreed. In the end, though, Morse countered that the venality of the conspirators simply didn't matter. They would be held accountable for their behavior but so, too, would Kennedy. The rule of law had to be maintained.

Morse, speaking from notes hammered out and agreed to in a caucus, stated that sufficient numbers of senators now felt they could no longer support JFK's acquittal, given some of the blatant missteps made by the President and the team working for him.

Kennedy smiled, by all accounts. "Thank you, Senator," he said, "it's always nice to know where the Senate stands on the issues of our day." The President had heard nothing about a bargain, and nodded to his brother.

Bobby was certainly more candid. "Senator Morse, if you have come to the White House simply to tell us we have lost your vote, I believe we could all have used our time more wisely. I had been led to believe that the censure option was still viable."

Morse put aside his notes and shook his head. He did not address his answer to the Attorney General but to the President. "With time, you will be seen as a whole man and, on that measure, you will do very well." Morse paused, placed a paternal hand on JFK's forearm, "We still need a clean slate, Mr. President."

THE LONG COUNT

On February 10, President Kennedy swam in the ninety-degree waters of the White House pool. When the President emerged this time, he was wearing trunks. Since the "Secret Life" story had broken the year before, there had been no more nude swimming, let alone in the company of White House interns with names like Fiddle and Faddle. While the President toweled off, Bobby Kennedy showed him a handwritten sheet of numbers and names, all sketched out, erased and redone again and again. Bobby watched his brother and waited.

"You certainly seem to have done your homework," said the President, handing the paper back to his brother.

"Every way you can look at it." The Attorney General, always one to preempt one argument with his own, simply stated the one essential fact. "The numbers just aren't there for us."

For us. The President would later say he was touched by this phrasing. It would have been so easy for his younger brother to say "for you," but he held back.

The two men, these brothers, who had gained the political authority of the most powerful nation on Earth were about to have it taken away. Still, their lives had been spared.

"You were always better at math than I was," said Jack Kennedy, still managing a trace of a grin. Bobby noticed how old he looked, how tired.

"Jack, the math doesn't get any simpler than this."

"What if you're wrong about some of these yes votes? They might not be as firm as you think they are," said Jack Kennedy, knowing Bobby never missed his count. "We only need to turn two or three."

Bobby shook his head and bit at his pencil. Jack could see in his eyes the cold, unforgiving finality of political reality. Both of them knew what had to be done. Bobby reached for the phone. "We're going to need a secure line and then to dictate a letter." The President asked the Attorney General if perhaps Ted Sorenson should come in and work his magic. "It's not that kind of letter," said RFK.

After moving to the Oval Office, Robert Kennedy, referring to notes he had made about resignation letters for the encounter with Lyndon Johnson over a year ago, dictated the actual letter. President Kennedy stared out the window behind his desk, turned to suggest a few words, but mostly remained silent. After it was done, Evelyn Lincoln typed it up at her desk, dabbing at her moistening eyes with Kleenex.

She gave it to the President first. Lincoln said later that he read it and pursed his lips, something she'd seen him do many times when he was experiencing a twinge of severe pain from his various conditions. Then he handed the document to his brother and said, "Getting out of Dallas was the easy part."

That night, President Kennedy dismissed his staff early and spent the night alone in the White House Oval Office. Evelyn Lincoln stayed outside, refusing to leave him alone. Bobby contacted the White House Secret Service agent-in-charge and told him to immediately bring Abraham Bolden back on shift to stand on the President's watch. He wanted to be updated hourly throughout the night, as Bobby put it, "just in case."

Closing arguments were made that night. Clark Clifford spoke for President Kennedy, and Melvin Laird and Leslie Arends spoke for the House, specifically the House Republicans.

During the non-televised, closed session, each senator had fifteen minutes to speak in the debate. Looming ahead were separate votes to be taken on each article. If a single one passed with a two-thirds majority, Kennedy would be convicted and, under Article Two, Section Four of the Constitution, must step down. If the senators were feeling particularly harsh, they could take a further vote to bar Kennedy from future office.

Fall from Grace

If Dallas had come to be known as "the day JFK dodged a bullet," then February 24, 1966 would become "the day JFK bit the bullet."

The Senate was close to wrapping up the comments from individual senators. All that was left was a short wait and then instructions from Chief Justice Warren. The vote was scheduled for the next day.

At that moment, Senator Edward Kennedy approached the Senate leadership and spoke quietly with them. Soon he left the room. Within a half hour, all the seats in the Senate were taken by their elected occupants.

Although it was never photographed, the image of Senator Kennedy escorting his oldest brother, President Kennedy, into the Senate chambers was never forgotten by anyone who had seen it. Teddy opened the door, and JFK strode through it. There had been no formal announcement, nothing from the sergeant-at-arms introducing "the President of the United States," as was the custom.

In this daring climax, President Kennedy stood at the lectern before one hundred members of the U.S. Senate, all of whom were extremely mindful that their own careers, too, would be in jeopardy in the next election. He began speaking without notes. Those who heard him said there was no hesitancy, no fumbling for words, no gathering of thoughts. In an emotional speech, Kennedy demanded the accountability of all the senators before him in the cause of preserving democracy. It was perhaps the most passionate speech of his career, and it came to be known as the "Finish What You Started" speech:

> Having served in this body with many of you sitting here today in judgment of me, I know this political trauma carries a personal cost for all of you as well. Because your business will not be finished when I walk out of the Senate chamber tonight; it will just be beginning. For you all know that a coup has been attempted in this country to replace the legitimate elected authority. While the identities of the conspirators are not known to everyone, their treasonous activity remains in plain sight for all to see. You must carry that serious burden forward, and see to it that this dark moment of history shall never be repeated. I wish you courage in that battle, and success. For

*while we are a divided nation, we are still a nation, one of laws that
command me to leave office now, and command you to finish the job
that has been started here.*

At the end, President Kennedy said he would discuss the details
of his resignation that night with "the American people who put me
in this office, rather than now, with the members of this body who
would ask me to leave it." Because the Senate deliberations were
closed, Kennedy was thus guaranteeing that history would never
record a vote on the matter of his Senate trial, but would maintain
a color TV archive of his final words. The bottom line was still
that, within twenty-four hours, the country would be President John
McCormack's to run. The Speaker of the House was next in the
line of succession, given that the nation had no Vice President with
Johnson now resigned and about to go to jail.

The Kennedy brothers left the Senate chambers together
and rode in the presidential limousine to the White House. There,
President Kennedy prepared to address the nation from the same
desk from which he had told them about the Cuban Missile Crisis
three and a half years earlier. In a statement barely four minutes
long, he revealed that he would tender his resignation, as the
Constitution stipulated, to Secretary of State Dean Rusk, effective
noon Friday, February 25. The speech is famous for this concluding
statement that JFK supporters in a Boston bar dubbed the "White
House Finger," a crude name that, nonetheless, has always had more
currency with the public than "the speech he made before he quit":

> *While mistakes were made and have not been denied even today,
> it's clear that two and a half years have taught us a great political
> lesson. There are many ways to assassinate a man, particularly
> in Washington. Considering the finality of the alternative to the
> resignation that I now offer, I accept this verdict gladly, and intend
> to start tomorrow behind a sail, and plot a new course for my life.*

After the speech, Kennedy was driven by the Secret Service
to the Georgetown apartment of Ben and Toni Bradlee. There he

had dinner with his estranged wife, Jacqueline, and the Bradlees, a couple JFK had not spoken to in the past year. When asked what they had discussed by reporters who had been waiting outside, Kennedy replied, "We talked about the children." Observers of the scene said they'd never seen John Kennedy as visibly disturbed as he seemed at that moment.

The next day at 9 a.m., Kennedy gave a farewell talk to an East Room assembly of White House staff and selected dignitaries, including the entire Cabinet and Speaker John McCormack. Many eyes were on the seventy-five-year-old Speaker, a tall, thin, teetotaling Irishman, whose House leadership had been challenged repeatedly by unruly Democrats. He also had history with the Kennedy family. His favorite nephew, Edward McCormack Jr., had been defeated by the President's brother, Edward Kennedy, in the 1962 Democratic senatorial primary.

While there was some concern from Robert Kennedy, Kenneth O'Donnell and others, that the occasion could descend into maudlin emotion, it instead turned out to be classic JFK. He shook hands, exchanged hugs and kisses, and smiled a lot. The most memorable moment came when he took Evelyn Lincoln aside, apologized for what he had put her through, asked for her forgiveness, and kissed her hand. When it was done, he signed the letter of resignation and handed it to Secretary Rusk. The nuclear codes were left in the care of Speaker-turned-President McCormack.

The now-former President Kennedy then was escorted by his senator brother and his attorney general brother to the Marine One helicopter, waiting on the White House lawn. The trio then flew to Andrews Air Force Base, where Air Force One waited to take JFK to Palm Beach, Florida. Bobby had urgent matters to take care of at the Department of Justice, but Teddy announced that he needed a vacation from the Senate and asked John if he'd mind a little company. The President was surprised but said yes.

The ride in Air Force One began the reshuffling of the deck for the Kennedy brothers. While Jack and Bobby always remained close, forged by fire as their relationship had been, they needed a break.

John Kennedy and Edward Kennedy began to spend more time together, something neither one of them had ever seen coming, let alone anyone else in the family.

Once the Kennedys were in the air, the White House staff began preparations for McCormack's swearing in. More chairs were added for a larger crowd of invited guests to witness the oath as administered by Chief Justice Earl Warren. President John McCormack addressed the nation shortly thereafter from a lectern in the East Room:

> *My fellow Americans, I am aware that the American people have not elected me President by their ballots, and so I ask you to guide me toward the justice and mercy and wisdom that this office demands. John Kennedy is a friend of mine; we come from the same state. History will judge President Kennedy, but I will not. Yet both he and I know that our great republic is a government of laws and not of men. The people have spoken through our constitutional process. Now, today, I humbly accept this great honor and will, as I have sworn today, protect this office to the best of my ability. God bless America.*

With McCormack's spare 113 words delivered, the new President met with the cabinet, including Robert Kennedy, and asked them all to stay on the job until he could determine what combination would work best to the advantage of the United States. President McCormack then took his daily nap. He was awake before his predecessor's plane had touched down to his new life far from Washington.

Top Story

NOVEMBER 17, 1969   50c

MOON MEN

Kennedy Relaunches?

Kennedy, Armstrong, Nixon
at the White House, November 5

Chapter 7:
Life After

Closing the Book

On March 16, 1966, President John McCormack asked for time on all three television networks. It was initially assumed that he wanted to address the American public about the situation near Palomares, Spain where a B-52 bomber had collided with a KC-135 jet tanker over Spain's Mediterranean coast two months earlier. Three seventy-kiloton hydrogen bombs were found on land but one was lost in the nearby sea. Although none of the bombs were armed, their loss created an international incident as more than two thousand U.S. military personnel were on site decontaminating the area and more than thirty U.S. Navy vessels had been engaged in the search for the lost hydrogen weapon. It had been located the day before.

McCormack, however, had a bomb of another kind to drop. The new President had been relatively silent about the fate of John Kennedy since the transition but, as was later revealed, that was his public position. In private, he had apparently lost a lot of sleep over the matter.

He began his address by relaying how he had come to a decision that he felt was good for America, one that he had struggled with, seeking the advice of God and conscience about the right thing to do with respect to his predecessor, John Kennedy:

> *What has happened in this country over the past two and a half years is an American tragedy in which we all have played a part. It*

*could go on and on and on, or someone must write the end to it. I
have concluded that only I can do that, and if I can, I must. There
are no historic or legal precedents to which I can turn in this matter,
none that precisely fit the circumstances of a private citizen who
has resigned the presidency of the United States. But it is common
knowledge that serious allegations and accusations hang like a sword
over our former President's head, threatening his health as he tries to
reshape his life, a great part of which was spent in the service of this
country and by the mandate of its people.*

With that, President McCormack granted the former president
a full pardon for "all offenses against the United States that he,
John Fitzgerald Kennedy, has committed, or may have committed"
during his time in office. McCormack said he had not spoken with
Kennedy, nor his representatives, and that he was unaware of any
specific attempts to bring charges against Kennedy.

*The simple fact is that a former President of the United States,
instead of enjoying equal treatment with any other citizen accused
of violating the law, would be cruelly and excessively penalized either
in preserving the presumption of his innocence or in obtaining a
speedy determination of his guilt in order to repay a legal debt to
society. During this long period of delay and potential litigation,
ugly passions would again be aroused. And our people would
again be polarized in their opinions. And the credibility of our
free institutions of government would again be challenged at home
and abroad.*

McCormack knew this decision would be controversial,
and because he had already lived a long life with a full career, he
concluded, "In order for this decision to be considered in the least
political environment possible, I have resolved to end my service as
President on January 1st, 1969 and not to seek the nomination of
my Party for a second term."

Later, acting as the lawyer for former President Kennedy, Clark
Clifford accepted the pardon. Asked if this meant the public could
assume Kennedy was admitting guilt on any of the potential charges

he might face, Clifford responded, "Former President Kennedy agrees with President McCormack that justice delayed is justice denied and has instructed me to end this chapter for both him and the nation at large."

ALL POLITICS IS LOCAL

While John Kennedy received a pardon from President McCormack, Lyndon Johnson did not. His plea deal with the Justice Department eventually derailed all continuing investigations, in both Washington, D.C., and Texas. He grumbled to Lady Bird, "They've turned me into Aaron Fucking Burr." On May 13, 1966, Lyndon Baines Johnson surrendered himself to authorities of the Federal Bureau of Prisons in Texarkana, just 175 miles east of Dallas, Texas, where his most serious crime had been committed, and began serving his ten-year sentence.

Johnson immediately unleashed the same skills he had honed on U.S. senators while running the United States Senate. Soon the inmates he served with knew him as "Lyndon," and he became extremely popular. The warden stated, "All issues here end up in Lyndon's cell before they get to my office."

LBJ, it turned out, was a born dealmaker. If he couldn't make them in the congress or the White House, the prison yard would serve just fine. He is widely credited with improving the quality of food served to inmates when he began a hunger strike to denounce the injustice of his own preferential prison menu, stating, "I won't eat another bite until everyone here gets the same square meal they give me." His hunger strike was ended with Texas steak and shared with every member of the penitentiary.

He died in prison at age 64, on January 22, 1973.

JUSTICE SWERVED

With the exception of a vice president in prison, what is most surprising about the constitutional crisis of the Kennedy years and their aftermath is how few people actually went to jail, given the magnitude of the original crime. The corollary irony, in retrospect, was that the intended victim of the crime, John Kennedy, was made to suffer such a humbling, public punishment in the immediate aftermath.

Although he had intended to stay on as attorney general through 1969 to continue his investigation, Robert Kennedy found immediately that his heart was not in it. He tendered his resignation, and the Working Group simply withered away without his leadership.

Other prosecutors faced the standard of overcoming reasonable doubt, and often found themselves simply unable to convince a jury of something they knew in their bones was based on fact. This was true because, even though the assassination attempt failed to kill President Kennedy, it had been constructed with a post-Dallas cover-up in mind and those plans had still been implemented. During the twilight war waged in the background of the 1964 election, forensic evidence was destroyed, documents shredded, and witnesses silenced through bribery or murder.

As a consequence, an exact identification of all the conspirators and participants in the Dallas ambush has never been fully accomplished. It has become something of a national parlor game, full of speculation. While shadowy, some definition has emerged with time.

First, it is generally accepted that Lee Harvey Oswald was aware of and recruited into the conspiracy, although his death before full evidence could be presented at his trial means we will never know for certain if he was an actual member of a shooting team or "just a patsy," as he had maintained. We do know that Corsican mobster Lucien Sarti was convicted of being Oswald's backup, with or without Oswald's knowledge. A jury said in 1976 that Sarti, dressed in a Dallas police uniform, had fired several of the bullets that hit the Kennedy motorcade from the grassy knoll area behind the picket fence.

We also know that the Central Intelligence Agency's Bill Harvey was convicted of having recruited Sarti and others to take part in the plot. Actual CIA planning was never shown, however, and Harvey has always contended that he acted as a classic rogue element within the agency. Harvey's boss, James Angleton, was a constant suspect. He denied any involvement and no prosecutor ever managed to mount a case against him.

Prosecutors never stopped leaning heavily on Dallas nightclub owner Jack Ruby to testify. They discovered many connections to organized crime, and this informed their prosecutions, but Ruby, serving a life sentence for his murder of Lee Harvey Oswald, remained steadfast in his refusal to testify and help them out.

This meant that multiple members of U.S.-based organized crime were under suspicion, but none ever made it to court. Johnny Roselli, Santos Trafficante, Sam Giancana and Carlos Marcello all were, to one degree or another, believed to have participated in CIA plots to assassinate Fidel Castro and suspected of transferring that working relationship to targeting John Kennedy. Active cases existed against Roselli and Marcello, who were both viciously murdered before charges could be filed. Trafficante and Giancana also later died mysteriously.

Federal prosecutors mounted a case against Antonio Veciana, the leader of the anti-Castro group Alpha 66. The jury found him not guilty. Even though the majority of jurors believed he had been involved, they simply felt the government had not proven its case.

Texas oilman Clint Murchison also was taken to court and, as with Veciana, the jury came away loathing him as a person and acquitting him as a conspirator.

And so it went. Trial and error.

Today, it is generally believed that the main plotters escaped punishment because they had planned carefully, never stating explicitly what they wanted or expected. The men who carried out their wishes either managed to stay silent or were silenced by violent means. Over and over, men were found to be victims of shocking suicides, or robbery-turned-homicides. In some cases, particularly with some of the Mafia leaders, the deaths were not mysterious at all. They were outright murders, designed to send a message not to talk, a message that was heard.

In the end, there was no doubt that a conspiracy had led to the ambush in Dallas, Texas on November 22, 1963. There were two and possibly three teams in Dealey Plaza that fired as many as seven shots. The plot involved Texas oil money that hired both foreign and domestic sharpshooters who were managed by CIA rogue agents working with organized crime leaders in concert with anti-Castro Cubans. It was as complicated as it sounds, wildly improbable, and yet it happened.

DAVID POWERS

A continuing source of pain and guilt to the former President was the incarceration of his great friend Dave Powers at the Massachusetts Correctional Institute at Norfolk. Powers had received an eight-year prison sentence for his role in disposing of the White House tapes and charges of interfering with the authority of the Secret Service to perform its duty to protect the President of the United States. The relatively spacious and campus-like atmosphere and architecture of MCI-Norfolk permitted a form of "community life" that was generally not available at other penal institutions of the time.

Kennedy knew that even though he had not asked Powers to destroy the tapes or to specifically thwart the Secret Service by bringing women into the White House, those acts had, indeed, been performed to his benefit. Kennedy visited Powers once a month, every month, from the time he left office until the time Powers was given early release in August of 1970. The two men were allowed to visit in private on the grounds and to smoke cigars together. After he was granted his freedom, Powers told friends that his privileges involved Scotch from a flask first used by Joseph Kennedy during the days of Prohibition, something that has always been officially denied.

AFTERMATH

Former President Kennedy moved his base of operations to the family compound in Palm Beach, Florida, and started his new life. He joked to friends that his situation proved to what extremes a man might go to escape the harsh winters of Washington, D.C. He stayed in Florida through the spring of 1966, living as a virtual recluse.

At the President's request, his housemate was Paul "Red" Fay Jr., who had served with JFK going back to their PT boat days in World War II and continuing through his Administration. Fay took a room in a separate wing of the house and was a constant companion. Because Kennedy could not venture into town without photographers following in great abundance, it was Fay who, along with a housekeeper, kept the place running. Evelyn Lincoln made occasional visits to work personally with Kennedy, although she spent most days at an office maintained by the Kennedy family in Washington, D.C.

Senator George Smathers often saw Kennedy when he was in his home state of Florida as well. Smathers, Kennedy, and Fay made several famous nighttime visits into town, but none of them ever provided a photographer with a single picture of the ex-President and a female. The trio provided a disappointing guys' night out to the nation's curious. Where JFK's buddies had once enabled his lifestyle, they now went out of their way to keep him from it. Kennedy took it all in stride, admitting to his friends that he had enough women in his life for all of them, and that as a military man, he knew when it was time to stand down.

THE EX-PRESIDENT AND THE EX-FIRST LADY

John Kennedy had left Washington, D.C., a President who was separated from his wife and landed in Florida as a Catholic trying to avoid a messy divorce. For more than a year, there remained avid interest in where the situation stood between Jackie and him. It was a source of endless speculation and interest from the American public on the part of both friend and foe.

During this time, Jacqueline Kennedy moved to New York City with the children and enrolled them in private school. She rarely saw the former President when Caroline and John Jr. were handed off. It was all done through family members or other intermediaries. The tables had clearly turned. She had several rumored affairs. He minded his own business. Even when she was seen in public on the arm of another man, it was always explained that the gentleman was acting as an escort only.

In May of 1967, both Jack and Jackie were seen in a red convertible Ford Mustang on Cape Cod just before tourist season. By the summer, Jackie and the kids had moved back into the Hyannis Port home (she loathed the Palm Beach house) with this complex man, who both infuriated and enchanted her. The divorce papers were withdrawn as quietly as possible, given the inflamed tempers of the times and the heightened public interest.

POLITICS CONTINUE

President McCormack kept his promise to be only a caretaker President and did not seek reelection in 1968. He turned seventy-seven that year, and most voters appreciated his discretion. Instead of curtailing partisan politics, however, his announcement had the opposite effect. From the moment President McCormack took office, it seemed, he was a lame duck, and politicians by the droves in both parties began floating one trial balloon after another.

There was serious talk of Bobby Kennedy running in 1968, but he chose to step back from such an emotionally overwrought race. He accepted a teaching position with Harvard Law School, where his courses were standing room only on everything from the legalities of the Cuban Missile Crisis to the appropriate legal course to pursue with regard to the conspirators who targeted his brother. (He felt the death penalty would be too harsh and believed they should spend as much time in prison as possible in order to consider their treasonous behavior.)

John Kennedy's 1960 nemesis, former Vice President Richard Nixon, took the Republican nomination that year, holding off a strong challenge from New York's liberal Governor Nelson Rockefeller. With Lyndon Johnson and both Kennedys out of the running for the Democrats, and Vietnam contained as an issue, Senator Hubert Humphrey of Minnesota and Senator Ed Muskie of Maine fought it out with a number of "favorite sons" holding on to blocks of votes, hoping to be kingmakers. Muskie took the nomination on a third ballot, when Humphrey threw his support behind him. None of the competition mattered in the end, as Nixon beat Muskie by a comfortable margin and returned the White House to Republican rule.

In 1969, former President Kennedy began a national book tour to promote what his publishers had hoped would be an autobiography but instead had become a call to action for Americans to retake control of their government. *Just Courage*—as the book was titled—led to a national reevaluation of his time in office, with sides being taken once again. The growing conservative movement focused on Kennedy's transgressions, and the liberal community said JFK's behavior simply could not be compared to the venal treason of the conspirators. His support, particularly among women, had dropped precipitously, but not enough to prevent his book from becoming the year's bestseller.

Although it took as much brokering as the Kennedy-Khrushchev Summit of 1965, eventually President Richard Nixon invited John Kennedy to the White House in November of 1969 to greet the astronauts who had returned from the Moon the past July. At the time, Nixon had gone to see the astronauts in their isolation quarters, where they had been placed to avoid lunar contamination. He had invited them to the White House after they completed a global goodwill tour on behalf of the United States.

The shadow that haunted Richard Nixon that summer and fall looked like his old rival John Kennedy, the man who had first challenged the United States to send a man to the Moon before the 1960s were over. Nixon's own advisers fretted that their boss might look like he was trying to take credit for something that wasn't his, particularly given that he had been in office less than a year. It only took some impertinent questions from some Democratic-leaning reporters to push them into the photo op of the decade.

The photo of an awkwardly smiling Neil Armstrong flanked by former President John Kennedy and current President Richard Nixon became almost as famous as the one with Kennedy and The Beatles. The odd men out, of course, were astronauts Buzz Aldrin and Michael Collins, both cropped from the photo by circumstance and artistic design. As JFK left the White House that day, he winked to Kenneth O'Donnell, who had accompanied him to their "old stomping grounds," and said, "I still got it." John Kennedy had begun the decade with his New Frontier and had left the decade with his flag firmly planted on the lunar surface.

That same summer, on July 18, 1969, a young political intern named Mary Jo Kopechne drowned under mysterious circumstances at a party Senator Edward Kennedy attended on Chappaquiddick, off the eastern end of Martha's Vineyard. No charges were filed, but Teddy's excuse, that he was too inebriated to drive and thus could not have been at the wheel of the car that she had drowned in, had most people convinced the night was not among his finest. The police report stated that a Kennedy cousin, Joseph "Joe" Gargan Jr., was the driver. An inquest into the incident failed to lead to charges in the case, but it left a lingering suspicion about Teddy's own behavior just over a year before he would face the voters in his reelection bid.

In 1970, Teddy surprised no one when he announced he would not be seeking reelection for a second Senate term. He told his close friends that he was following his brother Jack's example of leaving to avoid being a distraction from the important business facing the nation. At the news conference, however, the youngest Kennedy brother smiled and said he intended to serve as his brother Jack's chief of staff.

In a precedent-smashing, mind-blowing turn of events, the supposedly disgraced and humiliated ex-President was going to run for his old Senate job in his home state. The world simply could not believe this was happening. Most loved the move, particularly after they heard JFK's explanation, which he laid out in private more than once. "It's the biggest finger I can give the sons-of-bitches," said the former President. "I'm still standing, and they know I know who they are." It was never made clear if he was talking about the men who tried to kill him or the senators who saw to it that he was removed from office.

The legendary Kennedy self-deprecating humor was called into action again when reporters asked if it wasn't wrong to act like a Senate seat could just be handed from one brother to another. "Let's not jump to conclusions," warned JFK. "So far, Teddy is all talk."

END OF AN ERA

In November of 1970, the eldest still-living Kennedy brother was elected in a landslide by the Commonwealth of Massachusetts (defeating Josiah Spaulding) and became, once again, Senator John F. Kennedy. He was welcomed back to the U.S. Senate in January 1971 by a crowd that mostly contained the same names and faces as the crowd that came *this close* to voting him out of office for high crimes and misdemeanors five years earlier. He became the most sought-after guest in the Senate cloakroom and used his position to push aggressively on the issue of nuclear arms reduction treaties.

In his first years as a junior senator, from 1953 to 1960, the younger John Kennedy seemed to most to be a man in a hurry to get someplace else. The second time around, however, from 1971 to 1977, Kennedy was a man at peace with who he was and where he was. By all accounts, he was a far superior representative of the Commonwealth of Massachusetts in this twilight of his career.

Jack and Teddy became the new Kennedy power team. Edward Kennedy had never wanted anything more than to be trusted by John Kennedy to be his number two, a position that had seemed impossible to attain during the JFK presidency. But Bobby was now finding his own footing. He had served Jack nobly, loyally and passionately, and he was spent. He retreated into academia and practiced politics as an observer and not a participant whenever possible.

Together with Jacqueline Kennedy, former President Kennedy moved back to a Georgetown home just three blocks from the one they had lived in back in the 1950s. Friends noticed that they spent far more time together in the 1970s than they had when they were supposedly living in harmony in the White House.

They fell into old routines like having breakfast together while each read something different, occasionally interrupting to point out an item of interest. To the end of his days, John Kennedy found reading *The New York Times* a great diversion, telling his brother Robert, "The most goddamn frustrating thing is, I still read this crap and it's not even about me anymore." JFK, however, refused to read *Top Story*, preferring *Time* for his newsweekly. The magazine had selected JFK as its "Man of the Year" twice—once in 1962 and again in 1966—an honor commensurate with his fall from grace.

The former First Couple did not go out much, but when they did, they preferred a dinner party with old friends to a social engagement at some large Washington, D.C., event. Those always came stocked with photographers whose editors had told them to come back with Kennedy photos or not to bother coming back at all. Jack and Jackie were still the toast of the town, or at least the most interesting couple on the guest list.

The Kennedy family managed to hang together more closely, too. Jackie became more comfortable with the clan gatherings she had formerly despised and even played touch football with the boys once or twice. Jack, Bobby, and Teddy established an easy familiarity and comfort that had eluded them in the pressure cooker of the White House. Watching President McCormack and then President Nixon and commenting was so much easier and carried far less personal risk.

Even the haters of the Kennedys seemed to take a step back. They were still hated, of course, by the extreme right, but they were not considered an immediate threat to the safety of the nation. In later years, Robert Kennedy confessed that this was his motivation in not pursuing a political career of his own. He had lived through his brother's brush with martyrdom and had resolved that, however it turned out, he was through. In actual fact, all three of the Kennedy brothers—John, Robert, and Edward—had taken a private family oath to never seek the presidency. They agreed to be happy without it, and besides the occasional twinge of regret that comes from knowing one of them could probably have defeated the existing candidates of any particular year, they seemed to accept the decision with great high spirits.

For nearly six years, then, John Kennedy lived a life that he enjoyed immensely. He was able to watch his children grow up, to fall back in love (or, as doubters maintained, to fall in love for the first time) with Jackie, and to practice club politics in the United States Senate with his little brother Ted, who seemed to be naturally drawn to the rhythm and mood of the congressional lifestyle. There were family gatherings, sailing trips, old friends and a true appreciation for what it meant to be alive, something that only a man who has nearly been killed can ever truly experience.

In 1975, the former President's health began to fail beyond what could be seen from his increasing use of a wheel chair due to his back pain. Whether it was the long-term grinding down of his Addison's disease or the years of drug abuse to combat his various infirmities, he began to suffer one setback after another. Even so, after years of masking pain and disability, he was able to keep all but those closest to him unaware that he was actually dying.

In 1976, John Kennedy announced that he would not be a candidate for reelection, just as Teddy had done six years earlier. But Teddy did not step in to try to reclaim the so-called "Kennedy seat," because he had come to believe the voters might hand him the first defeat in an election that the Kennedys had ever suffered, a distinction that he did not want.

In presidential politics, John Kennedy even managed to stage a series of primary appearances with the young governor of California, Jerry Brown, the son of the man who had defeated Richard Nixon for the same office in 1962. His endorsement was sufficient to derail the candidacy of little-known Georgia Governor Jimmy Carter. The general election of that year came down to a choice between two California governors—Jerry Brown for the Democrats and Ronald Reagan for the Republicans. Reagan defeated his Golden State successor, a rebuke that hurt Kennedy as much as Brown. JFK knew he would not see another presidential election, while Brown knew he had another shot in 1980 for a rematch.

In the early summer of 1977, having celebrated his sixtieth birthday only a month earlier, John F. Kennedy died of heart failure. He was sailing with numerous members of the Kennedy clan on a hot summer afternoon and complained of indigestion. They came in early; Kennedy skipped dinner and went to bed. "Leave the light on," he said to Jackie as his wife kissed him goodnight. He passed away in his sleep.

In 1978, Jacqueline Kennedy wrote her own national bestseller, *Leave the Light On*. It detailed her life with John Kennedy in very personal terms and tried to reconcile the complex feelings she had about him as a leader, father and husband. She worked in the New York publishing industry until her own death in 1994.

WHODUNNIT?

To the extent that the Kennedy assassination attempt was ever "solved," it occurred on January 23, 1983, the day the confession of Lyndon Johnson was finally unsealed, ten years after his death. In the handwritten page, LBJ had stated, "To my eternal shame, I was aware of and may have indirectly encouraged the irresponsible actions of others to make an attempt on the life of President John Kennedy in Dallas, Texas on November 22, 1963." He concluded dramatically, "May God have mercy on my soul. Lyndon Baines Johnson." Critics of the way the confession was handled have argued that LBJ should have been forced to turn evidence against others, particularly Clint Murchison, something he had steadfastly resisted doing, saying that if he complied, his life in prison anywhere in the United States "wouldn't be worth the ass-hair on my beagles."

In national polls taken since that day, LBJ has consistently placed at the top of the least liked politicians in American history.

That history can pivot in an instant has been made crystal clear by the case of John Fitzgerald Kennedy. He had come so close to losing his life in Dallas. Had that happened, it is more than likely he would have become an instant martyr, and his many sins would have remained unknown. Lyndon Johnson, rather than being seen as one of the men who let the ambush happen, would have become President Lyndon Johnson, and all the charges and investigations involving him would likely have been forgotten. After all, the nation would have just suffered the death of a popular President; it might have been too much to bear to see Johnson impeached.

With a Lyndon Johnson in the Oval Office instead of a federal prison, the United States might have committed its blood and treasure to a losing cause in Vietnam. The 1960s might have been even more revolutionary than they were. Anything could have happened.

Instead, Lyndon Johnson is remembered today as a corrupt player of rough-and-tumble Texas politics who ended his life in jail when he confessed, more or less, that he was involved in the Kennedy assassination plot. If he was not a leader of the conspiracy, he was still its highest-ranking member.

STRANGELOVE'S IDENTITY REVEALED

On Memorial Day in 2005, Strangelove's identity, something that had become a national guessing game during and after the constitutional crisis, was finally revealed. The FBI's Mark Felt was the source for Altman and Berkowitz. He was close friends with Hoover's far closer friend, Clyde Tolson. Felt worked for Tolson since 1964 as the assistant director for the bureau's training division. In coming out as the anonymous source, Felt talked about the emotional cost of his actions in 1965:

> *I have never been proud of my role in leaking the Kennedy papers.*
> *At the time I rationalized that I was acting on behalf of Director*

Hoover, which I was, but I never asked the questions about what was in these files, how the information had been gathered, and whether it was appropriate to use it as a destructive force. I simply did my job as I was instructed by Clyde Tolson. President Kennedy made a lot of mistakes that these papers describe in detail, but he was the American people's elected President. Yet men in our own government tried to execute him, and then I was their assassin when it came to his character.

Felt managed to elude Altman or Berkowitz ever making his identity on the streets of Washington, D.C., by accepting a posting in Los Angeles before he leaked even the first document. He came forward near the fortieth anniversary of the Ali-Liston rematch and the "document dump." Fighting pancreatic cancer, he said, "If I see President Kennedy wherever I'm going next, I want him to know what I'm doing now, and understand that the shame is mine."

ANOTHER TORCH IS PASSED

While Jack, Bobby and Teddy had agreed informally that none of them should pursue the presidency, pressure developed to see that at least one of John Kennedy's children picked up his standard. Caroline was oldest, but she lacked the drive and ambition for a public life, and, being a woman in those days, could realistically see that her chance of being elected President of the United States was small.

The same could not be said of the former President's son, John Kennedy Jr. The nation had fallen in love with him as a little boy hiding under his father's desk. He had celebrated his third birthday just three days after the ambush in Dallas. The now famous photo of John Kennedy and his twelve-year-old son sailing together off Hyannis Port, wide grins on their faces, the wind in their hair, has become as classic as a Norman Rockwell painting. When his father passed away, John Jr. was just sixteen years old, an age that also coincided with the end of his Secret Service protection.

As he grew into young manhood, John Kennedy Jr. clearly had his father's good looks and magnetism, leading to his selection by People magazine in 1988 as the "Sexiest Man Alive." Yet he also seemed to exhibit his father's gene for risky behavior, both in his sexual exploits and his active lifestyle. He dated a succession of celebrities that included Darryl Hannah, Brooke Shields, Cindy Crawford, Sarah Jessica Parker and even Madonna.

In 1995, John Kennedy's son decided to enter politics his own way with the creation of *George*, a magazine that would focus on the intersection of politics and fame. At that time, three years after her separation from Prince Charles, Great Britain's Princess Diana was probably the biggest "get" in the business. She was already well on her way out of favor with the Royal family at the time. When she came to New York alone, John Jr. arranged to meet her to persuade her to do an interview for his magazine. He got the interview and more.

For nearly six months to follow, John Kennedy Jr. and Princess Diana became the most high-profile couple in the entire world. At first, Diana and John tried to keep their relationship secret, but that turned out to be impossible for the two.

Their celebrity simply transcended anything that Hollywood could confer. He was the son of the charismatic thirty-fifth President, and she was the blonde commoner who became a fairy-tale princess. Together they were explosive, both personally and publicly. And yet, for reasons that can never be fully understood, it worked for that brief moment in time. They each knew what it was like to be famous because of the fame of someone else.

Some commentators believed that John only pursued Diana because she reminded him of his mother, a classic beauty with intellectual passions of her own and only a passing tolerance for the formality of politics. "My parents stayed together," he wrote in *George*, the only public forum he found acceptable. "It was hard, hard work, particularly for my mother. But seeing their final success, that makes me believe I can have a successful relationship with anyone I choose."

Both John and Diana hated the amplified tabloid and paparazzi scrutiny that being together brought upon them. In a joint statement they asked the media to "respect our privacy" which, of course, was an impossible ask. Eventually, they agreed to go their separate ways.

Within two years, JFK Jr. married former model and fashion-industry saleswoman Carolyn Bessette, despite nearly breaking off their engagement a month before the ceremony. Diana was set to wed film producer Dodi Fayed, the son of an Egyptian billionaire. When the two couples met at a charitable event in New York City in 1999, the pictures sold to *Us* magazine which outbid *People* for their rights, paying over half a million dollars. Several weeks later, Diana and Fayed were dead, the result of a paparazzi chase in a Paris tunnel.

Diana's death, coupled with the tragic skiing accident death of his cousin Michael, seemed to affect the young Kennedy heir strongly. He saw it as a warning about his own mortality. His sister's friends had already been referring to him as the "Master of Disaster." He told his close friend, Bill Noonan, that he was going to find another way to express his penchant for risky behavior besides extreme sports and other dangerous pursuits like adventure travel, rappelling dangerous rock faces, and flying single engine planes.

Whatever was going through John Kennedy Jr.'s mind, he found himself increasingly considering the family business of politics. The reality of the Kennedy political experience had been that there had been the expectation of a dynasty when John Kennedy was elected in 1960. Bobby would run in 1968 and then, when the time was right, Teddy would follow. In his memoirs, Bobby discussed the irony.

Had Jack actually died in Dallas, I might have found it important to carry on the flame of his unfinished life. The battle we fought together, however, made us all feel as if politics was just not going to be something that Kennedys did. When Jack, Teddy and myself discussed this, we knew that others would carry that flame but that we had become marked men. All of us would have liked to have enjoyed the continuing battle of elected office and public life, but we

*saw clearly that the price it would exact on our families was simply
too great to bear.*

John Kennedy Jr. had followed the position of his father and
his uncles dutifully, confining his work to his magazine. Increasingly,
however, he began to question if Bobby's feelings were valid.
Perhaps, he wondered, a new generation of Kennedys could pick
up that flame and run with it. He also knew that of all the younger
generation he had the best chance. Plus, politics had the added
dividend of being risky, a place where a man could test himself and
actually vanquish an opponent on the field of battle.

Still, in November 1998, when Kennedy was having these
feelings about entering politics, there was not a clear field for him
to run in. Republican incumbent Senator Al D'Amato narrowly
defeated Democratic challenger Congressman Chuck Schumer
that month and would hold the seat until 2004. New York's other
senator, Democratic incumbent Senator Daniel Patrick Moynihan,
had one of the most secure seats in the U.S. Senate. The Governor's
mansion would not be open for challenge until 2002.

Then Moynihan shocked everyone and shuffled New York's
electoral landscape days after D'Amato's re-election when he
announced he would not be running in 2000 when his own seat
was up. Tired and ill, Moynihan wanted to give Democrats a chance
to find their champion to replace him, given that New York City
Mayor Rudy Giuliani was clearly planning to run. The idea that
liberal New York might be represented by two Republicans in the
Senate was something that liberal lion Moynihan deemed completely
unacceptable. Moynihan had served as Assistant Secretary of
Labor in the JFK Administration and his fondness for a Kennedy
restoration of sorts was palpable. He wanted John Jr. to run.

Most other Democrats, however, had taken John at his word
that he would not follow the family lead and pursue politics outside
of seeking public office. As a consequence, the Democratic primary
already had a favorite in Chuck Schumer. It also had interest from
First Lady Hillary Clinton who was considering a run now that

her husband's first term was winding down (he had been narrowly defeated by incumbent President George H. W. Bush in 1992 and elected to a first term in 1996, defeating Senator Robert Dole.)

The Kennedy camp let John's interest become public with an eye toward keeping Schumer out of the race. Instead, as is often the case in politics, it had the opposite effect. Clinton bowed out, opting to support her husband's 2000 re-election campaign that was expected to be a tough one against Senator John McCain of Arizona. Schumer, on the other hand, doubled down, saying that whatever John Kennedy Jr. wanted to do made no difference to him. When it came to running for the U.S. Senate, said Schumer, "I'm all in."

The primary campaign pitted John Kennedy Jr. against Chuck Schumer on the Democratic side and Rudy Giuliani against himself on the Republican side. Giuliani was forced to weather a perfect storm of bad health news with a prostate cancer diagnosis and a separation from his wife, actress Donna Hanover. Kennedy and Schumer traded leads in the statewide polls throughout their contest but when the actual polls closed, John Kennedy Jr. stopped Schumer's comeback in its tracks with a ten-point win.

The fall election between Kennedy and Giuliani featured successful strategies, painful mistakes and the unexpected impact of current events. It also took place against the backdrop of an equally bitter presidential contest where President Bill Clinton got a chance to run against another Bush, in this case the former President George H. W. Bush's son, former Texas Governor George W. Bush (who took the nomination over Senator McCain). While there was no connection between the younger Bush and the younger Kennedy besides them both being the sons of former presidents, the comparisons didn't seem to help either man.

When it came to debates, President Clinton savaged his opponent, who gave one of the weakest performances of any modern presidential candidate, losing both the debates and the election. John Kennedy Jr. and Rudy Giuliani, on the other hand, reminded people in their meetings of the intensity that was on display in 1964 when JFK took on Senator Barry Goldwater. There was no doubt in any voter's mind that Kennedy was the nicer man but Giuliani managed to make that seem like a disqualifying trait for the expected rough-and-tumble of Washington, D.C., politics.

All the Kennedys campaigned with John. The sight of Kennedys coming together to support the handsome son of President John F. Kennedy proved too irresistible for the electorate to resist. Voters gave him a victory with a solid fifty-three percent of the vote to Giuliani's forty-five percent.

Senator John Kennedy Jr. was reelected in 2006 and 2012. In 2016, on the fiftieth anniversary of his father's resignation from the office of the presidency, John Kennedy Jr. is the odds-on favorite to win his Party's nomination for President.

Asked about his feelings on the eve of this anniversary of his father's political undoing, Senator Kennedy said, "My father was my hero when he was alive, and now that he's gone my feelings in that regard have only deepened. We were all lucky to know him."

The Unmaking of the President

Thinking about how our world would have been so different had President Kennedy's brilliant flame been extinguished on that bright and clear Dallas afternoon is a "what-if " that our scholars have been playing out for decades. They wonder if a President Lyndon Johnson would have pursued a war in Vietnam, what the success of the conspirators would have meant to America's sense of itself, and whether Kennedy would have become a martyr in his death.

In the real world, however, even historians now consider the struggle between the Kennedys and their enemies to be the most shattering constitutional crisis our government has faced since the Civil War. The President fought back with everything he had. His adversaries spared nothing in return. In the end, the epic battle waged in the mid-1960s made it seem that JFK's political survival was not the point anyway.

Since the Kennedy case, however, impeachment has been

threatened or acted upon with sufficient regularity by both parties that it seems more like a parliamentary vote of no confidence than the last-ditch constitutional remedy the Founding Fathers intended it to be. Both Democrats and Republicans have embraced the process in what many now view as a partisan tit-for-tat.

Had John F. Kennedy died from the bullets fired by his would-be assassins on November 22, 1963, it is possible his reputation today would still burn brightly. Yet in a preternatural display of anticipation, lightning reflexes and bravery, Secret Service agent Clint Hill sacrificed his life to ensure the President of the United States would escape.

For Americans under age fifty, the wrenching agony of the assassination attempt on President Kennedy and the subsequent events that led to the premature end of his presidency are events from their parents' past, things they've read about in history books. For those who lived through the political tumult of the mid-'60s, however, the memories brought to the surface by a phrase or a photo can be as stark and vivid today as they were so many years ago.

Two strands of political DNA were twisted together by the incredible events that transpired during the twenty-seven months between November 1963 and February 1966. The first was JFK's battle with the dark forces of conspiracy. Could faith in our democracy be restored in the face of the powerful expansion of a national security state that would try to execute the nation's elected leader? The second strand was Kennedy's personal fall from grace, a monumental series of events, because we as a people had placed him on such a high pedestal.

Kennedy's response to the failure of the conspiracy was to plot against its members in the same way they had plotted against him. Their counter-response was to try to change the subject away from their own shadowy crimes and place the issue of Kennedy's intimately personal foibles before the public. That Kennedy was forced to pay such a high price, even as many of the men who sought his death walked free, was the ultimate irony of that turbulent period.

John Kennedy cheated death in Dallas only to face a fate that for him might have been even worse: the public exposure of his private double-life. Learning the truth was just as difficult for many Americans, who loved and admired him when they knew him less well. Being forced to face the whole picture—for Kennedy and for the nation—was something no one ultimately was prepared for, yet we all took the journey together.

The sense of denial, anger and tragedy which hung over those days leading up to February 1966 may even have caused some to have secretly wished that our charismatic and vigorous leader had died in Dallas, leaving only cherished memories.

Yet even through the dissolution of both his marriage and his political administration, John Kennedy found a way to give meaning to it all. He fought long and hard enough to ensure that all thinking people in the United States understood that far more importance hung on these matters than whether the President's relationship with his wife was sound or his health perfect.

There is one matter on which all sources agree: on November 22, 1963, most of this nation admired John F. Kennedy and approved of his job performance. What has turned out to be so vexing about the post-Dallas revelations is how so many others could have wished him dead at a time when his personal popularity with the majority of the American people was authentic and solid. The collision of these two forces outside the Texas School Book Depository near the fateful overpass at Dealey Plaza reverberates to this day.

In the final analysis, the venal men who tried to kill President Kennedy with actual bullets in Dallas switched tactics to political assassination in Washington, D.C. They saw a chance to break his career into pieces with his own actions. This is not to make excuses for the President, or to argue for pardon, but only to state the obvious: he himself had given vicious enemies the weapons they would use against him.

John Kennedy survived his brush with death on November 22, 1963 and then suffered an almost unimaginable fate. He became a mere mortal.

ADDENDUM
THE FINAL KENNEDY
INTERVIEW

Former President and Senator John F. Kennedy gave his final interview to *Washington Post* editor Benjamin Bradlee on November 10-11, 1976, just four days after the year's election results. Kennedy and Bradlee had been close friends during the early White House years but had become estranged during the slide into impeachment and its aftermath. Although they had seen each other socially a few times (most poignantly on the day of his resignation), the relationship was not the same and many observers took JFK's granting of this special interview to Bradlee as a dying man's acknowledgement that their friendship triumphed over politics in the end.

The interview took place at the Kennedy Compound in Hyannis Port over two days, spanning over four hours of conversation. It is excerpted here and is not a complete transcription.

Bradlee: Were you surprised by Tuesday's results?

Kennedy: Which ones?

Bradlee: Well, let's start with Ronald Reagan defeating Jerry Brown in the presidential election.

Kennedy: Not at all. I predicted all along that the winner would be a California governor of some kind.

Bradlee: I can't let you off with a joke.

Kennedy: I'm disappointed but not surprised. Ronald Reagan is an effective campaigner. He's very good on television.

Bradlee: Many people reading this interview will say that you would know.

Kennedy: I'll take that as a compliment, Ben. I do believe that, as they were in 1960 and 1964, these debates were a turning point but, unfortunately this time, not in a way that favored the Democratic candidate.

Bradlee: You think that Governor Brown lost the debates?

Kennedy: No. Not on the issues certainly. But I do think that Governor Brown has an intensity that I personally like but that a certain part of the electorate may have felt was unwarranted, given his youth. Remember that I was considered a young president and Governor Brown was even five years younger when he ran. In any case, many people seemed to feel that he was somehow being disrespectful to Reagan, something that seemed related to the disparity in age between the two men. And, of course, Governor Reagan had served eight years in that office while Governor Brown had served only two. There were many factors and I doubt they've all been sorted out yet.

Bradlee: Do you think his defeat had anything to do with his belief that America was entering an era of limits? Governor Reagan certainly seemed to use that against him quite effectively.

Kennedy: Governor Brown was correct. America can't do everything for everybody, nor should we. This point was distorted by the Reagan campaign to make it seem like Brown was pessimistic about our country's future. Only by understanding the limitations of our resources—political, economic, military—can we make intelligent decisions about where to put them to the most effective use. I can say that, Ben, and still be an optimist about our country and I am, very much so.

Bradlee: Brown will go back to running California and may run again in four years. But this year you decided not to pursue reelection to your Senate seat. Is this the end of your political life?

Kennedy: It's certainly the end of my seeking office but politics runs in the blood of my family and I imagine I will continue to think about it and speak out about my feelings as long as I'm around. And if members of our family choose to seek office in the future and they ask for my help and I'm able to give it, then I certainly will do that.

Bradlee: Which will you miss most, the Senate or the White House?

Kennedy: The Senate.

Bradlee: Care to elaborate?

Kennedy: To the best of my knowledge, when I was in the Senate no one was plotting to murder me. I have to emphasize I'm only talking about my personal feelings. There's no question that we made substantial change possible during my term as president and we accomplished some important work.

Bradlee: What would you describe as your Administration's most important achievement?

Kennedy: While our Civil Rights work slowed down during the post-Dallas distractions, I believe we set the nation on the right track there. I'm proud of reaching out to Dr. King and supporting Voting Rights legislation, among many strategies to heal this terrible national wound. His death in Chicago in 1967 was a terrible blow to the nation and to me personally, of course. Had he survived, I'm certain he would be pushing for greater change and faster even now, as would be correct.

Bradlee: Other accomplishments?

Kennedy: Stopping the march to war in Vietnam. I know many, many people disagreed with my choice not to expand the nation's role beyond advisers, but I feel it was the right policy for the security of the United States. Vietnam would have fallen anyway, in my judgment, but many thousands of American soldiers would have perished. I think the challenge to go to the Moon was accomplished beautifully and has been good for America and good for the world at the same time. It showed also that the country can make a commitment to a goal that can be pursued across multiple Administrations and congresses, something that is extremely important for our future growth. And in the same way that Civil Rights is unfinished business, I think addressing the issue of the Cold War from the point-of-view that nuclear war was completely un-survivable for either side has established a framework that will enable a breakthrough between the nuclear powers of the world.

Bradlee: How close to nuclear war did we come?

Kennedy: It could have happened. The fact that it nearly did on my watch is a terrible thing that I live with even today. I did everything I could to stop it, of course, but I wonder now if I should have done even more. I mean, I was already impeached. What more could they have done if I had negotiated a full peace treaty with the Soviets?

Bradlee: If you had done that in 1966, it would not have passed the Senate.

Kennedy: No, it wouldn't. You're correct.

Bradlee: Let's pick up on that political question you raise. Now that it's been over a decade since you left the presidency, do you have any regrets about resigning rather than face trial in the United States Senate?

Kennedy: I regretted resigning the day I signed my letter of resignation. I regret it today. Having said that, Ben, I think it's fair to argue that it was the correct decision at the time and, given the same set of circumstances, I would have taken the same action.

Bradlee: Because the votes weren't there?

Kennedy: That's certainly what Bobby felt and I had gotten pretty far listening to his opinion on those kinds of matters.

Bradlee: Did you deserve to be impeached?

Kennedy: Impeachment is only a decision by the House of Representatives to send a case against a president to the Senate. It is possible that with the suspicions and vitriol that had been raised that impeachment could have served the purpose of clearing the way for a resumption of normalcy for the rest of my term.

Bradlee: Did you deserve, then, to be convicted by the United States Senate and removed from office?

Kennedy: I believe the personal issues overwhelmed the others. Had that dynamic not existed and only the charges based on my official conduct while in office been forwarded to the Senate then, no, I don't believe I would have deserved conviction. And, frankly, I believe that as time goes on, historians are apt to agree with me on that score.

Bradlee: Let's clear up some issues that historians are already disagreeing about. There have been claims that you and Mrs. Kennedy argued more after Dallas about security than anything else, and that it nearly ended your marriage. Is that true?

Kennedy: No. At least I hope not. Remember that no one had any experience with something as shocking as what happened at Dealey Plaza. All of us who survived that event knew that our lives had changed because of it but none of us knew exactly what that meant. Jackie had come to me within a few weeks, maybe a month, with some rather strongly held opinions about how I should reconcile my public life with her desire to pursue a more normal personal life for our family. While I wouldn't call it a list of demands, she wanted to see changes made. I started to argue with her but I thought she was right.

Bradlee: What changes did you make?

Kennedy: Mostly we followed the recommendations of our security team. There was a feeling immediately following Dallas that whoever had done that might want to finish the job and that we should not make it easy for them.

Bradlee: The country was being told that Lee Harvey Oswald had done it. He was in jail.

Kennedy: I think it's very clear now that he did not act alone. So we were right to be concerned.

Bradlee: We know that now, yes. But you make it sound like you knew that from the beginning.

Kennedy: I certainly suspected it.

Bradlee: Why?

Kennedy: Why not?

Bradlee: Mister President…

Kennedy: Many reasons. The most obvious one was how dangerous the times were. Because of Civil Rights, I wasn't popular in the

South. Because of Cuba and the impasse with the Soviet Union, I wasn't popular with some of our own people in the military or the CIA. Because of our battle with organized crime, I wasn't popular with the Mob. I had a lot of enemies, and most of them had a lot of resources.

Bradlee: Did you favor one theory over another initially?

Kennedy: The sad truth is that I did not. I felt that there was a strong case to be made for all of them, at least the ones I just mentioned to you. You have to understand that every president gets briefed regularly on the real intelligence about potential threats to their life. It's part of the job.

Bradlee: Can you tell us your feelings about Lyndon Johnson?

Kennedy: It seems clear to me that Lyndon, at minimum, knew something was coming and got out of the way and certainly that is what he acknowledged in the plea deal he made with the Department of Justice. Bobby's feelings go beyond that in that he believes the Vice President was told directly, in order to see if he would play ball after my death, and that he basically said that he would. Either way, I believe Lyndon Johnson still went to his grave protecting at least a few secrets.

Bradlee: I believe it was in January of '64 that you were threatened in order to prevent you from running for reelection. Can you tell me about that?

Kennedy: I knew it was something big. Bobby called me from his office and said, "Wrap up whatever you're doing. I'll be there in ten minutes." I think we had some farm lobbyists over at the time. I gave them cufflinks and sent them on their way. To be honest, I had been feeling better for almost a week at this point, starting to see some daylight. This news from the Attorney General, well, I hadn't felt that way since the shooting happened.

Bradlee: What did he say?

Kennedy: He said that Ed [Guthman] had been contacted by people who said I had a week to get out of the race.

Bradlee: Or what?

Kennedy: They didn't feel the need to elaborate. After Dallas, it didn't take much imagination to figure out what they had in mind. Understand that this was exactly the time when I was making my mind up to get in after all.

Bradlee: You never seriously considered not running up to that point, did you?

Kennedy: I did. Looking back, I'm not certain how serious I was. I think I was very serious. And, of course, I made everyone around me very nervous because I refused to discuss it. And the more quiet I got on the subject, the more panicked they appeared to get.

Bradlee: I can't imagine Bobby panicked.

Kennedy: No, you're correct. Bobby doesn't panic. He works the problem. In this case, he was very deferential to my own feelings and readiness but I could tell that every atom in his body was ready for this fight. When you tell Bobby Kennedy that he can't do something, you've guaranteed that he will.

Bradlee: You practically announced on the Ed Sullivan Show with The Beatles.

Kennedy: That is how some people put it, Ben, but you know that's not true. Showing up to see The Beatles was something I could do and wanted to do. I'd been incarcerated in the White House more or less night and day for over two months. I was going stir-crazy. The timing of going to New York coinciding with the threat was not a timing of my choosing.

Bradlee: What did you think of The Beatles, by the way?

Kennedy: I knew very little about them at the time except that I wished I could have their level of popular support in the '64 election. Both Caroline and John, however, have bought every one of their albums including that latest reunion album that's been so controversial. Certain of their albums we had to buy twice because the kids couldn't agree to share it. My favorite one, I believe, was, I can't remember the name now, wait, yes, it was the one called "Rubber Soul." I like that one a lot. Having said all that, I still want to make the point that seeing them in

New York was not intended to be political.

Bradlee: You brought all three network anchors into the Oval Office and made it seem like you were almost announcing your intention to run by accident.

Kennedy: Is there a question to that?

Bradlee: The whole thing was planned, right?

Kennedy: Not entirely. We had discussed doing it that way and had literally made no decision as the interview began. Once I was in the middle of it, though, I just thought, why not?

Bradlee: I'm sure what happened at Dallas was a key factor in your reticence to seek a second term, but were you also concerned that details of your personal life would be exploited by the Republican Party during the campaign?

Kennedy: We agreed that we wouldn't be discussing this.

Bradlee: We agreed that you would not discuss the details of the relationships themselves.

Kennedy: Those kinds of issues had not come up in previous campaigns. There was an assumption that the situation would not change in that regard.

Bradlee: Really?

Kennedy: I've answered your question as fully as I intend to.

Bradlee: All right, then, jumping ahead to the end of 1965, did you believe that the alleged affairs you had with various women were impeachable offenses?

Kennedy: Both my attorney, Clark Clifford, and my brother, the Attorney General, advised me that they were not.

Bradlee: Mr. President, I understand that we agreed to restrict this area of questioning, but I wonder if you might reconsider? The point of the interview was to give you a chance to look back on your entire career, and it seems clear that your public and private lives had impact on each other.

Kennedy: What do you want to know?

Bradlee: There are several questions that I've heard many, many times from other people, questions that are not mine exactly, but from average Americans. I would like to ask those. The first question, the one that comes up most often, is how could you have relationships with so many other women outside of your marriage?

Kennedy: The honest answer is that there is no good answer to that.

Bradlee: What's the bad answer?

Kennedy: The behavior began long before I was married. Many men play the field. I just never seemed to stop. A number of years ago, seeing how deeply and profoundly it had hurt Jackie, I knew it couldn't continue. I knew that I might never have her back, even if I changed, so I changed for myself. It just became clear.

Bradlee: Second question. People want to know if you loved any of these other women?

Kennedy: I've read the same articles you have, people speculating that I never really understood love. I don't know if that's something I'll ever be able to speak to. I had fondness and affection for some, not all, but not what I would call love. I do love my wife very much. That's what I know.

Bradlee: Marilyn Monroe told her friends she was going to marry you and move into the White House.

Kennedy: No. Never.

Bradlee: Did you do drugs with any of these women while you were the President? Marijuana? Even LSD?

Kennedy: No. I have stated this under oath and I have not committed perjury. I have taken more than my share of drugs to deal with medical issues and that has been well-documented but that behavior never extended to recreational drugs of any kind. I think we're done with this line of questioning. Let's move on, it's getting late.

Bradlee: Were you surprised, then, at how things went for you after Dallas?

Kennedy: Yes. But probably not as surprised as many of my constituents, it's fair to say. I expected to win reelection, particularly if they nominated Barry Goldwater. I expected my second term to be as difficult or more so than my first.

Bradlee: In what way?

Kennedy: I had made up my mind to fight what my predecessor, President Eisenhower, warned about—the so-called "military-industrial complex." That meant I would not have let anyone railroad me into a disaster in Southeast Asia, or an invasion of Cuba, or war with the Soviet Union. I simply was not going to go there. Based on my experience in my first term, I would have imagined some strong pushback. On the other hand, looking at it now, after Dallas, I was on borrowed time anyway.

Bradlee: Mr. President, you're looking a bit tired. Would you like us to wind this down?

Kennedy: Please. Maybe another question.

Bradlee: What do you think would have happened had you been assassinated in Dallas, Texas on November 22nd, 1963?

Kennedy: That is the ultimate "what if," isn't it? If I had died that day, we know that Lyndon Johnson would have assumed the presidency. That probably would have saved his career. He would never have been held accountable for his role in the ambush and, quite likely, those who were investigating his other crimes probably would have been persuaded that losing one president through gunfire should not be followed by losing the next through impeachment. Lyndon would have consolidated his power. It's possible he would have invaded Cuba but I think more likely he would have acquiesced and given the Joint Chiefs their war in Vietnam.

Bradlee: How would that have changed America?

Kennedy: It would have made us deeply unpopular. And, because the war would have been based on false assumptions, the war would have been lost. This would have led to a loss of national confidence. There is only one area where I see an LBJ presidency as being a positive. That would have been Civil Rights. He would have been shrewd enough to seize the moment of my death to push forward our Civil Rights agenda, and he might have gotten all of it, something I was unable to do, given my other problems.

Bradlee: We started this conversation talking about politics. Do you think your death would have changed the men who held the presidency afterward?

Kennedy: I haven't thought that deeply about my possible death, to tell you the truth. Nixon would probably have made his comeback either way, but you never know.

Bradlee: President Nixon has said that watching what happened to your Administration, particularly your taping system and the destruction of the taped evidence by Dave Powers, taught him a valuable lesson that he was able to apply when his own Watergate scandal broke. How do you feel about getting credit for two terms of Richard Nixon?

Kennedy: It's an honor I surely would decline, if possible. The Nixon presidency in my view has been a disaster from its aggressive foreign policy to the suppression of dissent here at home. If presidents are learning lessons from each other, I do hope that President-elect Reagan will learn a few from his predecessor.

Bradlee: I'll wind this down now. The public, overall, seems to have forgiven you for whatever trespasses may or may not have happened on your watch. Among many, in fact, there remains enormous public affection. Does that surprise you?

Kennedy: A bit. But I'm deeply grateful. Maybe the American people understand that we're all flawed and they leave it to God to judge us. Probably part of it is that no one really wants to see a presidency terminated by any means other than the end of a term or a defeat in an election.

Bradlee: Mr. President, people would like to know, how is your health?

Kennedy: I have good days and bad. It's wonderful to be alive. I try to take it as it comes these days. Spending time on crutches or even in a wheelchair is not how I would like matters to be, but that condition still beats the alternative.

Bradlee: Have you given any thought to how you would like to be remembered?

Kennedy: We've covered that, I believe. Although I would also like to be remembered as a man who spent a decade not speaking to an old friend such as yourself but who, when it was time to call it a night, was very happy to have put those hard feelings aside.

Bradlee: I feel the same way. Thank you, Mr. President.

Kennedy: Thank you, Ben. Goodnight.

ACKNOWLEDGEMENTS

This labor began with a love of President Kennedy, whom I shed tears for as a student in Laura Braden's fourth-grade class at Peter Boscow Elementary in Hillsboro, Oregon. All students came to lunch learning the President had been hit by gunfire, and we left knowing that he was dead. Mrs. Braden, a tough old cookie, cried at the table and didn't force us to eat our vegetables as she normally did. Then we went home and watched TV with our parents all weekend.

My father, Harvey Zabel, worked as a high school history teacher and left me a treasured thirty-five-cent paperback edition of *Profiles in Courage* with its underlined highlights and his handwritten side comments. Through his eyes and his library, I've been able to see how history often springs from a series of close calls that, had they gone another way, would have had dramatic and profound impacts. Equally important to this literary exercise, however, was the influence of my mother, Lucile Zabel, who gave me permission from a young age to think differently than all the other kids and go my own way.

After years of laying out the structure of this book, I approached the gifted alternative history writer Harry Turtledove about collaborating to bring it to market in the mid-2000s. Harry and I only briefly worked together but deadlines and commitments pulled us apart, and I've carried on with his blessing. I'm grateful to Harry for his continued support, particularly of this final version, for which he has generously contributed an important foreword. If you'd like to dive deeper into alternate history, I highly recommend Harry Turtledove's work.

The first person to engage my passion for an alternative version of the Kennedy assassination was Brent V. Friedman, my creative partner on the primetime NBC series *Dark Skies*. Back in 1996, Brent and I co-created that series and produced twenty hours of television drama that made Jack Kennedy's death and Bobby Kennedy's life central parts of the story.

My mentor out in Hollywood, Bill Asher, was a close friend of the Rat Pack and, by extension, the Kennedys. Bill directed JFK's inaugural party the night before his famous "Ask Not" speech and Marilyn Monroe's famous "Happy Birthday, Mr. President" performance. He also told me about being at parties where the President-to-be acted in ways that seem wildly dangerous from today's perspective. He gave me a clear understanding of how those times were so different from today.

To all the researchers who have written about President Kennedy and the circumstances of his death over the years, it can only be said that anything published today is informed by your work and dedication. In this group I include everyone from author Mark Lane to filmmaker Oliver Stone, two men whose pursuit of clarity, justice and closure in the death of John Kennedy has made it easier for others.

This edition would not exist without the insight of Jason Leibovitch who recognized instantly that *Surrounded by Enemies* was not only a great read but deserved to be the launch of a book series dealing with some of the great "what-ifs" of our times.

I'm also grateful to Steven Silver who suggested that an earlier edition of this book might be a good submission for the Sidewise Award for Alternate History. Given that the novel went on to win the 2014 competition, I've resolved to always take his suggestions seriously.

My appreciation for making this book possible in crisp, clean, readable form goes to editor Randall Klein, who managed to suggest cuts that, when done, were so beautifully realized that I don't miss a thing that went before. On the previous edition, I'd worked with editor Eric Estrin whose insights elevated the content and the form throughout.

Graphic artist Lynda Karr gets a special shout-out for assembling the striking *Top Story* magazine cover images that make the words seem more real than ever. Cover artist Kit Foster managed to create a book cover that is as bold as it is poignant.

Finally, I'd like to thank my family for allowing me to keep my collection of *Time* and *Newsweek* in all its pre-digital bulk for all these years. Jackie, Lauren, Jonathan and Jared have indulged this storage challenge and so many other peculiarities I've brought into their lives, and I am eternally grateful. They have given me the motivation to carry on whenever doubts have threatened to overtake me, and, always, courage.

About the Author

CNN correspondent-turned-screenwriter Bryce Zabel has created five primetime network television series and worked on a dozen TV writing staffs. A produced feature writer in both live-action and animation, he has written and produced for nearly all major networks and studios and collaborated with talents that include Steven Spielberg and Stan Lee. He has worked for ABC, NBC, CBS, FOX, HBO, Showtime, Syfy, Sony, Warner Bros., 20th Century Fox, Universal, Paramount, Hallmark, USA, and Animal Planet, among others.

In 2008, Zabel received the Writers Guild of America (WGA) award for writing his third four-hour Hallmark mini-series, *Pandemic*. He has received credit on other produced films and miniseries that include *Atlantis: The Lost Empire*, *Mortal Kombat: Annihilation*, *Blackbeard* and *The Poseidon Adventure*. He wrote SyFy's first original film, *Official Denial*, and the first film in the Unsolved Mysteries MOW franchise, *Victim of Love*. His end-of-World War II true story, *The Last Battle*, is currently in pre-production with Studio Canal.

Zabel served as the elected chairman/CEO of the Academy of Television Arts & Sciences, the first writer in that position since Rod Serling. During his term, he was responsible for handling the post 9/11 Emmy awards, the negotiations that led to an unprecedented 250 percent license fee increase for the telecast, and the move to the Microsoft Theater at L.A. Live.

He has been an award-winning on-air journalist for PBS (investigative reporter), CNN (correspondent) and NBC (local news).

In addition to the Emmy-winning *Dark Skies* (NBC), Zabel

has received the WGA "created by" or "developed by" credit on *Kay O'Brien* (CBS), *M.A.N.T.I.S.* (FOX), *The Crow: Stairway to Heaven* (SYN) and *E.N.G.* (CTV). His other series work includes *Steven Spielberg's Taken*, *L.A. Law*, *Life Goes On* and *Lois and Clark: The New Adventures of Superman*.

Besides two WGA nominations and one win, his work has won the coveted Sidewise Award for Alternate History, the Gemini Award, Golden Mike and Emmy. He has also been nominated by the Environmental Media Association and the Mystery Writers of America. He is a member of the DGA (Directors Guild of America), SAG (Screen Actors Guild) and the WGA. As an adjunct professor for the USC School of Cinematic Arts for the last decade, Zabel has taught graduate-level classes on producing film and television as well as writing one-hour TV drama.

Zabel is an often-featured speaker, moderator, keynoter and panelist, who has appeared in numerous TV interviews that include *The Today Show*, *CBS Morning News*, *Politically Incorrect*, *Entertainment Tonight*, *Access Hollywood*, and *Extra*, as well as being interviewed by news organizations that include *Time*, *The Washington Post*, *The New York Times*, *The Los Angeles Times*, *Daily Variety*, *Hollywood Reporter* and others.

He is also the co-author of *A.D. After Disclosure: When the Government Finally Reveals the Truth about Alien Contact*. His Breakpoint book series will continue next with *Once There Was a Way: What if The Beatles Stayed Together?* from Diversion Books.

**Find out more about Bryce Zabel and
the Breakpoint series on Twitter and Facebook!**

@BryceZabel

www.facebook.com/SurroundedByEnemies

Printed in the United States
by Baker & Taylor Publisher Services